BRIDGE OF ASH

BRIDGE OF ASH

BOOK 3 of THE LONDON CHARISMATICS

WITH THE NOVELLA

A WRATH OF SPARROWS

VAUGHAN WOODS
PUBLISHING

Content warning for A Wrath of Sparrows:
Contains references to past sexual assault and human trafficking, murder, injuries, use of minors in criminal acts, alcohol consumption, a child in danger, murder, graphic injuries, war, gun violence, physical fights, off-page sexual content, bombing, and depictions of surgery.

A Wrath of Sparrows

"The opportunity of defeating the enemy is provided by the enemy himself."

Sun Tzu

~

"All the gods, all the heavens, all the hells are within you."

Joseph Campbell

ONE

Sunday, November 15th, 1914
Mid-afternoon
Marylebone, London

THE GRAY SKIES of London promised a rain they had no intention of delivering.

Lily had buttoned her wool driving coat to the chin to ward off both the cold and the damp as she zipped across the city on her Triumph, gliding through the afternoon traffic.

The season for riding was coming to an end. Lily mourned it more this year than she had before. She had become accustomed to using her motorbike for everyday transport instead of reserving it for those rare and luxurious races through the open countryside beyond the sprawling edges of the city. Returning to a life of trams, underground trains and hackney carriages held a note of tragedy.

A bright spray of golden chrysanthemums was carefully strapped to the luggage rack, their colors bold against the unrelenting dullness of the day. People's eyes were drawn more to the flowers than to the woman in trousers straddling the vehicle.

That much had changed in the three months since the outbreak of the war. There were far stranger sights in London these days than a woman motorcyclist, like the endless lines of soldiers drilling on the wide greens of Regent's Park. The marching men blurred along the periphery of Lily's vision as she turned onto Park Lane. They were arrayed in a ragged assortment of civilian clothes, carrying wooden dummy rifles on their shoulders. The Army's supplies had not been able to keep up with the flood of volunteers who had answered the call to arms.

Requisitioned lorries lined the circular lane at the heart of the park like the caravan of a utilitarian carnival. The red, white and blue bunting that had been euphorically strung between the rows of houses in August was now stained with soot. Shops plastered their windows with the latest edition of the newspaper, the vague headlines that made it past the censors lined up against the minuscule print of the lists of the known dead.

The celebratory mood that followed the declaration of war had not endured long against those merciless rows of type.

Lily turned from the park, maneuvering the Triumph down the roads that twisted to the west. She could glimpse the pale ribbon of Regent's Canal here and there through the gaps between the houses. A small dog barked at her furiously from the end of its lead, the owner hissing a reprove.

Sparrows danced overhead, quick brown rags fluttering against the featureless backdrop of the sky.

She arrived at Kensal Green.

The cemetery sprawled along the banks of the canal, gray mausoleums mingling with pale tilted crosses under the watchful eye of the gasometer that loomed on the far side of the water.

Lily dismounted, chaining her motorbike to the black iron of the gate. She plucked the golden burst of the chrysanthemums from the rack.

She had not been to Kensal Green since the day of the funeral. She still remembered perfectly well which of the many crisscrossing paths she needed to take. At the end of it, a cluster of somber figures came into view, gathered on a patch of vibrant green lawn.

There was the tall, lanky form of James Cairncross beside plump, trim Miss Bard in her brown tailored suit. Estelle had dressed in gold and black for the occasion, her caftan seeming to billow around her in spite of the lack of any breeze.

Lily, in her driving coat and trousers, her bobbed hair tucked under a cap, joined them by Robert Ash's tomb.

"Darling," Estelle noted in greeting, wrapping Lily in a fragrant embrace as though they hadn't just run into each other in the hall that morning. Lately, it seemed that was all Lily saw of Estelle, just quick exchanges in the hall or at the door as she ran out to one appointment or another.

Estelle's services had been in particularly high demand for all the terribly obvious reasons since the outbreak of the war. She had added more séances each week, and yet Lily no longer heard screams and thumps and bleating trumpets through the thin floor of her flat. Estelle's current clients weren't thrill-seekers out for a bit of entertainment. They were mothers desperate to connect with the sons who would never return from the mud of Flanders.

Lily could have made more of an effort to spend time with Estelle and Miss Bard, but it was hard when every casual chat was a reminder of what was no longer there.

The glue that bound them all together had dissolved, and Lily did not know how to fill the space it had left behind. She didn't have words for what she was feeling, and yet pretending everything was fine exhausted her.

It was different with Strangford, where pretenses were impossible and language was irrelevant. With a touch, Lily knew she was understood.

Those moments were a stolen rarity. The attention of the world had drifted since the outbreak of the war but there were still limits to the time she and Strangford could spend together alone. All of that would change in a month when they were married, at which point she would no longer have to sneak through the garden gate when it all became too much to bear.

At least Strangford had neglected to repair the lock since the afternoon Lily had kicked her way through it into his life.

Strangford would not be joining this gathering. He had been forced to return to Allerhope, the family estate in Northumberland. The Army had issued a requisition order for the estate's horses, and his mother, Lady Strangford, had her hands full wrangling over which of the animals should be considered essential breeding stock and which would be sacrificed to the war effort.

It would mean some terrible choices. Strangford and his family were under no illusions that any of the horses taken would ever be returned. She did not envy him the errand.

Strangford was not the only one missing. Dr. Gardner, now an officer of the Royal Army Medical Corps, was stationed at a new military hospital opened in a requisitioned girls school in Portsmouth. He had managed to dash off a letter or two since his appointment, enough to tell Lily that the flood of wounded men arriving daily from the continent was both horrible and desperate. Gardner would not leave his post while there were lives on the line.

A small brown bird alighted onto one of the nearby headstones, ruffling its feathers against the damp. It reminded Lily of someone else who should have been there. It seemed like Sam Wu was always accompanied by sparrows, his little auxiliaries in whatever mischief he was getting up to. He would set them to monitoring his father or Ash when he was intent on something one or both of them would undoubtedly disapprove of.

The last Lily knew, Sam was at the enormous Army home base in Aldershot completing his basic training. She had written to him every week since he enlisted in August.

There had been no reply.

She told herself he must be terribly busy, but in her heart she knew it was more than that. He had left London in a tangled snarl of anger and grief, torn apart by the death of the man they had come to see today.

"Shall we get on with it, then?" Cairncross gruffly announced. Without waiting for an answer, he turned and crossed the remaining distance to the slab of marble that marked the grave.

The gasworks rose above the silver line of the canal with iron crowns, blackened bricks and the steady rumble of some secret engine. A barge chugged quietly along the water, loaded with cargo.

A lone gull swung overhead.

Lily looked down at the unremarkable stone engraved with the name of the man who had told her she must become something more, then deserted her to figure out the rest of it alone.

The stone was a farce, of course. Ash didn't lie in the ground under her worn leather boots. There had been nothing left of him to bury. The gleaming coffin held only an assortment of objects Cairncross had chosen, quietly and alone. Lily had never asked what it contained. It would have felt like an invasion of some sacred privacy.

She supposed they could have executed this little ceremony anywhere, and it would have made no difference.

If Sam were here, he would have said as much. He had never been one to hold back from speaking the truth, however much trouble it was going to cause.

Lily knew she was being unfair. It didn't matter that Ash's physical remains weren't here in Kensal Green. Estelle would say as much if Lily mentioned it, and she knew death better than anyone. She could almost imagine the response.

It's not about the bones. It's about the heart.

Cairncross cleared his throat.

"I have prepared a reading," he announced. He unfolded a piece of paper from his pocket and began to recite something in a language Lily supposed might be Arabic.

She listened politely until he had finished, his voice roughening with emotion as he reached the end. He tucked the paper back in his pocket.

Miss Bard stepped forward. A folklore scholar, she held a wreath of yew branches, bright with their bell-like red berries. She set it down against the stone.

"I brought a traditional Celtic blessing with me," she said. "Deep peace of the running wave to you. Deep peace of the flowing air to you. Deep peace of the quiet earth to you. And deep peace of the shining stars to you."

"Is that yew?" Cairncross demanded.

"Yes," Miss Bard replied.

"Isn't that a bit macabre?" Cairncross pushed.

"Only if you ignore the clear symbolic associations with resurrection," Miss Bard retorted.

"It's bloody poisonous," Cairncross complained.

"James," Estelle warned.

The librarian and the folklorist glared at each other for a moment across the lawn. Miss Bard brushed off her skirt and graciously turned to Lily.

"Go on, Miss Albright. It's your turn," she urged.

Lily scooted forward and set down her golden bouquet. The color felt garish. She stepped back again, having nothing more to offer.

Cairncross frowned a little but refrained from saying whatever it was he clearly wanted to say.

Estelle moved forward, the black and gold of her robe dancing around her feet. She crouched gracefully before the stone, running her fine-boned hand across the delicate leaves of the grass.

"Happy birthday, my old friend," she said softly, and Lily felt a shard of glass twist inside her heart.

~

Miss Bard was deliberately cheerful as they walked back to the gate, pressing one-word answers out of Cairncross about his new position at a ladies teaching college in Rotherham. The students, it seemed, were "fine." The library was "adequate."

They divided as they reached the gate. Estelle was headed to a private session in the home of a well-off client who had just lost her younger brother to an artillery shell in Ypres. Miss Bard had a meeting of her women's suffrage group, who were to vote tonight on whether to postpone their next demonstration and instead devote their efforts to raising funds for wounded soldiers.

The two women flagged a hackney. Cairncross lingered on the curb as Lily unlocked her motorbike.

"Would you walk with me for a moment?" he asked bluntly.

Lily, surprised, gave him a nod.

She wheeled the Triumph alongside her as they moved down the pavement.

"I was able to find some information related to the new khárisma you manifested after your… fall," Cairncross finished.

Death, Lily silently corrected him.

After she had drowned in Regent's Canal and been resurrected on a slab of cement across from the King's Cross rail yard.

"I believe it has a name," the librarian continued. "Or at least, it does in one part of the world."

"What is it?" Lily demanded, stopping.

"Onmyōdō," Cairncross replied, turning to face her.

The rhythm of the word danced across her skin—*onmyōdō*.

"It was an institutionalized system of supernatural practice in ancient Japan," he continued, moving back into their walk, Lily matching his stride beside him. "For a thousand years, its masters held immense influence in the imperial court. They were highly valued for their ability to pinpoint adjustments one needed to make in the present to avoid misfortune in the future. The position of a chair, the birth date of the man who should be offered a promotion. How a palace should be oriented, what route the emperor should take to prayer…and for their power to curse the enemies of the dynasty."

"Curse?" Lily echoed, surprised.

He looked down at her, the wind tugging at the cropped gray hair under his hat.

"Onmyōdō is the art of discerning the path to both good and evil fortune," he replied. "The way to both balance and imbalance. It was a very elaborate science requiring years of study to master."

"Nothing about what I do feels scientific," Lily said.

"Yes. Well," Cairncross returned. "Perhaps it would be different if you had a proper teacher."

He sounded tired. He stopped, pausing to look across the canal.

"Mr. Ash…Robert," he corrected himself, the two syllables of Ash's given name roughed by emotion as they emerged from his throat. "Had a gift for it. An instinct that made up for any lack of experience or longstanding tradition. All I have are books—my own inadequate interpretations of books. I can't…do what he could do, Miss Albright."

The pain was a lump in her throat. Lily spoke past it.

"Why did you come to study this?" she asked. She did not say what she really meant—*to study us*. "Was it because you met Ash?"

Cairncross didn't look at her. His eyes were on the water of the canal and there was a stiffness in his shoulders she had not seen before.

"No," he replied shortly. He pushed out the rest. "I had an experience with khárisma."

Lily waited for more. The old soldier beside her didn't offer it. He shifted as though shaking off some moment of the past he had deemed best forgotten.

"I'll translate the most relevant passages from the original

Japanese for you. It is not my strongest language, so I am afraid it might take me a while." He glanced over at Lily. "They would call you an onmyōji."

She wanted to press Cairncross on his secrets, but it was clear that conversation was through. Instead, she let the word soak in: *onmyōji*. It was a name, an identity... though for what, she still wasn't sure.

She was so far from understanding the strange new power she had brought back with her from the other side of her fall into the canal. It loomed inside of her as both a promise and a threat, a spark of strange and unsettling instinct.

There should have been someone there to guide her through it, to bring her to an understanding of who she was and what she was meant to do.

There wasn't.

"There's ... something else I should tell you," Cairncross went on, his change in tone sending a warning note through Lily. "I have had an offer to let out The Refuge."

"You can't possibly be thinking of accepting it," Lily blurted.

Cairncross did not flinch. His long face was as serious as Lily had ever seen it.

"There isn't enough money in the trust," he said. "I can't afford to maintain the place. There are already issues with the damp, and I spent the last two weeks fighting an infestation of mice. Buildings do not fare well when they are empty. They slowly crumble into themselves. The rental money would be enough to pay for upkeep and secure an appropriate storage area for the artifacts and the books in the collection."

"A storage area somewhere else," Lily filled in, biting out the words.

"They are all just things," Cairncross replied with some effort. "They can be moved."

"Not all of them," Lily shot back. "Not the mural."

"No," Cairncross agreed. "Not the mural."

There would be no moving the last work of Robert Ash's wife, Evangeline. Her sprawling opus covered every inch of the walls and ceiling of the attic of The Refuge, woven through with the symbols and secrets of a woman with the power to perceive fate itself.

"I could lock it away, or board up the attic door, but it doesn't feel like enough," Cairncross admitted. "None of it feels like enough."

Lily could see the weight of it bowing his shoulders. The retort she had been about to make died on her tongue.

It wasn't fair for her to rail against Cairncross. He had not created the situation they found themselves in. He had simply been left holding the key to an impossible and heartbreaking responsibility.

She could not reassure him, either. She was not that good a liar.

They had reached the place where Great Western Road crossed the canal. The Westbourne Park station lay on the far side. Lily stopped, knowing this was where they must part ways.

"Thank you for the name," she said.

The old soldier nodded awkwardly. He turned to go, then paused.

"I hope you'll call. If you're ever in Rotherham," he said.

"Of course," Lily replied. The words felt wholly inadequate, but no others offered themselves.

He left. She watched his long stride eat up the distance between her and the station, then slipped her leg over the Triumph and spun it into ignition.

She flew back to Bloomsbury. She took the direct route this time instead of the more circuitous path that had become habitual over the last three months. It took her past the tidy green of Bedford Square.

Lily stopped.

From astride her motorbike, she stared at the two white-bricked buildings that stood out so starkly from the staid red facades of their neighbors. The paint on the blue door had not yet begun to flake. The brass plaque that hung on the wall beside it was as-yet untarnished.

The steps had not been swept.

The Refuge did not yet show obvious signs of decay, at least not from the outside. There was still something terribly off about it, something that reminded her of an empty shell—another vacant tomb like the one she had just left on Kensal Green.

The sight of it hurt. It threatened to tear open a wound inside of her that was only scabbed over, not healed.

She spun the Triumph away from it and raced down the road, leaving the memory behind her.

TWO

ILY TURNED THE TRIUMPH into the narrow mews that ran behind March Place. The rattle of the engine died, the echo of its sound fading from the high brick walls of the surrounding buildings. She pushed open the old gate that led into the yard behind her flat and wheeled the motorbike inside.

The yard was an unremarkable patch of cement her landlady, Mrs. Bramble, unironically referred to as "the garden." The only plants it was ever graced with were the odd weeds that found their way up through the neglected cracks in the pavement.

Lily had made a space for her Triumph inside the tiny, weather-beaten shed in the corner. She slid the motorbike into place between the old rakes and chipped plant pots.

She was distracted. The notion of strangers taking up residence in The Refuge was terrible to her in a way she knew was unreasonable. She could hear Estelle's infinitely patient voice in her mind and knew what her friend would say to her about it if she were to bring the matter up.

Everything passes, darling.

Would Strangford agree? Lily wasn't sure. He could discern everything she was hiding inside her heart with a touch, but his own thoughts and feelings were more obscure.

The man she was set to marry was often an enigma to her.

Sam Wu, on the other hand . . . Lily knew exactly what he would think of the choice Cairncross was contemplating.

Sam felt that The Refuge was his home. That his father and

grandmother now lived in a lovely little flat in Limehouse would not change that.

She thought of the expression on his face the last time she had seen him, that twisted storm of grief and unresolved anger. Losing The Refuge would not be good for him.

Lily slipped her key into the lock of the back entrance to her building. Her heart was in such a tumult that the little frisson of warning didn't register until she had gone through the quick and automatic motion of opening the door.

Then they were upon her.

Rough hands grabbed her arms with the clear intention of yanking her inside.

Lily lacked her usual means of defense. The walking stick she used for her kali, the art of self-defense she had trained in for years, was upstairs in her flat. She reacted in spite of it, twisting her body and throwing the weight of it backwards.

Both she and the man who held her tumbled down the three short steps to the yard. Lily landed hard on the pavement as a dull brown sparrow fluttered wildly out of her way. Her head bounced against the cement, pain blazing through her skull.

She ignored it, rolling free of her attacker and scrambling to her feet. She snatched at a broom that leaned against the brick wall of the garden. Without pausing to think, she whirled it at the stranger, who had also regained his feet and was already coming at her again.

The broom was not her staff. It was a length of cheap pine, made awkward by the weight of the wide brush at the far end. It snapped as it connected with her attacker's shoulder. The brush fell away and Lily was left with a splintered length of stick a little longer than her arm, jagged at the end.

She would make it work.

The man who had attacked her was tall and thin with cropped ginger hair. He had already recovered from her blow. He swung at her with his left hand. As Lily deflected it, she was conscious of two other strangers leaping down the steps, their faces and figures a blur.

She snapped the broom handle against the ginger-haired man's wrist, then swung it back into his jaw. His head wrenched to the side and he howled out a curse.

Someone else grabbed her from behind. Lily was prepared for it. She broke his hold with a twist of the broom handle, then jabbed her makeshift weapon back into his gut.

He let out a whoosh of breath at the impact, but it would not slow him for long.

There were too many of them. Even with her walking stick, Lily would have been challenged to overcome three men on her own, and she had started the whole encounter completely off guard. Her mind was still whirling to catch up, her body going through the motions of her defense on instinct.

Lily needed to level the odds. She had to find a way to take at least one of her attackers out of the equation.

The third stranger rushed at her. The jagged end of her broom handle offered itself. Lily spun, aiming the sharp point of it at her assailant's throat—and then realized that the threat she faced was a boy of no more than fourteen.

She fought against her own momentum. It softened the strike to a mere scratch across his neck, but left her dangerously off-balance.

The ginger-haired man, recovered now, barreled into her from the side. Lily was thrown against the bricks of the garden wall, his weight pinning her arms. His accomplice joined him, shoving her face against the wall as the boy yanked the broom handle from her hands. Lily opened her mouth to scream, conscious of the rows of closed windows on the upper floors of the houses that surrounded her. A wool sleeve was shoved against her teeth, muffling the sound and half choking her. She tried to bite at whoever was holding her but the fabric of his coat was too thick for it to matter.

Her arms were wrenched behind her back and locked there. She kicked out with her feet, landing a blow on a solid shoulder, but then her ankles were securely grabbed. She was hefted from the ground, hauled quickly and efficiently into the dark mouth of the house.

The men forced her into the kitchen and threw her face-first onto Mrs. Bramble's solid oak worktable.

A rope looped around her wrists, pulling tight. Another secured her ankles.

"Go ahead and bind her to the chair as well, boys," said a comfortable voice from the other side of the room.

There was a fourth man in this ambush—and Lily had met him before.

As his accomplices shoved her into one of the kitchen chairs, tying her into place with another length of rope, Lily turned her glare to Jack Cannon.

The ordinary-looking man in the well-cut suit was the uncrowned criminal lord of Limehouse, and Sam Wu's former boss. He reclined in the cushioned rocking chair by the stove, his boots crossed lazily in front of him.

Lily stopped fighting. She would not be getting out of this situation by way of physical force.

She kept her eyes on Cannon, knowing perfectly well that it was only Cannon that mattered. He looked much as he had in the brewery in Limehouse three months before, where he had cheerfully encouraged members of the Irish Republican Brotherhood to torture Sam to get the answers they wanted out of Lily.

Silently, inwardly, she cursed herself for foolishly letting down her guard. She should have expected that Cannon would turn up at some point after that encounter, which had ended with Lily and Sam staging a spectacular and risky escape. Picking the lock to get inside her building would have been easy for the man who had turned Sam into a consummate housebreaker.

Sam had warned her. When they had first discussed using Cannon to get to the IRB, Sam had promised there would be a price to pay for it.

Lily should have listened.

There were four of them altogether. Now that she was not being actively attacked, Lily could take a moment to assess them. Besides the tall, ginger-haired man who had rushed her at the door, there was a middle-aged fellow with a thick black beard and solid shoulders. He had the look of a sailor about him.

The boy she had nearly stabbed was thin, his lank dark hair falling into his eyes. There was a scar on his cheek from some sort of burn.

Something else registered as off about the kitchen besides the presence of four attackers. Mrs. Bramble's work table was normally kept clear of everything save her jar of cookies. Currently, an odd rectangular object sat on the scarred boards, covered by a piece of canvas.

Lily was certain it did not belong to Mrs. Bramble.

The boy was glaring at her. Lily was conscious of the red scratch on his throat she had left with her broomstick. His eyes were hard, as if he would happily have gutted her if Cannon had given him the word.

The yellow of an old bruise marred the boy's chin.

"You've met wee Davy," Cannon noted. "He's a replacement for one of his less fortunate colleagues. That boy was foolish enough to get caught. They gave him ten years of hard labor. I doubt he'll be much use to me when he gets out. It's a challenge, finding good help these days."

The lad in front of her was another child taken off the streets and forced into crime to avoid starvation. Sam had never told Lily the details of how Cannon secured the cooperation of such boys, but she could well imagine. Nor did it surprise her that Cannon showed no remorse when the children took the fall for the crimes he himself had organized.

The thought acted as a catalyst on her fear, transforming it into a quiet and potent rage.

The ordinary-looking man in her landlady's chair used the lives of the weak like pieces on an enormous chessboard. Now he had the gall to assault her in her own home.

He had the upper hand—for the moment. But Lily was conscious of a burning sense of her own power as she looked at him.

"You don't approve," Cannon said. "Rather I let the lads starve, then? Work puts food in their bellies and a bit more besides to keep the family. They don't get that from any school."

"If charity was your motive, then you wouldn't force them into committing felonies to provide for themselves," Lily snapped back.

Cannon leaned in, darkly and uncharacteristically serious for a moment.

"You can't keep giving from a pot that's empty," he said. "There ain't no one looking out for the people of Limehouse—least of all grand lords like your dad. My people could rot in the street for all they care, and they'd clear the debris for a new housing block. Lime-house must look out for itself, but desperate people will claw each other to pieces for a scrap of bread. It takes a leader to organize them."

"And you believe yourself to be that leader," Lily filled in.

Cannon leaned back, spreading his hands comfortably.

"I'm here, ain't I?"

It painted a tidy picture, but Lily knew better.

"What about the women?" Lily threw back. "You can hardly claim your treatment of them is for their own benefit."

There was one woman in particular Lily had in mind as she made the challenge—Wu Zhao Min, Sam's sister, whom Lily knew had been subjected to unimaginable horror at Cannon's instigation.

"Women are good for baking bread or providing one's heirs. If she ain't baking or breeding—well, there's really only one other use for her. Isn't that right, boys?"

The cold-eyed adolescent spat onto the floor, his rage at Lily still a palpable force in the room.

"Guessing you ain't much of a baker. Are you, Miss Albright?"

Cannon's threat was all the more chilling for how easily he delivered it.

Lily was conscious of her vulnerability, tied to a chair and alone in the house. The red-haired man was regarding her now with a different sort of interest.

She held fast to her anger. It was far more useful than terror.

"What do you want?" she demanded.

Cannon stood. He plucked the poker from the stand by the stove and used it to nudge open the iron door to the firebox. The coals were glowing comfortably. Mrs. Bramble would have filled it before stepping out to run her errands. Lily could feel the soft warmth of the embers. Cannon gave them a little stir and they flared to a brighter orange life.

"Nothing too gutty, love. We just came to conduct a little experiment," he replied.

"You can hardly expect me to be amenable after assaulting me at the door," Lily noted.

"I don't expect you to be amenable at all," Cannon returned. He left the poker buried in the glowing coals. "But you see, I've been puzzling over that show you put on during our little swarry with the Fenians this summer."

Lily inwardly cursed.

The meeting with the Irish Republicans had not gone as planned. With the situation rapidly veering out of control, Lily had been left with no time and no alternative but to use both her and Sam's respective powers to bluff their way into an escape. Sam had called on the favor of his rats, and Lily had summoned her own precognitive abilities to intimidate the men in the room into allowing her and Sam to slip away.

She had known it was risky. There were very good reasons for her and her fellow charismatics to keep their powers secret. By some interpretations, what they did was technically illegal. Estelle lived the most publicly out of them all, using her ability to earn an income. There were enough other men and women in London who claimed to communicate with the dead that she could mostly blend in with the crowd. Still, she had been forced to pay a hefty settlement back in September when an unhappy client filed suit against her.

Lily, Sam, Strangford and Dr. Gardner all kept the truth of their abilities very carefully hidden from a world that wouldn't understand—or the even more dangerous people who would believe it all and wish to exploit it.

When Cannon had returned Lily's lost staff to the steps of her building last August, she had known it was not the act of a generous spirit. It had been a warning that he knew where to find her.

Now he had decided to make use of that knowledge.

There were two ways she could play this—denial or intimidation. Cannon would not be easily convinced by a denial, which left her with only one option.

Lily summoned her courage, forcing herself to meet his gaze unflinchingly.

"So, then," she said with a boldness she didn't quite feel. "Come to find out how you're going to die?"

The sailor frowned. The ginger-haired man regarded her with a sneer.

The boy gave a blink of surprise.

Deliberately, forcefully, Lily burned toward a connection with her power. It rose up in her as though answering to the simmering call of her rage, and the foresight she had been granted in that brewery three months before flooded back to her.

Lily looked at the crime lord by the stove and recalled how she had foreseen his throat splitting into a wide red smile, the blood spilling down over his chest.

The grace in his movements as he fell to the ground, collapsing before a pair of worn leather boots.

"I will grant you, Miss Albright—that was finely done," Cannon mused. "Your mother would've been proud of that little performance. You've a future on the stage if you ever want it. But I didn't get where I am in the world by taking show for substance, and there weren't no more substance in what you said than I could've had from any two-penny fortune teller on a Saturday evening."

"Then why are you here?" Lily demanded.

"For the other bit," Cannon returned. "Davy, would you do the honors?"

The boy took a handful of the canvas covering the rectangular object on the table. He tugged it free, revealing a battered metal cage containing a single thin brown rat.

"You had these little buggers dancing to your tune at the brewery," Cannon said. "The boys here would like another show."

Lily consciously kept herself from reacting, though her heart was pounding in time with her sense of threat.

"I'm tied to a chair," she evenly replied.

"Didn't stop you before," Cannon noted.

Lily swallowed thickly.

"It doesn't work like that," she lied.

Cannon returned his attention to the stove. He gave the poker another stir, seemingly unperturbed by her refusal.

The boy, Davy, glared at her from across the room, his face utterly lacking any sympathy.

Cannon pulled the poker from the embers and thoughtfully regarded the red-hot tip of it.

"Perhaps we must raise the stakes," he said.

The words were a blow. Lily felt them hit and willed herself not to shatter.

The thug by the stove could not possibly know the significance of that phrase, a phrase she had last heard on the lips of someone else.

Someone she had trusted. Someone who was gone.

We must raise the stakes.

The grief flared up in her, fresh and sharp, with the sight of Robert Ash's empty grave and the hollow shell of The Refuge still fresh in her mind.

Cannon gave a little wave of his hand. At the signal, the sailor came behind Lily. He took hold of a handful of her hair, using it to force her head back against the bulk of his stomach.

Smoke rose from the tip of the poker.

"Do the trick again, or I'll burn you . . . right . . . here," Cannon finished, holding the smoking iron a breath away from Lily's cheek.

She could feel the heat blistering off of it.

"I am afraid it will leave a mark," Cannon apologized. "Pity to scar such a pretty face. You've a wedding next month, haven't you? Wonder if your grand lord will still want you if you ain't so fine-looking anymore."

To all appearances, there was nothing extraordinary about Jack Cannon. His hair was streaked with a little gray, the lines of his face soft and friendly. He might have been any tradesman or shop owner, a fellow you could easily pass on the street without giving a second look—if you missed the sharp intelligence in his eyes.

So unremarkable, and yet a nexus for such immense suffering.

Sam. Zhao Min. The child glaring at her from across the table and countless unnamed others.

As Cannon stood there in her kitchen with the heat of a brand at her face, Lily was certain he felt not one ounce of misgiving about any of it.

There was one obvious way for Lily to stop him from burning her. She could tell him the truth. She could admit that it was Sam who manipulated the rats.

She'd far rather take the scar.

Lily met Cannon's gaze, channeling every ounce of her rage and defiance into that look.

Then the front door opened.

The creak of the hinges easily penetrated the quiet tension of the kitchen. Lily heard the shuffle of a coat, the slide of an umbrella into the stand.

"Which will that be, do you think?" Cannon murmured. "The skinny spiritualist? Or the plump little suffragette?"

Something must have changed with Estelle's or Miss Bard's appointments. One of them had come home.

She was conscious of the lean and hungry shadows of the four men in the kitchen, more than enough force to overcome either of her friends.

It was Cannon who had casually suggested to the Fenians that torturing Sam would be a more effective way of forcing Lily to talk than inflicting pain on her directly. He would make merciless use of whoever was outside.

Lily had to keep him in the kitchen. There was only one way she could think of to do that.

"I can do it," she blurted. She spoke as forcefully as she could without raising the volume of her voice above a whisper.

She gave Cannon a look that dared him to contradict her. His expression was thoughtful, measuring.

He drew back the poker.

"Let's have a demonstration."

He spoke graciously, as though he were inviting her to tap out a favorite tune on the pianoforte. At a nod from his boss, the ginger-haired man opened the door to the cage.

For a terrified moment, Lily wondered if perhaps she could find some way to communicate with the rat. If she tried hard enough, could she be momentarily graced with some fragment of Sam's khárisma? Would the animal listen to her for his sake?

Lily had never had a particularly good relationship with God, but she began to pray as hard as she ever had in her life.

Please, she thought, willing the question at the rat, at the universe, at the forces of fate Robert Ash's wife had painted onto the attic walls of The Refuge. *Please will you listen to me?*

No new magic graced her. The room remained as it had been before. The rat sniffed thoughtfully at the opening of the cage, then turned to scrabble at some unseen mark in the corner.

Overhead, the stairs creaked as someone she loved walked by.

"We're waiting," Cannon noted.

The panic and despair threatened to overwhelm her. Lily anchored herself against them, refusing to give in.

She could not talk to rats, but she did have another kind of power.

A plan started to take shape. It was a reckless bluff … but perhaps it might be just enough to get her out of this.

Lily dug into the heart of her foresight, focusing it on the animal in the cage beside her. She felt the connection catch and spark, forging an electric and unstable link.

The rat would not take her orders, but Lily could still know what it was going to do next.

"Come out of the cage," she said, making it sound like an order.

Tentatively, carefully sniffing the air around it, the rat approached the open door, then tumbled out onto the surface of the table.

"Turn left," Lily said.

Following some rodent impulse, the creature whirled to the left.

"Freeze," she ordered, knowing that the rat would do it as its sensitive ears caught some shuffle of sound in the room.

She paused for what would come next. When the knowledge arrived, it was something less than she might have hoped.

"Just … sniff around for a bit," she said, trying to make the words sound forceful.

The men in the room looked confused.

"But it's just doing rattish things," Davy protested. "Can't you make it do something else?"

Lily lifted her chin defiantly, brazening it out.

"That isn't how it works," she retorted. "I can't make it do something it has no desire to do. It's more of a … nudge."

"And at the brewery, the rats desired to crawl all over your pretty self," Cannon cut back slowly. His eyes were sharp and clear in the gloom of the kitchen.

"That's right," Lily replied with far more confidence than she was feeling.

Cannon absorbed it thoughtfully as though he weren't still holding the poker he threatened to scar her with.

"I wonder," he mused. "How might this little experiment go if we tried it with our old friend Sam Wu?"

It took all her self-control not to react, to refrain from showing the spike of fear Cannon's words sent through her.

"He was always a curious lad, our Mr. Wu," Cannon went on. "Uncanny, one might say, how he pulled things off."

Lily thought of all the myriad ways Sam's remarkable power casually manifested itself in the world. The clear affection shown to him by Ash's horses, Pickford and Mary, nudging the back of his head with their noses. The hopeful, excited look he received from every dog he happened to pass in the street. The little brown sparrows that followed him everywhere, his tiny spies and messengers.

The fat black bodies of the ravens, their pebble eyes watching from the bare branches of trees as though waiting for Sam to make them an offer.

The purpose of this little audition in the kitchen became clear to her.

It had never been about Lily. Cannon was simply cleaning up a loose end. His threat to torture her was due diligence.

He had always suspected it was Sam.

Sam would not reveal his secrets easily. He could brazen out a great deal of pain.

Cannon would know perfectly well what Sam couldn't tolerate.

Lily thought of Sam's father and grandmother running their prosperous medicine shop in Pennyfields in Limehouse, selling the herbs that Mr. Wu carefully cultivated on a little rented plot in Crouch End. It would be easy enough for Cannon to get hold of either of them.

The thought of Sam's solemn father or his busy, loving năinai being subject to Cannon's brutality filled her with horror.

"You can't reach him," Lily asserted. "Sam is in the Army now. He belongs to them."

"It complicates the matter. I'll grant you that," Cannon replied. "But there are plenty of Limehouse boys in the Army, Miss Albright. And they're always happy to do a favor for their old friend Jack Cannon."

He set the poker back into the rack by the stove.

"I believe our business here is done, gentlemen," he announced. "And the lady's face is still intact. A right cordial little exchange. You needn't get up, my dear. We shall see ourselves out."

They filed past her. The sailor who had held her while Cannon threatened her with the poker gave her a polite tip of his hat.

The boy spat a vile curse at her feet as he passed, punctuating it with a vicious grin.

Cannon paused at the threshold. He turned back to regard her thoughtfully.

"It weren't quite of the same caliber," he mused. "But there is something to that little show you just put on. I can feel it tickling at the back of my brain. Never mind it now. I can always look you up again if it comes to me. His lordship's abode is in Lancaster Gate, isn't it? Fine establishment, that is. Look at you moving up in the world."

Lily's rage flared up, potent and powerful.

She was not like the women he had abused and dominated in the past. She was capable of things Jack Cannon could not possibly dream of.

If he came for her again, she would relish the opportunity to provide him with a demonstration.

Let him try, she thought, and some wild and dangerous thing inside of her danced with joy at the thought.

Cannon's gaze shifted from casually taunting to thoughtful in the face of her unflinching glare.

"Good evening, then, Miss Albright," he said and slipped away into the darkness of the hall.

She heard the click of the lock.

Lily struggled against the ropes. They held fast.

The rat sniffed at the edge of the table, still lingering close to its cage. She would get no help from there.

She contemplated shouting, calling down whoever it was that had returned home upstairs. The thought of the alarm in Miss Bard's or Estelle's face when they saw her like this was terrible. No, she would find a way out of this herself.

She looked around for some other advantage. Her eyes fell on the knife block on the counter.

Throwing her weight, she managed to hop the chair a few inches across the floor.

Lily repeated the action, slowly bouncing herself over to the counter. The chair was still far too low for her to reach the knives.

Carefully, painstakingly, she shifted her balance forward onto her toes, lifting the back legs of the chair up off of the floor. She shuffled closer to the counter, fingers reaching toward the knife block.

A key turned in the lock of the back door. It swung open and Mrs. Bramble stepped into the hall, carrying a crate of produce.

Lily's landlady froze at the sight of her tenant tied to a chair in the kitchen. She blinked with surprise.

Then her gaze moved to the rat on the table.

Cabbage and turnips exploded across the floor as Mrs. Bramble's scream echoed through the house.

THREE

Monday, November 16th
Early evening
March Place, Bloomsbury

THE GRAY SKY brought an early gloom to London, catching Lily off guard. It had been an unseasonably warm day, a last fleeing taste of late summer as the dry leaves skittered across the pavement, almost making her forget that autumn was already well advanced toward winter.

That dusk settling in at four in the afternoon set her straight.

Lily loosened some of the buttons on her coat as she slipped into the house. She had just completed a very awkward conversation with Strangford's sister, Virginia Eversleigh. Virginia had summoned her for tea that afternoon and then carefully inquired whether Lily might consider getting married in a Church of England establishment instead of a Catholic one.

Lily's wedding with Strangford next month was set to take place at St. Patrick's in Soho, the Roman church Lily had attended with her mother every Sunday when she was a girl.

Lily's appearances at Mass were far less regular now, but it had been ground into her from birth that for a Catholic, any wedding that took place outside a Catholic church didn't count.

Lily had been illegitimate all her life. It had become surprisingly important to her that her wedding feel entirely up to code.

She knew Virginia wasn't the source of the inquiry. Strangford's sister was merely playing uncomfortable messenger for her mother, Lady Strangford, who had her own notions of what "up to code" meant.

For his own part, Strangford was perfectly content with St. Patrick's. This was not surprising for a man who kept William Blake's inkpot on his desk.

"I have never thought God cared very much about denominations," he said. "I would gladly marry you in one of Miss Bard's pagan field ceremonies if that was what you wanted."

Lily wondered whether the folklorist had told Strangford the whole story of those pagan field ceremonies. Knowing it herself, Lily could not have referenced it without a significant blush to her cheeks.

Lily had been on guard since Cannon's attack the night before. As she reached the top of the stairs and set her hand to the door to her attic flat, she paused for a breath to reach out with her power.

A warning instinct flared.

She shifted her hold on her walking stick, balancing it in her right hand. With her left, she turned the key and then the knob.

Pushing the door open, Lily ran into the flat.

She swung at the tall, shadowy figure she had known would be inside, making a direct hit to his chest.

The wind came out of him with a gasp, but it wasn't enough. When she moved for another hit, he fluidly deflected her thrust.

Lily pressed her advantage, having quickly assessed there was only one person in the gloom of her parlor. Though alone, unarmed and winded, he was still a threat, naturally parrying her quick blows.

Lily's rage flared, the events of the day before having substantially shortened her fuse. Her power unfurled in response, and abruptly she knew exactly what her opponent's next move would be.

The knowledge snapped into focus—how he would grab for her staff, trying to wrench it from her grip.

Lily knew exactly how to turn that to her advantage.

She feinted with the stick as the shadowy figure reached out, then snapped back with a vicious hit against his shoulder.

"Bloody hell—it's me!" he gasped, and the sound of his voice stopped Lily from making a potentially disabling jab at his face.

"Sam?" she blurted.

"Yes! Now will you please stop trying to kill me?" he pleaded, hands raised. His voice was still raspy from the blow she had struck to his chest.

Lily slipped her staff into the stand by the door. She grabbed the matchbox from the table, her hands shaking a bit. She struck a light and put it to the wick of the lamp.

The room brightened into the familiar space she knew. In the middle of it stood a man who was absolutely not supposed to be there.

It had been three months since she had seen Sam. Already, he looked older. Something had changed in his face, the lines of it growing leaner and more defined. His arms filled out the sleeves of his coat more than they used to.

"Why were you lurking in here in the dark?" she demanded.

"It weren't dark when I got here," he retorted. "I was having a bit of a palaver with your cat and the gloom snuck up on me."

Lily noticed the fat, orange form of Cat shedding onto a pile of magazines. He looked not the least bit perturbed by the battle that had just taken place in the parlor.

"Anyway, I didn't think you'd say 'what do you know' by trying to knock my block off," Sam added.

"You were in my flat!"

"I'm always in places!" he countered, rubbing his bruised ribs. His look shifted, turning thoughtful. "You knew when I was going to grab for your stick, didn't you?"

"I might've," Lily returned carefully, slipping out of her coat and hanging it on the rack.

"That could be right handy in a scrap," Sam mused.

Lily didn't answer. She sat down in the more comfortable of her two chairs and regarded Sam with a frown.

"Cat's not mine," she announced. "He came with the house."

"Ain't what he says," Sam replied, taking the other chair. He frowned, shifting uncomfortably. "This chair is horrible."

"I don't have many visitors," Lily noted.

"No bloody wonder."

"Aren't you supposed to be in Aldershot?" she asked, naming the enormous base where the Army had been training thousands of new recruits before sending them to the continent.

"What, ain't you happy to see me?"

The scare he had given her was still rattling through her. It made her answer a touch less enthusiastic than it might have been.

"You know that I am," she said. "You haven't written. Didn't you receive my letters?"

Sam looked uneasy.

"I got them."

Lily had not known until then that she was hoping there had been some misdirection. The alternative hurt.

"Why didn't you write back?" she demanded.

Three months ago, that question would have earned her an insolent shrug. Instead, Sam just looked worn-out.

Things had changed.

"I guess I didn't know what to say," he finally answered.

"You might have said anything. What you had for breakfast. How the uniforms itch. I just would have liked to know…"

"Know what?" he pushed when her words trailed off.

Lily didn't have an answer.

There was an enormous weight hanging over their words, the leaden tangle of everything they had lost.

Of the moment on the Blackfriars rail bridge when Lily dragged Sam away from the bomb Robert Ash held in his hands, pitting her strength against the force of his grief and rage.

She recalled Sam's face when he surfaced through the ashy water of the Thames, twisted into a howl she could only see, not hear.

Now a war loomed between them, with Sam on one side of it, woven into a uniform. Lily stood safely on the other, cushioned from the shells and mud and death that he would inevitably face.

He rubbed his face with his hands.

"I'm sorry," he finally announced.

Lily accepted it in silence.

"What are you doing here?" she quietly asked.

"I heard you had a spot of trouble," Sam replied.

A little brown bird fluttered from the top of her bookcase to Sam's shoulder. Cat eyed it with lazy interest.

Lily recognized the familiar, mottled brown of an ordinary

London sparrow, and the pieces fell into place.

"You were watching me," she accused.

Sam shifted awkwardly in the uncomfortable chair.

"Not watching," he said. "More just…monitoring your situation."

"Were you concerned about my situation?"

He met her gaze evenly.

"Thought maybe I should be," he replied.

Lily sat back.

"You knew he would come for me. Cannon."

"I knew it was a possibility. Cannon misses nothing. That little show we put on in the brewery would have caught his attention." His mouth set into a grim line. "It isn't good to have Cannon's attention. You alright?"

There was a weight to the question that made it clear it was more than a casual inquiry.

"Just a few bumps and bruises," Lily assured him.

His visible relief told her a great deal of how much Sam knew about the threat Cannon could pose.

Her friend was not wearing a uniform. Sam was clad in his usual tweed coat and trousers over a clean white shirt.

"Why aren't you at Aldershot?" Lily pressed again.

"I'm en route to Dover. I ship out tomorrow. I'm just…making a small detour on my way to report in."

"Ship out?" Lily echoed.

The words twisted inside of her. She thought of Cairncross's furious expression in the library of The Refuge the day Sam told them he had joined the Army.

You'll be bloody cannon fodder.

"I'm headed to Gravelines in France," Sam replied. "The boat leaves at ten in the morning."

"And from Gravelines?" Lily asked. She kept her tone casual though her heart was hammering in her chest.

"Dunno," Sam returned. "I don't have my assignment yet. They said they'd wire my old man if it came through in time. Otherwise, they'll tell me when I get there. Seems there's a high demand for mechanics at the moment. Bit of a confab over who gets priority."

She tried not to let Sam's announcement that he was headed for the continent terrify her. She deliberately recalled what Dr. Gardner had said after Ash's funeral.

They'll not waste a good mechanic on the infantry.

With his skills, Sam would be very valuable to the military. That must count for something.

Lily hated this constant, low-frequency fear she had to feel—for Sam, for Gardner. For all the men she knew who had taken up the uniform when the call to war resounded over England.

Sam stood up, plucking his hat from the table. Lily had forgotten how tall he was.

"I won't keep you. Just wanted to tell you that you won't have to worry about Cannon."

Alarm rang through her.

"Why not?" she demanded.

Sam's face shifted into that familiar stubborn look.

"I'm going to take care of it, is all," he replied.

"What does that mean?"

"Best you don't know the details," Sam said.

Lily rose from the chair.

"You shouldn't do that," she ordered.

"I don't recall asking for your opinion," Sam returned.

"It isn't necessary. Cannon isn't interested in me anymore," Lily pressed.

The lines of Sam's face grew even more grim.

"Jack Cannon's never done with you," he said. The words rang with the flat truth of hard experience.

Something inside of Lily ached at hearing it.

"Even if he comes back, I'm entirely capable of defending myself. He won't catch me off guard again," she asserted.

"What about everybody else?" Sam shot back. "You ain't the only one he's a threat to. A man like Cannon doesn't stop until he's made to."

"That doesn't mean it has to be you who stops him," Lily protested.

"I stood by while Jack Cannon wreaked havoc for eight years. I was his bloody hand for it. You don't know half the things I done for Cannon."

He was raw. The words shook with the force of it.

Lily thought of Davy, the child she had nearly murdered in the back garden—the one who had watched with approval as Cannon threatened to sear her face with a burning iron.

It was true. She did not know what Sam had done in the past, what he had been coerced into as a vulnerable boy dependent on Cannon for his life, for the lives of his family.

"I can't pretend it ain't my business anymore," Sam said. It had the weight of a vow. "Not now I know what he did to Jiějie."

Jiějie—the Mandarin term Sam used for his sister, Zhao Min, summoned the woman's face back into Lily's mind. Her image was burned there, sitting across the table of an illegal nightclub, an oasis of perfect control in the middle of a bacchanal.

The gleaming white of her suit.

Strangford crumbling to his knees as she put her long fingers into his bare hand.

He had read Zhao Min's past in that touch and the pain in it had been potent enough to cripple him.

Lily only knew a fraction of the woman's history. It was enough. She would not wish what Zhao Min had suffered on her worst enemy.

Sam stood as though the chair was too small to contain the potent storm of emotion coursing through him. Lily couldn't read him with a touch like Strangford might have, but she knew something of what must be roiling under his skin—guilt, regret, and so much rage it was astonishing he did not come apart at the seams with it.

"There's no one else," he said, staring out the window so that Lily could not see his face. "Cannon has half the Limehouse division of the police in his pocket. The rest of the borough is too afraid."

He looked down at his hands. They were clenched into fists.

He didn't say the rest, but Lily knew what it would have been. Cannon had used him. He had arranged the rape and enslavement of his sister. Sam had changed so much in the months she had known him, smashing from the last lingering vestiges of boyhood into the soldier who stood before her. The metamorphosis was not yet complete. To burst into the man he wanted to be, he believed he needed this.

She watched Sam wrench back his control. His shoulders shifted, moving from that rigid determination to the casual pose he showed the world.

"Anyway, it's me who knows where he's vulnerable." He turned to face her again, leaning against the glass, arms folded across his chest.

"And how is that?" Lily demanded.

"He's got a secret. Something that would tear his whole empire apart if it came out. I'm going to see that it does in a way Cannon can't possibly brazen away."

"How exactly will you do that?"

"I'll fight him," Sam said. "He can't refuse a challenge, not one thrown down in public. It'd make him look weak if he did, and Cannon can't afford to look weak. When I have him pinned, I'll force him to admit what he did in front of all his men. There won't be nothing left of him after that. He'll be done."

"What happens if you lose?" Lily pushed, deliberately ruthless. "A man like Cannon doesn't fight without stakes. What will he demand you put on the table?"

"He'll want me to desert," Sam returned flatly. "And go back to work for him."

The horror of that took the life out of her anger.

"Desertion is a capital offense," she blurted. "You'd be in hiding for the rest of your days. Jack Cannon would have power of life or death over you."

"You don't have to worry about that because it ain't going to happen."

"You can't possibly know that," Lily snapped.

Her anger was fueled by fear. Sam was going into this fight for all the wrong reasons. He was twisted up with guilt, weighed down by a history of exploitation and helplessness. They were emotions that would make him reckless.

Lily felt certain a man like Cannon would know exactly how to leverage recklessness.

She could see Sam hold back his retort. He knew full well which of them was the one who could see the future.

"It doesn't matter anyway. The thing's done," he said. "The meeting's set for tonight."

"And he agreed to it? Just like that? Surely that shows you how clearly he knows he's going to win."

Sam didn't meet her eyes.

"I didn't exactly tell him the truth of it."

"Then what did you tell him?" Lily demanded.

"He thinks he's meeting you," he said. "I faked a telegram. Pretended you were wiring to offer to show him the truth behind the trick with the rats. Told him he had to bring an audience and made it sound like you wanted to cut a deal. You give him the trick, he agrees not to bother any of us again."

Fury sparked, caught. It burned through her, hot and fierce. Her next words spilled out before she could consider them.

"This is a childish, foolish, and entirely selfish debacle," she blazed.

Sam's eyes narrowed. She could feel his anger, but he held it under an iron control.

"I'm doing it to keep you safe," he said.

"This has nothing to do with me," Lily retorted. "This is about you. This is about not being able to forgive yourself for what happened to your sister. You're trying to make up for how you think you failed her, but it doesn't work like that. You can't earn your absolution by sacrificing yourself to Jack Cannon."

"I ain't asking for your approval," Sam snapped. His words were sharp as a whip.

He slammed his hat down onto his head and stalked to the exit. He paused on the threshold.

"See you around," he bit out, then slammed the door shut behind him.

The sound echoed dully through the cramped space of her little attic parlor. Lily closed her eyes against it, overwhelmed by the whirlwind of those few moments with Sam.

The shock quickly dissipated, leaving behind an urgent sense of purpose.

She raced into the bedroom, tearing off her dress so quickly one of the buttons popped from the wool, spinning across the floor. She threw open the wardrobe and yanked out her trousers. It took her only a few moments to throw on her motorcycling gear.

She strode to the door, pausing only to yank her walking stick from the stand.

Jack Cannon wouldn't be attending the meeting he expected to tonight—but neither would Sam Wu.

FOUR

Ten o'clock in the evening
Soho, London

AUTUMN LEAVES SKITTERED across the ground of Golden Square. Lights blinked on in the windows of the surrounding buildings as the sky overhead shifted to a deep violet. The night was warm for late autumn, and several flats had left their sashes open to enjoy the evening air. Lily could hear families chattering in Yiddish and Italian as she passed by.

A group of old men held court on a ring of benches in the square itself, the smoke of their cigars rising up in thin curls. Their laughter echoed off the bricks, comfortable as an old shoe.

A stoop-shouldered fellow with a cane made his farewell. He had the medal of some foreign war pinned to his lapel and paused to give Lily a curious glance as he passed by. He made her a polite tip of the hat and ambled on to his building.

The bench behind her was empty. Lily didn't sit on it. She was restless, itching for movement. It was all she could do to refrain from pacing up and down the pavement.

The lamplighter had finished his rounds. Lily could hear the soft hiss of the gas.

Time was moving too fast.

She had followed the clue her father had dropped into their conversation in St. John's Wood four months before.

To arrange a meeting I send a runner to a chip shop in Soho with a note.

After visiting her fifth chip shop that evening, Lily had cause to curse that he hadn't been more specific.

The sixth was a narrow tiled room sandwiched into the ground floor of a building that also housed a smoke shop. The proprietress was a tall, broad-shouldered Russian woman with a face that was likely once quite pretty before it was marred by a vicious scar from ear to chin.

She quietly accepted the folded message Lily presented before dismissing her with a curt jerk of her head.

Lily tried not to think of what she would do if the person she had summoned to this place failed to turn up. Would she simply shrink back to March Place and wait to see what the morning brought? The notion was intolerable, even though the course of action she had chosen instead barely deserved to be called a plan.

A black carriage rolled to a stop a few yards away. It was of the same make as half the hackneys that crowded the streets of the city, pulled by a single black gelding, but a closer glance revealed that the vehicle was exceptionally well-kept. The ebony paint gleamed with wax.

Lily gave an equally careful look to the driver. The figure on the box had short dark hair and a sturdy build, clad in the same dull wool coat and trousers you might see on any other London cabby.

But this cabby was a woman.

The woman noted Lily's scrutiny and made a thoughtful tip of her hat.

The door to the carriage opened and a more obviously feminine figure stepped out. She wore a gown of pale, elegant gray. A neat black feathered cap sat on the coiled pile of her dark hair, a veil falling to obscure her face. She had the look of a lady in half-mourning, of which there were plenty in the city at the moment.

Wu Zhao Min therefore attracted little notice as she sat down on the bench behind Lily's motorbike.

Lily reined in her restlessness and joined Sam's sister.

"Why the veil?" Lily asked without preamble.

"I'm grieving," Zhao Min replied.

The answer surprised Lily.

"For whom?" she said.

Zhao Min paused for a moment before answering, as though deciding how much she was willing to share.

"I pay women for information," she finally said. "Women who are . . . trapped in intolerable circumstances. When they have earned enough, I help them use it to escape."

Lily refrained from looking to the driver of the hackney. The woman sat comfortably on her perch, out of earshot of their conversation. She thought also of the Russian with the scar at the chip shop on Greek Street where one could leave messages that would somehow find their way to Wu Zhao Min.

"For some women, escape means removal from the sphere of influence of certain powerful individuals who would prefer that they remain entrapped. It means removal from England," Zhao Min clarified flatly. "I placed several of those women at an inn I purchased in Dinant. In Belgium."

Lily began to have an itching notion of where this story was going. It made her queasy.

"The Germans occupied Dinant in August," Zhao Min continued. "They became convinced that local saboteurs were undermining their efforts to fortify the city. To discourage such insurrection, they executed a series of reprisals against the civilians of the city. The inn was sacked, then burned. Six of the ten women there are now dead."

Zhao Min's voice was even, but Lily could see a dark fire blazing in her eyes even through the obfuscation of the veil.

"I'm sorry," Lily said. The words felt inadequate, but she found that she meant them.

"If men simply chose to kill each other, it would be their own business. But that is never the way of it. To occupy another country is to rape it. So they rape. It is always the women who pay. Their weakness is exploited, and only chance holds the monsters accountable for it."

Though she continued to sit straight and still on the bench, Zhao Min's rage was a palpable thing. Lily was shocked she had not noticed it the minute Sam's sister stepped from the carriage. It rolled off of her skin, an electric current that heightened the atmosphere around them, and yet was ruthlessly controlled.

"But you did not call me here for an exchange of pleasantries," Zhao Min said.

"No," Lily confirmed. She knew better than to waste any more of Zhao Min's time, especially in her current mood. "Sam has arranged a meeting with Jack Cannon in my name tonight. Do you know where it is?"

"Yes," Zhao Min replied.

Lily's hands clenched on her knees, the fear and anger racing through her. It took effort to hold them in check.

"Sam plans to force Cannon to admit to some sort of transgression. Something he says will ruin him," Lily said.

"He is talking about Nathan Vance," Zhao Min replied.

"Nathan Vance?" Lily echoed.

"Vance was one of Cannon's top lieutenants. He was younger. Strong. Had the sort of energy people are drawn to. Charisma," Zhao Min said. She gave Lily a look as she named it. "He was also ambitious."

"Cannon saw him as a threat," Lily filled in.

"Vance *was* a threat," Zhao Min corrected her. "So Cannon assigned him to punish an importer who had stopped paying his protection money. On the night Vance went to do the job, Cannon tipped off the police. Vance was shot along with three other men."

Lily put the pieces together.

"Sam plans to force Cannon to admit to betraying Vance, out loud in front of his men."

"Vance was loved," Zhao Min continued. "Knowing that Cannon had him killed—and in a way that involved collaborating with the police, no less—would turn many powerful men against him. But Jack Cannon is like a spider in a drain. You might think you have washed him down, but he will always climb back up again. There is only one way to remove the threat of a man like Cannon. If that was what Sam truly wanted, he would not be staging this charade. He would simply set his rats to tearing him to pieces in an alley."

The image of it horrified Lily. Surely something like that was beyond Sam's power. She knew he couldn't force an animal to do something it didn't want to do. His gift was for charm and communication, not coercion.

"I don't think the rats would do it," she blurted, recalling the day she had carried one of them around in her pocket for hours, the warm weight of it dozing happily against her leg.

"There are other ways to kill a man," Zhao Min replied.

She stood. Her pale gray skirts required no straightening. Everything about her fell neatly into place.

"This is not about taking out Cannon," she announced coldly. "This is about Xiang's pride."

Her voice was hot with contempt as she spoke her brother's Chinese name.

She began to walk away. Lily stood, calling out.

"He's not wrong."

Zhao Min stopped. Even through the veil, Lily could see the twist of fury in the woman's features. It was the fury that had driven Zhao Min to leave. She was not a woman accustomed to allowing anyone to see what she was truly feeling.

"Someone has to hold them accountable. The men like Cannon. Not just chance," Lily declared.

Zhao Min lifted her chin, her dark eyes blazing with challenge.

"Is that what you are offering? To hold them accountable?"

"I just want to stop Sam from making a mistake," Lily returned.

"You have the power to do far more than that," Zhao Min snapped.

"You are hardly lacking in power yourself," Lily shot back. The retort was automatic, the words slipping out before she could think better of them.

They weren't meant to be a blow, but clearly struck the woman like one. There was so much happening under Zhao Min's surface, a tumult of pain and rage and determination Lily could not begin to understand. She burned like a star at the verge of the square. Lily wondered what it would look like if Zhao Min ever let the hot light of it escape her skin and blaze out into the world.

"Tell me where it will be," Lily begged. "Please."

"The Poplar Hippodrome," Zhao Min replied at last, her voice thin with the tension of it. "At eleven o'clock."

"Thank you," Lily said.

Eleven o'clock. That was less than an hour from now.

Zhao Min slipped into the gloom of her carriage as Lily took hold of the motorbike. She swung her leg over the saddle, primed the fuel and spun the pedals into igniting the engine. The Triumph roared to life and Lily snapped back the stand. Her tires tore at the pavement as she jerked into motion, tearing out into the November night.

~

The streets of the East End were still alive with activity. Lily wove through tight-packed clusters of hackneys and carriages, omnibuses and carts. She rode on her Triumph with her walking stick tucked into her belt against her back.

She flew past a cluster of South Asian sailors who laughed as they turned the corner from the docks. The crowd around a sausage cart had spilled into the road, forcing her to swerve.

She watched closely as she rode past a group of men fighting outside a pub, one young tough tossing another across the hood of a parked automobile.

The street widened as she turned onto the East India Dock Road, and Lily opened the throttle, pushing for more speed. Each beat of her heart punctuated a fierce sense of urgency. She could not be late.

She still had no idea what she would do once she arrived.

However she interfered with the events about to unfold at the Poplar Hippodrome, Lily knew with a grim certainty that Sam would not thank her for it.

She was willing to accept that. She would take his rage over losing him to Jack Cannon.

The theater loomed into view.

Lily knew the elaborate art deco facade of the place well. Her actress mother had pointed it out a dozen times when Lily had passed this way as a child. Deirdre Albright's performance in *The Bachelor's Remorse* had catapulted her from the ribald music halls of the East End to the prestigious stages of the West. It was at the Hippodrome that Deirdre transformed into the star who would later dominate the theaters of Shaftsbury Avenue and Covent Garden.

The modern lines of the building were usually illuminated by glaring rows of electric lights. The bulbs were dark as Lily approached, the theater shuttered for the night.

A cluster of men lingered at the back of the building, marked by the pinpoint orange glow of the tips of their cigarettes.

The sight of them was a splash of cold water on her nerves. She had nearly forgotten what Sam had told her of his instructions to Cannon.

Bring an audience.

There were perhaps a dozen men gathered in the alley. She wondered how many more were already inside.

Lily swung the Triumph into a narrow lane just shy of her destination. A stretch of fence heavily overgrown by an unruly rhododendron offered a suitable hiding place for the motorbike. Lily chained it securely.

She tugged the walking stick free of her belt and headed for the theater.

The mood of the crowd gathered by the stage door of the Hippodrome shifted as Lily approached. A casual glance or two multiplied into a murmur of more defined interest, and Lily knew she had been recognized.

The wall of shadowy bodies, bearded faces and lingering tobacco smoke parted to allow her to pass. No one challenged her as she reached the door. The man who had clearly been set to guard the entrance gave her a simple once-over, then swung it open, granting her access to the gloom of the Hippodrome's backstage.

After all, as far as every man there knew, it was Lily who had called this meeting.

Lily had never been backstage at the Hippodrome, but the space she found herself in was still familiar to her. It had the same smell of sawdust and paint and old cloth she knew so well from other theaters around the city. She had haunted them as a child, following in her mother's wake, and again as a young woman freshly escaped from finishing school. Lily had swept halls, scraped and painted set pieces, sewn rents in costumes and finally donned them herself, kicking up her legs with a line of sequined chorus girls or allowing herself to be caught in the rings of an illusionist.

It had not been a comfortable life. The expectations for what constituted an evening's performance had been rapidly and unpleasantly shifting when Lily finally inherited her mother's trust at the age of 21. It had been nearly four years now since she had walked the boards of a stage—but she remembered all of it.

The occasional paraffin lamp punctuated the gloom, illuminating the scattered bodies that lingered in the hall. Most of them were men, though here and there Lily caught sight of a painted face and ruffled skirts. Some of the few women present were clearly actresses. Others were of a related profession.

The buzz of their conversation dipped as she moved by.

Lily aimed for a deeper rumble of sound. It emanated from the brighter light that spilled across the far end of the hall—the eager hum of a waiting audience.

A short set of stairs led up to the stage. Lily mounted them without hesitating and stepped into the glare of the electric floodlights.

The hum of the audience opened into a roar. The theater was packed. Bodies lounged in the luxury boxes overhead. Others crowded the seats of the orchestra. The stage itself was ringed with men, leaving a broad circle of bare wood in the center of it.

A few of the orange-and-cigarette girls had been called into service. They roamed the aisles, one of them shrieking as a man made a grab at something other than the fruit on her tray.

There were men in evening dress and men in coveralls, men in tweed and men in gold-threaded brocade. Lily spotted one fellow in a British Army uniform in the orchestra. She caught another glimpse of that same unmistakable olive khaki in one of the boxes, a young soldier laughing with a girl on his lap.

The women were fewer in number and more uniform in class, whether they wore the garish colors of whores or the sober dress of a pub mistress.

There were no ladies present.

Jack Cannon stood in the center of the stage. The crowd that filled the Hippodrome was a testament to his empire. It was Cannon who had brought them all together. Every person in the theater was there because they needed him, wanted something from him—or owed something to him. Cannon held just as much authority here as the men Lily's father mingled with all day in the halls of Parliament, however much he lacked the bloodline or the title.

He was the Lord of Limehouse, and only a fool would fail to recognize how dangerous that made him.

Sam Wu stood among the men lining the back of the stage. His body was rigid with a tension that grew worse as he spotted Lily at the top of the stairs.

His face creased into a frown. He stalked over to where she waited.

He did not bother with a greeting.

"You shouldn't be here," he said. He looked as though he wanted to shake her.

"You're making a mistake," Lily retorted.

"If it's a mistake, it's already made," he hissed, glaring at her. "I'm not backing down from it now."

A murmur of interest rose from the crowd. The men on the opposite end of the stage parted to make way for a slender figure in dove-gray silk.

Zhao Min had done away with the veil.

Sam shifted beside her, the anger Lily had felt radiating off of him mingling with a note of uncertainty.

He had not spoken to his sister since the brief and painful storm of words they exchanged in a wasteland outside a makeshift night-club in King's Cross. Lily remembered it well, every phrase burned into her memory.

You are as guilty as the worst of them.

The words were daggers that struck at the heart of Sam's guilt, tearing open the old wound of how he believed he had failed Zhao Min.

That pain was still raw in him. For a moment, Lily ached to try to comfort it.

He tore his eyes from the estranged sister on the far side of the stage and threw a dagger of his own at the woman beside him.

"I'm doing this," he snapped. "And you'd bloody well better stay out of it."

Sam turned for Cannon, but Cannon was already moving. The Lord of Limehouse took the center of the stage, spreading his arms in an expansive welcome, his voice booming through the rafters of the theater.

"Good evening, Miss Albright," he bellowed cheerfully.

The crowd settled into an anticipatory silence. Lily could hear only the shuffling of cloth as people adjusted to their seats, preparing to watch the show.

"And our own Mr. Wu has decided to join us. What a delightful surprise," Cannon noted.

His voice was pitched for the space, carrying beautifully across the acoustic curves of the ceiling. A trained thespian could not have done it better.

"I ain't never been your own, Jack Cannon," Sam shot back.

The crowd gasped as if at a twist in a play.

Cannon projected his response to the audience, half-turned to share a conspiratorial look with them like an actor breaking the fourth wall.

"What's that, Mr. Wu? And me the one who plucked you off the street. Showed you which end of a knife to hold. Got you your first woman."

He punctuated that with a ribald wink at the crowd, who chimed in with an approving laugh.

"Showed you which end of her to use as well," Cannon finished.

The chime turned to a roar, a wild note of approval.

It was the casual cruelty of a pantomime, a perfect act of theater, and Cannon played it like a master. He knew exactly how to manipulate the mood of those gathered to watch, acting out the part they wanted to see—that of the ruthless and witty ringmaster.

Lily was capable of recognizing that power. Cannon would feed off their energy, riding it like a wave.

Beside her, Sam seethed with rage, his body taut as a bowstring. His own energy was raw and wild, a feral thing barely kept under rein. It would take almost nothing to break his hold on it and spill it out into the world.

Against Cannon's mastery, his potent and instinctive control of the room, Sam didn't stand a chance.

Cannon was going to crush him.

Disaster loomed. Lily felt it with more than mere logic. Her khárisma sang in warning, lifting the hairs at the back of her neck.

She needed to know more of it. She had to find some way to shift the balance.

With a practice that was becoming more natural to her every day, Lily opened herself up to the impossible knowledge that loomed inside of her.

She saw what was coming next.

Time slowed, running like honey. Certain bodies in the crowd bloomed with significance, their colors brighter and deeper than those around them.

The man in the box seat in the uniform of a sergeant, teasing a girl on his lap. Two privates in the orchestra and on the far side of the stage, near Zhao Min, an older man with the double chevrons of a corporal on his shoulder.

Why were they all in uniform? If they were soldiers on leave, like Sam, why had they not worn their civilian clothes?

The moment stretched like rubber—then snapped as the vision washed over her.

Sam attacks.

He shoves past Lily to the center of the stage, meeting Cannon in a clash of fists.

The moves flash at her like slides in a lantern show.

Sam dodges, strikes.

He lands a blow.

An alarm shrieks from across the theater, the cry of a diving hawk. The corporal stands with a whistle to his lips.

Sam's head snaps back against the force of Cannon's fist.

The soldiers in the orchestra launch onto the stage.

A private tackles Sam from the side. The second joins him, and Sam is pinned.

The sergeant in the box seat has put on his hat. It blazes with the crowned wreath of a military police badge.

A pair of handcuffs glimmer in the electric lights, swinging from his hand.

Lily dropped back into the present with a sick lurch in her gut.

The crowd jeered. Sam was still beside her, his jaw rigid with the urge to find a comeback that would unsettle Cannon.

The game had been rigged.

Cannon must have known that it was Sam, not Lily, who had arranged the night's meeting. He had gone along with it because he had seen a clear way to turn it to his advantage.

He had warned Lily himself that there were Limehouse men in

the Army. That had been no idle bluff. Cannon had summoned them here tonight to put Sam under arrest.

She could already see the list of charges—violating leave, disorderly conduct. There would be a court martial. With a dishonorable discharge on his record, Sam would have no chance of finding respectable work in the future. There would be nothing left for him—nothing but Jack Cannon waiting to welcome him back into the fold.

Waiting to make use of the mysterious power he must now be all but certain Sam possessed, thanks to Lily.

Sam couldn't win this. He would never get to finish the fight. Cannon had set the trap, and Sam—in his guilt and anger and grief—was about to stumble right into it . . . unless Lily could find a way to stop him.

The need washed over her, cold and desperate. This future could not come to pass. There had to be a way to change it.

Lily had the power to find that. It had been born in her when she had fallen into the cold waters of Regent's Canal, when she died and split apart and was somehow knit back together again. She had come back with the ability not just to see the future but know the threads that wove it to the present. She could know what tug, what nudge, would send the whole of fate cascading in another direction.

She had a name for it now. Cairncross had given it to her.

Onmyōji.

It was merely a sound, a tumble of breath, and yet it served as an anchor.

She had no training, no practice. No lessons in what this strange new ability meant or how to use it. The one who should have given her those answers was gone.

Robert Ash couldn't help her anymore.

Lily was on her own with nothing but a word to guide her.

It would have to be enough.

She felt the challenge rising up in Sam, readying itself to spill from his lips, binding them irrevocably to the terrible outcome she had just foreseen.

Cannon gave a little nod to the corporal, a signal no one but Lily took note of.

In the orchestra, the two privates stood, uniformed bodies quietly working their way toward the stairs that would take them up onto the stage.

The sergeant in the box tapped his hat against his knee.

Lily swallowed her dread and guilt and uncertainty. She drew her will into a single vivid point and focused it on that subtle place inside of her, the silent and secret core where she felt her power live.

She asked it one simple, desperate question.

How do I stop this?

The point hit. Connection arced. The world blazed into daylight. Colors shone, lights dazzling her. The crowd was an agonizing roar in her ears, the crash of an unruly sea. Electricity skittered across her skin and centered itself on the staff of yew she held in her right hand.

It flooded with something like fire, twisting and alive in her grasp.

Dangerous. Powerful.

The answer.

Lily gasped aloud under the force of it, the certainty crashing through her brain. The implications of it terrified her. It was madness. Possibly suicide…and without doubt a brutal betrayal of someone she knew trusted her completely.

Her power sang it, and it burned with the call of a siren.

The Poplar Hippodrome slammed back into motion.

She must have made some sound. Sam had turned and looked down at her now with concern.

"Lily?" he asked, and then Cannon's voice rang out from the center of the stage.

"We done now, Sam Wu?" he drawled cheerfully. "Or have you something more than running your mouth to offer tonight?"

From his place beside her, Lily felt Sam rise to Cannon's bait, the call to battle ready to spill from his lips.

None of it would happen. Lily was about to rewrite the script. With the knowledge blazing inside of her, she didn't have any choice.

As Sam opened his mouth to speak, Lily pointed her yew staff at the Lord of Limehouse, the wood pulsing in her hand, and said the words she knew might end their friendship.

"Jack Cannon," she called out in a voice that rang across the theater, spelling the crowd of the Hippodrome into an abrupt and shocked silence. "I challenge you to a fight."

FIVE

HE SILENCE HELD for the space of a breath after the shock of Lily's announcement. It broke with a roar.

The men and women filling the seats of the theater knew they had just been promised a show. They leapt from their seats, cheering like spectators at a Roman circus—all but three of them.

Jack Cannon regarded Lily with bemused surprise as though some part of him were pleased to learn he could still be taken off guard.

Behind Cannon, Zhao Min raised a dark eyebrow.

Sam Wu glared down at her with absolute fury.

The palpable force of his rage took her breath away.

Lily had known it must come to this. She had stolen his plan, robbed him of his chance for vengeance. He trusted her and she had turned that on him in what must inevitably feel like a betrayal.

The truth of that tore her apart, but to refuse would condemn him to far worse.

Her onmyōdō gave her no choice. Lily had asked for it and her strange power had answered in a way that was undeniable.

She had to fight Cannon, even if it cost her Sam.

Even if it meant risking her life.

Lily had overcome thugs in the street before. This would be different. Cannon might underestimate her for a moment or two, but he would very quickly recognize that he must treat Lily the same as any other genuine opponent he had faced in his life.

She was quite certain he had faced many of them.

Sam stepped closer, his voice a cawing whisper in her ear.

"This was my fight," he rasped, the rage seeping off of him.

"Not anymore," she replied.

"He's going to flog you," Sam promised. "He has you by three inches and three stone, and he ain't some windbag. He will whip you, Lily, and when he does, he's going to make you pay for it."

Lily turned to him, refusing to be bowed by his anger.

"Look around you. Look at the uniforms, Sam. There's a military police sergeant in the box watching every move you make. The minute you swing a fist they'll be on you. You'll be discharged, with nothing left for you but Cannon. He was on to you. This whole thing is a trap. You never stood a chance."

He hated it—every word that came out of her mouth. It added fuel to his fury, turning it to something deeper and wilder, more indiscriminate in its target. It flared out of him, electrifying the atmosphere—all his pent-up rage at Cannon, at Robert Ash. At this world that kept twisting his life into knots.

The force of it broke Lily's heart.

There was no time to do anything about it. The familiar weight of her staff was a beacon in her hand, calling her forward. Following it, Lily turned from Sam and stepped out onto the stage.

Cannon hadn't yet spoken. His gaze shifted from surprise to a careful measuring. Lily knew he was making his own attempt to see the future, assessing what he could best gain from this unexpected opportunity that had presented itself.

Lily knew better than to give him too much time to do that.

Thankfully, there was another weapon at her disposal besides her walking stick—the crowd that packed the theater.

Lily had some notion of how to use it.

"What's the matter, Jack?" she called out boldly. "Afraid of being bested by a woman?"

The words had exactly the result she had anticipated. The crowd roared with approval at the taunt.

Lily knew better than to mistake the cheering for an endorsement. There would be plenty of appetite here to see a woman beaten, but a riled-up audience would not tolerate Cannon putting her off. This was a show they wanted to see, and Lily was banking on Cannon being savvy enough to recognize that.

She was right.

"Name your stakes," Cannon returned.

There was no time to consider it. Lily shot back the first thing that came into her head.

"If I win, you leave England—and you never come back," she replied.

Gasps and laughter bounced through the theater. Her demand was audacious, far beyond the usual stakes for a contest like this. Had a man made the same declaration, he would have been derided or refused.

Lily was not a man.

Cannon had no doubt he'd win. The considering look he was giving her had nothing to do with doubt over the outcome of the contest.

He was mulling over what he could best gain from his victory.

Cannon stepped closer, pitching his words for Lily alone instead of the audience.

"And when I trim you, girl, I want your father. You'll give me something on Lord Torrington that puts him in my pocket for good. If you don't, I'll send you back to him one little piece at a time until he provides it himself."

Her heart felt like a cold weight in her chest. Of course Cannon would want to use this opportunity to gain leverage over one of the most powerful men in England. Though Lily's father held no official position in Parliament, he wielded immense influence.

Cannon would understand very well how to use that.

Lily didn't have the information Cannon was looking for. The transgressions she knew her father had committed were more or less public record. His affair with her actress mother was old news. That he had deserted Lily to a boarding school after her mother died was a betrayal to her alone. In the eyes of the world, it had been a perfectly sensible thing to do.

There would be more. Her father lived a complicated life. She did not doubt there were things in his past that could cause a great deal of trouble if they came out, and not just for himself, but potentially for the entire nation.

She could not give Cannon what he was demanding, and yet if she refused the stakes, he could easily refuse the fight. Sam still waited in the wings, all his rage aching for a target.

If Lily didn't see this through—if she left Sam any sort of opening—she couldn't say what he might do, even with the military police in the room.

"I accept," she replied, and the cheers of the crowd battered at her ears.

"Sticks, is it?" Cannon said, noting the presence of her staff.

Lily nodded.

He shrugged out of his coat and waved to an associate among the men ringing the stage. Cannon was solidly in his middle years, but in his shirtsleeves, it was clear he had not let himself go soft with age. He was a solidly built man, and as Sam had pointed out, he both outsized and outweighed Lily. She knew better than to dismiss the significance of that in a fight.

The man Cannon had singled out came forward and handed him a club. The wood was shorter than Lily's yew staff but thicker and heavier. A well-placed blow from it could easily snap her arm like a twig or crack her skull.

More than her father's freedom was at stake in this match.

Lily pulled off her own coat. She tossed it at Sam, who caught it more out of instinct than a desire to help. Freedom of movement was far more important to Lily than the impropriety of stripping to her shirt in front of a room of strangers. Thanks to her days as a chorus girl, she had trodden the boards of a stage in less.

She tested the balance of the staff. Her hand knew just where to grasp it. The wood she had practiced with for so many years was an extension of her body, as natural to move as her arm or her leg.

Recalling that gave her a brief burst of confidence. Cannon would not find her as easy to take down as he supposed.

His club was heavier, but she had a longer reach—and she was fast.

"What do you say, then, lads?" Cannon shouted at the crowd as he stalked back into the open ring at the center of the stage. "Shall I give it to her quick and hard or draw it out for the night?"

The crowd howled with approval at Cannon's blatant innuendo.

The reality of what she was doing swept over her and Lily felt ill. She fought it back, grasping at a more useful emotion—fury.

Jack Cannon deserved to fall, and Lily was going to do everything she could to bring him down.

Without further warning, he turned and came for her.

Cannon moved quickly. With practiced instinct, he threw the momentum of his body into the blow he aimed at her shoulder.

Lily parried it with her staff, deflecting the energy of his attack as she had trained to do for years. She spun her stick to prepare for the return swing she was almost certain he would make and Cannon's club slid harmlessly past her side.

She had first picked up this staff on a stage in Covent Garden. She could still recall the sting of wood against her arm as Bay exploited a weakness in her raw technique. The stern East Indian light rigger had engaged in an act of mercy when he decided to teach a skinny English girl how to defend herself. The first time her staff collided with Bay's, Lily had dropped the stick.

She had quickly learned not to let go.

Cannon circled her, adjusting his approach now that he knew his opponent was not entirely defenseless.

He attacked again. Nothing in his movements spoke of the kind of training Lily had received from Bay. It was all strength and rough experience.

Fast. Brutal.

Blow followed blow. Lily twisted, parried, joints aching from the impact. The faces around her were a blur, fists in the air, the roaring in her ears thirsty for violence. The noise was a barrage. She fought to block it out. She needed everything she had to protect herself from Cannon, even as she recognized that there was something casual in the unrelenting swing of his club.

He was toying with her.

An opening presented itself, brief as a flashbulb. Lily took it, landing a glancing blow on his gut.

The wind of the crowd shifted. The cheer that rose was for Lily. They didn't care whose blood they saw tonight, so long as someone got hurt.

Rage flickered across Cannon's features as they circled each other. Lily knew it wasn't the blow that had done it but the change in the mood of the audience. It represented a loss of control.

Cannon did not like to lose control.

He came at her hard. That vicious playfulness was gone now, his attack all furious intent. Lily struggled to move her staff in front of one of his swings. The club slipped past, striking a glancing blow against her arm.

She deflected most of the momentum but it was still enough to send pain shooting from her fingers to her collarbone.

Shock stole her focus, and Cannon threw his left fist into her cheek.

The force of it snapped her halfway around.

Lily felt warm moisture drip down her face. He had split her skin with that blow.

Cannon paused for a moment, grinning as he preened to the crowd, waving them into an even wilder response. His confidence was back, that unquestioning certainty that he was going to win.

He could not win.

The truth of that swept through her like a gust of wind. *He could not win.*

In its wake, the steady pulse of her heart slowed, beats stretching out along with the passing of time. Her hands were slick against the wood of the yew staff.

A drop of blood fell gracefully from her cheek to the floor. She could hear the soft sound of it hitting the boards as though the room around her were silent as a church and not screaming with bloodlust.

Her power woke, merging into her bones and flesh and wood.

The connection was complete in a way she had known only once before as she moved like a ghost through the rooms of an abandoned manor on Hampstead Heath, the lingering tendrils of a drug still seeping through her veins.

The future spilled out before her, unrolling like a carpet, and Lily understood that the game had just fundamentally changed.

He would come at her next from the right.

The abrupt swing of his club was intended to take her off guard, a quick diversion from playing to the crowd back to an unrelenting assault. It was to be a disabling blow, one that would send Lily to the floor.

She was ready for it.

She easily parried, then snapped her staff into a backswing that sliced across Cannon's jaw.

His head snapped to the side, forcing him to stagger a half-step back. His eyes widened with surprise at the blood he wiped from his lip.

Then they darkened with rage.

He came at her like a bull, mercilessly wielding every ounce of his superior weight and size. The strikes were meant to break her, to snap bone and split skin.

Lily caught the energy of each swing and spun it harmlessly past her. She moved flawlessly into every opening she had already known would be there, her staff striking home again and again.

It felt like fighting a blind man, someone incapable of perceiving that which came so perfectly and obviously to Lily.

A fierce and ruthless joy rose in her, growing stronger with every shivering impact of her yew against his flesh.

The man who fought her thought that he would win. He had attacked her certain of his own superiority—and he had unwittingly stepped into the ring with something he could not possibly comprehend.

Pride had brought him to this. Now he would pay the price for it.

She shifted from defense to attack. Lily was no longer anticipating and countering his moves. She forced him to react to her own.

It was pathetic. His clumsy attempts to protect himself were clear to her before he had lifted his club. Every deflection was another opportunity she could easily exploit. Every attempt he made to give himself the upper hand exposed a weakness she ruthlessly moved against.

The power raced through her brain with a drunk sort of ecstasy. The crowd fed it, screaming with approval, and the beat of that dark song resonated in the blood pulsing through her veins.

She expanded. She was *more*.

And she would tear him apart.

A red spray arced across the stage as Lily's staff blew across Cannon's face once more. The next opening revealed itself. Lily saw how she would sweep him, sending him plummeting to the ground.

He landed like a sack of grain.

She strode in for the finish. Raising her staff, she could feel how it would thrust down into the soft cavity of his eye, blast through until it struck the hard oak of the stage behind his head.

Victory would be hers. The blood of the man who had dared to oppose her would spill across the ground at her feet.

Lily realized what she was about to do.

The horror of it washed over her like a fever. She stumbled back, fighting the need to vomit.

The crowd was on its feet, howling with savage pleasure at the spectacle she had just provided.

Cannon rolled on the ground, gasping out a curse. His face bled. He held his ribs against some invisible damage Lily had inflicted on his gut.

She had very nearly murdered him.

She would have gloried in it.

She raised her head to the bodies ringing the stage, desperate for some way to anchor herself to the present—to the person she had always thought she was. Her eyes found Sam.

He stared at her with a mixture of horror and awe. Lily wanted to shout to him, to make herself heard over the blistering joy of the crowd.

It wasn't me!

But it had been.

Behind her, Cannon staggered to his feet. A few of the men on the stage surged forward to help him up. Lily was only vaguely aware of it, her eyes still on Sam, begging him to understand.

His expression shifted, the horror dropping away into the deep concern of a friend as he realized how stricken she was.

In another moment, he would be running to her—and then his glance darted to the right.

"Lily!" he screamed.

Her power was wrung out, collapsed under the tremendous and violent energy it had just expended, but at the sound of his cry it gasped out one last abrupt flash of insight.

It told her which way to lean.

Lily twisted her body and the knife flew past her to embed itself in one of the pillars that lined the stage.

She turned to see Cannon pulling a second blade from his sleeve.

His eyes were murder. His face twisted into a violent outrage.

Her staff was on the floor at his feet. Her power was dry, choked by that last burst of effort.

There was nowhere to hide.

Cannon knew it.

His battered face stretched into a grin. He raised the blade—and a pale white hand flashed out from behind him, slipping across the thick column of his throat.

It drew a thin, smiling red line that slowly widened into a crevasse.

Blood welled up and spilled over Cannon's collar.

He dropped gracefully to his knees, revealing Zhao Min standing at his back, a straight razor in her hand.

Cannon tipped to the floor. A red pool spread beneath him, slipping across the boards of the stage. It formed a shore near the tips of Lily's brown leather riding boots.

Behind Cannon's corpse, Zhao Min flicked the blood from her blade. She snapped it shut with a practiced twist of her wrist and slipped it back into the pocket of her gown.

There was no roar of approval. The crowd watched in cold and uncomfortable silence.

The murmurs started from the farthest reaches of the hall. Bodies rose, moved furtively toward the exits, slipping out into the night.

The momentum was infectious. The boxes drained, orchestra emptying. The exodus reminded Lily unsettlingly of every other show she had performed in, the low murmur of voices as the audience returned to normal life.

Zhao Min stepped around Cannon's body and walked sedately from the stage.

No one stopped her. Cannon's fall had been too shocking, too wildly unexpected. No one had yet dreamed of how to turn it to advantage.

It would not take them long.

Sam's hand slipped firmly under Lily's arm.

"Come on," he ordered and tugged her to the stairs.

She let him pull her into action. They moved quickly through the dark halls backstage, passing odd clusters of men who looked up in distraction from their dice and cigarettes. As Lily and Sam passed, then they returned to their conversations, ignorant of what had just taken place out under the lights.

Sam broke through the door into the alley. Night air washed over Lily like a balm.

He tugged her purposefully around a corner and down a twist of narrow lanes. Finally they came to a gate in a high brick wall.

Sam shoved at it. The lock was broken and the gate gave easily, admitting them into a dark and deserted schoolyard.

He released her, pacing to the skeleton of a swing set.

"What was that?" he demanded. "What you did back there."

"I just…" Lily started. The words failed her.

"Your khárisma," he filled in. In Sam's mouth, Ash's archaic and musical term sounded like a curse. "That's what it was. Wasn't it?"

A hopscotch field was painted onto the tarmac, faded with years and hundreds of small feet. Someone had hung a sign from the brick wall.

Wait your turn, it read.

Lily nodded.

The memory of it was monstrous—the burning pleasure, the bloodlust. She shuddered to think of it. It made her feel like something alien, something she did not know and was not sure she wanted to.

"You looked like…" he started.

"Don't say it," she cut in.

They watched each other across the shadowy sandbox, the frozen silhouette of a see-saw. There was so much in Sam's face—awe, fear, concern, and the lingering ghost of his rage. She searched for a twist of revulsion and thought she might have seen it.

"That was my fight, Lily."

It was a plea, the protest of someone who had something taken from him that he very badly needed.

"I'm sorry," she whispered.

He left. The schoolyard gate swung shut behind him, bouncing against the broken lock with a dull clang.

Lily remained alone in the dark.

SIX

Tuesday, November 17th
Morning
March Place, Bloomsbury

THE RING OF LILY's alarm was like a blast of water hitting her in the face. She tore herself into wakefulness. Every movement hurt, from the soreness in her arms to the bruises on her face. The events of the night before spilled across her brain, ripping any last vestige of sleep from her body.

The slide of yew under her hands. The dull vibration as it struck flesh.

The terrible joy of it.

The blood pooling at her boots.

Why hadn't he warned her?

Ash should have known. He should have understood that Lily's khárisma could potentially take this form. He should have prepared her for it, told her what it must mean . . .

She pushed that useless stream of thought aside. Her stomach, indifferent to any moral dilemma, growled, warring with her body over what she needed more—breakfast or another four hours of sleep.

There wasn't time. It was already quarter past seven, and there was someplace she needed to be—an errand likely to be as painful as it was necessary.

Ten minutes later she was dressed and standing at her door. She hesitated by the stand that held her walking stick.

Fifty-two inches of polished yew topped by a simple brass knob. There was a knot in the wood two-thirds of the way down, an amber eye. A tiny nick marred the surface just under the knob. It was hard to see, but Lily could always feel it.

She had carried it through the alleys behind theaters and the comfortable respectability of Bloomsbury, into ambushes and the home of her worst enemy. It had saved her from assault or worse, protected her when she had only herself to rely on in the world. It was a companion—something she had trusted—and as she looked at it leaning against the dull pewter of the stand she could not help but feel as though it had betrayed her.

Of course, that was nonsense. The staff was only wood and brass, a mere object. It was incapable of betrayal. It was Lily who had done that.

She still could not quite bring her hand to draw it from the stand.

~

She cut across the University of London campus. The grass of the lawn was still vibrantly green, though the students hurried across it, collars turned up against the cutting chill of the breeze. One of them cast a startled look at Lily as she passed, and she knew he had noticed the bruises and scabs that marred her face. She had done nothing to conceal them before leaving the house.

Someone waited for her on the other side of the square, a slender figure in charcoal silk.

Zhao Min was still in mourning.

She waited patiently for Lily to join her. An exceptionally well-kept hackney carriage was parked discretely on the other side of the road. Lily knew that a closer inspection would reveal the wool-clad driver on the box to be a quiet and fiercely loyal woman.

"How did you know I would come this way?" Lily demanded.

"It is rather obvious where you would be going," Zhao Min replied. "People are nothing if not predictable. Though you are still capable of some surprises. You surprised me twice last night—first when you challenged him and again when you won."

The dark-haired woman regarded her carefully, a cool challenge in her eyes.

"What you can do . . . it is rather more than I had suspected."

Lily remembered the thrill of knowing, the certain power of staff and flesh and technique.

The glittering confidence that she could tear her enemy apart if she chose.

She closed her eyes against it, her gut twisted with discomfort.

"That wasn't me," she protested.

Zhao Min arched a black eyebrow.

"Don't be a fool," she retorted. "It was precisely you."

Lily knew it was true. It drove her unease even deeper.

"I was just doing what I had to do," she returned, meeting the other woman's gaze with a confidence she did not feel.

Zhao Min's eyes drifted to Lily's empty hand—the hand that should have been wrapped around the wood of her walking stick.

"Not entirely," Zhao Min countered.

The final moments of the fight raced through Lily's mind—Cannon prone and battered on the floor, her walking stick raised for the finishing blow.

"I'm not a killer," Lily blurted, fear lending a hard edge to the words.

"Not killing is a luxury. Most of the people who need evil to die lack the power to accomplish it. You possess a great deal of power."

"I never asked for it," Lily returned.

"That is hardly relevant." Zhao Min's tone was dismissive.

Lily's hands had clenched into fists at her sides.

"I have no right to decide who lives or dies," she protested, the words raw.

"Who, then?" Zhao Min demanded. "God? Fate? We call it bàoyìng—that good or evil deeds are repaid in kind. But who does the repaying? Your God has no hands of his own. If those who can refuse to act, what instrument should he use?"

Her words snapped like a flag in the wind, and Lily was thrown back to a carriage ride three months before. She recalled the rain tapping against the windows as they rolled to the funeral of the man who should have been here to give her the answers to those questions.

Remembered how Estelle had calmly delivered a devastating

message from the dead.

A key transforms into a weapon.

There will be blood on your hands.

"I don't want this," Lily ground out in reply. "I don't want to be anyone's instrument."

"Those who do are likely unqualified for the job."

Zhao Min's voice carried a note of weariness, one that deflated Lily's reflex to defend herself.

This woman had saved her life last night. Lily could not know if that was a victory, or what it had cost her.

"Will there be trouble for you?" she asked.

"I have a great deal of practice being hard to find," Zhao Min replied.

Lily was struck for the first time by how much Zhao Min resembled her brother. She wondered how she could have been ignorant for so much as a moment that Zhao Min and Sam were siblings.

The woman in gray turned for her carriage. Pressed by the uncertainty of knowing when—or if—she would ever see Zhao Min again, Lily called after her.

"I'm not the only one with power. What will you do with yours?" Lily demanded.

Zhao Min hesitated, looked away—across the city, perhaps beyond it.

"I thought I knew the answer to that question," she replied. "Now I am not so sure."

A pair of automobiles slipped past them, engines rumbling comfortably. A paperboy dropped his wares onto the doorsteps of the tidy row houses that lined the road.

Distantly, a train whistle sounded.

A feeling of strange kinship bloomed in Lily for the woman beside her. It surprised her with its warmth. Lily explored it carefully, far from certain it would be welcome.

"I hope you find out," she finally said, meaning every word.

"And you as well," Zhao Min returned.

The phrase felt like a challenge.

Lily considered what else she might say—how she might urge this woman to heal at least one of the great wounds of her past, reknit a bond that never should have been rent. She kept those words inside. It was not her place. Zhao Min would make that choice in her own time and her own way.

Zhao Min signaled to her driver and stepped into the shadows of the carriage. The woman perched on the box snapped her reins and the vehicle slipped into the flow of traffic, blending with the countless others that looked almost exactly like it crowding the streets of London.

As it slipped away, Lily became aware of a truth glowing softly inside of her, edged with the familiar hue of her khárisma.

She would see Wu Zhao Min again.

~

St. Pancras Station had the look of a red-bricked cathedral with its Gothic peaks and tall shining windows. Lily merged with the stream of bodies moving through the doors and passed from the bright glare of the street to the shining womb of glass and steel that was the platform.

She paused to look up at the timetable. The train she wanted would be leaving from Platform 12.

Lily let herself be carried in a whirling current of black-suited businessmen and families hauling traveling trunks. She passed a sailor bidding goodbye to a beautiful woman with a kiss, heedless of the crowd that surrounded them.

She reached the top of the platform and stopped to wait. It was ten minutes to eight.

Two minutes later, Sam arrived.

He was wearing his uniform, the wool a rough olive in hue. A wide leather belt cinched his waist and a khaki rucksack was slung over his shoulder. His dark hair was crowned with the distinctive peaked cap of the British Army.

He was walking with two other figures that were very familiar to her—Mr. Wu and Mrs. Liu, his father and grandmother.

They stopped several yards shy of the platform and Mr. Wu put a hand on his son's shoulder.

Sam responded with a deep bow of his head. It was a simple movement with a volume of meaning.

Emotion shifted across Mr. Wu's weathered features. Lily saw a change in the pressure of his hand, and then he was drawing Sam closer.

He pulled his son into an embrace.

Sam's face fell against his father's shoulder, and Lily felt a quick note of shame as though she were witnessing something that should have enjoyed the anonymity of happening in a crowd where nobody knows or cares about you.

Sam bent down to hug his năinai, her arms coming around him fully and generously. He held her for a long moment and then straightened, squaring his shoulders and making certain his cap was still in place.

He did not see Lily when he turned away from them, exposing a secret glimpse of his face twisted into an almost childlike sadness. That Lily witnessed it left her feeling even more awkward, but she forced herself to stay, planted in his path to the platform. The purpose she had come here for was more important than her own discomfort.

Sam glanced up and saw her.

He stopped, forcing the crowd to shift and part around him. The people moving toward the train barely looked as they made the adjustment. They were all city-dwellers, accustomed to altering the flow of their steps.

Lily went to him.

"Did you get your orders?" she asked.

"I've been transferred," he replied. His hand moved automatically to the yellow edge of a telegram emerging from his breast pocket. "They're moving me to the Royal Flying Corps."

"You'll be working on airplanes," Lily filled in. She pushed herself into a smile. "That's wonderful."

She did not have to force a genuine note of happiness into her voice. It felt right that Sam would be using his skills to take men up into the sky—that he should somehow become even closer to the birds that were always following him around. There was also a relief in it. Airplanes weren't maintained in the trenches of Ypres. There would be some distance between Sam and the front lines.

And a greater chance he might come back home to England again someday in one piece.

Lily was conscious of the hands of the big station clock, slicing towards the moment at which he would have to leave. There was no time to do anything but say what she had come there to say. She could read his impatience in the straightness of his back, the grim line of his mouth. He was still angry at her. She could not fix that. She knew better than to try. There was something else she had come to set right.

"I need you to know," she said, looking up to meet his eyes, "That I believe in you. That I will always believe in you, Sam Wu."

With a quick dart of panic, Lily realized she was dangerously close to starting to cry.

She pulled herself together, but her voice was not as level as she might have hoped as she continued.

"You are capable of so very much … bravery and loyalty, intelligence, strength. I never want you to feel that I doubt…"

The words failed, her throat running dry. She closed her eyes, pulling for some way to communicate the truth she so desperately wanted him to know.

"It's just this blasted thing inside of me. Sometimes it demands so much…" Her voice broke. "I can't pretend I don't know the things that I know," she spilled out at last.

He was quiet. She reached for more words, for some perfect way to articulate what she was trying to say—the language that would reach into his heart and fix the damage she feared she had wrought there with her actions the night before. She was left with only air.

A hand slipped over her own, took hold of fingers she had not realized were shaking.

She let herself fall against him, her face pressed against the rough wool of his uniform. After a moment, his arms came around her and he held her back.

A wave of sparrows burst from the elegant iron lattice that supported the domed glass roof of the station. They danced overhead in a wild spiral, then rushed out into the clear air of the morning.

Sam released her, self-consciously adjusting the straps of his bag. He gave her a nod. There was something in it that reminded her of the formal gesture he had made to his father a moment before, and her heart twisted.

He didn't speak. She was left with reading the look in his

eyes—both loving and hard at the edges, wrought through with threads of grief.

The bell of the clock echoed through the station. She had run out of time.

He turned and moved quickly down the steaming length of the waiting train.

Lily stayed where she was and watched him go, the dull green of his uniform visible between the moving bodies of tradesmen and governesses and sailors climbing into the passenger coaches.

There, at the far end of the platform, came the briefest flash of gray silk.

Steam billowed toward the glass roof. The long, soot-darkened line of the train slipped into motion, gliding away from her into the unknown.

~

Outside St. Pancras, London buzzed with the morning. The newsmen swapped coins for papers while a small boy tugged a puppy along at the end of a lead. A pair of lorry drivers were arguing over a collision as pigeons fluttered out of the way of a passing Daimler.

A few yards down the road, an exceptionally well-kept hackney gleamed where it sat parked at the curb. The driver lounged in her seat, flipping the pages of a magazine.

She was settled in for a wait.

The woman noted Lily's attention. She tipped her black cap in a meaningful little salute, then returned to her reading.

Lily thought of the flash of gray on the platform.

A return trip to Dover took roughly three hours. The driver would indeed be waiting for a while.

And perhaps on a train steaming its way to the war, an old wound was finally beginning to heal.

Bridge of Ash

"It is a mistake to try to look too far ahead. The chain of destiny can only be grasped one link at a time."

Winston S. Churchill

ONE

Monday, December 14, 1914
Ten-thirty in the morning
The Hampshire Coast

THE SLATE WATERS of the Portsmouth Estuary churned outside the train's window as it wound across the grassy coast of Hampshire. The sky was pale as snow, the chill wind stirring up little caps of foam on the dark water.

It was a mid-morning run to the city, but even for that quieter hour, the train car was oddly uncrowded. The young men were disproportionately missing. Since the outbreak of the war last August, so many of them had enlisted and were now packed into hastily expanded barracks across the country.

Or they were already gone, shipped off to Europe from which it seemed very few ever returned intact.

Lily sat on the bench with a wicker hamper at her feet. She was dressed for the cold in a wool skirt, jacket, boots, and a coat. Her walking stick was conspicuously absent. The polished yew staff meant far more to her than an accessory or physical aid. Lily felt oddly naked without it, but carrying the hamper required both of her hands.

The countryside glided past the other side of the glass, pastures giving way to little farmhouses or the occasional punctuation mark of a village. The tracks ran no more than two miles from the sea, and Lily could smell the briny tang of the water even through the ever-present veil of coal smoke.

She had been in Hampshire for a week, staying with Strangford at his sister's country house on the coast. It should have been something out of a dream—a sprawling, cozy manor stuffed with garlands and candles, filled with people who laughed and fought and chatted every hour of the day. Lily had never experienced that before, and for many years had been convinced she never would.

She was far from comfortable with the reality of it. It was like visiting a foreign country, one where she was unsure of her ability to speak the language. At any moment, those around her would recognize that she didn't belong.

Going on this errand to Portsmouth had been a relief. It was easier to sit alone on the wooden bench of the local train, staring out the window at the dull procession of fields and houses until it threatened to lull her to sleep.

The tracks turned, and the tumbling hedgerows and white clusters of sheep gave way to a broad green expanse of mingled grass, mud, and water. They had reached the marshes.

Lily's pulse thickened, the world around her slowing. The wool of her skirt scratched softly at the palms of her hands.

As she looked out over that endless sprawl of soft land and shallow streams, unease crawled over her flesh. It reminded her of somewhere else—somewhere she had been before. For a moment, that strange twilit place felt ever so close. It whispered at the back of her neck, tugging for her to return.

A release of breath, a step sideways through the veil, and she would slip from the train to the soft rustling grass. There would be a path, a pale cord twining her toward the place where she must go. She would be free of all of it—the doubt, the longing, the pitched energy of desire.

The train moved past the gnarled shadow of an old oak. A raven perched on the stripped branches. It cawed harshly at her, a rebuke like a slap across her face. The sound anchored her to the wooden bench and the clatter of iron wheels, lifelines she clung to until the marsh ended, broken by a cluster of row houses and a post office.

The tracks turned inland again, following a course through shorn wheat fields and grazing cattle. The elderly gentleman across from her turned the pages of his newspaper, the mother beside him quietly scolding the toddler in her lap.

Lily clenched her hands and forced herself to breathe—drawing air in, then forcing it out again. She was shaking.

She had been changed by what happened to her last August—the fall into the cool water of the canal, the liquid fire that burned through her air-starved lungs.

The place she had gone afterward until Strangford dragged her back to life.

She still did not understand the whole of it—the uncomfortable new powers, the way certain places seemed to shift in opacity, blurring into somewhere else. The person she would have looked to for answers to those questions was gone.

It was another ten minutes before Lily felt safe again.

~

Hefting the hamper, Lily stepped out of Fratton Station in Portsmouth, emerging into the cool, sea-scented December day. A few hackneys waited at the curb, but Lily moved past them. Her destination was not far.

The city was close-packed with terraced brick houses and shops. The masts of ships in the harbor were visible here and there over the rooftops. The more modern shapes of the vessels in the great Navy yard were hidden from view, lying further to the south.

Lily's arms were strong from her training in kali, the martial school of self-defense she practiced with her walking stick, but the hamper was starting to make them ache.

Recruitment posters were plastered to the walls of the shops that lined the road. Some of them were faded with the weather, peeling at the edges. Flags hung in the windows, and a strand of ragged bunting crisscrossed overhead, relics of the celebrations that had broken out when war was first declared months before.

She passed another artifact of the war. It was a bakery with a German name. The windows were nailed over with plywood, and smoke stains marked the bricks above. The shop must be the victim of one of the anti-German riots that had peppered the country, targeting businesses with names like Gertz and Schmidt even if the families who owned them had been in England for generations.

At the newsstand on the corner, the latest war casualty list was pinned to the boards, columns of names marching down the page in tiny black print.

Lily moved past, shifting the weight of the hamper in her arms.

A group of sailors from the Navy yard strolled up the pavement, their bold voices mingling with the cough of lorry engines and the clop of hooves. One of them, who could not have been more than eighteen, looked over at her and flashed a charming smile.

"Want me to carry that for you, love?" he offered, jogging back to her, his tone blatantly flirtatious.

"Thank you, but no," Lily answered coolly.

His companions laughed as she moved on, pounding his shoulders as the boy returned to them.

A formation of the new seaplanes buzzed overhead as she reached the school. Of course, the grand brick building was not currently functioning as a place of learning. The twin flags of the empire and the British Army hung from the upper floor, flapping a bit in the crisp breeze off the harbor. It was a hospital, one of many that had sprouted up like mushrooms in the southern counties since the outbreak of the war.

They were direly needed. The beds were filled almost as fast as the Army could build them.

The whole country had been similarly transformed. New bases sprung up from the ground seemingly overnight and were filled with recruits who drilled in sheep pastures with wooden rifles. Uniforms and guns couldn't be made fast enough to supply them, but it didn't matter. They had to be trained. The more experienced soldiers who had been shipped to Belgium were already returning, packed into overcrowded hospital ships—or they never came back at all. The war was a thresher, crushing through bushels of men.

She hefted her hamper over the step and entered the lobby.

It still looked like a school, with rugby trophies in a case by the wall and the scent of chalk dust in the air. A pair of nurses strode purposefully by in their crisp white uniforms, and a young woman dressed in her Sunday clothes hugged an older man in a wheelchair, tears running silently down her cheeks.

Her father, Lily guessed as she approached the desk.

The soldier behind it hung up a telephone. The wires were strung along the ceiling, falling in makeshift arcs from the water pipes.

"I'm here to see Dr. Gardner, please," Lily said politely as the sergeant turned to her. "I mean Captain Gardner," she abruptly corrected herself.

"St. Andrew's Building," he replied impatiently. "Next one down."

He jerked his thumb to the left as the phone rang again, then turned to answer it, clearly done with her.

"Fifth Southern General," he barked into the receiver.

Lily pushed back outside, then shifted quickly out of the way as a pair of orderlies hurried past, carrying a bandaged man on a stretcher. He was missing an arm. An ambulance was parked at the curb, the vehicle rather obviously a requisitioned milk lorry that had been quickly painted gray. She could see the rows of beds bolted to the inside. Save for the one the orderlies had just emptied, they were all full of ragged men in dirty uniforms and blood-stained gauze.

She slipped quickly past, turning in the direction the desk sergeant had indicated. The St. Andrew's Building was marked by a small plaque on the wall by a pretty blue door.

The halls were bright, still lined with bulletin boards punctuated by tacks that would have held school notices a few months before. Big windows looked into what had once been classrooms. They were wards now, packed with beds holding men with burned faces, flat sheets where limbs had once been. Another ward echoed with coughs. A man vomited into a basin as she passed.

Lily stepped aside to make way for a gurney wheeled along by a bored-looking attendant. The body on the metal slab was covered in a sheet.

She waited until it had gone, her hands cold, then stopped a passing nurse whose uniform apron was splashed with a dark stain.

"Captain Gardner?" she asked as the woman frowned at her, clearly intent on a more important purpose.

"He stepped out," the nurse snapped in reply.

"Do you know where he might have gone?" Lily pressed, a little desperate.

The woman slid a quick glare over her, taking in her civilian clothes, bobbed auburn hair, and the hamper in her hand. Her eyes flashed with quick disapproval.

"Try the chapel," she bit out and moved on.

~

The chapel had not yet been touched by the war. The vestibule was cool and quiet. A rack by the door was stuffed with the requisite pamphlets on the dangers of drink. A small lost-and-found box held a pair of bright green gloves and a knit shawl.

Lily hesitated at the door to the nave. She knew it was foolish of her. Dr. Gardner was her friend. It shouldn't matter that she hadn't seen him since the day they put Robert Ash's coffin in the ground.

She steeled herself and pushed inside.

The door opened silently on well-oiled hinges. As Lily stepped through, her boots tapping softly on the slates of the floor, she heard the low gasp of someone crying. The sound pinned her at the threshold. The hamper pulled at her arms, and her shoulders began to ache. She shifted to adjust the burden, the movement making a small sound that seemed louder in the stillness of the church.

"Don't mind me. I'm just finishing up."

The voice came from the front pew. It was deep and familiar if a little ragged at the edges.

The nave was dim and quiet. Light streamed softly through the stained glass window above the altar, painting patches of muted color across the high, arched ceiling.

"It's me," she finally announced, her voice echoing uncomfortably through the empty air.

"Ah," Gardner replied. "In that case, you can join me while I keep at it."

She made her way quietly up the aisle and sat down beside him on the hard, polished surface of the pew. She set the hamper down on the floor, her arms sighing with relief.

The doctor was in uniform. It was the first time Lily had seen him like that. The khaki wool fit his broad shoulders well, and yet something about it still felt off, as though she had caught him playing in a pantomime. Gardner was a middle-aged physician with a gentle empathy that belied his substantial size and crooked nose, which Lily was fairly certain had once been broken. Despite the insignia on his shoulders, he was not a warrior.

The Ulsterman cradled a photograph in his big hands. It was an image of two little girls, stained with something ruddy at the corner. Lily guessed their age at about four. One was smiling, her hair a little blurred with motion as though she had been unable to hold completely still while the image was taken.

"Twins," Gardner said, answering a question Lily had not spoken aloud. "I just sent their father on to the morgue. Got the better of me for a moment. I came in here so that the nurses didn't need to keep watching me sob like a wet handkerchief in the chair next to the poor lad's bed."

With an uncomfortable jolt, Lily realized she knew exactly how Gardner must have looked in that moment—because she had seen it before.

Ten months earlier on the floor of Strangford's study, the bitter, woodsy taste of the Wine of Jurema on her tongue. The visions had taken her like a whirlwind, spinning her through things she had no desire to know before they finally gave her what she was looking for.

Gardner's body had been bowed by grief beside an empty hospital bed. In the vision, he had been in one of the wards at St. Bart's in London, the hospital where Gardner then worked, but Lily knew that her foresight was far from literal. Her mind showed her a hospital she was familiar with because she couldn't yet have imagined the one she currently sat in.

A chill crawled up her arms that had nothing to do with the December cold. The spill of premonitions she had inflicted on herself that night had been far from pleasant, and this was now the second of them to come to fruition.

The first to come to pass had been a fleeting glimpse of James Cairncross locking the door to The Refuge, the place which had become more of a home to her than anywhere else Lily had ever known—a building which now stood shuttered and hollow at the edge of Bedford Square.

She did not like to think of the other things she had foreseen— of Sam standing in a whirlwind of ravens or Strangford shouting at her to run as the ground tore itself apart around them, his uniform obliterated in an avalanche of mud and splintered wood.

She reminded herself she had nothing to fear from that last one anymore. Strangford had lost his eye in August, a sacrifice that disqualified him for service even if the government did pass the threatened draft she knew was being whispered about in the halls of Parliament.

The fact should have reassured her, but her unease lingered. Lily's visions weren't usually so easily thwarted.

She thought of the hall of wounded men that lay just outside the quiet of the church. The war was merciless, devouring arms and legs and souls without a blink of remorse. Sam was relatively safe from it, stationed at an airfield some distance from the front thanks to his mechanical skills. And Strangford was here. But for so many others…

Her gaze fell to the photograph in Gardner's hand again. He was still staring at it, his eyes rimmed with red.

"I knew he was dying."

His words had the feel of a confession, startling her out of her dark reverie. Lily stayed silent, listening, unsure of how to respond.

"There was a bacterial infection inflaming the tissues of his heart," he went on relentlessly. "I could feel it."

I could feel it.

The words meant more coming from Gardner. Like Lily, he was gifted with the power to know things ordinary people couldn't. His ability took the form of a deep and detailed medical intuition. By laying his hands on the body of a patient, he could sense what had gone amiss under their skin.

Like Lily's foresight, it was something Gardner had to keep carefully concealed from those around him. As the son of a mere Belfast tailor, his background already gave his higher-class peers in the field cause to look down on him. Claims to be able to read a person's ailments with arcane powers would surely have made him even more of a target. It could even mean the loss of his license and, therefore, his power to practice medicine. At least as a licensed physician, Gardner could quietly use his power to aid his more conventional work. Were he labeled a quack or charlatan, he would be pushed to the fringes and perhaps made vulnerable to charges of fraud.

"He wasn't manifesting any arrhythmia," he continued. "Short of sawing open his ribcage, there was no way I could get the other doctors to recognize what was happening, and even if I did . . . what would it matter? We don't have anything to treat it."

Lily could see the tension in his hands though he still held the photograph as delicately as he would some precious artifact.

"I didn't tell him," he said. "He kept rattling on about his girls— how maybe he'd get a chance to go home to see them before they shipped him back to the front. I knew it would take him quickly when it happened."

The doctor looked up at the stained glass window above the altar. The light was pale today, muting the vivid colors. Lily followed Gardner's gaze. Thanks to her Catholic upbringing, she would have recognized the saint in the center panel even if he had lacked the handy label painted in Gothic letters at his sandaled feet. He wore the robes and long gray beard quintessential to the depictions of many holy men, but the great wooden planks he stood before formed the shape of an X, the sign of St. Andrew.

"They say he struck a staff in Cyprus and called up waters that could restore sight to the blind," Gardner said, his eyes on the martyr in the glass. "I always thought it was a fairy story until I heard Cairncross going on about all of them being like us."

He didn't have to tell Lily what he meant by *them*. She had heard Cairncross's theories as well. The librarian of The Refuge believed that many of the saints and martyrs of history had been charismatics like her and Gardner. He said the same of Hindu gurus, Taoist adepts, Sufi mystics, and the witches lit up like candles across Europe during the Dark Ages.

"I don't know them like your people would," Gardner admitted. "But I've heard there were dozens of saints blessed with the power to heal. I've never known of one who just told everybody what was wrong with them without doing anything about it. I know . . . that's not entirely fair. I don't wish it away. It's helped me treat a great many people with more accuracy than they might have found otherwise. But sometimes it feels like I'm only half of what I should be."

Lily knew what he meant all too well. She had seen the future for as long as she could remember but had never been able to change it until recently. For years, she had wished for a way to be rid of her power. She would have given almost anything to be free of it.

Her relationship with her clairvoyance was more complicated now. Something had shifted in her—something she still didn't entirely understand.

She remembered the acrid stench of burning paint in the attic of The Refuge. The cold water of Regent's Canal closing over her face. The call of the raven from the branch of a sea-bleached tree.

The endless expanse of the marsh and the dead woman who rose from the water.

There is more than one right path.

A new power had bloomed in her after that night. Lily wasn't sure whether she'd quietly possessed it all along or if it had been born in her through her passage into that strange, twilit place between life and death. She still didn't know how to use it or what it meant.

Perhaps Robert Ash could have explained it to her. He had always had such faith in Lily and her fellow charismatics, in the powers that moved the universe—his Parliament of Stars. Lily didn't share it. Where faith should be, she found only doubt and confusion and no small degree of fear.

There will be ample time to discuss all of this, Ash had told her.

He had lied.

Gardner was quiet beside her, lost in his grief and frustration. Cairncross might have pulled a half-dozen historical examples out of his prodigious memory to provide context for what the doctor was feeling. Estelle might have known the perfect words to say to comfort him—she usually did, since comforting people was more or less her line of work. Sam could have disarmed him with a joke or roped him into some legally dubious escapade to distract him.

None of them were here. They were scattered. The glue that held them together had dissolved in the explosion that took out half of Blackfriars rail bridge. Lily wasn't sure what remained.

Gardner sighed, the sound long and eloquent.

"Thank you," he said.

Lily startled.

"For what?" she blurted.

The big doctor glanced over at her.

"A little quiet company can be excellent medicine," he replied.

Lily supposed that was true, even if she offered it to him only because she was incapable of thinking of anything better.

"I see you brought me some treats," he noted, glancing at the basket.

"They're from Mrs. Eversleigh," Lily admitted, feeling a little guilty.

She didn't want to take credit for Strangford's sister's thoughtfulness. When Virginia had learned that Lily and Strangford's friend was with the Royal Army Medical Corps in Portsmouth, she had insisted Lily bring him some holiday goodies to cheer him up.

Virginia was good at being thoughtful. She approached it with the same crisp efficiency and enthusiasm she did with everything else in life. It made Lily feel inadequate. She had spent most of her life alone. Her blood was too noble for the many, too low for the few. She fell between the cracks of other families, other circles of friends, and her strange power and the unwelcome knowledge it forced on her only served to isolate her further. She didn't know how to do the little things that made friendships work, the things that seemed to come so naturally to people like Virginia. It was like navigating a foreign country.

"There are two pints of jam, some candy straws, powdered cocoa, meringues, and a fruitcake," she listed automatically, unsure of what else to say.

"I have always felt fruitcake was unfairly maligned," Gardner sagely replied.

He flipped open the basket, taking stock. He pulled out the box of meringues, opened it, and held it out to Lily.

Lily knew she shouldn't. The biscuits were for Gardner, and who knew how hard it would be to come by more? Eggs and butter were already getting scarce.

"They won't keep long," the doctor noted.

Lily gave in and pulled one from the box. Gardner did so as well. They sat together in the soft quiet of the pew, munching on their meringues, the sound of the lorries and carriages passing outside muffled by the old walls of the church.

"Where's his lordship?" Gardner asked. "He ought to have come along to shoulder the burden for you. That arm should be healed up nicely by now."

Strangford had broken his arm in August in the tangled nightmare of events that had cost Robert Ash his life. The cast had come off three weeks before, and he had been working to rebuild his strength. That damage, at least, seemed as though it could be entirely repaired. Other wounds he sustained were permanent.

"We're spending the week with the Eversleighs," Lily explained. "Strangford went with them to hunt for a Christmas tree."

"You didn't want to join them?" Gardner asked.

Lily shrugged.

The truth was that tagging along with the loud, chaotic parade of Strangford's sister's family left her feeling like an impostor. That Virginia and her husband, Walford, were so easy and welcoming almost made it worse. They seemed to have entirely accepted her into their lives as though her presence there was an undisputed fact, but how could that be? They didn't know her. She was practically a stranger to them, having spent only a few afternoons or evenings with them before this week's house party in their country estate on the Hampshire coast.

For the last five days, she had been embedded in a whirlwind of squabbling children and convivial holiday preparations that was utterly strange to her. Even when Lily's mother had still been alive, she had never lived in a world of cozy dinners or bedtime routines. Deirdre wasn't that kind of parent. She had been loving and affectionate, indulgent and distant, drifting through a reality that only brushed up against the one the rest of the world lived in.

Lily wanted to find a way to belong but wasn't sure she was capable of it. That conflict inside of her had been rising to something near panic as the day of her wedding to Strangford approached.

"Is Lady Strangford there as well?" Gardner asked.

"Yes," Lily replied.

The next words spilled out of her.

"She doesn't..."

"Doesn't what?" Gardner gently pressed.

"Entirely approve, I think," Lily finished lamely.

She was a little shocked at herself for admitting this, but Gardner had a natural way of making one feel safe. He wasn't the sort of person who would judge her for being a little different, or a little less.

Lily's fears weren't entirely unfounded. Lady Strangford had clearly stated her opposition to Lily's relationship with her son last summer. Since Ash's funeral and the announcement of her and Strangford's engagement, the woman hadn't made any further efforts to dissuade him from the marriage. In fact, she hadn't said anything about the matter at all. Lily was left feeling deeply unsure of what Lady Strangford really thought of her.

She hadn't admitted that fear out loud to anyone, not even Strangford. Not that it mattered. Strangford would know anyway. It would be written under her skin for him to read the next time he touched her.

"Has she said anything to you about it?" Gardner pressed.

"No," Lily admitted. "Not since August, but she's just so . . . cold. She never says anything to me at all unless it's something practical, like passing the jelly or telling me I'll need boots rather than shoes to walk the cliff path. I think she must be keeping it to herself out of consideration for Strangford, but it seems blatantly obvious to me that she'd rather I wasn't there."

Gardner sighed. It was a heavy sound.

"It might not be about you, Lily."

Something in his tone snagged at her attention.

"What do you mean?" she demanded.

"There's often more going on under someone's skin than you realize."

Her nerves tingled. Instinct told her there was more to Gardner's words than their face value. It occurred to her that for someone like Gardner, the words *under someone's skin* had a very different meaning.

"You know something," she blurted.

Gardner didn't answer, which was more or less a confirmation.

"What is it?" she pressed.

He sighed.

"It's not my place to say."

"Why not?"

He gave her a frank look, one that clearly said she was being overly pushy about this.

"I didn't come by the information voluntarily," he said.

The words set her back a pace, as they were meant to. Lily had also kept information to herself that she had learned using her powers, both to protect herself from being called a liar or a madwoman and because she'd seen the harm the truth could do.

She knew she should respect Gardner's gentle set-down, but the urge to know was desperate. Gardner didn't read objects like Strangford. His power only worked with people—living people. Had he been in physical proximity to Lady Strangford? The woman spent most of her time at the family estate, Allerhope, in Northumberland, where she was working to establish a horse stud.

The answer came to her in a flash of memory—the green lawn of Kensal Green cemetery on a damp August afternoon. She recalled how Gardner's solid hand reached out to steady Strangford's mother as she stumbled over the uneven ground.

"It was at the funeral," she said before she could think better of it. "You took her arm. You read her."

"It wasn't intentional," Gardner replied.

"But you saw something was wrong. Why didn't you say anything?"

"I can't just run around telling people they're ill when they haven't come to me for treatment," he countered sharply.

Lily's words had clearly struck a sore spot, but she couldn't stop to worry over it. She was horrified by the possible implication.

"You mean she doesn't know?"

"She knows," Gardner returned flatly.

"How can you know that if you didn't speak to her about it?" Lily demanded.

"Because it'd hurt," he snapped.

The flash of temper was exceedingly rare for Gardner. It showed how far Lily was pushing him. She felt terrible about it, but how could she back away? She thought of how carefully Strangford avoided touching his family or the objects they came into contact with. He shielded himself with wool and linen and the black leather gloves that perpetually covered his hands. It was particularly trying for him at times like this, pressed into a house full of objects saturated by impressions from others.

Was it possible he didn't know about his mother's illness? Of course, it was. If he knew, she would have seen it in him. There would have been something more careful or solicitous in his interactions with Lady Strangford over the last week.

Thoughts of the Eversleighs rolled over her—of bright Virginia and kind-hearted Walford and their boisterous crowd of children. They had been tearing around Lady Strangford all week, and none of them *knew*.

"How do you know she's getting the right treatment? Even if she knows something is wrong, that doesn't mean her doctors have properly diagnosed it. How can you keep something like that to yourself?"

"It's not treatable," Gardner shot back. His shoulders were tense, but he took a breath, forcing them to relax.

The shock of it was like cold water in her face.

"She's dying."

"Lily…" Gardner groaned.

"But what does that mean? How long does she have?"

The words tumbled out of her as she rose to her feet.

He looked up, meeting her eyes. He had regained his calm, and his gaze was firm.

"I'm not going to tell you that."

As reprimands went, it was a gentle one, but it struck her all the same. Her next questions died on her lips, and the quiet of the church rose back up around them. Lily heard the ruffling of feathers overhead. A bird must have found its way inside.

Shame washed over her as she sat back down. Of all people, she ought to have known better than to push Gardner to reveal information he didn't want to. She wondered if she had just broken something between her and the man who sat beside her. The thought of it tore at her.

She searched for the right words, the ones that might make it all better, and failed to find them.

It was Gardner who spoke first.

"I don't know the perfect way to handle the things I know. I have lived with it for forty-nine years, and it only gets harder."

"I'm sorry I pushed you," Lily said softly.

"You're worried about Lord Strangford. It's natural," he replied with a hint of weariness. "Have you heard from Sam since he shipped out?"

It was a deliberate change of subject, but she accepted it.

"No," she admitted. "I've been writing, but he hasn't replied."

It wasn't the entire truth, of course. She didn't tell Gardner that the letters she had written were superficial little things stuffed with comments about the weather and what horrors her landlady, Mrs. Bramble, had manufactured in the kitchen. She had dropped envelopes in the post twice a week since the day Sam left, and they were all full of air.

She thought of the last time she saw him. It had been on the platform at St. Pancras Station, the steam of the train engine wreathing around him as he stood tall and straight in his drab uniform. Her heart twisted with a now-familiar doubt and regret. During Sam's last few days in London, Lily had made decisions she knew could very well mean the end of their friendship.

Sam had left with a great deal on his shoulders, like the discovery that his sister was still alive and the revelations of what she had suffered in order to survive. That, and the death of the man who had been employer, mentor, and foster-father to him—all of those things riddled through with resentment and complication that must be far from resolved.

Lily knew something about that torrid mess of grief and anger. Her own feelings about Robert Ash and his terrible sacrifice weren't exactly uncomplicated.

Writing about Mrs. Bramble's cooking was much easier than trying to find the words for all that.

"Keep writing," Gardner softly ordered. "It matters to him. Even if he doesn't know how to say it."

Lily wondered if Gardner's advice would be different if he knew just how much of a mess she'd made of things. Maybe not. The doctor had always understood people better than Lily did.

The thought tangled her up, tripping her into the morass of emotion that surrounded her thoughts about the events last summer at Blackfriars rail bridge—about the loss that had changed everything, scattering the people she loved like dandelion seeds in the wind.

"Do you miss him?" Lily abruptly demanded.

She didn't have to specify whom she was talking about.

His big hand reached out and clasped her own where it sat on her knee, warm and firm.

"Every day," he replied.

~

He walked her to the blue door of the St. Andrew's Building, carrying the hamper in one hand as though it weighed nothing. They paused at the threshold.

"A week from tomorrow, isn't it?" Gardner noted.

She realized with a little start of surprise that he was talking about the date of her wedding and that it was indeed only a little over a week away.

It still seemed surreal to her—that in eight days, she would exchange vows with Strangford, stepping out of the life she had known and into something different. There would be no more of the small, familiar flat on March Place with the rattle and noise of Estelle's seances echoing up through the floorboards.

"Yes," she confirmed.

"I'm not sure I'll be able to get away for it," Gardner warned. "But I will try."

"Of course."

"He suits you," the doctor concluded.

The observation warmed her.

"Pass my thanks on to Mrs. Eversleigh for the fruitcake," he added, lifting the hamper.

Then he was gone.

TWO

*L*ILY HANDED THE hackney driver her fare and stepped out onto the drive of Taddiford Hall.

The big house rambled atop the high clay cliffs. Rows of shining windows looked out over the gray water that separated the Hampshire coast from the Isle of Wight, the island faded but still visible in the distance. The water was choppy today, the wind whipping at her as she stepped out of the relative warmth of the carriage. It carried a note of rain, a promise echoed in the thickening clouds to the west.

Taddiford itself was an eclectic arrangement of gray stone. A square main building four stories tall was attached to a long two-story wing presumably built to maximize the number of rooms with views of the sea. The wing concluded in an incongruously delicate glasshouse conservatory. Lily knew that Walford Eversleigh's father had added the octagonal structure to house his orchid collection.

The place lacked the pretension of the palatial country manors of many of the nouveau riche, nor did it have the eternal grace of a centuries-old institution like Brede Abbey, her father's estate in the Sussex Wold. It still felt woven through with wealth and security.

Despite being the daughter of the Earl of Torrington, Lily had spent her life living in flats or boarding houses. Her mother's rented rooms on Oxford Street had been the largest and most well-appointed of those lodgings. Taddiford had nine bedrooms, not including the apartments over the carriage house where the footman and chauffeur slept. Even after staying there for a week, Lily still felt out of place.

The manor technically belonged to Virginia Eversleigh's

father-in-law, the semi-retired king of the Eversleigh steel empire, but he mostly stayed at the big house in Leicester near the foundries. Strangford's sister and her family clearly considered this rambling pile on the Hampshire coast home, perhaps even more so than their townhouse in London.

The Eversleigh's tall, ginger-haired footman, James, opened the front door as Lily approached. Lily had never once had to knock at Taddiford. James seemed to have an uncanny knack for knowing precisely when someone was arriving at the house. It struck Lily as oddly unnecessary. She was perfectly capable of turning a doorknob.

"Did you enjoy your excursion, Miss Albright?" James asked as she came in. Despite his youth—he could not have been more than twenty—he was always consummately professional. Lily felt more comfortable around Strangford's footman, Roddie, who was far more likely to blurt out *'his lordship's in his bathrobe'* than greet her properly when she arrived. Of course, Strangford hired his staff for reasons that had little to do with professionalism. He needed to be surrounded by people whose hearts and minds he didn't mind occasionally falling into.

"Yes. Thank you," Lily replied, allowing James to help her out of her coat.

Was this what it would mean to be a lady—standing around while someone else did things for her she was perfectly capable of managing on her own? Lily knew how to go through the motions of being upper-class thanks to her years at the finishing school her father had banished her to after her mother's death, but the few times she'd done it, it had felt like a blatant illusion.

At least Strangford was a rather minor baron of limited means. Life with him would be different than the years she had spent in her flat on March Place, but it would not be like Taddiford. Lily was fairly certain Roddie would routinely forget to take her coat. The thought gave her some relief.

James was patiently waiting for her gloves. Lily tugged them off and handed them over. The footman glided away, moving with the quiet grace of a dancer, and she found herself alone.

The entry hall was large, paneled entirely in rich, aged hardwood. More holiday decorations had sprouted up in it since Lily had left earlier that morning. A garland wove around the banister of the stairs. Holly sprigs were tucked around the gilt-framed mirror.

Like the rest of the house, the room was furnished with exceptional taste, both elegant and comfortable. A bow-legged Queen Anne cabinet held the estate's new telephone. A Georgian silver salver waited for calling cards. A perfectly aged Turkish carpet covered the floor.

The vase on the side table demanded to be moved.

The need pushed at her so strongly, she glanced in the direction of the hall, half expecting James to come back in and ask her what was amiss. The room stayed empty, silent save for the distant sound of someone pushing a tea trolley elsewhere in the house.

There was nothing particularly interesting about the vase. It was a piece of faux Chinese porcelain like one might find at any decent furniture store, decorated with an interlocking geometric pattern of blue glaze on a pale white background. It had been precisely set in the exact center of the burled walnut accent table on the opposite end of the room from the telephone.

Lily recognized the flavor of the impulse that consumed her. It was an outburst of the new power she had developed after her fall into Regent's Canal that summer—the one James Cairncross called her onmyōdō.

The name was Japanese and referred to an art that had flourished in that empire for hundreds of years. Practitioners had claimed to be able to see the changes that must be made in the present to shift the future, swinging it towards a favorable or unfavorable outcome.

For most of her life, Lily had experienced the future as something immutable and inherently antagonistic. Though her precognition allowed her to see what was coming, she had never been able to perceive how to avoid it. Every time she tried, her efforts twisted to bring about the very outcome she hoped to prevent.

That had changed after Regent's Canal. Lily had changed. Where once the future had been fixed, now it whispered to her of strange and uncomfortable possibilities.

Cairncross had described the Japanese practice of onmyōdō as a precise science of charts and calculations that took ages to master. It was a lost art now, popular opinion having swung against its masters, the onmyōji, who were labeled sorcerers or frauds. Cairncross said that was often how it went for charismatics—men and women who possessed unusual and extraordinary abilities. Whenever they rose into prominence, they were inevitably heading for a fall.

Those falls had historically been rather violent, which was why Cairncross cautioned that moving through the world as quietly and inconspicuously as possible was the best course a charismatic could choose.

Lily's strange new power felt nothing like science. Her onmyōdō was a thing of feeling and instinct, like a halo she could feel humming around some object or person or action that her power promised could make the difference between one future outcome or another. Lily thought of them as pivots, points at which everything was balanced more lightly—and where the right push could topple them from possibility into certainty.

Some of those pivots took a tremendous effort to move, like stopping a train from reaching the next bridge or challenging the most dangerous man in Limehouse to a duel.

Moving a vase would take almost no effort at all. It left Lily wondering how something so inane could possibly matter.

The onmyōdō didn't bother to provide her with an answer. There was nothing in this ferocious impulse that revealed why the vase needed to be moved. The need was simply there, as strong as if a dear friend had turned up to lunch with her hat on upside-down. The current position of the vase felt wrong. Of course, Lily must correct it. She might have thought she had gone slightly mad except that the impulse was threaded through with that now-familiar aura of her new power.

This wasn't her home, but Virginia and Walford Eversleigh had been extremely welcoming, folding her wholeheartedly into the rhythm of their lives here over the last week. Lily wondered if that would change should she start inexplicably moving the decor around.

The vase continued to demand her interference. It was indifferent to the possible social consequences.

Taking a breath and hoping rather desperately that no one was about to come into the hall, Lily pushed at the impulse, posing it the question of why moving this vase could possibly be so important.

The answer slammed into her, buffeting her with impressions that swung back and forth like the pendulum of some enormous and arcane device.

The delicate smell of unfamiliar flowers. A smear of blood on the white fabric of her gown.

Flags flapping over Whitehall, colored the black of absence, like moving holes cut in space.

Strangford's hands flexing terribly inside the dark leather of his gloves. The pain in his voice as he spoke.

There must be some point to it.

The pale, massive underbelly of a whale moving slowly across the sky.

The fog of her breath in a room made of ice.

The rumble of a lorry engine. Boots pounding regularly against the pavement, striking out a rhythm that pulsed dread through her heart.

The growl of monsters in the dark.

Lily snapped back to the wood-paneled hallway, the silence ticking around her like the counter on a bomb.

Every nerve was on fire. She was sweating through her blouse, chest heaving like she had just run a sprint. The vase had grown louder, blaring at her with its jangling sense of wrongness until her will finally crumbled, and she darted forward, pulling it from the center of the table to just within an inch of the forward edge.

The room quieted. Her breath found space to even, though it did so slowly. Her hands shook badly enough that she forced them under her arms, pinning them tightly to her sides. She waited for the tidal wave to sweep over her, for someone to come rushing in and demand to know what she had just done, but there was nothing but the fine carpet and the potted fern and the distant rush of the sea.

Claws scuffed against wood behind her, and Lily jumped, biting back the urge to scream. With an eloquent huff, Virginia's aging pug, Horatio, waddled into the hall. He stared up at Lily, his wide dark eyes clouded over with cataracts.

The dog let out a long, slow wheeze, lowering himself to the floor. He puddled there, skin pooling on the carpet as though he had judged Lily and found her just barely sufficient.

James came in, and Lily startled again, wincing back from him. The footman didn't notice. His attention was focused on the door. He opened it to reveal the figure of a naval officer just raising his hand to knock.

The newcomer was roughly Strangford's age and had a vigorous air about him. He was not particularly tall but solid in his build, with brown hair and bright eyes. He carried a briefcase in his hand and wore the uniform of a Navy officer.

"Lieutenant Felix Brockmeyer to see Mr. Eversleigh," he announced.

"You are expected, Lieutenant," James replied. "Do come in."

As the lieutenant stepped inside, Lily found herself in the awkward position of lingering where she had no particular reason to be.

"Sorry to disturb you, ma'am," Brockmeyer said with a bow as James took his coat and hat.

Things were right again. The vase spoke that fact to her clearly, and yet Lily was still far from at ease. She forced herself not to show it.

"It's 'miss,'" Lily corrected, extending a hand. "Miss Albright."

"Pleasure to meet you," the lieutenant replied.

He took Lily's hand, and the world turned.

He moves through a dim jungle. Glossy leaves brush his shoulders, the air dancing with the scent of foreign blooms.

Footsteps scratch softly behind him. Somewhere nearby, something is burning.

Lily forced the vision back with a desperate effort, conscious that the lieutenant was still looking at her. She could not afford to give any sign that she was other than what she appeared to be—a young woman who happened to be passing through the hall.

"Are you here to join the house party?"

She forced out the question and was relieved to hear that it was steadier than it had any right to be.

"No. I'm afraid it's business," Brockmeyer replied. "I have some papers for Mr. Eversleigh. Is he in the study?"

"I'm not actually sure . . ." Lily began. She was interrupted as the door flew open once more, and the gentleman in question strode into the house in a blast of country air.

Walford Eversleigh might have modeled for a poster of the ideal of vigorous English manhood. He was tall and blond-haired, his broad shoulders nicely filling out his tweed field jacket. Coupled with his wealth and the blessing of an enormous family, he had the sort of privilege that ought to have spoiled a man, yet he approached the world with the genuine enthusiasm of a Golden Retriever. It made him rather impossible to dislike.

Even though Lily was far from certain of her place in the Eversleigh family, she was incapable of doubting the sincerity of the easy affection Walford showed to her. He was so obviously uncomplicated. It had sparked an answering warmth in her for her soon-to-be brother-in-law, even as she continued to be twisted with doubt about how well she could possibly fit here.

"Trunk first!" Walford called as he stepped over the threshold. The doorway behind him filled with the dark green boughs of an enormous spruce.

Taddiford's gardener and the family chauffeur wrangled with the trunk of the great tree, pressing it through the door with a spray of needles.

"Brockmeyer!" Walford exclaimed cheerfully, striding over to the new arrival. He pumped the lieutenant's hand. "I wasn't expecting you until two."

"It's half-past now," Brockmeyer pointed out comfortably.

"Blast it, so it is! The tree took all morning to hunt down. Terribly sorry to keep you waiting, but I see you've already met Miss Albright. Afternoon, Lily," Walford said, planting a kiss on her cheek. The gesture held a comfortable intimacy Lily still wasn't sure she deserved.

"Best step back," he warned. "Mind the chandelier!"

The ornate brass light fixture swung precariously. Walford jumped up to catch it. He was just tall enough to reach.

With the tree now entirely through the door, the rest of the spruce-hunting party poured into the room.

The children came first. The Eversleigh brood was led by Lysander. The four-year-old sported his father's bright blue eyes under a mop of dark hair. He left a trail of mud behind him and promptly emptied his pockets of a pile of sand, which he deposited—more or less—on the card salver.

Rosalind, his sister, was thirteen and more solid than pretty with the bearing of a small major general.

"You must swing it toward the door to the water closet and then bring it round," she ordered, marching in behind the screen of boughs.

The youngest of the Eversleigh girls followed. Dorcas was nine years old with a scattering of missing teeth in her wide grin.

She cast an appraising eye over the tree. "I'm really not sure it's big enough. We ought to have taken the bigger one."

"We would have had to remove a wall to get it inside," Virginia Eversleigh countered, slipping in behind her daughter.

Strangford's sister was petite and pretty. She shared her brother's thick hair and dark eyes. Even in her country walking dress, she looked perfectly turned out, as though the mud splatters on her boots were carefully designed accessories.

Wrangling with the enormous tree, the chauffeur's feet clomped precariously close to where the old pug sprawled on the carpet, seemingly unmoved by the chaos.

"Get Horatio out of the way!" Rosalind barked.

Lysander ducked in, nearly tripping the chauffeur for the second time, and scooped up the dog.

"Don't forget to hold his bottom," Dorcas said, rushing in to assist with the drooping animal.

Lily knew the noise and mess of the children was greater this week than usual as their governess had been granted leave to go tend to her ailing mother. Virginia had been making do with the help of the maid, Bonnie.

At last, the eldest Eversleigh child drifted inside. Portia was a lovely girl of sixteen with her father's golden hair and her mother's dark eyes, which were framed in spectacles and firmly planted on the pages of a book. She moved unerringly through the maelstrom of tree and dog and siblings to slip up the stairs.

"Morning, Weewee," Lysander said in greeting, jogging past Lily with the dog. He was still short on a few key consonants.

Dorcas threw a quick hug around her waist.

"Auntie," she said before darting around the tree into the hallway.

The word sent a panicked lurch through Lily's gut. Her conversation with Gardner that morning came rushing back to her, lending the familiar discomfort a new note of guilt. Their grandmother was dying, and none of them knew.

"Into the drawing room, lads," Walford ordered.

"Mind the Turner on the wall!" Rosalind shouted, stalking after them.

Walford turned to Brockmeyer and Lily as he shrugged out of his coat and popped it into the adjacent closet, James being occupied with a mound of small gloves and scarves.

"I hope Lily kept you entertained while we were out. Lieutenant Brockmeyer here is quite a VIP. He's from the First Lord's office—works directly with Admiral Churchill."

Walford's brag wasn't entirely out of place. Winston Churchill, the First Lord of the Admiralty, oversaw the operations of the entire Royal Navy.

"Mr. Eversleigh is exaggerating," Brockmeyer returned. "I am merely a glorified errand boy."

"We've another of your colleagues at the Admiralty staying with us," Walford noted. "Dicky Anstruther-Fields. He's a civilian, works in the Department of the Accountant-General. His wife is a dear friend of Virginia's."

"Yes, we've met," Brockmeyer noted.

"I believe Mrs. Anstruther-Fields is lying down at the moment. Had a bit of a migraine and missed all the fun. Dicky's out for a walk but should be back shortly. You'll see him at dinner."

"I couldn't possibly impose," Brockmeyer protested. "I've already made arrangements in town."

"Have you sent round your things yet?" Walford pressed.

"No. I planned to nip over after we went through the papers."

"That's settled, then," Walford announced. "We've a room in the East Wing for you. No point in suffering through an inn when you can enjoy the comforts of home. I'll have James call and cancel your reservation."

He gave the footman a nod.

"Very good, sir," James replied and moved away, carrying an armload of mittens.

"That's very kind of you," Brockmeyer said.

"Nonsense. Least I can do after you came all this way. Lily, would you be a dear and let the others know not to wait for me? Shall we?"

He gestured Brockmeyer through the door, and the two men moved away towards the study. As they exited, the final member of the tree-hunting party stepped into the hall.

Lady Strangford was a tall, strong-featured woman who resembled her son more than her elegant daughter. She was dressed for the country in a wool coat and rubber boots, carrying a walking stick. Lily frantically wondered whether she had seen the woman rely on one before. Was she even relying on it now? Perhaps it was just for show. Perhaps Gardner had no idea what he was talking about when he let slip that Strangford's mother was ill.

The woman looked up, and Lily's mind echoed with the words her future mother-in-law had spoken in Lord Bexley's garden nearly five months before.

I will not stand by while you destroy your standing in society and curse my grandchildren to a life of whispers and ignominy.

There had been no rancor in it, just a mere statement of fact from someone who did not see the value in mincing words or veiling hard truths. Lily was the bastard daughter of an actress. Strangford was a member of the nobility, a class that used gossip about social weaknesses as a weapon to tear someone to shrapnel.

Lady Strangford had seemingly dropped her open opposition to Lily and Strangford's marriage after Robert Ash's funeral, but Lily had still never seen any warmth from the woman. There was no indication she was ready to welcome Lily into her family. She remained as hard and impenetrable as the rocks of her Northumberland home.

"James, please see that my trunk is packed," Lady Strangford said. She slipped the walking stick neatly into a stand by the door.

"My lady," the footman replied.

"You're leaving already?" Lily blurted as the footman climbed the stairs.

"Directly after tea," Lady Strangford replied flatly, removing her hat.

Lily's panic heightened. Lady Strangford couldn't possibly leave now. Lily hadn't yet found a moment to process what Gardner had told her.

"But… must you?" Lily protested, unable to stop herself.

"King's Ransom is due to foal this week," she replied. "I should prefer to be there when it happens."

Lady Strangford managed a horse stud at the family's estate in Northumberland. Lily already knew about the prize mare she was breeding, the result of a match that had taken quite a bit of work and money to arrange.

"I shall see you next Monday when I return to London for the wedding. Bonnie!" Lady Strangford called, catching the maid as she turned into the hall. The girl jumped, startled at being spotted.

"Have the cook pack a sandwich for me for the train," Lady Strangford ordered.

"Yes, my lady," Bonnie replied, making a quick curtsy and dashing away to find the cook.

It was all moving too fast. Lily forced herself to focus on what mattered most right now.

"My lady, do you happen to know where Lord Strangford has gone?"

"He broke off from the party as we returned to the house," the older woman reported. "I believe he has gone down to the strand."

"Thank you," Lily replied.

She hesitated for a moment, feeling certain there was something more she ought to say, but the words refused to come. It was always like this with Strangford's mother—stilted and formal, a mere exchange of information. Even the rote pleasantries of polite conversation seemed beneath her notice.

A crash resounded from the drawing room. Lily heard Virginia call out.

"Lysander, don't touch the ornaments! No, Dorcas, you may not decorate Horatio."

"Are you coming in?" Lady Strangford demanded.

"Not just yet," Lily awkwardly replied.

Lady Strangford turned without further comment and marched in to where her family waited, leaving Lily to the deserted hall.

The vase perched at the edge of the table. It radiated a quiet satisfaction that did nothing to calm Lily's nerves.

She plucked her coat from the closet and slammed back out into the chill of the afternoon.

THREE

HE WIND TUGGED at Lily's hair as she stepped outside, making her momentarily consider going back for her hat. She didn't want to face anyone else inside the house—not yet—and pressed on without it.

The air smelled cleanly of the sea under the pale gray sky. Long green beach grasses undulated on either side of the narrow dirt path leading her to the cliffs.

Taddiford sat atop a great shelf of red clay that broke off as it reached the sea, tumbling thirty feet to a long, broad shore. Lily pulled up her collar against the wind and looked down as she reached the edge.

Strangford pivoted on the sand, going through the moves of his tàijí. His head was bare, the breeze from the sea rippling the dark waves of his hair. Bare toes gripped the beach as he shifted his weight, hands gliding before him. His fist arrowed out, his body following the move, turning to block an imaginary strike, then flashing out with another blow. It was a dance both elegant and violent. He moved through it with the facility of someone who had done this a thousand times before.

Lily never tired of watching him move. Her pull toward Strangford had only grown stronger over the last few months until, at times, she felt like she must explode from it, and yet uncertainties continued to haunt her. Strangford could know everything about her with a touch, but that connection only worked one way. There were things that had passed over the last months they had not yet spoken of. He hadn't brought them up, and Lily was afraid to ask.

Things like Jack Cannon and what had happened that November night in Limehouse just before Sam left for the continent.

Sam had been about to throw himself into a situation that would have destroyed him. Lily's new power, her onmyōdō, had illuminated a way to keep him safe—but only at very great risk to Lily herself, involving her in a conflict that could easily have cost her life.

She chose it. It was nearly impossible not to. When the onmyōdō spoke, as she'd just experienced inexplicably with that blasted vase in the hall, she was compelled to listen, even if everything in her head and heart screamed for her not to.

Lily had survived the fight, though she still didn't like to think of how. While facing Cannon, her once-simple ability to sense the immediate future had twisted with a thread of her onmyōdō into something she barely recognized, showing her each move her enemy would make and exactly what she needed to do in order to defeat them. It had been an exhilarating power—too exhilarating. Lily still felt a dark, yearning attraction to that merciless violence when she thought about the fight.

Frankly, it terrified her.

She wished she could talk to someone about it, but the only ones who knew were Sam because he was there and Strangford because he touched her.

Sam was on the other side of the channel, not even bothering to answer the empty little missives Lily regularly sent his way. Strangford was here, but he had never so much as mentioned Jack Cannon and the events that took place in Limehouse, even though Lily had been certain he would rail against her for putting herself at such risk.

Lily had no idea why Strangford hadn't brought it up. Perhaps he was trying to respect her privacy. They had fought before about Strangford's disapproval of decisions Lily had never chosen to share with him. She supposed she should simply be glad he hadn't been openly furious with her for how she'd put herself in danger.

Or perhaps, deep down, it was because her fiancé was uncomfortable with what he had sensed in her.

She tried not to think about it, setting it all firmly in the past where it belonged. It helped that Strangford himself was increasingly distracting. The longer she knew him, the more compelling she found him until, at times, she thought she must shatter with it. New facets of him had emerged here at Taddiford that only increased that attraction, and they were abundantly present at the moment.

Until they had come to Hampshire, Lily had only ever seen Strangford dressed in one of his plain black suits, attire that gave him the air of a country vicar who'd lost his collar. Today he wore dark trousers and a navy-blue jumper. Lily knew the garment had been knit for him by his housekeeper, Mrs. Jutson, using wool her great-uncle had raised in Otterburn, Northumberland. When Strangford wore it, he would feel only Mrs. Jutson's habitual warmth and the rolling moorland of his home.

It made him seem more casual, even a little roguish, when paired with the dark circle of the patch over his missing eye. He was more comfortable here in the country, Lily admitted. His guard went up once he was inside the house, where every object might reveal the secret thoughts of members of his family. He was so careful not to violate their privacy, but out in the wild air, there was a kind of peace in him that Lily had only rarely glimpsed in the past.

Lily felt it too. There was something open and fresh about Taddiford, as though the wind swept it clean. It reminded her of her motorbike rides across Hampstead Heath. Lily had been lonely for much of her life but rarely alone. There was something fiercely liberating in answering only to the rippling grass and the soft rush of waves against the stones.

She wondered if Allerhope felt like this. She hadn't yet been to Strangford's Northumberland home. She knew it sat inland, bordering the moors, and so it would inevitably be different from the Eversleigh's home. Would Strangford also be different there? It was his native element. Lily supposed she would find out. They were due to head there after the wedding. The thought was both intriguing and a little terrifying.

Of course, Lady Strangford would also be there—which reminded her of why she had come to the cliffs in the first place.

She set off along the soft ribbon of the path. It turned to descend through a narrow gap in the cliffs, winding back down to the beach. Lily could see the lighthouse on the headland in the distance marking the entrance to The Solent, the narrow water that separated Hampshire from the Isle of Wight. She caught the bright wink of the light from the tower as she made her way down.

The tall ocher face of the cliffs towered over the pale sand of the beach, punctuated by scrubby patches of shore grass. A dinghy sat not far from where the path met the shore. It was overturned, gray paint showing the impact of the weather, tied off to a bolt set in a great stone. Walford used the boat to paddle his daughters around the coast, though Lily suspected it should have been put away for the season long before.

She rounded the corner, and Strangford was once more revealed to her.

The rush of the waves masked the sound of her approach, granting Lily a moment to observe him. His hands were bare as they deflected the attack of an imaginary foe. It was rare for her to see them unprotected. Strangford nearly always shielded himself with specially made black leather gloves.

The tàijí was meant to help him balance the energy that moved through his body, the force Robert Ash had called qi. Ash had taught Strangford tàijí in the hopes that it would help him learn to control his powers, perhaps even reach a point where he didn't have to spend his whole life protecting himself from the impressions lurking under every surface he came into contact with.

Lily knew why Strangford retreated to the privacy of this remote beach to practice. He didn't show this side of himself to the rowdy, affectionate bunch of people she had left up at Taddiford. His family had no idea that Strangford was psychometric. He had never told them.

Strangford twisted into a kick, his movements suddenly out of balance. He stopped in the middle of the sequence, muttering an uncharacteristic curse, the word carried to her by a trick of the wind. His attention shifted to the sea. He gazed out beyond the pale shadow of the Isle of Wight. There was something more in that look than a testing of the weather. It had weight, and Lily's spine crawled with a sense of significance.

It was not the first time she had caught him like this. There had been something uneasy in him for weeks now. She had not asked him to explain it. If he wanted to, he would. She had to respect that—even if it was something he couldn't grant her in return. Strangford would always know what Lily was thinking and feeling the moment he touched her.

She began to feel as though she were spying on him.

"I'm sorry to interrupt," she called, intentionally pitching her voice to carry over the wind.

He turned to her, his gaze warming. He crossed the sand to where she waited.

"The sea air suits you," he said.

Lily felt that familiar hum of response under her skin at the low rumble of his voice. She wanted to put her hand to the soft wool of his jumper, feel the vibration of his words from inside of him.

"Does it?" she returned a little playfully.

"You look . . . tousled," he concluded.

The word sent a little shiver through her.

"And you look rather like a pirate," she returned, taking in his sandy bare feet, the easy cut of his jumper, his wind-tossed hair, and the black patch over his eye. She had never been drawn to cheap romantic novels, but at the moment, she could rather see the appeal. She found herself wishing he could carry her away to sea.

He raised one of his dark brows, his eye twinkling.

"That sounds disreputable," he noted.

Disreputable. It was another word with a particular appeal. She found herself thinking of a few more disreputable things she could say to him, but it was not the time.

"You were practicing," she said, deliberately changing the subject.

"I was," he admitted. "It's . . . different now."

She inwardly winced. Of course, it was different. In the past, Strangford hadn't practiced tàijí alone. Robert Ash had been his teacher, his sparring partner, and his friend. All of that had been lost in the explosion at Blackfriars last August.

Lily hadn't spoken to Strangford much about his own grief for Ash. She suspected she was avoiding it because she didn't want to talk about her own confused and uncomfortable feelings about the loss of her mentor.

She knew she ought to say something appropriate to him now it had come up.

"Would it help if I fought you?" she blurted instead.

Strangford looked a little surprised at the suggestion—but only for a moment before his mouth curved wickedly.

"That is a very intriguing offer," he replied, stepping closer to her.

Her pulse skipped, her breath coming a bit shorter. Strangford always had this effect on her. She wondered if he was aware of it.

Well—of course, he was aware of it.

She put her hands to the dark knit of his jumper. It was a caress as well as a means of holding him at bay. A kiss or a hand to the skin of her neck right now would reveal things she would far rather tell him upfront with words.

She was conscious of the solid plane of his chest through the wool.

"I would have to pad my staff," she forced out, clinging to that semblance of logical thought. "I should be rather upset with myself if I hurt you."

His mouth twisted into a wry smile.

"Is that a challenge?" he asked.

Lily's throat went a bit dry.

She needed to focus. She had to tell him what Gardner had revealed about Lady Strangford somewhere where they could be alone. It would be torture for him to discover it with a brush against her hand later in a drawing room surrounded by his nieces and nephew.

His expression shifted, growing more serious. Even without his hands, he could see the change in her. It reminded Lily of how well he knew her—how tuned he was to her frequency.

"Do you want to talk about it?" he asked gently.

The words tore a little rent in her heart. He tried so hard to be respectful of her emotional space. He would never push for things she didn't want to reveal. They walked such a delicate line, navigating what each of them did and did not know about the other.

If there was a perfect, painless way to say this, Lily didn't know it. She took a breath.

"Strangford, there's something—"

"Uncle Anthony!"

The voice blared like a foghorn from the top of the cliff. Lily looked up to see Dorcas standing at the top, hands cupped around her mouth to add unnecessary force to her already substantial volume.

Strangford's attention stayed locked on Lily.

"Later," she said, forcing out the word as she squeezed his arm through his jumper.

Strangford looked up at his niece.

"What is it, Dorrie?" he called back.

"Grandmama is leaving, and Mother won't let us put any ornaments on the tree until you're there!" Dorcas protested.

Strangford turned back to Lily, waiting for her response.

"We should head up," she replied, quietly admitting defeat.

Strangford plucked his boots from where they sat near the dinghy. He carried them as they mounted the cliff path, his feet irredeemably sandy. Dorcas kept pace with them at the top of the cliff, jogging to meet them where the path crested.

"You'll get sand in the hall," the girl shouted down to them.

"Most likely," Strangford admitted.

"James will be furious."

"I find that difficult to imagine," Strangford said. "But I shall have to find a way to make it up to him."

"He likes port," Dorcas called back.

A flicker of irrepressible humor brightened his face. Dorcas seemed particularly capable of drawing that out of him. Strangford had a weakness for precocious children.

"Tawny or ruby?" he asked.

Dorcas answered him with a grin.

"Did somebody say port?" a new voice cut in.

They mounted the last steep curve of the path to find Dicky Anstruther-Fields waiting for them, looking like an illustration from a country life magazine with his tweed flat cap and red waistcoat.

Dicky had joined the house party with his wife, Celia, two days before. Celia had been friends with Virginia since they were children. The two women still seemed close in a way that felt more like family than friendship, both in its intimacy and in how the pair seemed to take turns being quietly irritated with each other.

Though Dicky had been married to Celia for years, Lily had the impression his relationship with the Eversleighs was more superficial. In fact, she suspected that all of Dicky's relationships were a bit on the shallow side. He was admittedly charming, with a quick grin and warm chestnut hair thinning a bit at the temples, but his interests seemed limited entirely to horses, brandy, and cricket.

"Tawny. And it's for James," Dorcas firmly corrected.

"He's a generous soul. I'm sure he'll share," Dicky commented. His eyes dropped to Strangford's bare feet. "That's a bold choice, my lord."

Strangford didn't bother to answer. Lily quietly suspected he only really tolerated Dicky because doing otherwise would make things more complicated for Virginia. Strangford had never had much patience for the superficial.

"He's going to get sand in the hall," Dorcas proudly reported.

"Returning to the castle, are we?" Dicky continued. "I'll jog along. I'm desperate for tea—or something a bit stiffer."

They proceeded back to Taddiford, the narrow path forcing them into a kind of parade. Dorcas led the way, setting a brisk pace. The rambling pile of the manor rose from the wind-tossed grasses, the forest a dark line in the distance across the fields.

Gray light gleamed off of the Eversleigh's motor car as it pulled into the drive. Lily's heart fell.

They reached the drive as the chauffeur emerged from the driver's seat and circled around to open the boot. The well-tuned engine rumbled contentedly.

Strangford paused, glancing down at his sandy feet.

"I'll go in through the conservatory," he said. "I can rinse off in the basin."

Dorcas looked disappointed. It was likely an appealing novelty to have one of the adults in the house making the mess that raised the footman's ire.

Lily searched for an excuse to go with him, hoping to steal another moment to communicate her news. She had not seen the conservatory yet, which lay at the far end of Taddiford's long, low wing. That part of her tour of the house had been interrupted when Virginia had needed to stop Lysander from building a tower out of Italian crystal wine glasses. The octagonal glass structure was largely a workroom rather than a place where the family gathered, the shelves jammed with the plant starts the gardener was growing for the flower beds and the remnants of the elder Mr. Everleigh's brief and now-abandoned foray into orchid collecting.

Dorcas gave her no chance to slip away.

"Come along, Lily," the girl cheerfully ordered, marching through the open door.

"After you," Dicky gallantly said, sweeping out his arm.

Lily glanced back, offering Strangford a tight smile, and then allowed herself to be herded into the entry of the main house.

The hall was once again chaos.

The entire family was jammed inside, making the expansive wood-paneled space feel small. The three younger Eversleighs ran around in reckless circles. Lily flashed an uneasy look at her vase, still perched at the edge of the table, but the children miraculously avoided colliding with it. She tried to determine whether she was relieved by that or not.

Portia, the oldest, was still reading her book. James moved efficiently down the stairs with Lady Strangford's trunk as Bonnie hurried to the closet for her coat.

"Lysander, get out of the cabinet!" Virginia ordered.

In the midst of it all, Lady Strangford stood clad in practical layers of dark wool. She regarded the blur of noise and motion warily.

"Bye, Grandmama," Dorcas said, breaking off from chasing her brother to give Lady Strangford an unhesitating hug, throwing her arms tightly around her grandmother's waist and squeezing.

"Thank you, Dorcas," Lady Strangford said plainly.

"I do wish you would stay longer," Virginia complained.

Rosalind pulled Lysander from the cabinet and called out, frowning.

"Mother, he's sticky."

"Bonnie?" Virginia said, a note of desperation in her voice as she looked around.

Bonnie, clearly overwhelmed, pushed Lady Strangford's coat at Walford, who happened to be standing nearest, and dashed in to pluck the four-year-old from his sister's arms.

"Happy Christmas," Lysander yelled over the maid's shoulder, waving, as Horatio shuffled in and collapsed in an inconvenient spot on the floor.

Walford graciously held out the coat.

"It was lovely to have you, Mother," he said as Lady Strangford slipped her arms into the sleeves. "Do ring on the telephone when you reach Northumberland to let us know you've arrived safely."

"The trains are very reliable. Your telephone is not," Lady Strangford returned.

"The company promised the line is fixed," Walford protested.

Behind him, James was framed in the doorway, setting the woman's trunk into the boot of the waiting car.

It was all so terribly wrong, that tumbling, joyful noise. None of them had any idea that the woman they bid their cheerful farewells to was dying.

The children swept past, tumbling towards the drawing room and the attraction of the yet-undecorated Christmas tree. Strangford stepped easily aside to let them spill by. His boots and stockings were back on, as were his gloves.

Dicky and his wife Celia were making their farewells, Virginia and Walford waiting by the door. Portia stepped in, her book in her hand.

"May I kiss your cheek, Grandmother?" she asked.

"You may," Lady Strangford replied.

Her oldest granddaughter pressed cool lips firmly to her skin. The book rose up in front of her nose again as she strode from the room.

Strangford approached his mother. There were still too many people here. If he kissed her cheek as well—if he learned the truth from her before Lily had a chance to warn him, in front of his entire family, could he possibly conceal it? What would it mean if he burst out, exposing the truth about himself in that moment of shock and dismay?

It would be all her fault.

He crossed to his mother and clasped her hands in his gloved fingers.

"Good luck with the foaling," he said.

"The last telegram reported that the mare was waxing up, and she has delivered once before without intervention," Lady Strangford replied.

Clearly, she thought little of luck.

Strangford smiled at her and stepped back. Lily felt relief wash over her.

A crash resounded from the drawing room.

"Lysander!" Virginia shouted, pivoting to stalk toward the disturbance.

Lily realized it was her turn to bid the woman farewell.

She felt a quick flash of rage. Why had Lady Strangford kept her pain a secret from these people who so clearly loved and cared for her? If she would only say something, Lily's own awkward position would be eliminated.

She was angry at Gardner for revealing the truth to her and angry at herself for forcing him to do so. She was mad at Strangford for not providing her with a better opportunity to explain all of this.

Lily didn't have an easy routine for saying goodbye to her future mother-in-law, the handshake or kiss or comfortable words the others could fall back on. She was left only with what she had been trained to do in finishing school when addressing someone of a higher rank than her own.

With a solid six feet of space between them, Lily offered Strangford's mother a neat curtsy.

"Lady Strangford," she said.

"Miss Albright," Lady Strangford replied just as distantly, then turned and strode out the door.

Lily looked up to see Strangford's brow creasing with concern.

The vase on the side table hummed with satisfaction. Her head started to ache.

"Lily! Anthony! Are you coming?" Virginia called from the drawing room.

Lily took a breath, bracing herself, and went inside.

FOUR

 $\mathscr{A}$ FIRE GLOWED in the grate of the drawing room, which appeared to have suffered a minor explosion of holiday cheer. Bonnie was setting out tea and sandwiches on the table. The children had finally been permitted access to the ornament boxes, though Portia largely ignored them, content to curl up in an armchair in the corner and continue to read her book.

Rosalind took command of the tree trimming with an undisputed authority that belied her thirteen years.

"No, Lysander!" she barked. "Not that one."

She handed the boy a less fragile ornament, which he proceeded to place in exactly the same spot on the tree as the last five he had hung. As soon as he turned for another, Dorcas darted in to rearrange things.

Strangford intervened, easily plucking the four-year-old up in his gloved hands and lifting him to a higher point on the tree.

"Try here," he said.

"Better," Lysander happily declared.

Lily found an open spot on the settee near Virginia and Celia.

"We still need more holly," Rosalind noted critically.

"We can venture out after tea," Virginia declared, pouring a cup and handing it to Celia.

Dicky's wife was very lovely, if a little thin and pale. She had been upstairs most of the day with a headache. Celia had suffered several such headaches since she and Dicky joined the house party three days before. She was not a small woman, but something about her lacked solidity, as though one might blink and find she had faded away.

"Lily?" Virginia offered, holding up the teapot.

"Thank you," Lily replied.

Virginia handed her the cup with the same native grace she displayed in every action. Even shouting at her unruly children had a sort of elegance to it with Virginia. It would have been off-putting had Virginia not been equally skilled at making those around her feel welcome.

The thought turned sour as Lily recalled how much she was hiding from this woman who treated her with such warmth and acceptance. She hid her discomfort behind a sip of tea.

Walford came in from the study. He had changed, oddly, into a bright red shirt.

Lily blinked.

No—the shirt was white, as it had been all day.

Her nerves jangled. She recognized a faint whiff of her power, but the crowded drawing room was hardly the place to pursue it. She was too unsettled by the revelations about Lady Strangford. Everything felt raw and exposed.

Lieutenant Brockmeyer followed Walford into the drawing room.

"I should say another hour or so should cover it," Brockmeyer said.

"We'll be able to fit that in before dinner," Walford replied. "Of course, it would all go much faster if you no longer had to lecture me about putting the plans away every time I got up from my desk."

"I am afraid you must make a habit of it," Brockmeyer replied.

"Generally, nobody gives two figs for the stuff I'm manufacturing," Walford went on cheerfully, helping himself to a sandwich.

"Well, I suppose we should be glad the safe is being put to good use," Virginia noted.

"It was already holding his gun," Dorcas piped in. "Daddy has a Webley Self-Loader. It's very elegant."

She flashed Brockmeyer a gap-toothed smile. Rosalind fumbled with an ornament, shooting her younger sister a glare.

"When it isn't jamming," Walford returned, blushing a bit. "I honestly don't know why I've kept the thing."

"I think it's splendid," Dorcas returned. "I should like to carry one."

"Well, it will all be quite secure," Walford bravely pushed on after a clearly disapproving look from his wife. "Not even Virginia has the combination."

"Just Cicero," Portia calmly noted from her chair, turning a page of her book.

"Cicero?" Lily echoed, that tickle of unease returning.

"The house ghost. It's a bit of a running joke," Dicky offered.

He sat beside Celia, legs crossed, arm casually draped behind her shoulders.

Celia's back was rigidly straight. She leaned forward to set down her cup.

"Oh, it's quite true, I can assure you," Virginia cut in. "The last owners warned the elder Mr. Eversleigh about it when he purchased the place. We lost a maid over it four years ago."

"Lost?" Celia asked, looking a little alarmed.

"She quit," Walford explained.

"Said she couldn't stand the eyes on her during the night," Virginia added a touch more deliciously.

"And how did this haunt come by the name of Cicero?" Brockmeyer asked.

"There's an old Roman camp on the property, across the field by the woods," Walford said. "Our gardener, Mr. MacInnis, still occasionally turns up bits of glass and pottery on the grounds, though the prize find was the brass spearhead. We had it mounted on a replica staff. It's on the wall in the study."

"Likely a midden," Portia filled in without looking up.

"A what?" Dicky said.

"An ancient trash heap," she clarified, fixing him with her gaze, the afternoon light glinting off the round frames of her spectacles.

"Splendid," Dicky returned wryly.

He rose with smooth ease and turned to Walford and Brockmeyer, extending a hand to the lieutenant.

"Brockmeyer. Lovely to see you again," he said.

"Likewise, Mr. Anstruther-Fields," Brockmeyer replied, returning the handshake.

Dicky turned, pitching his next words for the rest of the room.

"I was singing Taddiford's praises to the lieutenant when we met at a luncheon at the Admiralty last week. I must have done an excellent job."

"It is a lovely estate," Brockmeyer agreed. "It reminds me of Rerik, where my grandparents lived."

"Is that in Germany?" Dorcas demanded.

The question was an awkward one, though Dorcas clearly didn't know it.

"It is," Brockmeyer replied.

If he was bothered by the reminder that he had connections in the country England was at war with, he didn't show it.

"That must be terribly difficult for you," Virginia noted with deliberate kindness. "Have you any family still living there?"

"An aunt and uncle, a handful of cousins," Brockmeyer said.

"Dicky's friend, the duke, is in Germany as well," Dorcas piped in helpfully.

Celia softly cleared her throat.

"His Grace Charles Edward of Saxe-Coburg and Gotha," Dicky explained easily.

Lily started a bit. She knew the name, of course. The Duke of Saxe-Coburg and Gotha was King George's first cousin, one of Queen Victoria's brood of grandchildren. The British royal family had deep and zigzagging ties to the noble houses of Europe. Even the Kaiser himself, with whom they were currently at war, was a cousin of the king, as was the czar in Russia. At least Nicholas fought on the same side as England.

"We were at Eton—got into all sorts of trouble together," Dicky said, directing the story to Brockmeyer. "Damned unfortunate he ended up on the wrong side of this war."

"His schloss at Callenberg is truly magnificent," Celia offered thinly. "Like something out of a fairy tale, set in the forest and topped with a tower. One feels like they could fall asleep for a hundred years in it, then wake up and look out to find nothing had changed."

"It's very fine. Excellent game preserve," Dicky cut in. "We stopped with Charles Edward for a week on our honeymoon. Didn't we, Peaches?"

At the mention of "honeymoon," Celia's mood shifted like a cloud slipping over the sun.

"Yes. Well. We won't be returning anytime soon," she concluded.

Lily felt a crawling unease, the fingers of it dancing up the back of her neck.

The schloss at Callenberg. *We won't be returning ...*

Something was about to happen.

The room glazed over, her mind shifting to someplace else—somewhere she hadn't been yet.

The smell of dust and old paper. A warm voice murmuring by her ear.

Shall we keep hunting?

She jumped, nearly spilling her tea, at the sound of a firm knock at the front door.

Strangford's gaze narrowed on her as if on instinct, his nephew still perched on his shoulder.

"I wonder who that could be?" Virginia said.

"A carpet salesman, I should think," Dicky returned. "Or perhaps someone seeking to show you the true path of our Lord and Savior."

His eyes rose to the heavens in mock beatitude.

"Really, Dicky," Celia scolded.

The low murmur of masculine voices sounded from the hall, and a moment later, James appeared in the doorway.

"Mr. George Carne is calling," he announced.

Lily's focus narrowed, her heart skipping a beat. The name conjured the image of a bright-eyed, light-haired gentleman enthusiastically wielding the sacred staff of the Black Rod of Parliament like a boy playing knights-and-dragons.

George Carne. He was Lord Torrington's second-oldest son—Lily's half-brother. She had met him twice before, each time briefly, and on neither occasion had she actually introduced herself.

He was little more than a name to her ... a name that shared half her blood.

Lily didn't know what George might think of his bastard sister. Unlike his older brother Simon, Viscount Deveral, George had never made his opinion on the subject clear. She didn't know that George would meet her with the same terrible disdain as Deveral. She didn't know how he would meet her at all, though she supposed she was about to find out.

Why on earth was he here?

Strangford met Lily's eyes from across the room as he held his nephew up to place another ornament. She could clearly read his concern for her at this unexpected intrusion, but there was nothing to be done about it. She could hardly flee the room without an explanation, and Strangford wasn't the only one watching her. His sister, Virginia, had quickly turned her eyes to Lily when George's name was spoken. Virginia was far too socially savvy not to recognize the connection between Lily and the man who had just shown up at the door.

"George Carne?" Walford echoed, surprised. "That's unexpected."

"But of course, you must show him in, James," Virginia cut in smoothly.

"Thank you, ma'am," James intoned, departing with a quick bow.

Lily took a breath, bracing herself, and a moment later, the footman reappeared in the doorway.

"The Honorable Mr. George Carne," he formally announced, then stepped aside to make way for the new arrival.

Lily's half-brother wore a driving suit of clearly excellent tailoring. He filled it out well, looking much the same as he had when Lily had last encountered him four months before, save that he appeared to be growing out a mustache.

His eyes flashed with recognition as he spotted her. His gaze lingered on her for only a moment before it snapped to take in the rest of the party, to whom he offered a broad smile.

"Mr. Eversleigh," George said, striding over to Walford, his hand extended. "I do hope you'll forgive the intrusion."

"It's no trouble at all, Mr. Carne," Walford returned easily. "You're a pleasant surprise. Is your mother, the countess, well?"

"She is," George replied. "I am sorry to barge in on you like this, but I was driving up the coast road when my motor started giving me a spot of trouble. I recalled your country place was nearby and hoofed it over to see if I might use your telephone to ring up the garage and perhaps beg a warm spot to wait until they can send someone along for me."

"Nonsense," Walford said. "We'll send our chauffeur, Mr. Lewis, out to look it over himself. He knows far more about an engine than any garage, and of course, you must join us in the meantime."

"That's most generous of you. I should be happy to accept."

Virginia rose, stepping forward and offering George her hand.

"Mrs. Eversleigh," he said, bowing over it. "You look splendid as always."

"You're too kind," Virginia said. "And we shall be very glad to add you to our party. Are you acquainted with Mr. Anstruther-Fields?"

She gestured to Dicky, who rose from the settee beside her.

"We met at Lady Castlereagh's," Dicky said as the two men exchanged a handshake. "Fundraiser for her orphanage, I believe."

"That's right," George confirmed.

Virginia stepped in once more.

"And I don't believe you have met my brother, Lord Strangford," she smoothly went on.

Strangford set Lysander down on the ground and straightened.

"He has," Strangford calmly corrected. "In Parliament last August."

Virginia's eyebrow cocked with interest at this revelation.

"Yes—we did," George said. "Very pleased to run into you again."

Was it only Lily's imagination that a strange tension had come into her half-brother's voice as he greeted her future husband?

George extended his hand. Strangford accepted it after the briefest hesitation, though Lily could still see the wariness in the firm line of his shoulders.

Virginia turned smoothly, and Lily tensed at what she knew must come next.

"And you may have seen the announcement that my brother is engaged to marry Miss Albright next week," Virginia said smoothly.

Lily had to admire it. The segue was perfectly chosen to avoid the awkward question of whether an introduction was necessary. But if her brother truly hadn't known that the auburn-haired woman he had encountered last August was actually his illegitimate half-sister, he must realize it now.

Lily waited for the inevitable reaction. Would it be shock? Dismay?

She saw none of those things. Instead, George looked a little nervous.

"I am pleased to offer you both my congratulations," George said, extending his hand to Lily.

She accepted it, and he made her an elegant bow, a practiced mark of respect. The exchange left Lily with only one possible conclusion—George had already known quite well who she was, and he had fully expected to find her here at Taddiford.

It was too much to believe that his car had just happened to run into trouble down the road from the house. Lily was suddenly quite certain that George's motor had not died from natural causes. Her brother was here for a reason—and it had something to do with her.

The tension this wrought in her was abruptly broken by the shriek of a four-year-old.

"I do it!" Lysander barked, reaching to snatch a particularly vulnerable glass bulb from Dorcas's hands.

"We were just about to hunt for a bit of holly," Virginia smoothly interjected, offering George a charming smile. "Would you care to join us?"

~

The happy screams of the children echoed across the cropped grass of the field as they tromped from the house toward the forest. The clouds had thickened overhead, the wind carrying a moist note that promised rain before nightfall.

Taddiford's gardener, Mr. MacInnis, led the way with a step ladder balanced on his shoulder. Dorcas chased Lysander out of the straggling line of their procession, the two of them cutting wide circles through the grass as the boy shrieked with delight. Rosalind strode to the front of the line, loudly discussing holly-cutting strategy with her father and the gardener.

The bushes in question lay at the edge of the wood near a place where the ground dipped sharply and then rose, a ditch giving way to a soft rampart of roughly five feet in height. The grass here had been left long, the dry blades of it swishing against Lily's skirts as she pushed through them.

Dicky scrambled energetically up the rampart, standing atop it like a conquering hero.

"That'll be the old camp," Mr. MacInnis called up to him, squinting against the pale glow of the sky. "Caesar's Second Legion, if my old man spoke true of it. Told me the place was marked on Ptolemy's map of Britain."

"Come on up, Brockmeyer," Dicky challenged. "Let's see how far we can survey it."

"Fair enough," Brockmeyer returned, mounting nimbly up the steep ground.

Under Rosalind's direction, the gardener set his ladder by the largest of the glossy green holly trees.

The only ones missing from their party were Portia, who had remained in her chair to read, and Celia, who had claimed another headache and retreated upstairs. Lily had caught a look of guilty concern on Virginia's face when her friend made the announcement.

Lysander wheeled through an uncut stretch of grass, startling a few brown sparrows up into the air. The birds reminded Lily of Sam—of the look on his face in St. Pancras Station the day he left and the silence that had so far answered the empty chatter of her letters.

Keep at it. It matters to him.

Strangford stepped to her side.

"Are you alright?" he asked softly. They were far enough from the others to have gained a sliver of privacy.

Lily glanced at the potential source of her trouble. George had turned to give an admiring glance at the rambling length of the house and the land that rolled down to the sea. His appreciation seemed genuine, but then, so had everything else about George from the moment she met him in the Black Rod's Study.

She still hadn't found a chance to talk to Strangford about Gardner's revelations that morning. Could she risk it now, with the rest of the party momentarily occupied?

"Uncle Anthony! Give us a hand!" Rosalind called from beside the holly trees.

Strangford looked to Lily.

"Go on," she told him softly.

She watched as he strode across the field to where Mr. MacInnis adjusted the ladder, and Rosalind pointed to a higher bough laden with bright red berries.

"Mama!" Dorcas shrieked from the field. "Lysander tried to bite me!"

Virginia picked up her skirts and stalked toward the children. Lily wondered if the governess would be up for a pay increase when she returned from her leave.

"They're a lovely family," George noted.

Lily glanced up at him, caught off guard by his arrival. He looked slightly more sun-kissed than he had been a few months ago, and his hair was cut shorter. Something about the burgeoning mustache, his cropped locks, and his tan came together in her mind. She blurted out the realization before she had time to think better of it.

"You've joined up, haven't you?"

George brightened.

"I have, as a matter of fact," he replied. "I'm with the Royal Sussex. I've been training at Chichester since October."

She felt a little jolt of fear.

"You'll be shipping out soon."

"I certainly hope so," George easily returned. "I'm itching to get a crack at Old Franz." He caught himself. "Not that I'm overly fond of the business, but someone has to step up. Can't let the Kaiser simply march all over Europe."

George spoke of the German Army as though they were naughty lads trespassing in someone else's garden. Lily recalled the rumors from Belgium, the long casualty lists in the papers, but said nothing. She didn't want to shatter George's enthusiasm. It was blindly upper-class, the attitude of a man who had never seen what true adversity looked like, but there was also something precious in it—something she found herself loathe to break.

She supposed the reality of the war in Flanders would do that quickly enough.

George cleared his throat awkwardly.

"Miss Albright . . . I must admit that it was no surprise to me to find you here this afternoon. I had rather hoped you would be."

The wind tugged at her coat. It had picked up more of a chill.

"There's something I need to speak to you about, and I wasn't sure you would welcome the call. I took the coward's way out and ambushed you," he admitted.

"Because I didn't tell you who I was when I saw you before," Lily filled in, feeling slightly dreadful.

"Simon let it slip," George said glumly, naming Lily's monstrous older half-brother. "He demanded to know why I would upset Mother by speaking to you."

The moment flooded back to her, just as uncomfortable now as it had been then—standing in Lord Bexley's drawing room, drowning in a vision of death dancing across the bodies and faces of the bright young men around her.

George's hand supporting her arm, the concern in his voice.

You had me worried for a moment there.

The countess had been there as well, pale and blonde with echoes of old beauty. Lily could still recall the expression on her face as she had realized who her son was speaking to across the room—the most exquisite fear.

"Mother is dreadfully sensitive about certain things," George blurted awkwardly.

Sensitive seemed an inadequate word. Lily was the living embodiment of the woman's years of shame. She knew her father had been relatively discreet in his relationship with his mistress, but there would still have been the whispers, the quiet pity or derision.

Had the countess been unfortunate enough to actually love her husband, there would also be the pain of a broken heart.

There was no reason for Lily herself to feel guilty about it, but Lady Torrington remained a very uncomfortable subject for her.

"I was engaged in urgent business both times I saw you before," Lily admitted. "I know it sounds a pale excuse, but there honestly wasn't any time."

"Well. That's better than thinking you preferred to have nothing to do with me," George replied.

In another mouth, like that of Dicky Anstruther-Fields, the remark would have held the sharpest sarcasm. With George, it sounded genuine. Somehow that made Lily feel even more rotten.

"What was it you wanted to ask me about?" she prompted.

"Oh!" George exclaimed, recalling himself. "It was just to ask if you met Father for lunch at The Holborn two weeks ago, on Thursday."

"No," Lily replied, surprised by the question. "I haven't seen Lord Torrington in some time. He's been . . . busy."

Lily and her father had made plans several times over the last month. He had canceled all of them. There had been little explanation as to why, but he clearly felt terrible about it. Lily could read between the lines easily enough. Torrington had involved himself somehow in the business of the war, and it was consuming him. She could only guess what his work must be. Her father had always moved outside the official lines of authority in the realm, leveraging relationships and forging compromises behind the public facade of the government.

"I see," George said.

Lily's answer was clearly not the one her half-brother hoped to hear. She was quickly learning that George had no skill for hiding his feelings. He wore them like a colorful necktie.

"What is it?" she quietly demanded.

"Mother has a friend—well, not really a friend," he corrected himself. "More one of those dreadful people who never give you an excuse to get rid of them. She told Mother she'd seen Father outside The Holborn with a younger woman, someone wearing a veil. Mother becomes rather… fixated on these things, but it occurred to me there was likely a very simple and innocent explanation for it."

"Me," Lily filled in.

"Except that it wasn't," George concluded glumly.

There was a crunch of gravel from the drive. Lily glanced over to see Mr. Lewis piloting the motor car back to the carriage house.

Walford had climbed the step ladder, leaning against it precariously to stretch the clippers towards another branch Rosalind was pointing out. Strangford reached out a hand, calmly bracing the ladder before his brother-in-law tumbled into the holly tree.

The awkwardness of it was terrible. Lily could read between the lines of George's story. Lady Torrington worried that her husband had taken up a new lover.

She considered whether it might be true. Torrington had done it once before. Many powerful men picked up and discarded mistresses throughout their lives. Why shouldn't her father do the same, particularly given his past record?

As soon as the thought occurred to her, Lily dismissed it. She had seen the deep lines of guilt on her father's face when he spoke of the pain his relationship with her mother had inflicted on his family. She couldn't believe he would willingly subject them to something like that again.

If the woman wasn't a new mistress, who could she have been?

As soon as Lily posed the question to herself, the answer was clear.

"She wore a veil?" Lily pressed.

"That's what Lady Colebrook said," George confirmed.

"Did Lady Colebrook happen to mention what color the woman was wearing?"

George blinked, surprised by the question.

"I'm not actually . . . No, wait. She said the woman was hardly out of mourning. Her dress was gray."

Lily knew of one other young woman who had a history with her father—a woman whom she had last seen clad in soft charcoal silk.

Wu Zhao Min.

It had been over a month since she'd last seen Sam's sister. Whatever business Zhao Min had with her father, Lily felt certain it was related to the events of last November—to what had happened in Limehouse with Jack Cannon. What seed had that conversation planted? What fruit would it bear?

Lily couldn't know, but she felt a shivering instinct that any collaboration between two extraordinary minds like those of Lord Torrington and Zhao Min portended something significant.

"There is a woman our father does business with who is currently in half-mourning," Lily reported firmly. "I can't tell you anything more than that. But it is not an affair."

George looked both relieved and disappointed.

"I'm not sure whether Mother will believe it. It might have been easier if it had been you," he joked awkwardly.

Lily thought back to the look on the countess's face in Lord Bexley's drawing room.

"I'm not so sure about that," she replied.

Across the field, Dicky and Brockmeyer stood on the apex of the Roman ruin, engaged in deep conversation. To their right, Lysander had found a ball. He kicked it wildly, and it soared toward the two men. Brockmeyer caught it neatly, then dropped and punted it with the practiced skill of an athlete. It surprised Lily just a little—she had not seen that physical prowess in the lieutenant before.

Mr. Lewis crossed the field from the carriage house, and Walford hopped down from the ladder, happily sacrificing his clippers to the gardener despite Rosalind's protests.

A trio of sparrows fluttered down to settle on the branches of a sprawling ash tree, its last leaves still dancing in the breeze.

"That wasn't the only reason for my 'car trouble,'" George sheepishly admitted.

Lily looked back to her half-brother, startled … and for a moment, she was somewhere else.

The front seat of a speeding automobile, road unwinding like a silk tie before them. George at the wheel, the wind tugging at his hair. A delighted gleam in his eye as he looked over at her.

We'll both be shot if we're caught for this.

The vision snapped, throwing Lily back to the field outside Taddiford, where George's expression had shifted to one of concern.

"Is something the matter?" he asked. "Dash it, if I've upset you—"

Lily stopped him.

"No," she countered firmly. "It's fine. Go on."

He flushed a bit, the tips of his ears going pink.

"I really did mean to ask you about that luncheon with Father… but I also hoped that finding you here might give me the chance to get to know you a little better."

The words tumbled out of him as though a dam had broken.

"You've been a terrible mystery to me for years now—that I have a sister! How marvelous is that? I would've given anything for the chance to speak to you, but I couldn't know whether you would welcome it, and there was this awful unspoken rule that none of us should so much as mention you existed. But I'm a grown man now. It is my right to make my own decisions about such matters, and I have decided I should like us to become friends," he concluded.

The flush came back, brightening his ears again.

"If you are willing, of course," he added a bit lamely before clamping his mouth shut.

Lily could not have been more surprised, both at George's outburst and at her own reaction to it. She was overwhelmed by a sense of longing.

She forced herself to face it. The thought of being friends with this man appealed to her deeply. From what she had seen so far, George was a man open-heartedly full of boyish enthusiasm for life. What else could one possibly wish for in a brother?

Yet she could not forget the rasp of Viscount Deveral's voice in the smoke-wreathed gloom of his drawing room. Her older half-brother had thrown words at her like daggers, designed to pierce the most vulnerable spaces in her heart.

He dared ask us to accept you?

It will never happen.

Even the memory of it hurt.

Her heart twisted, torn between that pain and this unsettling new desire—but only for a moment. Lily knew which side must win.

"It's rather more complicated than that," she said softly.

George's mouth firmed into a stubborn line.

"You mean because of Simon," he pushed back, using Deveral's given name. "As I understand it, he rather owes you his life. It was you who got him out of that ghastly business last spring."

"I am not sure he sees it that way," Lily returned carefully.

Memories assailed her—the pale fear on the face of her father's wife, the visceral hate in the glaring eyes of his heir. She wanted it terribly—what George was offering her—but that didn't make it possible.

Her brother waited for her answer with a puppy-like mixture of hope and trepidation. The idea of disappointing him was terrible to her, but what else could she do?

Lily opened her mouth to answer, and the sky broke into rain.

Mr. MacInnis snapped the ladder closed, neatly twisting it up onto his shoulder. Everyone rushed across the grass back to the house except for George, who blinked up at the sky as though surprised it could be capable of this.

"Ball!" Lysander cried from over Dorcas's shoulder as she tried to wrestle him across the threshold into the drawing room.

George startled, coming back to himself and spotting the football halfway across the field.

"I'll fetch it!" he shouted back, jogging over to it.

Strangford stopped at Lily's side.

"Is everything alright?" he asked.

Cold rain dripped from the dark hair that fell across his forehead. Lily brushed it back, tucking it behind his ear. It reminded her of the night he had come after her when she fled from Deveral's house, his overcoat abandoned, the icy sleet soaking through his shirt.

I don't want you to be alone right now.

It was the moment she had begun to fall in love with him.

"No," she replied. "Not really."

He didn't answer. Instead, he offered her his arm. She slipped inside of it, tucking herself against him, and let him walk her back toward the house.

FIVE

HE PARTY FLED through the French doors to the drawing room, the nearest entrance to the field where the rain now pounded against the stubble of the grass. Virginia was ordering her damp children upstairs as Lily and Strangford came inside.

"You as well, Portia," she added.

Her oldest child let out an eloquent sigh before closing her book and rising from her chair.

"You will join us for dinner, won't you, Mr. Carne?" Virginia demanded.

"Er—well. I wouldn't want to be any—"

"It's no trouble," she cut in firmly. "Mr. Lewis will have to wait for a break in the rain to go out with the tractor and pull your auto to the garage. We'll put you in the guest room above the study. James can show you up. James!" she hollered in finish.

The footman slid neatly into the doorway, his hands miraculously already clear of wet coats.

"This way, if you would, Mr. Carne," James said.

George shot Lily a look. He appeared a little helpless, as though looking to her for guidance on how to respond, but Virginia had already moved on, and the footman was waiting.

"Anthony, you are dripping all over the carpet," Virginia snapped. "Go change. Lysander—shoes!"

She pivoted without waiting for a response, stalking after the boy, who left a trail of muddy footprints behind him.

~

Twenty minutes later, Lily pulled a brush through her hair. She had hurried through the change in her costume, replacing her wool skirt, blouse, and jacket with a dinner dress. She had only a handful to choose from and had already worn the green silk with the ivory lace bodice. Lily was not invited to many dinners. The brush froze as the terrible thought occurred to her that as a baroness, she ought to dress for dinner every night once she took up residence in Strangford's house in Lancaster Gate.

She breathed out the worry, quickly dismissing it as she resumed the quick strokes of her brush. She felt quite certain Strangford could give two figs about what she wore to dinner. He possessed only one set of evening clothes, and those were a bit frayed at the cuffs. Strangford did tend to hang on to his clothes until they threatened to fall apart on him.

She could far more easily picture them eating off of trays by the fire in his study. The image warmed her.

The brush lowered as Lily studied the results in the mirror. There was not much she could do with her hair since most of it had been burned off last summer. Though she did not come by her bob voluntarily, she found she rather preferred it. It was easier to manage.

The mirror was three-sided like a painted altarpiece. It offered Lily a rare look at her profile in the glass. She was struck by how much the lines of it resembled those of George's face. They shared the same firm jaw and long, straight nose—traits they had both inherited from their father.

The thought made her a little dizzy. Lily set down the brush and closed her eyes.

A knock sounded on the door.

"Come in," Lily called.

The housemaid, Bonnie, slipped inside. She was a slight thing with dark-blonde hair and wide hazel eyes, but Lily had seen how hard she worked. She was stronger than she looked.

Bonnie made a quick curtsy.

"I'm sorry I'm late, Miss Albright."

Her cheeks were flushed with embarrassment.

Lily was ashamed to admit that she had forgotten all about Bonnie in her distraction over George. Virginia had ordered the girl to look after Lily in place of a lady's maid for the duration of her stay at the house. As Lily had never had a lady's maid before, it had been easy to forget and simply get on with doing things for herself.

She felt a little guilty that she was already dressed.

"I'm terribly sorry, Bonnie. I just buttoned myself in. I'm afraid I haven't any need of you."

"Oh," Bonnie replied. The girl wore her emotions almost as openly as George. Lily could see her flash of relief.

Between Brockmeyer and George, the house had two unexpected guests to contend with. Of course, the maid must be run ragged.

"Go on," Lily urged. "I'm sure you've a million things to do."

Bonnie turned for the door, then paused, glancing back.

"I could iron it for you if you like. Your hair," she explained when Lily looked at her blankly.

Lily touched the slightly unruly auburn waves. She knew that ironing was the fashionable way to style this particular cut, turning it sleek and modern, but something about it felt a little too close to being burned—to the way she had lost all that hair to begin with.

"Perhaps another time," she replied.

A few seconds after Bonnie had gone, Lily crossed to the door, placing her hand on the wood.

She could hear the swing and click of another door closing in the hall, then silence, but Lily didn't need to eavesdrop for this.

She took a breath, deepening her focus and pulling on the power that glimmered quietly inside of her. She drew it firmly up and *knew.*

The hall would be empty.

She opened the door and stepped out. Her room was in Taddi-ford's long wing rather than the main house. To the left, the hall ended at the staircase that descended to the library where James would be serving cocktails. She would be expected there eventually but had likely dressed faster than anyone else.

Lily turned to the right. Halfway along the hall, she was startled by the low murmur of voices through one of the doors.

"You are making a mountain out of a molehill."

It was Dicky. She was outside the room where he and Celia were staying.

Though Lily could not make out the words of the reply, she could hear the note of despair in it. She pushed on, not wishing to eavesdrop.

The door she was looking for was near the end of the hall. Lily raised her hand to knock and became aware that Bonnie was about to turn the corner.

There was no sound as yet, not so much as a footstep creaking on the stairs, but Lily did not doubt the knowledge. To allow Bonnie to find her in front of this particular door would put both Lily and the maid in an awkward position.

The solution to that problem was obvious if unconventional.

Lily put her hand to the knob, turned it, and slipped inside.

Strangford was only halfway into his suit. His braces hung from the sides of his trousers, his white undershirt revealing his arms and clinging nicely to the lines of his chest.

His hair was still wet.

It was a strongly appealing view, one Lily had not had a chance to enjoy before—that is, outside of the visions she'd had of her and this man entangled in far more compromising circumstances.

The thought brought the blood into her cheeks. Lily turned around, facing the door.

"I'm sorry. I didn't mean to catch you out," she said.

She could hear the rain pattering against the window, the brush of fabric as he moved.

"And here I thought it was intentional."

There was a low note of amusement in his tone. A moment later, his hand slipped around the silk at her waist. She could feel the warmth of his touch through the fabric, the close rumble of his voice by her ear.

"It's nothing too terribly scandalous," he noted, the sound of him sending a shiver of desire through her. "We are to be married in a week."

Lily turned to face him. His hand slid along the silk to accommodate her movement. She set her palms against the fabric of his undershirt. It was a very fine wool rather than the usual cotton. Strangford had once told her there was too much pain in cotton.

The possibilities of this stolen moment unfolded before her in all their delicious variety, but Lily knew she could not act on them—not yet. Not until she had told him what she came here to say.

He read the uncertainty on her face, and his own expression shifted from teasing to more serious.

"What is it?" he asked.

She didn't have the right words for this, but then again, with Strangford, she didn't need them. She could fumble her way through and let his power do the rest.

"Something Gardner told me this morning," she said. She moved her hand against the warm plane of his chest. "Take it. Please."

He was a little surprised but raised his bare hands from her waist and held her hand instead. She felt the soft electricity of his touch, the raw warmth of his skin.

"It's your mother," she spilled out. As she said it, she thought it, centering her mind on that moment with Gardner in the chapel. She knew he would feel it, that he would pick up more of the tone and meaning of things directly from her thoughts as she stumbled through the rest.

He breathed in sharply, and she knew that he had heard. She lifted her head to meet his eye.

"I can't tell you much more than that," she admitted. "He refused to say what was wrong."

"No. He wouldn't," Strangford muttered in reply.

He knew perhaps better than she did the delicate ethical territory Gardner had to walk with his power. Strangford's own gift often put him in a similar position.

"He just said that it was ..." Her voice drifted off, the words failing her.

"Serious," Strangford quietly filled in.

"Something a bit more than that," Lily choked out, not wanting to risk that terrible fact to any possible ambiguity. "Did you know?"

He released her hands, stepping back to pace the room.

"No."

The news hurt him. Lily felt as though it were her fault. In a way, it was. What she had to say next wouldn't make it any easier.

"According to Gardner, she must know she is ill, but I don't know that she understands ... what it means," she finished lamely. "Do we tell her?"

Strangford leaned against the window frame. His shoulders were heavy.

"How could we possibly explain that we know?" he replied steadily.

There was so much in those words—a lifetime of secrets, of hiding truths he had learned in impossible ways.

Lily struggled for a better answer. It couldn't be right to let Strangford's mother go on in ignorance of the fact that she was dying. Perhaps she could beg Gardner to admit his power to the woman, demonstrate that it was real, and then deliver his diagnosis. Even as Lily thought it, she knew Gardner would never agree to do it, not unless Lady Strangford asked him to.

And what about Strangford's own secrets? Any discussion like that would necessarily reveal the truth of his own power—a fact he had kept hidden from his mother for three decades. How would Lady Strangford feel about that? Would she believe him and feel betrayed that he kept it from her for so long, or think him a liar? Or a madman?

"I'm sorry," she blurted. "Gardner didn't want to tell me. I pushed him into doing it, and once I had, I knew that I ..."

"Would be incapable of keeping it from me," Strangford filled in.

Lily felt terrible.

Strangford pulled on his shirt, doing up the buttons. He shrugged into his braces and picked his gloves up from the nightstand.

"What about the vase?" he asked.

"You felt that?"

"It's very ... loud in you right now," he said, searching for the right word.

"I just needed to move it. I don't know why," she admitted a bit defensively.

He nodded, accepting that, but Lily could tell his thoughts were elsewhere—not on the vase but on the terrible tangle she had dropped him into over his mother.

"We should go down to dinner," he announced distantly.

Her throat was thick with things she did not know how to say, so Lily simply nodded.

"I'll see you there," she said and slipped back out into the hall.

~

Lily followed the sound of voices down the stairs and into the library. It was her favorite room in Taddiford, the walls lined with bookshelves framing big French doors looking out over the cliffs and the sea. There was something comforting about being surrounded by all those words.

She paused outside the door, steeling herself. She would have to channel some of her mother's energy and play the actress, pretending that everything was perfectly fine. In reality, all she wanted was to retreat to her room, curl up in her bed and watch the rain—or run back to Strangford and throw her arms around him until things somehow became right again.

She stepped inside.

A fire glowed in the hearth, contrasting with the cold gray drizzle spotting the windows. The world outside the house had drifted into the gloom of early twilight.

Everyone but Strangford was already there. Portia stood in front of a glass-topped display case that had been slid open to reveal the manuscript inside. Her figure was soft and feminine, her features as elegant as her mother's. She spoke with the straight-backed authority of a university lecturer.

"It is an illustrated thirteenth-century manuscript of *The Life of King Edward the Confessor*," she pronounced, the firelight glinting off her round spectacles.

Dorcas hovered beside her, bouncing a bit on her heels. George stood behind the girls, looking down at the book with studied polite interest.

"As you can see, the binding is relatively modern. It sat quite unnoticed on our shelves until Mrs. Bates discovered it during a visit six years ago."

"Constance Tyrrell's friend," Walford piped in helpfully from his chair by the fire, addressing the comment to Dicky and Celia.

"Yes, of course," Celia murmured.

She sat near to her husband, but Lily could feel the emotional distance between them. Dicky was all sprawling ease, his arm draped over the back of the settee. Celia sat up iron-straight, her hands folded in her lap.

"She's not Connie Tyrrell anymore, darling," Virginia easily corrected her husband. "It's Mrs. Fairfax now."

"When you have known someone since childhood, it takes a while to get your head around a new name," Walford returned, frowning.

"She has been married for nearly twenty years," Virginia noted.

"Most of the books came with the house," Walford said, shifting the subject as James handed him a cocktail. "I'm afraid I don't know half of what's in here."

"I am three-quarters of the way through a complete inventory," Portia noted, calmly turning the page. "The collection tends towards geography and animal husbandry. The only other illuminated volume I discovered was a standard hagiography, which Mrs. Bates rightly insisted be returned to Christchurch Priory, from which it had undoubtedly been stolen during the Reformation."

"Father didn't fight it," Walford offered. "He's not much for hagiographies."

George looked very fine in his evening dress. Lily suspected he was not particularly interested in the life of King Edward, but he did an excellent job of humoring the girls.

She had not yet given him an answer to his question about whether the two of them might have some sort of relationship moving forward. At some point, she would have to find a moment to disappoint him.

The thought hurt.

Portia turned another page.

"The illuminations are quite primitive, of course, which limits the book's value on the antiquarian market, but I find they provide useful insights into how the early Norman dynasties sought legitimacy through connection to the Anglo-Saxon past."

George nodded knowingly, then he blinked with surprise.

"Is that a severed leg?" he asked.

"Indeed," Portia replied.

Dorcas's face split into a grin as George leaned closer, clearly baffled.

"But how many of them are there?" he demanded.

"I say fifteen," Dorcas offered cheerfully. "But Portia thinks that one's an arm."

Walford and Virginia had clearly heard this lesson before and treated it with cheerful indifference. Dicky was providing James with detailed instructions for his cocktail while Celia radiated quiet misery.

Feeling that Portia deserved a bit more of an audience, Lily drifted over to the glass case. She took up a spot behind Dorcas and looked down.

The illumination was indeed primitive. Cartoonish ink was filled in here and there with pale, faded hues of blue, green, and red— rather a lot of red.

"The scene is the Battle of Stamford Bridge," Portia explained. "A single Danish axeman reportedly held the bridge against the entire English army, cutting down forty men before a soldier managed to float under the bridge and strike him from below with a spear."

"Sounds like quite the stout fellow," George noted.

Portia looked at him.

"He was a berserker," she corrected.

Lily felt a chill creep up the back of her neck.

"What is a berserker?" she asked quietly.

"A warrior capable of entering a heightened state of both savagery and strength in battle," Portia replied. "Berserkers were reportedly extraordinarily vicious and effective killers, far more powerful than ordinary men and impervious to pain and injury. The term is Teutonic in origin, but there are accounts of warriors with berserker-like capabilities across several cultures. Marcus Cassius, a centurion in Caesar's army, apparently blunted his sword on his victims before he tired of slaughter. There is an account of a Chinese general who was shot in the eye with an arrow during battle, only to pull out both the arrow and the eye which he promptly devoured and then continued fighting."

"He ate his own eyeball?" Dorcas asked with ghastly delight.

"That is the story," Portia loftily returned.

"Portia has always been rather fond of the darker sort of fairy tales," Virginia noted.

"This manuscript is a historical account," Portia retorted.

"I think we can safely assume the author took a few artistic liberties," Walford commented cheerfully.

Strangford stepped into the room. He was fully dressed in one of his typical dark suits, black gloves on his hands—a living, breathing example of the sort of myth of extraordinary powers that his brother-in-law had just dismissed as fantasy. Lieutenant Brockmeyer was beside him, clad in his Navy mess uniform. He wore it well.

Lily studied Strangford carefully as he greeted Virginia. Had his manner toward her changed? Would he be able to conceal what he'd learned about their mother?

Of course, he would. Lily knew that Strangford could put on an act when required. He had kept too many secrets in his life not to be rather good at it. The bigger question was what it would cost him.

James offered the lieutenant a glass. Bonnie slipped into the room behind him, carrying a fresh ice bucket.

Portia's eyes narrowed behind her spectacles.

"Just because we do not see berserkers now does not mean they never existed," she announced. "Mammoths no longer wander Russia and Norway, but we have certainly found clear evidence that they once did so."

Lily wondered whether she had just inadvertently been compared to a mammoth.

Strangford drifted over to the wall near to where Dicky and Celia sat. He studied the painting hung there in a gap between the book-shelves. It was an unremarkable landscape Lily knew was not at all to his taste. That he made a point of losing himself in it spoke to his unease.

Dicky glanced back at him.

"I have meant to say, Strangford, those gloves of yours are very fine. Might I have a closer look?"

Lily's hands clenched. She had to fight the urge to intervene. She reminded herself that Dicky could not possibly know what he was asking. His interest in Strangford's gloves was purely sartorial.

Virginia would likely know a perfect way to deflect Dicky's attention, but of course, that would require her to be aware of the true reason why Strangford wore his gloves. His sister was in as much ignorance of that as his mother.

There was no reasonable way for Strangford to refuse Dicky's request. He tugged off the gloves and handed them over.

"In the old days, writers had a looser relationship with the truth. One must take it all with a healthy grain of salt," Walford said.

Walford's gentle assertion was entirely reasonable. Lily was equally sure it was false. History abounded with stories of saints and heroes capable of extraordinary feats. Cairncross and Ash had both insisted those stories were actually about people like Lily and Strangford—people who were still very much alive and walking the world, albeit perhaps more quietly than they might have in the ancient past.

Lily knew of a slew of strange abilities the miracle-workers and witches of history had been said to possess, like the power to heal or read minds.

She gazed down at the pile of dead at the feet of the berserker on the page in Portia's hands. Lily was sure Cairncross had never mentioned a khárisma like this. Maybe that meant Walford was right. Maybe this one was simply made up.

Thinking about it kept her from staring at the gloves in Dicky's hands.

"Lambskin?" Dicky asked, running his fingers over the leather.

"Kid," Strangford replied a bit shortly.

His hands hung self-consciously at his sides as he very deliberately kept them from touching anything.

James extended a platter with a glass.

"Sherry again tonight, miss?" he prompted.

"I ... thank you," Lily mumbled, accepting the glass even though she had no intention of drinking it.

"Don't believe in flying saints, Eversleigh?" Dicky teased. "Or being in two places at once?"

"Being in two places at once?" Brockmeyer echoed, confused.

"Of course, with a name like Brockmeyer, you must be a Protestant," Dicky quipped. "No magic powers for Lutherans."

"The phenomenon Mr. Anstruther-Fields is referring to is bilocation," Portia filled in. "It is the reported ability of some holy men to be physically present in two locations at the same time."

"They mostly used it to preach twice as many sermons. You can be sure I'd find a better application for it," Dicky noted with a wicked grin.

The conversation was beginning to make Lily feel like a rabbit stumbled into a den of foxes. At any moment, Portia would turn those owl-like, knowing eyes on her and announce that Lily was rather a myth herself.

Aren't you, Miss Albright?

It was too much—George's cheery presence by her prescient soon-to-be-niece. Dicky's hands on Strangford's gloves and the terrible tension only she could feel over the looming question of what he would do with his knowledge of his mother's illness. His silence was a lie, and Lily was complicit in it. She was lying to them even now as she stood in the midst of them pretending not to be what she very surely was.

Bonnie dropped the ice tongs onto the carpet. She flinched with alarm.

Dicky's eyes flickered over to the maid, lingering for a moment on her figure as she stooped down to retrieve them.

"There was a holy virgin, I believe, who was impervious to fire," Dicky went on as Bonnie stood. "So, the Romans kept burning her over and over again. Girl refused to catch. Finally, they just cut off her head. She was that determined not to give it up."

"Really, Dicky," Celia noted with clear disapproval.

"It's just history, darling," Dicky easily replied, his eyes following Bonnie as she darted away.

The room felt too close. Lily was overwhelmed by the urge to throw open the French doors and dash out into the December rain.

Dorcas piped up from beside George, seeking to recapture his attention.

"My favorite part is this hacked-up torso over here," she noted, pointing at the page.

Virginia firmly set down her champagne.

"Portia, Dorcas, time to join Lysander and Rosalind upstairs. Mrs. Metzger will have your supper ready."

Portia neatly swung shut the manuscript, sliding the glass cover of the display case back into place. She drifted out of the room without complaint, which somehow made her banishment seem even more unjust.

Dorcas gave her mother a more obviously violent look, stomping out into the hall. She paused in the doorway to stick her tongue out at George.

George automatically returned the gesture, and Dorcas's face split into a grin of clear delight.

"James, please see if dinner is ready," Virginia ordered. Lily could hear the note of tiredness in her voice.

"Of course, ma'am," James replied.

The footman's gaze flickered over to a shawl draped on one of the chairs. Lily recognized it as Portia's, forgotten in her distraction over the books.

James murmured a quick word to Bonnie. As he left the room, she darted over to pick up the shawl and then hurried out with it.

Virginia turned a forcefully charming smile on her husband and Lieutenant Brockmeyer.

"Did you two accomplish what you needed to with those papers?"

"I believe we did," Walford cheerfully replied.

"Excuse me, darling," Dicky said quietly to his wife.

He set Strangford's gloves thoughtlessly down on the seat of the settee and rose, slipping out of the room.

Strangford leaned down to retrieve them. As his fingers clasped the black leather, Lily saw his shoulders stiffen.

Something was wrong.

Alarm sang through her as she realized that Strangford was having a vision—right here in the intimate crowd of the library.

Strangford's visions weren't just something he saw from a distance. They were visceral, a lived and immersive experience. Most of them he could endure without giving any outward sign of it, but Lily had witnessed others that drove him to painful extremes.

She prayed this wasn't one of them.

"We'll need to do a bit of calculating to modify the standard alloy, of course," Walford went on.

Brockmeyer cleared his throat, and Walford started.

"What—I can't even talk about the alloy? Well, it will take some work, is what I'm saying, but I'm confident we can pull the whole thing off in record time."

Strangford straightened, and Lily breathed a sigh of relief … until he tugged on the gloves and promptly stalked out of the room.

The rest of the party didn't seem to notice, but Virginia did not miss his abrupt exit, her eyes tracking him as he left.

Lily remained frozen with indecision for a moment, then stepped forward to follow him. Before she could go any further, James appeared in the doorway.

"Dinner is served," he announced.

SIX

ℒILY SAT IN the morning room, roast and potatoes lingering uncomfortably in her stomach. The world outside had gone dark, the rain still tapping at the windowpanes.

The morning room was intimate, the furnishings more obviously feminine than they were in the rest of the house. It was clearly Virginia's space, one designed for gathering with women. The fire had been glowing when they came in after dessert. Both tea and sherry were set out on the table, along with a few biscuits. Lily could not imagine trying to eat them.

Virginia and Celia sat opposite her in a pair of plush velvet upholstered armchairs. Lily could hear the rumble of male voices from the billiards room next door.

She knew that dividing the men and the women for a while after dinner was traditional in wealthier houses, but when it had been only family here, they had all gathered together in the evening. Lily far preferred that, even if she had felt a bit like an impostor in the midst of it.

There had been something odd going on between Dicky and Strangford when the two men came in for dinner. They had been the last to arrive after everyone else was seated. She wanted to ask Strangford why he had gone after Dicky, but there had been no opportunity for it before they were divided.

The last two nights that the women had gathered together in the morning room, Virginia had set out cards. The table remained empty tonight. Instead, Virginia sipped at another glass of wine.

"Really, they ought to look for more pilots from the working classes. A man who can navigate an omnibus through London traffic is likely far better suited to thread an airplane through artillery fire than someone who has spent most of his life being driven around from place to place," Virginia said.

Celia didn't answer. She had been silent through most of dinner as well. Celia didn't seem talkative even when at her best, but there was something exceptionally withdrawn about her tonight.

Lily supposed she wasn't helping much herself. Her own thoughts kept getting tangled in the unresolved tensions of the day, from Lady Strangford's illness to George's presence in the house.

The glimpse of Strangford with his braces hanging at his sides kept pushing its way back into her mind. It was unhelpfully distracting.

Her thoughts hitched on the line of his shoulders, the curve of his back. The little drops of water falling from his damp curls onto the white fabric of his shirt. The dark interest in his expression when he turned and realized she had come into the room.

"So, I asked her—could she really be bothered that a civilian who'd had a nervous breakdown at the outbreak of the war hadn't been chosen for War Secretary? Instead of Kitchener, the Hero of Khartoum?"

Virginia paused for the expected agreement, but Lily had completely lost track of the conversation, consumed as she was by mentally undressing the woman's brother.

"Sorry?" she blurted.

"The War Secretary, darling," Virginia patiently explained.

There was a secret glint in her eye, one that did not seem entirely displeased. Lily was left with the distinct impression that Virginia was able to guess precisely what she had been thinking.

The notion brought a blush to her cheeks. She hid it behind a sip of sherry.

"I was saying we are much better off with Lord Kitchener than we would have been with Lord Bexley," Virginia continued smoothly. "Particularly given that the man is now in an institution."

Thoughts of Strangford in his braces firmly vanished.

Lily had last seen Bexley in a whorehouse in Primrose Hill where she and Strangford had assaulted him, using Strangford's powers to rip secrets from his skin.

She had heard Bexley was gone to a rest home in Berkshire. The public story was that he was recovering from stress inflicted by the outbreak of the war and the disastrous decline of both his political career and his financial estate.

If Bexley made other ravings before being put away—stories of barons with the power to read minds, perhaps—no one seemed to be taking them very seriously.

Virginia knew nothing of all that, of course.

Lily took a deeper sip of the sherry.

Before she had to come up with a response, they were interrupted by a roar of laughter from the next room. Lily caught a whiff of cigar smoke. The click of billiards balls echoed through the fine Morris print paper covering the walls.

Celia cut in, her voice firm and even.

"He really is quite terrible," she calmly announced.

Her face crumpled. She set down her glass as though afraid she might otherwise drop it.

"Oh, Cissy," Virginia exclaimed. She rose and went to Celia's side, but the other woman held her off with a raised hand, working to recover herself.

"You needn't fuss about it," Celia asserted firmly. "And I apologize to you, Miss Albright. It was rude of me to blurt it out like that. It is just that sometimes it all becomes too much to stand, and one cannot help but give voice to it."

She was pale and straight. Her fingers trembled as she reached for her glass. Celia seemed to realize it and instead set her hand back on the arm of the chair.

"You have nothing to be sorry for," Lily asserted firmly.

Celia nodded, accepting this. Her shoulders slumped as some of the tension wrung out of them.

"Cissy hoped to come here on her own," Virginia explained. She knelt at her friend's side, leaning against Celia's dress. "She wrote last week, begging for a chance to escape for a few days. Of course, I said yes. I knew you and Strangford wouldn't mind."

"But I had to tell Dicky where I was going," Celia replied dully. "And then he insisted on joining me."

She managed a big sip from her glass.

"I am certain he's unfaithful," she said. "I know it the way a woman must always know these things, and yet I have never been able to prove it. Just when I think I have him, he turns up with a perfect alibi. Half a dozen men who saw him at the club, or the theater, or will swear he was in his office at the Admiralty working until the small hours of the morning."

Her eyes reddened, a tear escaping and running unacknowledged down her cheek.

"I have smelled another woman's scent on him. He'll start humming as he shaves as though he's so pleased with himself when he was supposedly doing nothing but filing papers the night before."

Lily struggled to absorb this revelation. She had never paid Dicky much mind. He seemed a frivolous thing, bouncing from one entertainment to another. She probed at how Celia's story fit with her impression of the man and found it entirely plausible. Dicky didn't seem to take anything very seriously. Why should his marriage be any different?

"Perhaps I'm simply going mad," Celia burst out, her voice shaking. "I am not sure which is worse. To be wrong and be so poisoned with suspicion, or to be right and be unloved."

Virginia reached over and clasped her friend's hand, saying nothing.

Lily could still hear the men next door—the clink of glassware and the low, comfortable chatter of their voices. It was as though they sat in the bubbles of two distinct worlds separated by one thin silk-papered wall.

A quick knock sounded on the door.

"Come in," Virginia ordered.

Bonnie slipped inside. She plucked a pair of empty glasses from the table, setting down a fresh bottle of sherry. An awkward silence reigned while she worked. This was not the sort of thing one discussed in front of the help.

Bonnie took her tray and opened the door, trying to spin quickly through it. She nearly crashed into Felix Brockmeyer, who was walking down the hall.

"Oh! Terribly sorry," he apologized.

Virginia glanced up at the sound of his voice.

"Is everything alright, Lieutenant?" she asked.

"Quite, madam. I just needed to use your telephone if that isn't too much trouble."

"Of course. You'll find it in the hall," Virginia replied. Lily could hear the note of tiredness in her voice.

Brockmeyer made her a quick bow and then disappeared. Recovering herself, Bonnie hurried out, pulling the door shut behind her.

As the latch clicked into place, the room around Lily tightened, squeezing the breath from her lungs.

Her heart pounded. She tasted the bitter spice of her onmyōdō.

Something was happening.

She was torn between the need to freeze or run, the conflict of it driving her to her feet. She was distantly conscious of how odd it was—Lily bolting from her chair as a woman who barely knew her exposed a raw sliver of her soul—but it didn't matter. She fought an urge to scream as Virginia looked up at her with surprise.

A delicate crash pierced the quiet of the room.

Lily's world splintered, shattering into fragments.

The scrape of a footstep amid glossy leaves.

The sharp stink of burnt cordite.

Slick wet blood on her hands.

The elegantly appointed morning room twisted around her until Lily felt certain she was going to be sick, and then abruptly snapped back into place.

Celia blinked.

"What was that noise?" Virginia's friend wondered aloud.

Lily forced herself to move, her body still shaking. She sprinted for the door, yanking it open, needing desperately to know the source of that terrible little sound.

George had emerged from the billiards room, frowning curiously, a glass of scotch in his hand. Lily turned from him and ran in the opposite direction, toward the main house. She slipped around the corner to see Brockmeyer holding the telephone receiver. He was staring in surprise at the shattered remains of a blue-glazed porcelain vase.

The world narrowed, tunneling down to those broken shards on the floor. The regular geometric pattern of the glaze was interrupted.

Distantly, like a voice speaking from far away, it occurred to Lily that the delicate blue marks on the clay now looked like so many interlocking keys.

One thought rang through her mind, cutting through the fog of her inexplicable shock.

What have I done?

A tinny voice was just audible through the receiver of the telephone.

"...believe it's who, then?" it demanded.

"I must go," Brockmeyer murmured distractedly, his gaze swinging to where Lily stood in the doorway.

He set down the receiver as the others flooded into the hall. George was first, followed closely by Strangford and Walford, with Virginia and Celia behind them.

Dicky sauntered up to join them.

"Did I miss something?" he demanded.

Lily didn't respond. She wasn't yet capable of it.

"I'm terribly sorry," Brockmeyer said. "It just fell over while I was standing here by the telephone. I've no idea what set it off."

"Don't concern yourself about it, Lieutenant. It is merely a bit of decor," Virginia assured him.

Celia stepped over to where the vase had fallen, across the room from where Brockmeyer had been standing.

"How very odd," she murmured.

"Perhaps it was old Cicero," Walford offered.

"Cicero?" George echoed.

"The ghost," Celia flatly replied.

"I am rather more certain one of the children had something to do with it," Virginia sighed.

Lily's heart continued to beat, the regular push of her blood throbbing in her ears.

James slipped past the cluster of house guests.

"I'll see to it, ma'am," he intoned.

"Back to the whiskey, then," Dicky declared. He rambled in the direction of the billiards room.

The others followed, the incident already forgotten. After all, it was insignificant—a mere accident. An event of no possible consequence.

Strangford touched a black-gloved hand to her arm.

"What is it?" he asked.

"Nothing," she replied, knowing the words were a lie.

~

The voice was a whisper in her ear carried on the wind of a dream. It smelled of grass and horse, the sweat of sleeping men, and rang with the clatter of brass.

Mendax ambulat.

Lily stood on the earthen rampart of the ancient camp at the edge of Taddiford's field. The uncut grass rustled at her feet, bending and dancing in the breeze. It was a flat, moonless night, but she could see the waving of each distinct blade.

A raven settled onto the branch of the ash tree with a heavy beat of dark wings. It dug its claws into the wood and croaked.

The sea rose against the cliffs, waves breaking in foam and mist against the clay—and then the water was everywhere. The flood spilled past her, pulling Lily's legs from the rampart. She fell, plunging into the cold tide, the current tossing her like a leaf. Water pushed at her mouth, her nose, fighting for a way inside.

Lily had drowned once before. She knew what came next would be terrible.

She heard the creak of leather—smelled, impossibly, a whiff of woodsmoke.

The words bit at her through the torrent, edged like oiled metal.

Saga, excita.

The sea poured inside.

~

Lily woke, gasping. Her chest ached as though someone had struck her. She clutched at it, bolting upright, legs tangling in the blankets.

The panic was blinding, visceral, every instinct fighting against the memory of that water—but it was gone. She lay in the bed of the room assigned to her at Taddiford.

It was still dark. The rain had stopped. A brief flash of light spilled over the quilts, brightening the pale marble of the fireplace. The lighthouse, Lily remembered. The beam from that outpost on the headland reached as far as the manor.

She'd had a nightmare. The memory of it was already fading. As it drifted back, something else rose in its place, familiar and unmistakable.

A premonition.

It offered her no insight, only a fierce sense of threat. It pulsed through her with an urgency Lily had not felt in months, not since that February night when she woke knowing that Annalise Boyden was about to die.

Her legs tensed with the urge to run. She forced herself to still, taking a breath and reaching for the thread of energy that pulsed through her. How could she act when there was no detail, not so much as the ghost of an image of what was about to go wrong?

The knowledge throbbed back at her mercilessly, unresponsive to her attempts to probe it into revealing more. It beat out its terrible truth with every frantic contraction of her heart.

Now. Now. Now.

Lily threw back the quilts and slipped from the warm safety of the bed. She hurried to the chair and yanked on her wrapper—and as abruptly as it had started, the feeling snapped.

The urgency was gone. She was left standing in her bare feet and nightdress, shivering in the chill of the dying fire.

The lighthouse beam swept by once more. It revealed the wind tossing the silhouettes of the trees outside the window. Lily could hear the low whistle of it through the darkness. She considered climbing back under the covers. They would still be warm.

Grimly, she pinned closed the wrapper and stepped out into the hall.

A small lamp had been left lit near the door to the water closet. It provided enough illumination for Lily to read the hands of the clock. It was eleven forty-three.

She headed for the nearest staircase, which lay not in the wing but in the main house. Turning the corner, she passed the door to the master bedroom. A soft light spilled from beneath it.

Lily heard a low sob, then a murmur of comfort. It was Virginia's voice, though she couldn't make out the words. The mournful reply was recognizably Celia's.

Lily slipped past them, her bare feet light on the carpet. The rest of the building was silent, the rooms cloaked in darkness.

Her hand on the banister, she descended the stairs.

She didn't know where she was going, only that a lingering unease demanded she ascertain the state of the household. Lily followed that instinct past the gloom of the dark drawing room and study, moving along the ground floor of the wing.

A light had been left on in the lower hall just as it had upstairs. Lily heard a soft burst of laughter. It came from the cracked-open door to the billiards room.

She tiptoed up to it and peered inside.

George and Walford reclined in two of the chairs, a nearly empty bottle of scotch resting on the table between them. They were both quite comfortable and rather obviously intoxicated. The whisky appeared to have deepened their relationship to one of easy intimacy.

"So you see, if we just invested in a fleet of lorries, we wouldn't be held hostage to the vagaries of freight schedules," Walford complained with great feeling.

"That seems perfectly sensible to me," George replied sincerely.

"It's a matter of national security," Walford emphasized, thumping his fist on his knee.

Opposite them, Dicky snored on the settee, his head lolled back.

There was nothing amiss beyond the headaches all three men would likely be suffering from in the morning. Lily moved on.

Light glowed under the next door as well, the one that led to the library. Lily turned the knob quietly and pushed it open.

Strangford was alone. He sat in a chair with a book in his bare hands. He still wore his suit, though his tie had been discarded. His shirt was a bit open at the collar, and he rested his stockinged feet on an ottoman.

The December wind rattled the glass of the French doors behind him. Lily could see nothing through them, just her own reflection in the glass.

She came inside and moved to his chair. She glanced down at the book.

"Poetry?"

"It's actually rather awful," he admitted.

Lily ran a finger over the back of his bare hand.

"No gloves," she noted.

He smiled a little sadly.

"Sometimes, I just need to feel something," he replied. "This seemed a relatively safe option."

His gloves sat on the walnut table by his side. Lily picked them up, running her fingers over the soft leather. They were showing wear in places, widening a bit at the seams.

"I seem to have misplaced the newer pair," Strangford noted.

That struck Lily as odd. Strangford's gloves were far too important to him for him to leave them lying around carelessly. Of course, they were staying in a busy house full of people and servants. His attention had been called in a thousand different directions over the last few days. There were also the children to consider. Lily could easily imagine them snatching things up and moving them about without giving it a second thought.

"Couldn't sleep?" Strangford asked.

Lily considered how to answer.

"I think I heard a ghost," she replied.

One of his dark eyebrows rose.

"Is that even possible?" she asked. "I'm not like Estelle. I don't talk to the dead."

"I don't know that it requires khárisma to hear a ghost," Strangford said. "Was it anyone you know?"

She recalled the foreign sound of the words in the wind, the aura of brass, leather and horse.

"I think it may have been Cicero."

He set aside the book, pulling back on his gloves.

"Would you like me to walk you back up? I'm sure I can intimidate any ghosts out of the way should the need arise."

"That could be rather scandalous," Lily returned.

Strangford's mouth curved into a smile. He put down the book and took a step closer, slipping a hand around her waist. She recalled that she was clad in her nightgown and wrapper.

"No more than getting caught together in the library," he said, his voice low in her ear. "Just imagine what we might get up to amid all these books."

Lily began to do precisely that and felt a bit warmer.

She was distracted by the sound of a dull knock.

It was not a particularly loud or alarming sound, but it felt distinctly out of place in this otherwise quiet hour of the night. It had not come from the billiards room next door, where she could still make out the contented murmur of George and Walford's voices.

"What is it?" Strangford asked, sensitive to the abrupt change in her attention.

"I heard something," Lily replied distractedly.

It came again, soft and a little distant—a single, unmistakable knock.

In her mind's eye, Lily found herself vividly picturing a Roman soldier, muscular and brown-skinned in a breastplate and skirt. She wondered if the ghost in the house had resorted to pounding the walls for her attention.

"Come on," Strangford said, leading her to the door.

He nudged it open and stepped into the empty hall, then paused, listening. The careful tension in the lines of his body told her that he was poised for a fight. The thought both alarmed and reassured her.

The knock sounded again, more distinct now.

"It's in the conservatory," Strangford said.

The glass octagon was tacked on to the far end of the wing, past the other staircase that emerged near Brockmeyer and Strangford's rooms. The door to it was slightly ajar, the space beyond it black.

"I'll have a look," Strangford said.

He did not expect her to follow, but Lily went along anyway. As she approached the door, she found herself irrationally afraid that he would turn on the light to reveal the ghastly figure of a dead Roman centurion.

It was the grossest superstition. Estelle had made it quite clear the dead had no interest in deliberately horrifying the living.

Strangford pushed the button, switching on the single electric bulb that lit the conservatory. It was not very bright—this wasn't a room routinely used after dark.

The space was thick with life. Plants packed the rows of wrought-iron shelves from tidy lines of little flower seedlings to rich, spilling pots of tropical blooms. A lemon tree sprawled in the corner, branches heavy with small green fruits.

The stone floors were neatly swept, but the potting table at the back was covered with tools. Walford's father, the senior Mr. Eversleigh, had once dabbled in orchid collecting, and the surviving evidence of his hobby was still packed against the dark glass walls. Lily could smell the subtle fragrance of the blooms in the warmer, humid air and for a moment, she felt transported to somewhere equatorial. The stove the gardener used on cold nights like this one sat in the corner. The door to it was slightly ajar, revealing the orange glow of the coals.

The knock came again, far sharper now. Lily's gaze flashed to the door on the far side of the room. It was made of wood and opened into the yard. A gust of wind caught it, bouncing it against the frame.

"I'll get it," Strangford said. He took a step forward—then Lily's hand flashed out, grabbing him by the sleeve.

"Strangford," she uttered, the word half-strangled with shock.

Her eyes were locked on the floor. Just beyond the nearest shelf of plants, a pair of polished black shoes emerged from a set of navy-blue trousers.

Surprise only froze her for a moment. Lily rushed forward, spinning around the corner to see Felix Brockmeyer lying face-down on the flagstones in a pool of blood.

She dove to her knees beside him, grabbing his arm.

"Lieutenant," she called.

She shook him, but the texture was off. He felt too loose, too still. Lily let out a wild cry.

"Somebody help!"

"Lily," Strangford said from behind her.

The rest of the picture came into focus. Her eyes fell on Brockmeyer's mangled and blood-soaked hair, on the pale shards of bone.

A shovel rested on the floor, long-handled and rugged, the blade marred with blood.

Fragments of a vision came back to her—Brockmeyer's uniformed back moving through the thick greenery as a threat stalked him from among the dark leaves.

What have I done?

The thought rose automatically and inexplicably.

The glow of the stove demanded her attention. It was too bright. Something was flaring inside of it, burning at a rate faster than that of coal. The smell of it had a chemical edge.

Lily scrambled to her feet. She dashed past Brockmeyer to wrench open the door of the stove, singeing her fingers on the handle. There was something black smoldering inside. She snatched up the fire tongs and plucked it out, dropping it on the ground.

The shape became recognizable. It was the remnants of a leather glove.

She turned to Strangford, horror bolting through her like a shock of electricity. His expression was grim.

"He was hit from behind," he noted.

His gaze moved to the shovel. No—the murder weapon, Lily corrected herself. She could read his intention before he moved. The notion terrified her.

"No!" she hissed.

Strangford ignored her. He pulled off his gloves, shoved them into his pocket, and dropped to his knees.

He put his bare hands to the handle of the shovel.

Voices echoed from the hall, mingling with the sound of heavy footsteps.

Lily pivoted, pushing to her feet and sprinting to Strangford. She wrenched the shovel from his grip. He slumped against the potting bench, catching himself with a hand on the flat surface.

She quickly wiped down the wooden handle with the blood-stained hem of her nightgown. She set it down and staggered back a step just as Walford and George raced into the room.

"Dear God!" Walford exclaimed.

George pushed past him, hurrying to Brockmeyer's side. He knelt more carefully than Lily had, avoiding the pool of blood. It was smeared at the edges.

Lily looked down at the front of her pale wrapper and realized it was soaked crimson.

George put his fingers to the lieutenant's neck. The entire world paused for a breath.

"He's dead," he announced.

Walford went pale.

"But that's ... He was just..."

Virginia pushed past him, Celia lingering tentatively in the frame of the door. Strangford's sister held a paraffin lantern high, casting a more clear and ghastly light across the scene.

Celia gasped in horror, clutching at the wall for support.

Dicky strolled up behind her, yawning.

"What's all this, then?" he mumbled.

Lily pushed past the shock, finally accepting that what lay at her feet was real.

"Lieutenant Brockmeyer has been murdered," she said, her voice surprisingly even. "Walford, please telephone for the police."

SEVEN

Tuesday, December 15th
Nine o'clock in the morning
Taddiford Hall, New Forest, Hampshire

THE GLASS BAUBLES on the Christmas tree glittered in the sunlight through the windows. A fire crackled in the grate. The drawing room should have felt cozy, but instead, the mood was decidedly sober.

Celia and Virginia sat on the settee, the two women holding hands. Celia looked even more pale than usual. Walford stood by the fireplace, tapping his fingers restlessly on the mantel.

"I should have checked the conservatory door," Walford said again.

"Mrs. Metzger said it was locked," Virginia repeated.

They had already spun their way around the fact three times. Taddiford's cook, a handsome and broad-shouldered blonde in her fifties, lived in the village with her husband. She made it a routine to check that all the doors were locked before she left for the night.

"The thief must have picked the lock," George offered helpfully.

George and the others had all settled on this explanation for Brockmeyer's death—that the lieutenant had been unfortunate enough to surprise a burglar in the process of breaking into the house.

Lily glanced over at Strangford. He stood at the window, looking across the dry grass of the field to the dark line of the forest. Blue-clad bodies moved slowly across the field, a quartet of private constables who appeared to be painstakingly examining the grass. A plainclothes officer walked with them, barking an occasional order and pointing.

There were more of them in the conservatory, carefully cataloging the scene of the crime. Others had combed through the bedrooms. They would surely have had their hands all over Strangford's things. Lily winced at the thought.

She brushed at the wool of her skirt, needing something to do with her hands. At least she was wearing a skirt. It had taken Virginia unleashing the full force of her fury on a clearly uncomfortable sergeant from the station in Highcliffe for Lily to be allowed to remove her blood-soaked nightgown and wrapper.

She wondered if Strangford had more answers. There had been no opportunity to discuss what he had learned in the conservatory. After Walford dashed to telephone the police, they had been rounded up like stray cattle and herded from one room to the next until they were planted here in the drawing room. So far, Strangford had managed only a brief whisper to her since he read the murder weapon.

He was waiting.

"I still don't know why that dreadful man had to bother the children," Celia complained.

The dreadful man in question was a lean, elegant police inspector who had arrived on the scene at around seven in the morning, a few hours after the clearly rattled Highcliffe sergeant had blinked down at poor Brockmeyer's corpse and pronounced it a murder.

The inspector was clearly not from Highcliffe. Lily could smell London in his urbane self-possession and the controlled grace of his movements. He was also of South Asian descent, with black hair and a copper complexion. That was rare enough in the city, never mind on the remote Hampshire coast.

"Because they might have seen something," Virginia replied to Celia.

Lily could hear her exhaustion.

"He was very polite with them, even when Lysander insisted on untying and retying that constable's shoes," Walford noted from his place by the fire.

"I did not find him polite," Celia countered. "I thought him pushy and tedious."

"The poor chap's simply doing his job," George offered.

Lily wondered why a murder in Hampshire required the services of a London inspector. Certainly, violent deaths must be rare in this quiet slice of countryside, but had the local sergeant required assistance, might he not have received it from Bournemouth or Southampton? Those cities were far closer and surely had a detective or two on hand.

The inspector had interviewed the servants first, taking ample time with each of them, even those who lived in town and therefore hadn't arrived at the estate until the morning. He had moved on to the children next, Virginia and Walford being called upstairs to chaperone.

The younger Eversleighs, thankfully, had slept through the night's events. Lily wondered how much they had been told, though she felt certain they would know the whole of the matter before long. All four of them were tenacious about satisfying their curiosity once it was roused.

Had they also been fingerprinted? She recalled the cold press of the ink, the pressure of the constable's hand as he pushed her fingers one by one onto the soft yellow card stock. She'd stood by helpless as it became Strangford's turn. She recalled the flinch in the muscles of his jaw as the young officer had grasped his bare hand and pressed it to the paper.

A constable had waited by the door to the water closet as she washed her hands. The ink had turned the water a hazy purple. It was the second time she had stained a basin of water that morning. Brockmeyer's blood had turned it a translucent red.

The image of Brockmeyer's corpse continued to haunt her—that kind, solid man turned to something pale and crushed on the conservatory floor as the delicate perfume of the orchids wove through the air.

"The inspector is with Special Branch," George noted distractedly.

"Special Branch?" Celia echoed in surprise. "What could they have to do with it? They're meant to be guarding ambassadors or chasing anarchists."

"Haven't the foggiest," George replied. "I thought it was a bit odd he and his constables arrived five hours after the other fellows, so I asked. One of the local bobbies spilled it."

Lily absorbed this with quiet alarm. Special Branch was a division of the London Metropolitan Police specially tasked with thwarting revolutionaries. They were most visible as blue-helmeted heads surrounding visiting foreign dignitaries—men like the Kaiser before England had gone to war with him. What business did Special Branch have with a murder in a remote Hampshire country house?

She recalled that Brockmeyer had worked in Churchill's office in the Admiralty. Perhaps that warranted special consideration.

Her thoughts were interrupted by the creak of the drawing room door.

The London inspector stood framed in it, dressed in a plain but well-tailored charcoal suit. Dicky leaned against the wall behind him, looking wan. Lily recalled her glimpse of him the night before passed out in the chair in the billiards room. He was clearly paying for that overindulgence now.

The room went even more silent.

"Miss Albright," the inspector said, looking straight at her. "Would you join me for a moment?"

His voice was deep and firm, his accent clearly educated. Only a subtle care in his enunciation suggested that his origins were not entirely English.

Lily had known this was coming. He had interviewed everyone in the house with unrelenting thoroughness. Only she and Strangford remained. She reminded herself that it must be routine procedure after a murder.

"Of course," she calmly agreed.

She met the inspector at the door as Dicky slumped back into the room, dropping heavily into a vacant armchair. He laid back his head and promptly closed his eyes.

"This way," the inspector said, directing her into Walford's study.

The study lay beside the drawing room and offered an equally pleasant view across the grounds. One wall was covered with shelves. They clearly housed a working collection rather than an ornamental one. Thick reference volumes were sandwiched beside bound journals and file boxes. One shelf was completely taken up with ledgers, another with what looked like sample cases. A few curiosities brightened things up—rocks with lines of mica running through them or intricate knots of driftwood. A bright, sea-weathered blue bottle caught her eye beside a little lump of iron ore shaped vaguely like a rabbit.

On the wall above Walford's desk, a pair of hooks served to mount a martial-looking spear. A long, polished staff of modern hardwood was topped with an ancient blade, the brass tarnished to a pale green. It must be the Roman artifact Virginia had mentioned the day before.

"Detective Inspector Tariq Kazi," her interrogator said, taking up a position behind the desk. He gestured to a chair.

"Please."

Lily adjusted her skirt and sat down.

The desk itself was clear. Lily recalled that any papers Walford had been working on with Brockmeyer must be stashed in the safe. She couldn't see any safe in the room, but her eye lit for a moment on a fine oil seascape hanging on the wall that adjoined the staircase. There would be space behind it, beneath the stairs.

The inspector noted the direction of her gaze. His brown eyes were a rich hue with hints of gold, but there was nothing warm in them. He lowered himself into Walford's chair and opened a slender notebook.

"You are affianced to Anthony Rivers, Lord Strangford," he said, his eyes on the book.

"That is correct," Lily confirmed.

"How long have you been engaged?"

"Since August," she replied.

"And for how long before that were you acquainted with his lordship?"

"We met in February," she said.

"Was your immediate acquaintance casual or intimate?"

She startled at the question. It was abruptly personal, an inquiry with no apparent relevance to the crime the man was investigating, but there was nothing prurient in his expression. His interest seemed both focused and entirely impersonal.

Lily had never really belonged with the upper classes, but she knew enough of their ways to know how a woman of privilege would respond to that sort of question.

Lily straightened her spine, icing her words.

"I beg your pardon," she returned.

"Was your initial relationship with Lord Strangford distant, or have you been very closely connected since February?"

His tone was patient and relentless, as though she merely required clarification of the question. It might have been another insult, but once again, there was nothing personal or vicious that she could see in it.

The disconnect rattled her.

For a moment, she was thrown back to that cool February morning—to Strangford's windblown hair and open collar as he looked down at where she lay on the ground.

You are dripping blood onto the road.

"May I ask why the question is relevant?" she pushed back.

She watched his response for some clue as to what he was thinking. He gave her none, smoothly changing the subject.

"Your father is Lord Torrington. Correct?"

Everything about this conversation was raising Lily's hackles. She felt unnaturally defensive and was unable to entirely contain it.

"I am Lord Torrington's bastard," she returned sharply.

She wanted to provoke him, to stir up some reaction that would reveal what the man was thinking.

"How close are you to your father?"

"We did not speak for fourteen years," Lily retorted.

"But you are speaking now," Kazi pressed back calmly.

Silence extended awkwardly as he waited for her response, his pencil poised over his little book.

"Yes," Lily finally bit back.

He made a note.

The fury rose up in her, as visceral as it was unjustified. There was nothing in his manner that indicated he intended to insult her.

"How close is Lord Strangford to your father?" Kazi continued.

The question threw her. It was not at all what she had expected. Alarm slowly bloomed.

This was not the snide curiosity of society gossip. It felt more like the careful stalking of a fox than a bout of thoughtless bullying.

Everything about Kazi screamed of deliberation. He had a reason for pressing her about Strangford and her father. Lily simply couldn't guess what it was—which meant she couldn't guess what answer was the right or wrong one to give him.

It made her vulnerable. Even her power couldn't help her here.

"They have spoken once or twice," she replied.

He raised his gold eyes from his notebook.

"Once? Or twice?" he calmly demanded.

The fury snapped in her again, threatening to explode. Lily fought it back.

"They had an exchange in a hallway in the House of Lords five months ago," she replied. "Then spoke again briefly at the funeral of a mutual acquaintance later that week. Lord Strangford met with my father privately at his club a month later to discuss our engagement."

She wracked her memory, wanting to be as pedantically thorough as he seemed to demand, as though doing so would serve as some kind of slight to him.

"I believe Lord Torrington also asked for Strangford's support for a bill he was interested in. That would have been sometime in October."

The only sound was the delicate scratch of his pencil against the page. Behind him, through the glass, Lily watched the constables combing the field.

"And I understand Lord Strangford is fluent in German," Kazi continued without looking up at her.

The question felt like another terrible non sequitur.

"Yes, and French and Latin. He works as a translator," Lily replied.

"Thank you," Kazi said.

He set down the pencil, folding his hands.

"You and Lord Strangford were the ones who discovered Lieutenant Brockmeyer's body."

"We did," Lily carefully confirmed.

"Can you tell me what happened? In your own words," he prompted, then waited.

"I woke at around a quarter to twelve—"

"Why?" Kazi cut in.

The interruption startled her into blurting out the truth.

"I heard a ghost."

At last, his face revealed a flash of emotion—a focusing of interest. He took up his pencil again.

"You mean a rattling? Something at the glass?"

"I mean a voice in my ear," she returned.

"And this was at precisely eleven forty-five?" he pressed.

"A little earlier," Lily corrected. "When I went into the hall, the clock read eleven forty-three."

"Your room is directly above the morning room," Kazi said, flipping unerringly back three pages in his notes. "Could this voice have been coming from the terrace outside those doors?"

"No," Lily replied.

"Sound can move in unexpected ways, especially in the quiet of the night," he challenged.

"It was in the room," she returned.

"And what did it sound like?" he pushed back, revealing just a hint of irritation.

"Latin," Lily replied.

She knew it was likely a mistake. Every instinct told her she should offer this man only as much as she absolutely must, but the urge to discomfit him with the truth was too compelling to resist.

It worked. His eyes widened softly with surprise.

"Latin," he echoed carefully. "Do you speak Latin, Miss Albright?"

"No," Lily replied.

"Then how do you know that's what you heard?"

"*Mendax ambulat*," Lily returned.

Kazi blinked at her. The blink felt infinitely satisfying, a small but thrilling victory.

"How is your Latin, Inspector?" Lily asked.

"I studied it at university," he admitted.

"Tell me what it means," she ordered.

He did not reply right away. He watched her thoughtfully, weighing it.

"The liar walks," he finally replied.

The words sent a chill of gooseflesh over her arms.

"And *Saga, excita?*" she continued carefully.

Kazi stared at her from across the table, his eyes sharp.

"Witch, rise."

That electric unease crawled from her arms to the back of her neck, raising her hair. She could hear the dry whisper in her ear again, recalling every rasping tone of it.

Saga, excita.

She settled back into her chair, forcibly making herself comfortable.

"That's what it said, then," she concluded.

Kazi's eyes drifted back down to his notebook. His hand hovered over it with the pencil, but for the first time, he hesitated to make a mark. He set the pencil down and turned his gaze on her again.

"And after that?"

"I went downstairs to see if anyone else was awake. I passed Mr. Carne, Mr. Eversleigh, and Mr. Anstruther-Fields in the billiards room. Mr. Carne and Mr. Eversleigh were talking. I believe Mr. Anstruther-Fields was asleep. I saw the light on in the library and found Lord Strangford there."

"The library has French doors leading out onto the terrace," Kazi cut in. "Were these opened or closed?"

"Closed," Lily replied. "It was cold out."

He motioned for her to continue.

"We spoke for perhaps five minutes and then heard something banging. We left the room to investigate and determined the noise was coming from the conservatory. Strangford supposed someone must have forgotten to latch the exterior door. It was quite windy here last night. We went in to check and when we turned on the light, we found Lieutenant Brockmeyer on the floor."

"You called for the others immediately?" Kazi asked.

The images flashed back to her—the blood on the floor, the flare of the firebox. Strangford pulling off his gloves and laying his hands on the handle of the murder weapon.

"I . . . yes. I suppose I did. I'm sorry, it's hard to recall the details. I was mostly concerned with whether the lieutenant needed help."

He glanced back a few pages in his notes.

"Sergeant Taylor of the Highcliffe station reported that your nightgown was covered in blood when he arrived."

"It was," Lily admitted, skin crawling with the memory of it.

"Why?" Kazi demanded.

"I went to him—Brockmeyer. I thought he had been hurt. Maybe slipped and fallen. I must have been kneeling in the blood."

The words spilled out without much feeling, but inside she was shaking. She could still feel the wet chill against her knees.

"And then?" the inspector prompted.

Lily forced herself to continue.

"It was clear very quickly that he was dead. I looked up and noticed something burning in the stove. I plucked it out with the tongs and dropped it on the flagstone. I thought perhaps it might be important."

She swallowed. Her throat had become quite dry.

"Then the others came in," she said.

It was a lie, but how could she tell him the rest?

Then my fiancé picked up the murder weapon and tried to pull the memories out of it with his hands.

The inspector was looking at her. Lily felt unsettlingly certain that he knew she was leaving something out.

He couldn't possibly know. No one had seen it, and Lily was better than most at passing a lie.

"Which others?" he finally asked, pencil in his hand again.

"Mr. Eversleigh and Mr. Carne at first. Mrs. Eversleigh and Mrs. Anstruther-Fields arrived shortly after that. Then Dicky—Mr. Anstruther-Fields, I mean."

"Did you see any of the servants?"

"No," Lily replied. "But only Bonnie sleeps in the house, and she's up on the third floor. I'm not sure she would've heard us. James and Mr. Lewis have apartments in the carriage house. Mrs. Metzger and the gardener, Mr. MacInnis, live in town."

The pencil scratched on the page, the sound itching at the back of Lily's skull.

"And was Lord Strangford wearing his gloves all this time?" the inspector casually asked.

The question dropped into the room like a bomb. The quick terror of it electrified her. He could not possibly know what he was asking.

"Miss Albright?" Kazi prompted, watching her with that awful focus.

She was making it worse by hesitating. Lily forced herself to respond. The image flashed in front of her mind of the black leather covering his fingers as he pushed open the door.

"He was," she replied, the words clipped.

Kazi gazed at her, and Lily was certain he was studying every nuance of her reaction.

"Are you certain of that?" he quietly demanded.

Her mind spun through the horror of those few moments in the glass room—the blood, the fire. The over-rich scent of the orchids. Strangford's hands on the wooden handle of the shovel.

Had she succeeded in erasing those marks when she frantically wiped the handle down? What else had he touched?

They had all been fingerprinted. Men had been over every inch of that room since Kazi arrived a few hours ago.

She had to remember to breathe.

"I'm sorry. I am mistaken," she said, forcing the words out as casually as she could. "He did not have them on at the time."

Everything around her felt brittle.

"That would have been unusual, wouldn't it?" Kazi noted. "I understand that Lord Strangford wears the gloves quite habitually, even when indoors."

"Yes. It is rather a quirk of his."

The lightness in her tone sounded false even to Lily's ears.

"I suppose that's why I initially made the mistake. I am so used to seeing him wearing them, but then it was very late in the evening. I can assure you he did not have them on when we found Lieutenant Brockmeyer."

"I see," Kazi said.

Something about the moment felt horribly wrong. It was written into the clutter on the shelves, the innocuous painting on the wall. The blue-uniformed policemen she could still see out in the field through the window behind the inspector. Lily realized what it was a moment later.

Kazi had not made a mark in his book.

"Have you found any indication of how the murderer got onto the property?" Lily demanded.

"I have found that the murderer must already have been here," Kazi replied.

"But that's impossible," she blurted.

"What is impossible is accessing the conservatory after a heavy rain without leaving tracks in the saturated ground," he replied. He stood, looking out the window. "The paved terrace runs along the length of the wing from the morning room to the conservatory, with means of egress from each of the rooms that line it—the morning room, the billiards room, the library, the breakfast room, and the conservatory. The terrace is otherwise surrounded by lawn. Mr. Anstruther-Fields reportedly stepped out to relieve himself at around eleven o'clock. His footprints can clearly be discerned at the edge of the grass. Mr. Carne recalled needing to rise to close the door after he returned—apparently, the gentleman was fairly intoxicated and neglected to do so himself. Lieutenant Brockmeyer retired for the evening a half-hour later. There are no other footprints, Miss Albright. Whoever entered the conservatory last night did so by way of the hallway or the terrace. Either way, that means they began their journey from inside this house."

She thought of the words Strangford had managed to whisper to her earlier that morning.

He was waiting.

Lily finally had a name for the unease she'd been feeling since her conversation with the inspector began—suspicion. If Kazi believed the killer came from inside the house, then the members of the house party were his suspects.

She searched for a way he must be wrong.

"The killer might have entered the house during the day," she pointed out. "He might have hidden until the night and then surprised the lieutenant."

"Then where did he go?" the inspector demanded.

"Out the driveway, perhaps," Lily suggested. "It is paved with gravel. It wouldn't show footprints, even in the rain."

"The front door to the house was locked. Mr. Bradley had to turn the latch to admit Sergeant Taylor when he arrived from Highcliffe."

"Mr. Bradley?" Lily echoed, confused.

"The footman," Kazi replied.

Lily realized she had never heard James referred to by his surname.

"Only the kitchen door was open. Mr. Bradley has a key and claimed he opened it himself when he arrived for work in the morning. His tracks can clearly be seen from the carriage house where he has his apartment. All other entrances to the house were found to be locked when the Highcliffe police arrived," Kazi continued relentlessly. "If our killer fled down the drive, Miss Albright, who locked the door behind him?"

Lily knew it was possible to reset a lock with picks. She was aware of one enterprising young East Ender capable of that feat, but why would someone fleeing a murder scene take time to reset the lock?

The alternative was that someone inside the house was an accomplice to the murder—or had committed it themselves.

Lily had heard Virginia and Celia talking in the bedroom on her way through the house. They sounded as if they had been at it for a while—not as though they had just made a mad dash through the corridors after committing a murder. George, Walford, and Dicky had all been together in the billiards room.

She felt she could safely rule out the children. Bonnie had been alone in her bedroom, but Lily found it hard to believe that the girl, who was rather small, could have possessed enough force to strike Brockmeyer down with a shovel.

She thought of the wound she had seen on his skull, forcing herself to think of it without feeling sick. It seemed most likely to be caused by something from above—a powerful downward stroke with the blade.

James had a key. He was tall and strong enough to have done it, but Lily recalled hearing him arrive early in the morning. She had gone with Virginia and Celia to the morning room while the men still lingered in the hall. There had been a rise in the volume of their voices when James turned up and was filled in on what had happened.

Kazi said only one set of prints led from the carriage house. Had the footman found some roundabout way to get into the estate? Or come earlier to murder the lieutenant and then hidden somewhere in the house for a few hours?

Even as she considered it, she felt how implausible it was, especially when compared to the opportunity the last suspect on Kazi's list would have had.

Strangford was already in the house. He had been alone in the library with a door leading directly onto the terrace. He might easily have walked into the conservatory, murdered Brockmeyer, and then returned to where he was sitting.

Lily knew that was impossible. Strangford wasn't a killer, but the picture might look very different to a sharp-eyed police inspector—and suddenly, more of Kazi's questions began to make a terrible sort of sense.

She thought of the black leather glove smoldering on the flagstones, his hands on the handle of the shovel. Had she wiped it down thoroughly enough? Did it even matter?

Kazi thought it was Strangford—Strangford who had no alibi and was certainly strong enough to have done the deed.

The inspector closed his notebook.

"Thank you for your assistance, Miss Albright," he said smoothly. "You have been most helpful."

It was a dismissal. Lily stood, turning for the door, suddenly rather desperate to escape. She had just put her hand to the knob when Kazi spoke again.

"I do hope you understand how serious the matter is."

She turned back to look at him. The inspector was standing behind the desk. The light through the window cast deeper shadows across his face.

"We found fragments of fabric in the fire. The pattern matches that of a missing garden smock. Mr. MacInnis was able to identify it. He was adamant that he had not burned a smock that day—that, in fact, he would have turned a damaged smock into rags rather than burning it. That suggests the murderer burned the smock and did so because the item had become stained. If the killer took the time to don a covering before attacking the lieutenant, it speaks of clear and undeniable premeditation. I'm sure you are aware of how much more serious a charge of premeditated murder must be."

He stepped toward her around the desk. He was a tall man.

"If you knew anything that might shed light on the motives of the killer—the involvement of another party, perhaps, in the planning of the crime?—it could mean the difference between imprisonment and execution for the man found guilty of holding the weapon."

Lily's heart was pounding. Her hands were cold. Kazi's words were both an offer and a threat.

"Should I find the killer, Inspector, I shall be certain to ask him that," Lily replied, then pulled open the door.

EIGHT

Two officers waited in the hall. One was a seasoned sergeant, the other a young constable who smelled of the country.

"Ready for the last one, then?" the sergeant demanded.

Kazi nodded.

"Take her back to the others," he ordered.

The inspector closed the door to the study, retreating behind it to prepare for his next interview—the one he would have with Strangford. Lily was left with the two other policemen, who were under clear orders to shuffle her back to the makeshift prison of the drawing room.

She could not allow herself to be simply carried along by a series of events that might end with Strangford's neck in a noose.

"I need to visit the restroom," she announced.

The constable blushed. The sergeant frowned.

"Take her," he barked at the younger officer. "I'll grab the lord."

"Sergeant," the constable quickly replied, nodding acknowledgment of the order.

The sergeant stalked towards the drawing room. Lily watched him go, then pointed the opposite way, toward the hall to the wing.

"It's this way," she said.

"Right," the constable blurted awkwardly.

There were closer restrooms, but a plan had abruptly taken shape in her mind. If she were caught, it would very likely make her seem an accessory to the crime Kazi supposed Strangford had committed. She had to take the chance.

She stopped at the narrow door to the water closet between the library and the breakfast room. The library door was open. Two officers were inside, dusting fine powder over the table where Strangford had sat his book the night before.

She flashed the constable a thin smile and pushed into the restroom.

It was long and narrow, consisting only of a toilet and sink. Lily deliberately neglected to lock the door. She knew the constable wouldn't dare come in after her—not for quite a while.

A small window at the far end faced the terrace. Lily went to it, peering outside. The lawn looked empty, but she could be more sure of that.

She took a breath, calling on her power, demanding it show her what would come next. The answer was soft and clear.

She flipped over the tin waste bucket, noiselessly setting it on the ground. Standing on top of it, she turned the latch on the window and pushed it open. It swung sideways on silent hinges.

She pushed herself through the narrow opening, pulling her legs out after her. As she dropped to the pale gray paving stones of the terrace, she heard a rip. Glancing down, she could see a little tear in the fabric of her skirt.

There was nothing she could do about it now. She pushed the window closed once more. It wasn't latched, of course, but it would do.

The glass doors to the library lay just behind her. She was conscious of the two police officers still searching the room. One of them might step outside at any moment.

Her power tugged her the other way, toward the conservatory. Lily followed it, darting past the dark glass doors to the breakfast room to stop in the shadow of an enormous bay laurel. Beyond its thick green branches lay the intricate glass of the conservatory, panes glittering in the pale light of the gray morning.

She lingered, tuned to the careful knowing inside of her that whispered *wait ... wait ... move.*

Lily obeyed, stepping before one of the great panels of glass. Beyond it, inside the conservatory, stood two officers and a plainclothesman.

The sight froze her for a moment. Brockmeyer's body was gone, though his blood still marked the floor. One of the officers held a camera. The bulb flashed, momentarily blinding her.

She lost the thread of foresight and felt panic rising. It urged her to run. Lily resisted, digging into herself to reforge that connection.

Now, it told her.

As the plainclothesman turned, Lily moved. She strode around the glittering wall of glass, reaching a panel that fronted a tall rack of shelves covered in orchids and ferns. The knowing told her to pause, waiting for a breath as an officer walked by with a tray of glass sample jars.

She hurried on, slipping past the conservatory and rounding to the kitchen. She tugged open the weathered wooden door and slipped into the gloom of the mudroom.

"I just feel so awful about it."

Bonnie's tearful voice drifted to her where she hid. Lily heard Mrs. Metzger's murmured reply. She darted forward into the kitchen, passing soundlessly behind the cook's back as she watched Bonnie dig a few more potatoes out of the basket in the pantry.

Lily slipped through the door into the hall, then froze. She could hear the maid and the cook shuffling around in the space behind her. The hall in front of her looked empty—as much of it as she could see around the frame of a grandfather clock.

She was conscious of the conservatory door right in front of her. At any moment, one of the policemen inside might push through into the house and see her lingering. It left her feeling pinned and terribly vulnerable. The urge to move was overwhelming, but it was painted in the wrong colors—a motive of logic rather than instinct. Lily resisted it, though the effort made her grit her teeth as the clock beside her ticked.

Finally, the right time announced itself. Lily darted out, glancing down the hall to see the constable waiting outside the water closet turn his gaze toward the main house, obviously uncomfortable with how long Lily was taking.

Lily slipped into the stairwell. She mounted it quickly and quietly. At the top, she emerged into the hall to see two more officers walking away from her. She pivoted, reaching for the nearest door—then flinched back, catching herself. Her focus on her power had almost made her forget common sense.

Lily whipped a handkerchief from her pocket, wrapped it around the doorknob, and turned it, pushing inside.

Brockmeyer's room was empty.

The lieutenant had been given one of the smaller rooms in the house, though it was still very comfortable and well-furnished. The bed was neatly made, the surface of the desk clear. A window looked out at the dark blue line of the sea. A valise stood on a stand in the corner.

Lily's eyes moved to the desk. She carefully examined its surface. The wastebasket was empty, the notepad blank. She could see a fine black film on the paper, a little more on the surface of the desk. There were neat square spaces where the dust was missing. The police had already been through here, as Lily thought they must.

Working quickly and quietly, she checked the drawers, using the handkerchief to avoid leaving any more fingerprints. They were empty. She made a quick search of the valise, finding a shaving kit, a nightshirt, and spare underclothes tucked beneath a copy of yesterday's London newspaper.

She didn't know what she was looking for. She could have only a little time. The knowledge burned with both frustration and fear. There had to be something here that would help Strangford—that would explain why someone else might have a reason to bludgeon a perfectly nice young naval officer to death.

She threw open the wardrobe. Brockmeyer's day uniform hung neatly on the hangers, freshly brushed. His shoes, polished to a mirror-bright shine, were set side-by-side on the floor with military precision, his cap perfectly aligned on the shelf.

Nothing else.

Strangford would be able to do so much more with this. If Brockmeyer had secrets—like a reason someone might want to kill him—Strangford might have been able to pull them from the fabric of his coat. All Lily could do was fumble around.

Desperation rising, Lily plunged her hand into the dead man's trouser pockets. The first was empty. The second yielded a crinkle of paper. Using the handkerchief, Lily pulled it out.

The envelope was printed with the stationary of a gas company and had been forwarded to an address at the Admiralty. Lily eyed the original direction.

F. Brockmeyer
1 Merchant's Row
Scarborough, Yorkshire

There was nothing inside but a bill.

The urge to pop it into her skirt pocket was fierce. Lily resisted it, thinking back to her interview with Kazi—to how careful and thorough he was. She could not take the chance that he knew the envelope was here or that he might order her searched before he allowed them to leave the house.

She memorized the address, wiped the paper clean, and put it back.

Her power flashed a warning.

There had to be something more here, something she could use … but she had run out of time.

Lily ran to the door, yanking it open and dashing into the hall. Voices sounded from the far end where the corridor turned into the main house. She grabbed the knob of another door and darted inside, then waited, listening.

"The inspector says pack it all."

The voice echoed to her dully through the wood, moving closer.

"Bloody waste of time if you ask me," came the reply.

She heard the click of the latch and the creak of floorboards as the two policemen entered Brockmeyer's room. Her heart pounding, Lily slipped back into the hall.

She hurried toward the main house, tiptoeing down the stairs into the entry. She could hear the murmur of voices from the drawing room where the rest of the household was still sequestered. She turned toward it, then dodged back, a warning from her foresight mingling with the sound of footsteps from around the corner.

Could she linger here unseen? The answer wound out before her in a quick vision of Kazi stepping into the entry and finding her frozen like a deer.

She yanked open the front door, wincing at the creak of a hinge, and darted outside.

Her shoes crunched on the gravel of the drive. A pair of officers stood by a police carriage parked at the gate. They were chatting amicably and did not turn when she came out.

Lily darted around the corner of the house. She halted in front of the French door that led into the drawing room and found herself looking into the surprised face of her brother.

Her power had given her no warning of it, or perhaps she hadn't listened. Either way, there was little she could do now but trust him.

She mouthed the word.

Please.

George snapped to attention, flipped the lock, and opened the door.

Lily stepped inside, her entrance half-hidden by the bulk of the Christmas tree. George shut the door behind her. She heard the soft click of the lock as she stepped around the tree back into the room.

Virginia turned, her sharp eyes noting Lily's arrival. The others appeared oblivious. Dicky was dozing again while Celia stared down at her hands, clasped firmly in her lap. Walford was pacing.

The door from the hall opened, framing Lord Strangford and the older sergeant who had been stationed outside the study. The officer's sharp eyes moved immediately to Lily. He frowned.

"PC Edgars is still waiting at the restroom for you," he snapped.

"I didn't see him when I came out, so I made my own way back," Lily placidly returned.

It was hard to keep her voice even. All her attention was on Strangford as he made his way through the room. She tried to read his face to find some clue as to what had passed between him and the inspector. Had Kazi accused him outright? Or tricked Strangford into saying something that might make him look even more guilty?

Holding back the questions took effort. It highlighted her exhaustion. Drawing on her power to navigate the house for so long had left her feeling a little dizzy.

Then Kazi himself arrived, stepping past the sergeant into the room. His golden eyes snapped to Lily, then dropped unerringly to her skirt. She was conscious of the little tear and felt uncomfortably certain that he was looking at it.

She refused to look down herself to see if it was visible, straightening her back and waiting.

The inspector returned his attention to the room.

"I wish to thank all of you for your cooperation and patience this morning," he said.

He spoke graciously. There was something almost aristocratic about his bearing. It made it seem as though he belonged there in Taddiford's drawing room—as though he would've fit in nicely had they been gathering for an evening of cards rather than a murder.

"I know this has all been terribly shocking, but I assure you the persons responsible will be brought to justice."

Lily fought the urge to reach out and take Strangford's hand. She thought of the address on the envelope in Brockmeyer's pocket upstairs. Why hadn't she managed to find something more?

"Thank you, Inspector," Walford said. "I feel awful about the whole business. Can't help but feel responsible that it happened in my own house."

He looked miserable.

"You mustn't think like that, Walford," Celia cut in. "There are ruffians everywhere these days. It is only lucky he did not burn the house down with us in it."

Virginia's lips thinned. Lily wondered what she was not saying.

"My men will need the conservatory for another hour, but the rest of the house is cleared. You are all free to go about your business. Be assured I will call if I have any further inquiries."

His gaze drifted to Strangford as he said it.

Virginia rose, brushing down her skirts with self-assured elegance.

"Of course, we are all eager to cooperate with your investigation any way we can, Inspector," she said.

~

The room rapidly became crowded when the children descended the stairs. Bonnie trailed after them, clutching her hands a bit helplessly.

"The murderer might have come in by parachute," Dorcas suggested.

"We would have heard the plane," Rosalind snapped.

"Not if it was gliding," Portia noted. The oldest Eversleigh child sounded a bit distracted. Her attention was focused out the window, her sharp eyes studying the grass through her spectacles.

Strangford met Lily's eyes, then slipped from the room, dodging through the snarl of young people.

"I'm afraid we must be getting on," Celia said, standing. "I am rather eager to put this whole dreadful business behind us. James?"

"Yes, ma'am," James replied with a nod, turning for the hall.

"Quite understandable," Virginia replied, her voice just a little cool.

"Have you got any blood on you?"

The demand came from below. Lily looked down to see Lysander staring up at her.

"Not anymore," she replied. "Excuse me."

She wove past the four-year-old and the cluster of older children, escaping into the relative quiet of the hall. She hurried up the stairs, stopping to tap at the door to Strangford's room.

"Come in."

He stood by his suitcase, which rested on the bed. He was carefully folding and packing his clothes, his hands shielded by his gloves. His things must be covered in impressions from the police officers who had gone through all of them. The thought made her heart twist.

"What did he say to you?" she demanded.

Strangford set his blue jumper down in the suitcase. Lily vividly recalled what he'd looked like wearing it on the sand below the cliffs. Had that only been yesterday?

"The inspector has requested that I proceed directly to Bayswater and remain at home."

It only confirmed what Lily had already suspected. Still, the fear crawled in, icing her veins.

"For how long?" she demanded.

"For as long as he determines necessary," Strangford replied.

"He thinks it was you," Lily blurted, pain and worry giving the words force.

"It would appear that he does."

Strangford paused in his folding, his shoulders bending forward.

"They went through everything. I took the gloves off to check. All of it feels like suspicion."

She stepped closer and slipped her arm around his waist. Her head fell against his shoulder.

"The shovel," she said.

"You must have managed to clean it," he replied. "If the inspector had found a print on the murder weapon, he wouldn't be sending me back to Bayswater. But they did pick one up from the potting bench. I told them I had been in the room earlier in the day when I came back from the beach."

The truth settled over her, as awful as it was undeniable. Kazi had identified Strangford as his lead suspect. Unless evidence materialized that someone else was involved, that was where the suspicion would remain. That glove in the fire wouldn't have been burned if it hadn't been used, which means there would be no other fingerprints. The burned smock eliminated the possibility of any tell-tale bloodstain on someone else's clothes.

Kazi had a compelling argument that the killer must have come from inside the house, and Strangford was the only one who did not have an alibi—besides Lily herself, of course. That she wasn't competing with Strangford for the inspector's suspicions likely came down to her class and gender. The blow that killed Brockmeyer would have required significant strength, more than the inspector believed a respectable woman would possess.

He would not know, of course, about Lily's rather less than respectable regular training in kali, which made her arms significantly stronger than those of the average society miss.

It was Strangford who habitually wore the same gloves found burned in the stove, whose fingerprints had been recovered next to the corpse.

Strangford could go to prison for this. He could hang for it.

The terror of that tore at her, robbing her of words.

Lily looked up from Strangford's shoulder to see Virginia stalk into the room. She slammed the door behind her.

"The inspector suspects you," she declared.

"It would seem that he does," Strangford acknowledged.

Virginia stepped closer, her small frame radiating fury. She glared up at her younger brother.

"You must see how serious this is. You cannot simply endure it like you do all other adversity in your life. There must be something you could tell them that would make it clear you are not the man they're looking for."

The words had weight. They were true, of course. Strangford might tell the inspector that he was capable of pulling hidden truths from objects with his hands. He could ask to read the murder weapon or even Brockmeyer's corpse, and in doing so, might very well direct them to the real killer.

And Kazi could think him a liar. He might take the facts Strangford was able to reveal about the crime as further evidence of his own guilt.

Strangford had not felt safe revealing the truth about his hands even to his own mother and sister. Lily knew those fears were not unjustified. She could still vividly recall the glittering interest in Jack Cannon's eyes when he stood in the doorway of the kitchen in March Place, measuring her, assessing what she might be worth. Belief was almost more dangerous than skepticism.

Virginia was still waiting for Strangford's answer. Lily was painfully conscious of how much they had not shared with her, truths tangled up in the secret of Strangford's power.

"I have told him everything I can," he quietly replied.

Virginia glared back at him with simmering fury.

"Sometimes, Brother, you drive me to the edge," she said.

With that, she turned and stalked from the room.

She left a wave of guilt in her wake. Lily didn't like lying to Strangford's sister, even if it was one of omission.

Strangford sat down heavily on the edge of the bed. The lines of his face were deeply drawn, worn down by exhaustion and worry. Lily sat beside him.

"Someone planned this," she asserted carefully. "The garden smock in the fire, your gloves . . . You said a pair were missing. Anyone might have taken them from your room."

"The killer was waiting for Brockmeyer," Strangford said. "Only Brockmeyer."

Lily absorbed this revelation with a chill. She knew it made sense. It fit with Kazi's assertion that the killer must already have been inside the house and with what Strangford had managed to share with her earlier that morning. It had been more comforting to imagine that Walford's theory was right—that Brockmeyer had merely been unlucky enough to stumble across a would-be thief.

"Do you know who it was?" Lily swallowed thickly. "Was it one of us?"

"I don't know," he returned. He was frustrated, his shoulders tense. "I should. I ought to have been able to pull some sense of who held the shovel. There just wasn't enough time."

Her mind spun through the possible suspects—Virginia and Celia, Walford and Dicky. Her brother.

"I can't imagine which of them might have done it," she admitted. "Even forgetting that they all have alibis. None of them seems the type."

"People have secrets, Lily," Strangford replied, his voice dark with bitter experience.

It was why he had put on the gloves. As a boy, reading the hidden thoughts of the people he encountered was a game to him. That had changed when he grew old enough to understand the implications of those trespasses and lies—when he became a victim of them himself with Annalise Boyden.

Strangford didn't want to stumble across anyone's inner thoughts anymore. It had taken an enormous leap of faith for him to touch Lily for the first time. She'd more or less had to blackmail him into doing it.

She heard more than just that old pain in Strangford's voice.

"You know something about one of them," she guessed.

"Anstruther-Fields," he admitted flatly. "When he handled my gloves in the library, he was thinking about Bonnie. That's why he got up. He was planning to catch her in the hall and offer her two crowns to leave her door unlatched for him."

Fury rose up with a speed that surprised her.

"The rotter," she burst out. "Doesn't he realize she'd have no choice? That she'd be terrified he'd speak against her if she refused him?"

"He wasn't thinking of that," Strangford tiredly replied.

"Well, he bloody well ought to have been," Lily snapped.

"I know. That's why I went after him."

Lily remembered the tense moment when Strangford abruptly stalked out of the library and the tension in the air between the two men when they came into dinner a little later.

She knew all too well what it felt like to be cornered like that. During her time in the theater, Lily had encountered men who presumed they were entitled to whatever they liked from the women who worked on or behind the stage. Some of them had been oblivious to the terrible position their advances put on the girls. Others knew it perfectly well.

She had nearly been a victim of it herself. It was why she now carried a walking stick—why she had learned to use it to protect herself.

"I caught him where he'd cornered her in the upstairs hall. I don't believe he much appreciated the intervention," he admitted.

None of it felt hard to believe. Dicky was a dilettante, a man who had coasted through life on an easy wave of good birth, good looks, and a modicum of charm. He likely thought his advances to a housemaid were a gift. He would be bewildered and irritated by anyone who questioned that.

It made her grind her teeth.

Strangford's revelation about Dicky didn't make him a murderer. He had been passed out in the study with George and Walford when the crime took place, but it hammered home that Lily couldn't really know what the other members of the household might be hiding.

Not that it mattered. They all had alibis—all of them but Strangford. Something in Kazi's manner told Lily that the inspector believed Strangford had a motive, not that he'd given her enough clues to guess what it might be.

"We need to know more about Felix Brockmeyer," Lily declared.

"What did you find?" Strangford asked.

She could not be shocked that he had gleaned something of her adventure that morning from her touch.

"An address," she replied. "I'll go, see what I can learn."

Strangford stood.

"I'm coming too," he declared.

Lily felt a flash of alarm.

"If you leave Lancaster Gate, you'll look even more guilty. If the inspector told you to stay, it seems likely he'll put a watch on you."

"I can escape a watch," Strangford replied. "And I am better equipped than anyone to discover whatever information is there to be found."

Lily could not deny it, even though she hated the idea of him putting himself at even greater risk.

"It's me they're after," he pushed. "It's my choice, Lily."

There was something surprisingly fierce in his words.

She could not know what he was feeling about all of this. That insight only worked one way. His sudden intensity was an uncomfortable reminder of that.

Lily slipped a shaking hand through the dark fall of his hair, tucking it back behind the black silk that covered his missing eye. She took a breath, coming to a decision.

"We'll both go," she conceded. "But we won't do it alone."

NINE

Three o'clock that afternoon
King's Cross, London

$\mathcal{L}$ILY HURRIED THROUGH the crowded platform of the railway station, ticket clutched in her hand. The vaulted glass ceiling of the station glowed with the afternoon light even through the veil of soot that marred the panes. She glanced up at the massive clock, noted the direction of the hands, and quickened her pace.

The platform was wreathed in steam as Lily wove her way through clusters of families, small mountains of luggage, and businessmen clutching newspapers. The engine of the train gave a warning chuff as she approached, a conductor hanging out the door of one of the second-class compartments. He glanced up the length of the train, doing a final check before signaling to the engineer.

Lily raced up to him, extending her ticket and flashing him an apologetic smile. He gave the slip of paper a precursory glance and waved her on board, clearly a bit annoyed.

It had taken her longer to reach King's Cross than she had anticipated. She had made it as far as Gower Street when she realized the gentleman in the flat cap and brown tweed was shadowing her. Lily had stopped to read some advertisements on the wall of a haberdashery, and the fellow—almost certainly a plainclothes policeman—lingered behind her.

Halfway to Euston, she turned abruptly into a grocer's shop, weaving through the stands of kale and turnips to the service door she knew must be in the back. Hurrying up the alley to the next road, she had hailed a hackney and disappeared inside of it, instructing the driver to make an extra loop around the park before taking her to the station. She paid him a generous tip for his trouble.

She glanced out the window as the conductor shouted his final all-clear up the line. On the next platform, a noblewoman approached another carriage while her entourage of servants tried to wrangle her luggage. A trio of young women shrieked with delight at the blast of a train whistle, scurrying past. Behind them, a man in a bowler hat shouldered into the front of the line for the telephone office.

The carriage jerked, forcing Lily to catch her balance. The crowd by the other train began to glide smoothly past her, drifting until they vanished and were replaced by the dark gray gleam of the intricate weaving of rail tracks.

Lily carried her small suitcase up the aisle. It was narrower than the first-class compartment but also more familiar. Lily had never really possessed a first-class income. She wondered if her frugality would be more of an issue after she was married. Would it raise eyebrows if a baroness traveled in the more common section of the train?

Second class was reasonably comfortable even for a long journey like this one. It would be well after supper by the time she reached the terminus in York, and she would have to stay overnight there before catching an early local train to her destination.

Both sides of the carriage were lined with upholstered benches set facing each other, some with little tables down the center. As the train rattled down the tracks, Lily stuffed her bag into the luggage rack overhead, then sat down and looked to her travel companions.

"Tea?" Miss Gwendolyn Bard asked. The folklorist held up a flask and tin cup.

"A spot of vermouth would be better," Estelle remarked dryly. "I have never packed so quickly in my life."

Steam rose from the flask, pale ribbons rising toward the luggage rack, but there was something off about it.

"Why does it smell like smoke?" Lily blurted.

Miss Bard's eyes widened with surprise. She put the flask to her nose.

"It smells like tea to me," she asserted.

Lily shook her head. Of course, it smelled like tea. She wondered why she had ever thought differently.

"Are you well?" Estelle demanded.

Her head was wrapped in a soft green turban, and she wore a flowing caftan in marine hues, fringed in black. Her mode of dress drew a few eyes in the otherwise conservative environs of second class, but Estelle paid them no mind.

She made her living as a spiritualist medium. Her talent was genuine, though she had spent years putting on a show of illusions to attract clients. Her mode of dress fit the persona, though Estelle chose to wear it for other reasons, which included a love of bright colors and a contempt for corsets.

In contrast, her companion, Miss Bard, was clad in soft hues of white and brown. She had something of the air of a plump, pretty wren about her, while Estelle was more akin to the tropical plumage of an exotic parrot.

"Fine," Lily replied, dropping into her seat.

Estelle's complaint about packing was well justified. When Lily had burst into their flat, she had given them only an hour to prepare for this excursion. It had taken Lily half that time to stuff her own things into her bag, but then Estelle had never liked being rushed.

It had made sense for Strangford to take the risk of joining Lily on her mission to Scarborough. Estelle was a logical addition as well. After all, they were hoping to uncover the secrets of a dead man.

Lily had felt terrible asking her friends to drop everything and jump on a train to the far north, though she had never doubted they would do it. She was going to miss having them just downstairs. The imminence of that change rattled her. Lily still found it hard to imagine what her life in Lancaster Gate might be like ... if she got a chance to live it.

She forgot Miss Bard's offer of tea as her gaze moved to the empty chair beside the woman.

"Where is Strangford?" Lily demanded, alarm rising.

"Not here yet," Estelle replied, waving her hand.

Panic drove Lily to her feet. What had happened? She was frozen in the narrow aisle, unsure which way to go. Should she jump off the train at the next station?

Estelle's hand settled on her arm, her touch firm.

"Have faith, darling," she said blithely.

The door to their compartment clattered open. A country vicar in a plain black suit slipped through it, his head lowered under the brim of a slightly tatty hat. Lily only half noticed him, her thoughts whirling over how she might break Strangford out of Scotland Yard.

"Ladies," the vicar said, stopping at their section.

Lily startled, recognizing the low rumble of his voice.

"Good afternoon, my lord," Miss Bard said cheerfully. "Tea?"

Strangford pushed up the brim of the terrible hat, revealing his familiar features.

"That would be lovely," he replied, slipping into the seat beside her.

"See?" Estelle commented knowingly.

With a neat move of his gloved hand, he plucked the solid white collar from around his throat, tucking it discreetly into his pocket.

"Tickets, please," the conductor said, stopping at their row. Lily held her tongue until the man had punched their passes and moved on. Outside the window, the buildings grew lower and sparser as they rolled into the outskirts of north London.

"How did you get on the train?" she demanded.

"Third class," Strangford replied. "I nearly didn't make it. The fellow who was tracking me from Bayswater was uncommonly good at it."

He leaned back in the seat. The suit he wore was old, going a bit shiny at the cuffs.

The train slowed as it approached Hornsey Station. A few more passengers climbed on board for the haul north to Yorkshire. A stocky man in a navy sack suit and well-brushed brown hat joined their carriage, plopping into an empty seat and promptly unfolding a newspaper.

Estelle handed Lord Strangford a cup, which he accepted gratefully. Estelle's blue eyes glittered.

"Now that we're all here, perhaps you might tell us what all of this is about?" she said.

~

The early morning air in Scarborough was damp and salt-scented. The seaside town on the Yorkshire coast was quiet, streets all but deserted. This was not the time of year for holiday travelers, and many of the shops were closed.

Lily and the others had spent the night at an inn near the station in York, catching the first train out to the coast in the morning. It was an ungodly early hour for Estelle, who was more or less nocturnal in her habits. She hadn't complained. Instead, she endured the journey with a conspicuous fortitude that made Lily feel guilty.

The medium was dressed with uncharacteristic practicality in a black wool skirt and overcoat. The attire had surprised Lily when Estelle came downstairs at the inn.

"Caftans are impractical for housebreaking, darling," Estelle noted.

Her short brown hair was still wrapped in the green turban, secured with a paste brooch.

Mist hung over Scarborough's harbor. It veiled the sun, which had only just risen over the horizon, and put a deep chill in the air. Lily was grateful for the wool of her coat.

A few tradesmen lingered outside a bakery, sandwiches wrapped in paper tucked under their arms. The window glowed with warmth. A deliveryman rumbled by with a cart full of apples. A fellow in a brown hat knocked at the closed door of a telegram office.

The road from the station curved down the slope, ending at a fine and deserted sandy beach. On the crest of the hill above, Lily could see the ruined towers and crumbling ramparts of the old castle. The soft hush of the sea whispered against her ears.

They passed a few shuttered souvenir shops, stopping outside a cozy little restaurant that smelled of sausages. Lily's stomach grumbled. There had been time for only biscuits and tea before they left York.

A stout woman bustled through the door, tugging a small boy behind her. Strangford stepped neatly aside to avoid them.

"Sorry, love," she said.

Her eyes rose to Strangford's eye patch and widened, then took on a soft shine of emotion. She reached up and patted him on the shoulder.

"And thank you for your service," she added firmly. "See that, Robbie? That's a right decent fellow."

She tugged the boy down the road without waiting for any further response.

Strangford had gone utterly still, his body rigid with tension. Behind him, Estelle and Miss Bard exchanged a look.

"Strangford?" Lily said, concern rising.

"I'm fine," he returned flatly.

It was clearly a lie, but he strode forward, leaving Lily no choice but to follow.

Merchant's Row was a narrow crook of a road that ran behind the shops that fronted the strand. The house matching the address on Brockmeyer's envelope was small, two squat stories set at the end of the row.

The door was painted a cheery red and faced up the hill. The rest of the building was whitewashed and just a little stained with soot. The window boxes were empty, and a film of dust covered the glass.

If Sam were there, he might easily have picked the lock. In his absence, Lily wasn't entirely sure how they would get in.

"Keep a sharp eye," Strangford ordered.

He walked around the corner to the back of the row. Lily followed and watched as he looked quickly about, grasped the fence with his gloved hands, and scrambled over it. He dropped to the far side with a soft thump.

Lily turned her eyes to the road, watching for any passers-by. She heard the tinkle of breaking glass.

A moment later, the front door swung open. Lily hurried back to Estelle and Miss Bard, joining them as they stepped past Strangford and went inside.

The house was tidy but deserted. The air smelled musty.

They were standing in the living room. A shelf on the wall held a few decorative painted plates, done in German style. A quilt on the armchair looked handmade.

Miss Bard started nosing about, flipping through the handful of books on the shelf. Estelle wandered the space more idly, running a finger over the back of the sofa.

Strangford pulled off his gloves, tucking them into his pocket. He pressed his hands to the quilt, and his eyes lost their focus.

Unsure what use she could be, Lily passed through to the kitchen. A window there looked out over a scraggly back garden. One of the panes was broken, and the lock was turned, revealing how Strangford had come inside. Lily found she didn't feel terribly guilty about it. The man who had lived here was dead.

The icebox was empty. The cupboards held only a canister of oats and a box of sugar cubes. Mice had nibbled at the corners of it.

She tried all the drawers and cabinets but found nothing else of interest—a tin pan, a pair of mugs. One of the bowls had a chip in it.

Lily returned to the living room. She lingered in the doorway, not wanting to disturb Strangford as he brushed his fingers over the magazine rack, the silk flower arrangement.

"It's odd," he announced.

The remark surprised her. Nothing about the house looked odd to her. It was almost painfully ordinary.

"What do you mean?" she prompted.

"Everything is ... disparate," he said, searching for the right word. "The quilt was made by a widow for a church fundraiser. The plates belonged to a German shipwright. He dusted them frequently. They reminded him of home. This table had a batch of children eating at it until fairly recently."

"He must have got it all second hand," Miss Bard suggested. "Or perhaps some of those people were relations."

"It's more than that," Strangford pushed back. "Objects that are lived with together start to feel something alike, even if they came from different places. It's ... hard to describe. I don't feel that here. It's as though all of these things are samples cut from different bolts of cloth."

"Sounds like a rummage sale," Estelle noted.

"Yes," Strangford replied. "That's rather it. I don't think these things were lived with together for very long, if at all."

Lily ran a finger through the thin layer of dust on the table. She pushed aside a framed print on the wall. The paper behind it was slightly more vibrant in hue.

"Well, some of it has been here for a while," she said.

"Perhaps it was here," Strangford returned stubbornly. "But there's nothing of Felix Brockmeyer in it."

"Are you having any luck?" Miss Bard prompted, looking to her companion.

"Not with your dead lieutenant," Estelle replied. "But there is a helpful old gentleman who suggests we ought to go into the attic."

She frowned, reconsidering.

"Under the roof, rather. I'm not exactly sure what the difference is, but there you are."

Strangford turned to look at the narrow stairwell. He strode toward it, leaving the others to follow.

The upper floor of the house consisted only of a pair of bedrooms set under the peaked roof. One boasted a little gabled window that looked out over the sea. Lily could see the gray, mist-shrouded water of the harbor.

A narrow bed was covered in a blue wool blanket. The bookcase held a few volumes that even Lily could see didn't really belong together.

The other bedroom was empty. There was no attic.

It felt like a dead end.

Strangford ran his hands over the frame of the bed, then moved to the blanket.

At each side of the room where the roof sloped down lay a row of built-ins. Miss Bard opened one of the cabinets. The white-painted shelves held a spare blanket and pillow.

Lily tried a few of the drawers. They were all empty.

Estelle gazed out the window at the sea.

"Any ideas?" Lily demanded.

"I'm afraid not," Estelle replied. "The gentleman has moved on. I believe he was only peripherally interested in us."

Her gaze moved to Miss Bard, who had knelt down on the floor to peek under the bed, her brown tweed derriere raised into the air.

Strangford pulled out the drawers of a small dresser. He sighed with frustration.

There was so little here. Lily sat down in front of one of the cabinets Miss Bard had already searched. She stared into it, looking beyond the rust-hued blanket and the striped muslin cover of the bare pillow to the white-painted backing.

Something tickled at the back of her mind.

Reaching inside, Lily ran her fingers across the wood. Some part of her expected it to reveal a secret as though she were the psychometric in the room.

She looked up at the angle of the roof, following it down to where it met the built-in cabinets.

The tickling in her mind loudened to a buzz.

She pulled out the blanket and pillow, then tugged free the shelf. Pressing her hands to the backing, Lily pushed.

The wood popped loose, falling back an inch or so. Lily grasped the edge of it, shoved it aside, and revealed a narrow, sharply angled vacancy between the built-in fixtures and the place where the roof met the floor.

"Under the roof," she echoed softly, a little surprised at the uncanny accuracy of the information Estelle had reported to them downstairs.

She reached in, feeling blindly. Her fingers brushed against something regular in shape, discerning corners and edges covered in a thin layer of dust.

It had a handle.

Lily grasped it, tugging the object out onto the floor. It was a slender suitcase, smelling faintly of camphor.

Strangford crouched down beside her, Estelle and Miss Bard turning to look from behind.

"What is it?" he asked.

Lily flicked open the latches, raised the lid, and found herself staring down at something familiar—the collar and lapels of a precisely folded British Army officer's jacket.

It was made of that distinctive drab olive wool. Brass stars glinted from the lapels. Lily ran her fingers over the breast of it and was vividly reminded of how Sam's uniform had felt when she held on to him at St. Pancras Station.

"That's a captain's jacket," Miss Bard noted.

Lily lifted the coat out of the suitcase, revealing a pair of matching trousers and a peaked cap.

Something plinked to the floor by her knee. She looked down to see a thin aluminum disc strung on a leather cord.

She set down the coat and picked up the disk. Stamped letters rose against her fingertips.

Capt. H MacMahon
R Suss R
RC

"It's an identification tag. They put 'RC' on for 'Roman Catholic,'" Miss Bard said, kneeling beside Lily and picking up the jacket. She rifled through the pockets.

"And 'R Suss R?'" Lily asked.

"His regiment. The Royal Sussex," Miss Bard replied.

The Royal Sussex was also the regiment her half-brother George belonged to. Lily recognized that only distantly, most of her thoughts taken up by an infuriating frustration at the mysteries posed by the tag. They needed answers, not more questions. There was too much riding on all of this.

"What is a Royal Navy lieutenant doing with the uniform of a British Army captain under his eaves?" Lily demanded.

In answer, Strangford held out his hand. She placed the disk against his bare palm.

He breathed in, his gaze losing focus, going deeper. The room was silent, quiet enough that Lily could make out the soft hush of the sea.

"This was worn," he declared. "It hung next to a man's chest. It's his own name on the surface of it. He knows it by feel. Runs his fingers over it sometimes when he's thinking."

"But who is he?" Lily demanded.

"Brockmeyer."

Strangford said it as though it were the most obvious thing in the world, his voice still distant with his trance. He blinked, coming out of it, his eyebrows raised in surprise at his own words.

"It feels like Brockmeyer. It has his ... I'm sorry, I don't know the word for it. I suppose it's rather like a scent. I didn't have much contact with the man, but I can still recognize it."

Lily looked down at the British Army jacket in Miss Bard's hands.

"You're saying that Felix Brockmeyer is actually a British Army captain named MacMahon," she said slowly.

Strangford put the tag back in her hand. His dark gaze was steady. "Yes," he replied.

She knew better than to doubt it, as impossible as it seemed. Strangford wouldn't be wrong about something like this.

Miss Bard lifted her head, eyes widening with alarm.

"Someone's downstairs," she whispered.

Lily heard the subtle creak of a floorboard . . . and then was overwhelmed by the white-hot burst of a message from her power, vivid with urgency.

Danger.

Lily stood, the tag still clutched in her hand.

"We have to go," she announced, blurting out the words before she could question them.

Miss Bard looked up in surprise. Estelle's eyes narrowed.

Her head pounded with the need for it, screaming at her to move.

"Now!" Lily barked, fear roughening her throat.

Strangford half-lifted Miss Bard to her feet. Estelle caught her, pulling the startled folklorist to the door. He pushed Lily toward them into the narrow cave of the staircase.

At the bottom, a familiar figure stood framed by the dark wood. It was Inspector Kazi.

As he gazed up at them, a low whistle scratched distantly at the back of Lily's mind. It sounded like the wind moving across a bottle.

"Get out!" she screamed.

Then the wall above her exploded.

Bricks crashed, glass shattering. Plaster crumbled onto Lily's head, splintered pieces of lath clattering to the ground. The shock threw Lily to her knees, Strangford catching her before she could tumble further. Below them, Kazi lost his footing, falling backward.

A beam in the wall cracked, then shifted. It slammed down into the stairwell, striking a glancing blow against Miss Bard's head. It knocked her into Estelle, who caught her, falling back against the banister.

"Gwendolyn!" Estelle cried, turning Miss Bard in her arms.

"I'm alright—it's alright," Miss Bard insisted, pushing herself upright. A cut in her scalp dripped blood down her cheek.

Strangford set his shoulder under the beam, bracing it.

"Go," he shouted. "Outside—now!"

Lily ducked beneath the wreckage, catching Miss Bard's other arm and propelling the two women toward the front door. They stumbled past the inspector and spilled out into the gray morning light.

Strangford emerged a moment later, Kazi at his heels. The two men flinched at the sound of another great boom. It was like thunder, crackling thickly through the air.

Lily looked up at the hole blasted through the face of the bedroom in which they had just been standing. The shock of it froze her, rooting her to the pavement.

The window hung like a gaping jaw. Bricks crumbled, the debris still dropping soft clouds of plaster dust to the street. The back corner of the roof had been blown away.

Another crack echoed through the still morning air, followed by a richer boom and a shiver of impact she could feel through her boots.

The inspector whirled around to face the harbor, then stilled.

"Eie ki holo," he said softly, shock throwing him back to his native tongue.

"Lily," Strangford said.

He used a tone Lily had never heard before. She rushed to join him, confronting whatever had so clearly and terribly distressed him.

They emerged like prehistoric monsters from the mist of the harbor—the great gray hulks of destroyers flying the black cross of the German empire. As Lily stared out at the destroyers, their enormous guns recoiled with another volley of shells.

TEN

$\mathcal{L}$ILY COULD HEAR the sound of buildings crumbling, a soft rumble of falling brick. Plumes of smoke and dust rose here and there across the quaint hill of the town. Below them, on the Foreshore Road, someone screamed as people ran for cover.

Estelle pulled a handkerchief from her pocket, pushing the blood-sticky hair back from Miss Bard's forehead to press the cloth to her wound.

The horror of it washed over Lily, cutting through the dull veil of her shock.

The Germans were shelling Scarborough.

Rage rose, quick and hot. It burned like a fuse, and as it ignited, something washed over Lily, a familiar and consuming yearning for destruction.

She felt her power flare up in response, whipping out for a target. It lashed at the German battleships in the harbor, her anger focusing like a light through a lens . . . and then snapped back at her with a sharp and dangerous frustration.

She could do nothing about the guns on those great gray hulks on the water. They were beyond even her most improbable reach.

The rage swept out around her, searching for another target. It found Kazi.

She did not merely see how she could strike him down. She felt it burn through her fingers, her arms singing with the anticipation of impact.

A surprise blow to the gut, then a blocked fist—let him throw her

203

to the ground and then grasp the glittering shard of broken glass, driving it through the delicate tension of his skin ...

"Lily," Strangford called again, touching her shoulder.

She lurched back to herself, nearly choking on the impulse for violence. The ruined house loomed behind her. Shells burst on the hilltop, hiding the walls of the ruined castle in smoke.

Kazi still stood on the pavement, glaring with clenched fists at the enemy on the water.

Her guts churned. She could still feel the bite of the glass, the hot pulse of blood spilling across her fingers.

It had happened again—that quick, hungry urge for violence, the easy knowledge pouring in of how to destroy. She had tried to direct it at the ships in the harbor, but when that proved impossible, the power had been more than happy to seek an alternative target.

Behind her eyelids, Jack Cannon's blood pooled once more across the boards of the stage. She remembered his battered face under her boot, felt the perfect glory of the moment where she relished in her power to rip his life away.

Lily thought she might be ill.

"No," Lily blurted, protesting all of it—the continued pounding of the German shells, the monstrous horror that lurked beneath her skin.

Strangford's grip tightened. His hand was an anchor securing her to where she was even as his own gaze was directed out to the sea.

"There's no military target in Scarborough," Kazi said, the protest spilling out of him. "Why are they raiding a civilian town?"

"This isn't a raid," Strangford replied, his voice thin with tension. "It's bloody murder."

Kazi whirled at the sound of Strangford's voice, his dark gray greatcoat swirling around his ankles.

"You're supposed to be at home," he snapped, pointing an angry finger at Strangford.

Strangford released her arm. He reached into his pockets, yanked out his gloves, and tugged them on. Lily couldn't tell whether he was readying to run or to fight.

He took a breath to answer, and foresight crawled over Lily again, slipping up her spine and exploding across her brain.

"Down!" she screamed at Kazi.

The inspector flinched, then ducked, dropping to his knees. His hat blew away as the shell flew past him, slamming into the house he stood in front of.

It punched a neat hole in the upper floor, flying through it to land in the back garden, where it blasted a shed into splinters.

A few more bricks dropped from the ragged tear in the facade of the house, shattering in the road.

A woman's scream rose from inside, accompanied by the terrified wail of a child. The cry was clear as a bell, ringing out over the narrow street with ragged desperation.

Kazi rose from his crouch as he glared at Strangford. Then he cursed, bolting into the damaged house.

Strangford turned to her. His gaze was apologetic. Before she could ask why, he ran after the policeman.

Lily followed.

Dust shook down from the ceiling of the little house. Lily heard a crack as something shifted and fell upstairs.

"No!" a woman cried.

Strangford disappeared into the stairwell. Lily ran after him, crowding with the two men near the top where a young woman pounded desperately at a closed door. She rattled the knob, falling to her knees, her face pale with powdered plaster.

"I can't get it open. My baby's in there, and I can't get it open."

The long wail of a child resounded through the boards.

"Step back," Kazi ordered.

He tried the knob. It turned, but the door would only open an inch. Something blocked it from the far side. The inspector put his shoulder to it and shoved. He was a strong, solid man, but the door refused to move.

"Let me try," Strangford said.

Kazi took a breath to consider it, then nodded, stepping back, steering the woman into the opposite bedroom.

The space at the top of the stairs was narrow, but Strangford used every inch of it. He eyed the door, calculating, then shifted his balance and threw out his leg in a tàijí kick.

The door rattled with the force of it, shifting another half inch.

Overhead, something creaked. More debris sprinkled down on Lily's shoulders.

"It's too unstable," Kazi snapped.

"Outside," Lily said, picturing the layout of the house and making a quick calculation. "Through the window."

They ran back out onto the pavement. Lily stumbled at the sound of a crash as another shell impacted nearby. Strangford caught her arm.

She looked up. The shell had blown through the bottom corner of the window. The edge of the frame was gone, the glass hanging in jagged shards.

"You'll have to lift me up there," she said.

Kazi's eyes flashed with disapproval. He made a quick study of the hole. Lily could see him come to the same conclusion that she had. There was no time, no ladder, nothing they could roll or push under the window to allow access. There were three of them. It made far more sense for the two men to lift Lily onto their shoulders than the other way around.

"You'll have better balance without your shoes," Strangford said softly.

Lily tugged off her boots, tossing them aside.

"I'll brace myself against the wall as you stand. Inspector?"

Above them, the child wailed again. A few more bricks fell from the hole.

Kazi took a knee. Beside him, Strangford did the same.

Lily stepped up onto their shoulders, leaning forward to place her hands against the wall.

"On three," Kazi said. "One … two …"

They stood together. Lily reached up, scrabbling for whatever handholds she could find between the cracks of the bricks. She rose quickly and unevenly. Kazi was a bit taller than Strangford.

Her hands grasped the edge of the hole blown into the wall by the shell. She pulled at it. Lily's arms were strong, but she struggled.

Strangford's hands grasped her ankle, pushing her up.

Lily lurched, flailing through the gap until her fingers closed around the leg of a dresser. She used it to pull herself up, the bricks scraping against her torso.

She scrambled to her feet.

The dresser had fallen across the door. Part of the ceiling was collapsed on top of it. Those twin obstacles had been blocking the way inside.

On the far side of that damage, a red-faced toddler sat in his crib, sucking on his hand.

Broken glass littered the floor. Lily was conscious of her stockinged feet.

Above her, the ceiling groaned. It would take little stress for the rest of it to come crashing down on both her and the child.

"Hello, there."

Lily forced her voice to stay calm. She took a careful step forward, avoiding the glass.

The floor creaked ominously under her feet. A great split ran down through the boards. She wondered if it would be able to take her weight. She supposed she would have to find out.

"My name is Lily. I've come to help you. Do you want to see your mummy?" she asked.

The boy blinked wet eyes at her, then nodded slowly.

Lily took another step. A fresh fall of dust drifted down from the ceiling. She ducked carefully around the slanted, fallen timbers, making sure not to touch them.

She reached the crib, extending her arms.

"Come along with me. I'll bring you to her."

The child hesitated. The floor creaked again. The timbers beside her shifted, a few chunks of plaster falling to the ground.

Finally, he lifted his arms.

Lily plucked the boy from the crib. His body felt soft and solid. He melted into her shoulder, his little arms wrapping around her neck, grasping a handful of her hair.

Time shifted, spilling forward.

Dark curls against her cheek. The sweet, warm scent of his breath. His heartbeat is so fast.

Look, mama.

Lily gasped for breath. There was a fullness inside of her, something warm and strange that threatened to burst her into a thousand splinters.

"Where's mama?" the boy in her arms asked plaintively.

"Outside," Lily blurted, pulling herself together.

She hurried across the floor, less careful now, urgency pushing her on as the house continued to groan. She reached the window, now painfully conscious of those dangling shards of glass as she held the soft body of the child in her arms.

Kazi and Strangford had pulled the woman's kitchen table out into the yard. Kazi stood atop it as Lily looked down, black boots planted solidly on the worn surface. The child's mother hovered behind him, her hands clasped to her throat.

"Your mother is there—see?" Lily said, pointing. "Inspector Kazi will help you down to her."

The boy lifted his head with interest.

"Powiceman?" he asked.

"That's right, little chap," Kazi offered. "Come along now. Let's not keep your poor mother waiting any longer."

The boy's balance shifted in her arms, and Lily knew he was ready. She knelt in the shell hole, keeping her body between the boy and the glass daggers over her head.

There was no safe way to do this. Conscious of the shifting wreckage behind her, she gripped the toddler firmly under his arms and lowered him down to the inspector.

Kazi grasped the child around his waist, and Lily released him. He tucked the boy against his chest and stepped nimbly down from the table, passing him to his waiting mother.

She immediately collapsed into a heap on the pavement, clinging to her son and sobbing hysterically.

Kazi looked back up at where Lily perched in the hole on the second floor.

"I have her," Strangford said firmly.

He vaulted up onto the table.

Lily pushed her legs out through the gap, turned and lowered herself down, keeping low to avoid the glass. She felt strong arms wrap around her legs. Letting go, she slid down the front of Strangford's body. As her feet hit the table, she let herself lean back against him for a moment in relief.

Her legs wanted to shake. Her heart was pounding. His arms were strong around her waist.

"You're safe," he said, his voice low in her ear.

He released her, and Lily turned, letting him help her down from the table.

Estelle and Miss Bard waited across the road, sheltering by Brockmeyer's damaged house. Estelle had her arms around Miss Bard, still pressing the handkerchief to her head. The cloth was soaked with blood. Miss Bard looked pale and a little glassy-eyed.

Beyond the two women, in the harbor, the gray hulks of the ships turned away, steaming back to sea, finished with their morning's work.

It only occurred to her then that the bombardment could have easily been a precursor to invasion. The shells would have been followed by German boots pounding on the pavement, soldiers shooting their way through the battered town.

Smoke streamed from damaged buildings across the rolling hillside. The castle on the promontory appeared unchanged, but the rest of the town was in chaos. Lily could hear the shouts echo through the damp morning air. Someone wound up a fire alarm. It wailed across Scarborough like the cry of a banshee.

Strangford faced Kazi, his arm still at Lily's waist.

"There will be more like this," he said, nodding to the shattered house.

Lily could see the debate taking place inside the inspector's mind and knew the moment it had been settled.

"Come on, then," the policeman ordered.

Strangford released her and stepped forward. Lily moved to follow, then stopped short as her bare heel ground against a piece of shattered brick. She still did not have her shoes on.

"Get them somewhere safe," Strangford said, nodding to Estelle and Miss Bard.

Every instinct in her shouted to go with him, but Lily knew Strangford was right. Miss Bard looked ill. Estelle's face had a grim set to it that Lily had never seen on her friend before, and there was also the shattered mother still clinging to her bewildered child.

"I will," Lily agreed.

He took her hand, gripping her fingers. The pressure of that black leather said more than his words could. Then he was gone, pounding down the road after the inspector, headed for the nearest plume of smoke.

Lily turned to the woman with the toddler.

"I need a place on the far side of the hill," she said. "Low ground, sheltered from the harbor. A hall or a school, perhaps."

"The Wesleyan chapel," the woman replied. "It's in the valley, behind the train station."

There were other figures emerging from the houses and shops below. A young woman ushered a pair of small girls. An elderly man cradled his arm. There would be more of them, Lily thought.

"Show us where," she said.

~

Later that evening, in the dim, grand confines of the Westborough Methodist Church, Lily fought her exhaustion.

The nave was a grand space of gray stone, tall windows cloaked now in the gloom of dusk. It was packed with refugees of the bombardment. They crowded the pews, some lying down to sleep while others huddled together and talked in hushed voices.

Several of the more severely injured were being cared for by the altar. They were tended by a retired physician and a schoolteacher who had thrown on an apron to serve as a nurse.

Lily had been assisting the minister with searching the church stores for water, food, and blankets for the people who had gathered here. Some had homes too damaged to return to. Others lingered out of fear that the Germans would return and invade. Many others had crowded into trains leaving the town or fled on foot into the countryside, carrying their valuables in wheelbarrows.

The Germans were not coming back. Lily could feel that much. They had unleashed their quarter-hour burst of wild violence, left a mountain of destruction in their wake, and then gone.

France and Belgium had suffered much more. Villages and farms had been marched over by invaders or blasted into splinters. Lily recalled Zhao Min's brief, strained story of the women she had sheltered in Dinant where the Germans had lashed out at townspeople they perceived were resisting their occupation.

So much destruction. The thought of it threatened to overwhelm her as she looked around the packed church, watching as the doctor in the transept carefully put stitches into an older woman's leg in a circle of lamplight.

A Coast Guard officer who looked little more than a boy collapsed into the pew in front of Lily. His arm was braced in a sling.

"Most rotten luck," he said, his words slurred a bit with the laudanum the doctor had given him for his broken arm. "Blasted Krauts found the only break in the minefield for a hundred miles."

The bricklayer beside him nodded knowingly, though Lily could tell he wasn't really listening. His skin was still flecked with ash from whatever he had endured that morning.

Someone tugged at Lily's sleeve, recapturing her attention.

"Is there any more water, miss? Me ma needs it."

The girl was perhaps eight. She nodded toward a tired-looking woman three rows back. Two children slept with their heads on her lap.

"Of course," Lily said.

She pulled herself up and went for the pitcher.

~

Estelle reclined in another pew, her long legs stretched out in front of her. Miss Bard's head rested on her shoulder. She was asleep. Lily knew the doctor had told Estelle that Miss Bard could rest so long as someone was paying close attention to her breathing and color. When Miss Bard had protested that Estelle needed rest as well, Estelle had very calmly told her to shut up and close her eyes.

The smaller woman had a gauze bandage taped to her head. The doctor had put a couple of stitches into her wound.

Miss Bard had come so close to a far more serious injury, or something even worse. If they had lingered upstairs for even a moment longer...

How would Estelle look at Lily if it was her fault the woman she loved was gone? The notion was devastating. Even now, Lily was a little afraid to catch Estelle's attention.

Lily picked up a blanket from the pile the minister had brought up and carried it over to where the women were sitting.

"Here," she said.

"Thank you, darling," Estelle replied.

She sounded tired. Exhaustion and worry had deepened the fine lines on her elegant face, making her look more her age than she usually did.

"Would you lay it over her for me?" she asked.

Lily draped the blanket gently over Miss Bard's sleeping form, then sat down beside Estelle.

"How is she?"

"Still breathing," Estelle replied. She ran a long-fingered hand absently through Miss Bard's dark, thick hair.

The guilt welled up in Lily, threatening to spill over.

"It's my fault," she blurted. "I should never have asked you to join us. I should have known the Germans were coming. I should have warned you. You could both have been safely out of there if I'd just…"

Lily's words trailed off as she realized she was babbling.

"Done?" Estelle prompted.

Lily felt absolutely rotten.

"Yes," she bit out.

"Do I need to tell you what a pile of nonsense that was?" Estelle probed calmly.

"Estelle—" Lily began.

The older woman easily cut her off.

"When you are in need, we answer. We take whatever risks are necessary because that is what friends do for each other."

"But this time, it was too much," Lily protested. She could not stop looking at the blood on Miss Bard's collar.

Estelle's long mouth quirked into a sad smile.

"The dead never regret the chances they took for those they love," she replied.

The tears that had been threatening finally won. They slid down Lily's cheeks.

Estelle removed her hand from Miss Bard's hair and took a soft hold of Lily's fist. Lily forced herself to release the tension in her fingers and grasped her gently back as the night settled in.

~

She woke curled on a hard surface, a familiar hand on her shoulder.

"Wake up, Lily."

She opened her eyes to the sound of Strangford's voice. It took her a moment to recall where she was, rising disoriented from a pew at the back of the church. The nave was emptier than it had been when she closed her eyes a moment before, the windows purpling with the early light of dawn. Some of those who had sheltered here must have decided to brave a return to their homes rather than sleeping in the pews or on the floor.

"Estelle …" she began.

"A fisherman's wife offered Miss Bard a room to recover in. Estelle went with her. I had it from the doctor."

He nodded toward the old physician, who sat on the step to the altar. His shirt was open at the collar, and he was passing a flask back to the minister. Tea or whiskey—Lily couldn't be sure.

Strangford offered her a hand, and she let him help her off the pew. She picked up her coat, which she had been using as a blanket, and slipped it on. Her neck ached, her muscles sore from both the exertions of the day before and the rough sleeping arrangements.

He led her out of the church. Lily had barely noticed it when they had hurried inside the day before. Now she could see that it was monumental in proportions, with a peaked facade and soaring Grecian columns.

The air was chilly but clear, smelling of the sea.

Four men waited at the bottom of the steps. Two were in police uniforms. Another wore plainclothes and a brown hat. Lily realized she had seen him before. He had been on the train, the late arrival who joined their carriage at the last London stop.

The fourth was Inspector Kazi. He was wearing the same clothes he'd had on the day before, though he had brushed the dust from the dark hair under his hat. Lily wasn't sure whether it was the same one he'd had on when he accosted them on Merchant's Row. She felt certain he had not slept.

He crossed over to them as Strangford waited.

"I didn't kill Felix Brockmeyer," Strangford calmly announced.

"Words can lie. Evidence does not," Kazi replied. "I will follow it wherever it leads me."

It was both a promise and a threat. He swept his arm over the wreckage on the hillside, the buildings that had been within range of the German guns.

"This wasn't ill luck. It was the consequence of sensitive information falling into the wrong hands. You showed yourself well today, my lord, but I must ask you to think long and hard about where your loyalties lie," Kazi demanded.

"They lie with the people I love," Strangford replied. "And with what is right."

"And if those things conflict?" the inspector demanded.

Lily felt confused. Why was the inspector linking the bombardment of Scarborough to Brockmeyer's murder? It made no sense, and he did not strike her as someone who lacked logic.

Kazi didn't wait for an answer. He gestured to the man in the brown hat.

"Sergeant Cline will see you back to Lancaster Gate," he said. "If you leave the house again before I grant you permission to do so, I will have no choice but to put you under arrest, peer of the realm or no. Is that clear?"

"Perfectly," Strangford replied.

Lily could hear the low danger in his tone. Strangford was furious but doing a very careful job of reining it in.

Kazi had proved his decency over the last twenty-four hours. He was still a very real threat.

"And am I to be confined to my house as well?" Lily demanded, stepping forward to challenge him. She had to crane back her neck a bit to meet his eyes.

"Not for the moment," he coolly replied.

"Why not?" she snapped. "I was alone at the time of the murder. I also lack an alibi. Or do you think a woman incapable of such a thing?"

"I am well aware that women are capable of murder, Miss Albright," Kazi replied, unmoved. "But it was not your glove in the firebox, and it takes rather a great deal of force to crack a man's skull with a dull shovel blade. I am skeptical as to whether a woman would have the necessary strength."

"You have no idea how strong I am," she seethed in reply.

"Lily," Strangford said softly.

She heard the warning. She knew he was right. There was nothing to be gained from antagonizing the inspector and far more to lose. She had to get control of her anger.

She would find a way to prove Kazi was wrong. They would clear Strangford's name. That would be her vengeance for the fear he was making her feel now.

"Good day, then, my lord," Kazi said politely.

He strode off toward the still-smoking ruin of the town. Sergeant Cline and the two constables remained.

"See that Miss Deneuve and Miss Bard make it safely home?" Strangford said.

Lily's heart lurched with the realization that she and Strangford were about to be separated. It was so much more than merely a ride back to London. It felt as though her whole world was at stake—everything that mattered to her—but she couldn't abandon their friends.

The sergeant was watching. She didn't care. She put her arms around Strangford, dropping her head to his shoulder.

She felt him embrace her in return, his arms warm and solid around her back.

He raised her face with his hand, then gently brushed a lock of hair back from her face.

She wanted him to tell her that it would be fine—that they would get through this.

He stepped back, moving into the fold of policemen, and then he was gone.

ELEVEN

Thursday, December 17th
Three o'clock in the afternoon
Trafalgar Square, London

𝓛ILY LINGERED AT the edge of the busy crowd that eddied through the imperial splendor of Trafalgar Square, restlessly tapping her walking stick against the pavement. Nelson's Column loomed over the oyster sellers and the clerks carrying briefcases. The monstrous bronze lions were speckled with pigeon droppings.

A few of the ever-present birds waddled not far from where Lily stood. Behind her, the north wall of the square held a set of tarnished brass plaques with the standards for the foot, the yard, and the inch— the units by which Britain had marched across the world.

A parade of army lorries rumbled past, soldiers shivering on the open-air benches in the back. They looked like schoolchildren. The Union Jack snapped in the stiff breeze from the southwest.

Sam always said that Trafalgar's pigeons were a load of spoiled gluttons. A few vendors in the square were selling little bags of feed for the birds. A nanny purchased one for her charges. The little ones scattered the seeds about, the birds lazily pecking their way over. A few started flapping at each other in competition.

Lily couldn't communicate with animals the way Sam could, but they looked fairly gluttonous to her.

She missed him. The thought was like a hand twisting the soft places under her ribcage. What she had done to Jack Cannon in Limehouse had splintered their friendship. There had been no time to repair it before Sam shipped off to France. The letters she sent were nothing, ink and paper without substance. If Lily truly wanted Sam in her life, she needed to fight for him.

Gardner wasn't wrong. The letters mattered. They would matter more if Lily put the truth into them.

Somehow that notion was almost as frightening as going up against Kazi, the Special Branch, and whoever had murdered Brockmeyer in the conservatory.

Heads snapped up as a pair of airplanes droned overhead. The mood in the square tensed and then relaxed as the British colors on the rudder became visible. Everyone feared a raid, particularly one by the German empire's enormous pale gray zeppelins. Unlike the slight, delicate airplanes, the zeppelins were capable of carrying a truly dangerous payload.

Lily's tail lingered by the stairs. He was a short, stout man of roughly thirty with a blond mustache and a flat cap. Kazi had stepped things up after Scarborough, posting agents at both the front and rear entrances to her building on March Place. They seemed more skilled than those he had used before.

She still had one surefire way of escaping them stashed in her garden shed, but she had decided to save that surprise until it was truly needed. Today, she walked out the front door and let them follow her.

Kazi hadn't forbidden her from going out, but Lily was no fool. She knew that her freedom of movement had been granted because the inspector hoped her activities would provide him with more information he could use to build his case against Strangford.

Part of her worried that the meeting she had arranged here in the square would do just that, but she had to take the chance.

A tall, lean figure crossed toward her from Whitehall, scattering the pigeons.

Kazi had seemed oddly interested in Strangford's relationship with Lily's father. She had learned enough about the inspector to know he didn't indulge in idle curiosity. In Kazi's mind, Lord Torrington was connected somehow to Brockmeyer's death. Lily needed to know why.

"I'm sorry I'm late," Torrington apologized as he arrived.

There was no embrace, no perfunctory kiss on the cheek. Lily's relationship with her father had never been like that. Perhaps she might have shaken his hand, but that felt like a farce with someone who shared half her blood.

There were no easy gestures for navigating a relationship with the person who had hurt you more than anyone else in the world.

"I hope you weren't waiting long," he said.

"It's fine," Lily replied.

Her father's shoulders were still straight despite his age. There was something regal in his bearing, in that hawk-sharp nose and his distinctive gray eyes.

Lily had inherited those eyes. So had Simon, Lord Deveral, her father's heir—the brother who hated her.

She thought of George again, of his hopeful look at Taddiford when he asked whether the two of them might explore some connection that actually looked more like brother and sister.

She had yet to tell him that would be impossible . . . as impossible as thinking she and her father could ever have an uncomplicated relationship.

Torrington's gray eyes were more deeply set than usual, the lines on his face drawn. He was tired, worn at the edges.

She didn't precisely know what he'd been up to since the war broke out in August. As an earl, he held a seat on the House of Lords but had no other official role in the government. It didn't matter. He had his hands in everything, turning and manipulating the wheels that moved the nation. He spent more time with the Prime Minister than some of his cabinet secretaries, sometimes locked away until the small hours of the morning.

His name almost never appeared on bills or minutes or reports, but his influence was profound.

"I'm sorry I canceled our last lunch," Torrington said. "I feel I've been canceling terribly frequently these last months. It is not how I would have it be."

"You said it was urgent," Lily said, shrugging. She had to force the gesture.

"Everything is urgent these days," he returned. "But you didn't ask to see me today to talk about my schedule."

"No," Lily confirmed.

Kazi's agent still hovered by the newsstand. He was too close. Lily started to walk, and her father fell into step beside her.

The plainclothes policeman bought his newspaper, tucked it under his arm, and followed, but their movement meant he had to stay further back or risk attracting Torrington's attention. With the noise of the traffic and the wind through the square, Lily felt fairly confident their conversation would be inaudible.

"Do you know anything about a Navy lieutenant named Felix Brockmeyer?"

Torrington frowned. "Brockmeyer. The one who works in Churchill's office?"

"Yes," Lily confirmed.

"I've been in the room with him a few times, but that is more or less the extent of it."

"What about a Captain Hugh MacMahon with the Royal Sussex?" she asked.

"I don't know the name," he replied.

"Do you know any reason why the captain would have been masquerading as a Royal Navy lieutenant?"

Torrington stopped walking.

"Do you mean to tell me that an aide in the office of the First Lord of the Admiralty is an Army officer in disguise?" he demanded.

"Was," Lily corrected him. "He was murdered two nights ago in Walford Eversleigh's conservatory."

Her father's gaze lost focus, going distant. It meant that he was calculating, processing this new and unexpected piece of information, and working through the possibilities of what it might mean.

It relieved her. That he had to think about it meant he hadn't already known.

She trusted that her father would never intentionally put her or her fiancé in harm's way, but it was far from impossible to imagine that whatever conspiracy Brockmeyer—MacMahon—had been entangled in, Torrington might very well have been a part of it.

"What else can you tell me about this?" he demanded.

"The investigation into his death is being led by a Special Branch inspector named Kazi."

"Tariq Kazi is involved?" Torrington pressed.

"You know him?" Lily asked.

"There was some controversy when he was promoted to inspector. Kazi's father was a high-ranking officer with the Indian police force, serving directly under the commissioner. He was something of a mathematical genius. I believe he played a role in developing the system for fingerprint classification that Sir Edward brought back with him when he returned to London. As I heard it, Kazi was educated here in England with the understanding that he would return to Bengal to start his career there as his brothers had. He complicated matters by choosing to remain in London and join the Met."

"What was the controversy?" Lily asked.

"An inspector's position is highly coveted, and there were plenty of men at Scotland Yard who thought themselves better suited for it than a Muslim foreigner, whatever his skills and education."

Lily burned a little at the unfairness of that. She knew something of being thought less because of the circumstances of her birth. She did not know the inspector well, nor did she welcome his intrusion into her life, but it was clear he was well suited to his job—however troubling that made him to her at the moment.

"He was very interested in your relationship with Lord Strangford," she said.

"Strangford?" Torrington echoed, surprised.

"It would seem Kazi suspects Strangford of being the murderer," Lily casually replied.

They had reached the fountain. The pale water reflected the gray sky.

Her father was quiet. Lily didn't press him. She could feel his mind working, pulling together the various threads of what she had told him, weaving the revelations in with who-knew-what secrets he already possessed.

The pigeons cooed at a government minister eating a sandwich. A chestnut cart was doing a brisk trade, a pair of boys running up and down the line asking for pennies.

"There is a spy in the Royal Navy," Torrington finally said.

Lily's own mind whirled at this revelation. She was thrown back to the gray ships in the harbor, the crash of the shells. Screams and smoke.

The words of the Coast Guard man in the Methodist chapel.

…found the only break in the minefield for a hundred miles.

"Scarborough," she blurted, studying her father for a response.

The lines of his face had worn a bit deeper, spawning subtle new branches over the year since Lily had begun speaking to him once again. She wondered how much of it was age and how much of it was his skin giving way to the immense pressure of the role he must maintain.

"The entire Yorkshire coast is lined with mines, blockaded at either end by our vessels, and yet those ships somehow found their way through it to Scarborough. It was either blind luck, or they knew the heading that would take them through the minefield."

She thought of the injured men and women crowded into the church where she had brought Estelle and the others for refuge, the families who had fled their homes in terror. A fifteen-year-old Boy Scout had been carried off on a stretcher.

"Were it the only such incident, one might conclude on the side of luck," Torrington continued.

"But it's not," Lily filled in.

"No," he confirmed. His face was as drawn and serious as she had ever seen it. "The other leaks have been quieter, less destructive, but they have still raised alarm in certain circles."

"Which circles?" Lily demanded.

"There is a cooperative intelligence department in Whitehall, the Secret Service Bureau. A contingent of Special Branch officers was assigned to the SSB at the outbreak of the war, working under Major Vernon Kell, who leads the bureau's counter-espionage operation."

"Was Kazi one of them?" Lily asked.

"It's possible," her father replied.

Her mind was spinning.

"But what does any of this have to do with Brockmeyer's murder or Kazi's questions about you? It doesn't make any sense."

"It makes perfect sense if Major Kell thinks I am the spy," Torrington replied.

An engine backfired, startling a cluster of pigeons into the air. The breeze picked up, the chill cutting through her gloves.

"Why would he possibly think that?" Lily protested.

Torrington took a breath. There was an answer to her question. She could feel it in his hesitation. Would he tell her? It was hard to say.

He paused to turn his collar up against the wind. Kazi's agenthad been forced to stop some distance from their place by the fountain. She knew he could not hear them.

"I am the point of contact for a source recently placed in Germany," he replied.

"No one can get to Germany," Lily returned.

It was a fact. The borders had closed the minute war was declared, and a blockade of German destroyers guarded the coast. The frontier in Belgium and France was a morass of trenches. The borders were more porous between the neutral countries of Switzerland and the Netherlands, but they were also very closely watched.

"This individual managed it," Torrington replied. "The source is extremely capable but refuses to work within official channels. The information comes to me through means even I am not privy to understand, and I am charged with distributing it."

Torrington's was not the only mind capable of connecting information and drawing conclusions. Lily's thoughts leapt to George's story at Taddiford of her father's meeting with a younger woman in a black veil.

Wu Zhao Min.

She had last seen Sam's sister on the road to St. Pancras Station, when Lily had thrown a challenge down at her feet.

I am not the only one with power. What will you do with yours?

Zhao Min had been quietly burning with rage at the Germans for the violence they had inflicted upon the women she resettled in Dinant. Lily knew she had passed information to Torrington in the past. It was Zhao Min, after all, who had given Lily Lord Bexley's name back in August, providing her with the clue she needed to prevent an unimaginable disaster from obliterating half of London.

She was fierce, capable in ways Lily could only imagine. It was not hard to believe that Zhao Min might have found a way to smuggle herself into the heart of the German empire. Nor would she trust the

British government with her identity or her information. She knew too much about the men who ran it.

Sam's sister certainly felt no loyalty to the empire or its king, but she might take a side in the war for other reasons—like vengeance.

Lily didn't ask her father to confirm it. She'd be forcing him to lie to her.

Zhao Min had gone to spy against the Germans, and Lily was certain she would be very, very good at it.

"I cannot tell Major Kell or the other intelligence heads where I come by the information the source provides," Torrington said. "And so a question has arisen as to whether what I provide to them comes from the Kaiser himself."

"They think you are a tool of the Germans," Lily filled in.

The picture was all too plausible. Her father's connections and influence had always been international in scope. He was trusted by men in the highest circles of power, which granted him access to information some members of Cabinet likely weren't even privy to.

Those intricate tentacles of knowledge were a source of strength when political conflicts needed negotiating. When all of England was turned with suspicion towards a foreign threat, bristling with sensitivity to the possibility of foreign spies stealing British secrets, her father's unique position was a dangerous liability.

He had taken a great chance telling her as much as he had. Even half of what he had just admitted could ruin him if it fell on the wrong ears and was misinterpreted.

It could cost Zhao Min her life.

"Thank you for telling me," Lily said.

"You deserve to know why your fiancé is under suspicion," he replied.

A band of schoolchildren marched through the square, each of them clinging to a spot on a long blue ribbon. Their peacoats were neatly brushed, caps straight. The fountain continued to splash softly, the sound of the water mingling with the rattle of carriage wheels and the rumble of engines.

Lily didn't need to say the rest aloud—that Strangford was only at risk because of his connection with Lily, and therefore Torrington. She ought to have been a bride thoughtlessly anticipating her wedding day. Instead, because of who her father was, she was fighting to save the man she loved from a charge of murder and treason.

Two men lingered by the chestnut-seller's cart. Lily realized they had been standing there the whole time, their eyes only occasionally flickering to where she and Torrington stood.

"They're following you as well," she blurted.

"Special Branch men under Major Kell's supervision," Torrington confirmed. "They have been at it for the last fortnight."

"What about Brockmeyer?" Lily demanded. "Could he have been the spy?"

"You said his true identity was that of an Army captain. If the Germans had an agent in a position of authority in the Army, why would they take the chance of compromising him as an impostor in the Navy?" Torrington replied. "There is something missing, some key piece we need in order to see the picture clearly."

The wind cut across the square, biting with chill. Lily shivered.

"Why was Kazi there at all?" she thought aloud. "If you are right and he is, in fact, working for this Secret Service Bureau, why would he come to the Hampshire coast for what must have looked like the crime of a random housebreaker? Why not send a regular Special Branch detective, if one was needed at all? Or do you think perhaps the SSB is investigating the suspicious death of any military man in England right now?"

"They wouldn't have the manpower for that," Torrington countered.

He gazed down at the rippling water of the fountain. Something in that look reminded Lily of Strangford when he had his bare hands on an object.

"Walford Eversleigh is in steel," he announced.

"What has steel to do with it?"

His glance darted quickly right, then left, assessing who was near, but the noise and activity of the square were effectively a screen.

"The Navy is working on a new drive system for our Dreadnought battleships. It is very secret, very sensitive, and involves the manufacture of extremely strong and precise gears."

"Gears?" Lily echoed skeptically.

His gray eyes pinned her.

"Whoever controls the water controls the outcome of the war. The size and speed of our battleships are the pivot upon which victory rests."

She could hear how serious he was.

"If Walford Eversleigh has the contract for the gears, he would have the plans for the new drive system."

"Brockmeyer came with a briefcase," Lily whispered, the words falling from her lips with surprise.

No, not Brockmeyer, she corrected herself—Captain Hugh Mac-Mahon of the Royal Sussex.

She trusted her father's reasoning that MacMahon himself couldn't have been the spy, but if he wasn't... what was he? And why had he ended up dead?

"I am sorry, Lily," Torrington said quietly.

The new pain mingled with the relics of the old—the decision he had made to set her aside after her mother's death. How he had refused to answer her call when Joseph Hartwell was slaughtering his way through London's mediums.

He had done it again now by accepting Zhao Min's offer, knowing how critical it might prove to his country.

He was a man of honor and duty, a man who refused to flinch from responsibility. His decision was no less than Lily would have expected of him, and it put everyone around him at risk.

Would it always be like that with her father? Did she wish he was a different sort of man?

"I'll fix it," Lily quietly announced.

"I would not put that burden on you," he pushed back.

She thought of Scarborough, of the smoke and the blood and the destruction. Someone had done that. Someone would do it again. There was more at stake in this than her heart.

"You're not the only one who knows about duty," she replied.

The emotion shifted over his face like water—pride, regret, sorrow. As if by instinct, his hand found hers and held it, a quietly fierce pressure against her glove.

She squeezed it back, closing her eyes against the sharp burst of pain in her chest. She knew what he wanted to say—that if she needed help, she had only to ask for it. That he would find a way to make it all better.

But her father wasn't a liar.

Conscious of the other eyes upon them, she released his hand. Without another word, she turned and walked away.

The man with the blond mustache hovered by the pigeon feed seller, pretending to look nonchalant now that Lily was facing him once more. The act filled her with a burst of rage. She was tired of all the secrets, all the pretense.

She stopped as she passed, turning her own steel gaze onto him.

"This way now," she ordered curtly.

He blinked with quick surprise. To his credit—and that of Kazi, who had undoubtedly selected him for the job—he recovered quickly.

"As you like, Miss," he replied smoothly and fell into step behind her.

~

Dusk was falling as Lily stepped off the tram onto Bayswater Road. Her shadow, the sergeant with the blond mustache, hopped off the back of the carriage, landing neatly on the pavement.

The lamps across the gloom of the park were sparking to life, the lamplighters at their work early at this time of year. The wind cut cruelly across the great expanse of that open land. Lily turned from it to the quieter streets that lay further inside this elegant neighborhood.

She stopped at the house that would be her own in a few days' time—if the man she was supposed to live there with hadn't been arrested.

"I'll be quite alright from here," she neatly announced to the blond policeman, then mounted the steps.

He lingered behind, striking up a chat with the two uniformed constables who waited on either side of Strangford's front entrance.

Roderick opened the door. Strangford's footman looked nervous.

"Miss Albright," he said with a quick and awkward bow of greeting.

He didn't retreat to see whether Strangford was receiving. He knew better than to bother when it came to Lily.

"His lordship's in the study," Roderick said, jerking a shoulder toward the back of the hall.

He was tense, likely scenting trouble in the air. He was a sensitive young man.

"Thank you, Roderick," she replied, handing him her hat and coat.

Lily knew the study better than any other room in Strangford's house—the paintings that lined the walls, the neat bookshelf, the worn armchairs framing the low embers of the fire. It was the only room in the Bayswater house where she felt truly comfortable. That was partly because it bore such a striking imprint of the man who lived here, and because she had already experienced so much between its walls—blackmailing Strangford into touching her to break the hold of a dead woman over his soul, throwing herself into the embrace of a drug she didn't understand on the chance it might help her save someone she loved.

The books, the desk, and the battered inkwell might look ordinary, but Lily knew better. Every object in this room had been carefully chosen to serve as a potential refuge for someone whose senses were constantly assailed in a way Lily couldn't possibly understand.

Mrs. Jutson, Strangford's housekeeper, had been at work inside. A garland was hung over the fire, rich greenery studded with bright red berries. A wreath had been placed on the mantel.

Strangford had escaped his coat. He stood by the fire in his shirt-sleeves, glaring down at the glowing coals, tension threaded across his shoulders.

"You saw your father," he said.

He must have absorbed that flicker of her intention when they parted ways in the morning. It scratched at her, being known that intimately, but she set it aside. There was nothing she could do about it.

"I did," she confirmed, sitting down in one of the chairs.

"What did he have to say?" he demanded flatly.

It was not the welcome she might have hoped for.

"There is a German spy stealing secrets from the Admiralty," she informed him, parrying his sharp tone with her own matter-of-factness. "Kazi likely works for the bureau tasked with identifying him. They suspect it is Torrington."

"Are they right?" Strangford asked.

The question quietly infuriated her.

"You are better positioned to know than I am," she snapped back.

The knot in his shoulders tightened, then released as he let out a sigh. His gloved hand came to his temple.

"No," he admitted. "He wouldn't betray the crown. Other things, maybe, but not that."

He didn't have to say what 'other things' he meant. Lily knew.

You. Me. Those others that we love. Anyone who stood in the path of his duty.

"But he is involved in something," Strangford continued relentlessly.

"Yes," Lily admitted. "He is."

Silence descended, marked by the soft ticking of the clock and a shift in the coals. Something had changed since Scarborough. Lily could feel it but not name it.

"There must be a connection between Brockmeyer and the spy. That's why Kazi turned up after the murder. He suspects you committed the act at my father's behest."

The words were awful. Lily hated to say them, but they both needed the truth.

Did he blame her for all of this? She wanted him to answer the question but didn't want to ask it.

"We need to know more about why Captain Hugh MacMahon was posing as Lieutenant Felix Brockmeyer," she pressed. "There might be clues in the regimental records for the Royal Sussex. That's George Carne's regiment. I think I should ask him to get me inside the barracks at Chichester to examine them."

Finally, he turned to look at her. He was furious.

"We are at war, suspected of complicity in espionage and murder, and you want to trespass onto an Army barracks?"

"I can't know what I'm looking for until I find it," Lily returned. "And I can hardly ask George to smuggle out a trunk full of records."

"And you truly believe you can trust him?" Strangford demanded harshly.

It surprised her.

"Do you know any reason I shouldn't?" she threw back.

The bravado was something of a show. The truth was that Lily had asked herself the same thing on the ride here from Trafalgar Square. That George was her half-brother meant nothing. Her history with

Torrington's oldest son, Lord Deveral, was ample evidence of that.

She recalled the hopeful gleam in George's eye when he asked if they might share a role in each other's lives. That was a hope she still had to crush, sooner or later. That she planned to ask him to help her before she'd done so made Lily the dishonest one, but it might be the only way to save both Strangford and their father.

"No," Strangford thinly replied, his gloved hands clenched into fists at his side. "But what about me?"

"You?" Lily echoed, confused.

"Do you trust me?"

The question was harsh, striking at her like a whip. The clear antagonism in it shocked her.

"You know that I do," Lily replied. "Whatever would you ask that for?"

"Then why don't you want me to go to Chichester?"

Something was definitely wrong. There was a tumult raging behind the darkness of his eye. Lily pushed back against it, trying to reason with him.

"You know that doesn't make sense. The house is surrounded by police. Kazi has threatened to jail you the minute you walk outside. I am still capable of slipping away from them, and you know I can get into places most other people can't."

He moved closer, looming over her darkly. Firelight flickered across his scarred face.

"And so, I am to remain here," he growled. "Doing nothing."

"Strangford . . ." Lily protested.

She raised her hand to touch him, but he turned his back to her, the words pouring out of him like burning oil.

"They shelled a town full of civilians. They blew a hole in a child's bedroom, then simply turned out to sea again. There was no purpose in it. Nothing to gain beyond terror and pain. They have marched over half of Europe, leveled entire cities. They would march over all of us purely for the sake of conquest—"

He bit back the rest, his mouth firming into a hard line as he cut himself short.

The outburst frightened her. Of course, he must be rattled by what had happened yesterday in Yorkshire. It was only natural . . . and yet her mind snapped back to the vision she'd had on the floor of this room ten months before when the Wine of Jurema slid down her throat, and the world expanded into a maelstrom of foresight.

The roar of shells, the narrow channel of boards and wire. Damp clinging to her skin as the mud pulled at her boots. Strangford in front of her shouting, a blurred shadow over the place she now knew his eye no longer was.

Go go go go.

And then the world fell apart.

The memory of that premonition set her pulse pounding. The fear was still so close, so real. They weren't in France. They were in England, far away from the war.

Even with the threat of Kazi looming over them, it felt safer that he was here. Somehow Kazi frightened her less than that terrible pit of mud and wire.

His shoulders fell, the cord of that strange anger snapping.

"I can't stay here like this forever," he confessed, his voice hoarse with the truth of it.

Lily stood. She slipped her hand over his sleeve, holding the solid warmth of his arm through the fabric.

"Just let me go to Chichester," she quietly pleaded. "Let me do this for us, and then we'll decide what comes next. Together."

He nodded. There was something distant in it.

"Of course."

He had agreed, but Lily found she was far from reassured.

TWELVE

IT TOOK LILY the rest of the day to reach her brother.

She escaped her tail with the help of an urchin begging outside Victoria Station. Slipping him a few coins, she sent the boy to purchase a ticket to Chichester while she audibly bought one for the train on the next platform, headed for Kent, conscious of her shadow listening behind her.

The boy slipped the extra ticket into her pocket with a skill that reminded her of Sam. She was glad the child hadn't been inclined to try to rob her.

She boarded the Kent train, walked up two carriages—then unlocked the door and hopped onto the tracks, climbing up and letting herself on the Chichester train. Glimpsing the frustrated expression on the face of Kazi's agent through the windows as she rolled past was deeply satisfying.

Getting a message into George's barracks without alerting the censors who monitored the telephones and telegrams had been as simple as finding a man in uniform at a public house. The young private she approached had been perfectly happy to carry Lily's note back with him.

Lily received George's reply early the following morning at the inn where she'd overnighted. When he came to collect her, he brought along a uniform.

George had judged her size fairly well. Though the trousers Lily was wearing were a bit loose, they would stay up with the help of the suspenders. The drab wool overcoat wasn't as warm as her own.

"I'd lend you mine, but it's officer issue. Someone would be bound to notice. There's a fair bit of envy about coats going around at the moment," George admitted.

Lily had to wonder what poor private George had deprived of his clothes that morning.

He had managed to scrounge Lily a blanket from the boot of his gleaming two-seater Vauxhall before they set off. Lily tugged it around herself more tightly as George whipped the automobile around the narrow country roads of West Sussex, flying past tidy cottages and uninterested cattle.

He drove like a maniac. The windscreen of the vehicle blocked the worst of the cold winter wind, but it was still a small miracle that his hat managed to stay in place. He flashed her a pleased smile as he took a particularly sharp turn without slowing down.

Far from seeming uncomfortable with what Lily was asking of him, George was clearly delighted at the notion of executing a scheme that could get him court-martialed.

"Pull up the scarf when we get to the checkpoint," he shouted over the wind and the rumble of the engine.

Lily nodded. She would have had to shout for him to hear her. The Vauxhall was much louder and faster than her Triumph motorcycle. George drove it with a gleeful recklessness through the frost-touched landscape as they approached the barracks.

Roussillon Barracks, home of the Royal Sussex Regiment, sprouted like a cluster of mushrooms from the surrounding farms and pastures, appearing around a hair-raising curve in the road. It was surrounded by a high stone wall topped with what looked like fresh coils of razor wire. An embankment rose on one side, reminding her a bit of the Roman camp at Taddiford. Lily wondered whether this was a modern defensive structure or a relic of something far older—an echo of a fallen empire.

A little wooden hut perched at the place where the fence met the road, giving way to a simple hinged gate.

The thick waves of her hair pinned carefully under her borrowed cap would not pass more than a cursory inspection. She tugged the scarf up until it covered her ears, then hunched in her seat like a subordinate miserable at being dragged out to race through the countryside in the December cold.

"Cheerio, Sykes," George said as he slammed on the brakes, stopping the car dangerously near the gate.

The officer in the gatehouse slumped in his chair as he recognized who had come. He looked tired. Lily thought perhaps she had seen him at the pub the night before.

"What are you doing out?" the man grumbled.

"Throwing a bit of fresh Sussex air at my new friend here," George replied, hitching a thumb at where Lily huddled in the seat. "Courier from the Queen's Lancers. He's a bit worse for wear after finishing half a bottle of brandy last night."

Sykes sighed.

"Surprised he ain't heaved all over your dash, the way you drive."

George gave Lily a hearty slap on the shoulder.

"He's feeling better already. Aren't you, Private?"

It was not the strategy Lily would have chosen. Any cover story that drew more attention to her presence in the car seemed like courting danger.

She supposed she should not be surprised that George had chosen it.

She didn't answer, hugging the blanket more closely around her figure and shooting her half-brother a glare.

Sykes pulled a lever, and the gate swung up.

"On you go then," he said.

George flashed him a wide grin under the bright gold of his nascent mustache, then tore the Vauxhall onto the base road.

The barracks were busy. On the square, a battalion of recruits was drilling on the field, stamping through a round of calisthenics to the barking commands of a sergeant, their breath collectively steaming into the morning air.

George slipped the Vauxhall into a parking space behind a tidy row of officer's cottages, then vaulted nimbly over the door. He moved to Lily's side of the car, intending out of habit to open the door for her. She forced her half-frozen limbs into motion, beating him to it, conscious that eyes might be watching from the windows in the neighboring buildings.

"This way," George said cheerfully, setting off down the path.

He made no effort to lower his voice or blend in. It was like trying to commit espionage with a puppy. Lily only hoped that being so obviously brash made them seem less suspicious.

She hurried after him as he crossed the green, his long legs eating up the ground. The new recruits were jumping now, matching the rhythm of the sergeant's whistle.

"You'd think it would be quieter with most of the regiment in France," George noted. "But they've been bringing in new men as fast as they can ship the old ones out. I'm queued to go south myself in three more weeks, and I only finished officer's training at the end of November."

He looked back at her without slowing his pace, grinning.

"Between you and me, I can't wait. I've been bored out of my wits. At least the front won't be so blasted dull."

Lily missed a step. The notion that George would be shipping to the continent so soon impacted her more than she might have expected. She thought of the rooms of broken men in Gardner's hospital, the long black lists of the dead posted in the newspapers.

George was bright, optimistic, and so very alive. Even if she could not have him in her life, it felt terrible that he might become just another pound of flesh chewed up by the unfeeling machine of this war.

"Here's the place," George announced.

He had stopped at a building at the far end of the barracks. It was a low, single-story structure with small windows like squinting eyes.

"Let me do the talking," he said.

Lily grabbed his arm before he could step inside.

"Wait," she protested. "You've taken enough risks already. I can manage the rest on my own."

"What, and get past old Kolpecker?" George exclaimed. "He's a regular harpy. Leave it to me—I know how to handle him."

He didn't wait for a response. Her half-brother leapt up the few short steps to the door and pushed inside, leaving Lily to scramble after him.

"Morning, Kolpecker!" George announced cheerfully.

They were in a dark, narrow room dominated by a bland pine desk. A pale man of perhaps forty with the insignia of a sergeant on his sleeves sat behind it, frowning at George over his dull brown mustache. A pen hovered in his hand, signaling that he clearly hoped this interruption would be as brief as possible.

"Lieutenant Carne," the sergeant flatly replied.

"Books keeping you busy?" George said.

He sat down on the edge of the desk. Kolpecker's eyes shot to where George's thigh rested on the surface. His mouth twisted, fingers tightening on the pen.

"Nice if they'd give you a stove," George continued, oblivious to the man's obvious hostility. "This place is right chilly. I'm surprised you haven't lost one or two of your toes by now."

"I have excellent circulation," Kolpecker returned.

"I'm sure you do," George happily agreed. "Anyway, Corporal Sayers said you were to report to the mess immediately. Something about skipping kitchen duty."

Kolpecker stiffened.

"I am exempt from kitchen duty," Kolpecker snapped.

"You'd best clear that up with the corporal. He was in a terrible blather about it. I'd get on sharpish if I were you. Hate to see you saddled with latrines for the next fortnight."

Kolpecker's glare deepened. George answered it with a smile. At last, the sergeant stood. He methodically plucked his coat and cap from the rack.

With his back momentarily turned, George's long arm flashed out and snatched a key from a hook hanging behind the desk. He slipped it into his pocket. It was a move that Sam would have appreciated.

Kolpecker turned to find George and Lily's positions unchanged. His eyes raked over them. Lily tried to sink a bit further into her scarf.

"You have to get out," the sergeant snapped.

"Right," George agreed. "Come along, then, Private."

He hopped from the desk and strode out the door, Lily hurrying behind him. They reached the path and stopped as Kolpecker busily locked the door. He stalked past them, shooting another glare rather than offering any pleasantries.

George waited, still smiling, until Kolpecker had turned the corner, then plucked the key from his pocket.

"Come on, then."

He bounded back up the stairs, clearly certain that Lily would follow.

"What happens when he finds he isn't on kitchen duty?" she hissed.

"Oh, he'll have kitchen duty," George returned. "The minute he marches up to the corporal and tells him that he's above it, the old geezer will have him shunted to the dish line as fast as you can say, 'Yes, Sir!' Nothing Sayers hates quite like a shirker."

"How much time does that give us?"

"Thirty minutes, at least," George replied. "It was porridge this morning. It's the devil to scrub off. Sticks like cement."

She followed him through Kolpecker's gloomy office into a long room packed with shelves. The aisles were so narrow she had to turn sideways to fit down them. Some rows held bound books, others wooden crates or cardboard document boxes of unbound papers. There were piles of journals of varying ages, from old leather-wrapped volumes to more modern versions covered in waxed canvas.

As the home of the Royal Sussex, Roussillon was also where the records of the regiment were kept. Though some records, like enlistment forms, were sent on to the War Office in London, here they would find others, like the day records for each battalion, going back at least to the 18th century.

"What are we looking for, then?" George asked.

Lily hadn't expected or wanted George along for the entirety of this endeavor, but it seemed she was stuck with him. Facing the daunting rows of shelves with only a half-hour window of time, she realized she could use the help. She had already trusted him to get her in here. Did telling him a bit more really change the risk?

She also had to remember that George had been at Taddiford when Brockmeyer was murdered. He had a solid alibi—Lily had overheard him herself drunkenly discussing steel manufacturing logistics with Walford Eversleigh—but then, so did everyone else in the house that night, besides Strangford.

Someone had killed the man. George must be as likely a possibility as Virginia or Dicky or any of the others, but Lily found she couldn't quite bring herself to regard him with suspicion. George wasn't a murderer. She knew it like she knew the sun rose.

"We need to find anything we can about a Captain Hugh MacMahon," she said.

"Well, then," George replied, rubbing his hands together against the chill pervading the room. "Let's get started, shall we?"

~

Twenty minutes later, Lily came to the conclusion that the records were dreadfully unorganized. Half of the papers she had looked at appeared to be misfiled. The uptight Kolpecker was clearly the sort who thought himself indispensable while actually being terrible at his job.

The box she held was marked *Service Records, 1898-1910*. The most recent paper she found inside dated to 1864. Another had held nothing but a mountain of receipts for tinned beef and eggs.

George worked beside her in companionable silence. It surprised her to realize that her brother was, in fact, capable of quietly focusing on a task when it was required of him.

She really knew so little about him. It would have to stay that way once this was done. The thought made her feel sadder than it might have a day before.

"Hello, what's this?" George murmured, interrupting her thoughts.

Lily glanced over at the sheet of paper he had just pulled from a box marked *Quartering, S. African Expedition*. It was a printed form titled *Medical Record*, filled in with sprawling lines of ink.

Lily read the name scribbled at the top.

Hugh MacMahon

She plucked the page from George's hand, turned it over, then looked down at the box.

"Where's the rest?" she demanded.

"It's all on its own," George replied, flipping quickly through the rest of the contents. "Another misfile."

A warning energy trilled down the back of her neck, something that chilled in a way that had nothing to do with the unheated atmosphere of the room. She gripped George's arm instinctively.

"Hide," she ordered. "Now."

"But I don't hear any—"

He stopped at the sound of door hinges creaking in the

antechamber.

He stuffed the page into his coat, popped the top back on the box, and slid it into place, then took Lily's arm and tugged her toward one of the darker rows of shelves.

Lily dug in her heels, resisting. The room was too small, with only one door. If someone was coming, they needed to pick the right spot to hide—and she knew only one way to do that.

Breathing deep, she reached for her onmyōdō, feeling her way toward an outcome where they didn't end up getting dragged out onto the regimental lawn.

"Lily?" George whispered.

She knew she was taking a chance. What she was doing could raise questions she didn't want to answer. She didn't have a choice.

The answer came to her, glowing softly with certainty.

Without a word, she pushed George into the narrow space behind a tall oak cabinet. Lily followed, crushing herself into the gloom with him. She tried not to breathe.

Kolpecker stepped into the records room.

He held a pair of journals in his hand. He stopped halfway down the first aisle and slipped them into a gap on the shelf.

The sergeant turned to go, then hesitated, his eyes falling on a pile of books sitting on a table by the door.

"Nobody puts anything away around here," he muttered.

Picking up the files, he stalked toward them. Lily pressed George further back into their small hiding place, willing Kolpecker not to turn their way.

He pivoted to the left, going up the gloomy aisle George had nearly pulled them into.

Kolpecker popped the file into a box and returned, passing almost close enough for Lily to touch as he rounded the corner and headed back to the door. It closed a moment later, the sound of the latch echoing dully through the room.

Lily stepped out from the cabinet, George following behind her.

"That was bloody close," he muttered quietly. "Lucky you pulled us the other way."

"Yes," Lily agreed. "Lucky."

"I could jump him. Tie him to the chair for a bit," George cheerfully suggested.

"No," Lily quickly countered.

She thought of the single page they had found after all the risk they had taken to come here. It didn't seem like it could possibly be enough, but the sergeant could be back and any moment, and she couldn't help Strangford or her father if she got herself and George thrown into military prison.

"Best move on," she concluded.

George accepted that with the same ease with which he'd approached the rest of this adventure.

"I think we can squeeze out that little window in the back," he determined. "I'll pop you through."

George unlatched the window, then swept Lily up into his arms like a gallant knight with a helpless damsel. She bit back her protest, conscious of Kolpecker on the other side of the door.

Her brother fed her through the narrow opening feet-first, and she landed solidly on the scraggly grass behind the records building. George followed, hauling himself through and more or less tumbling to the ground.

The rectangle of glass, hinged at the top, fell back into place behind him.

"No graceful way of managing that," he concluded, brushing off his trousers. "This way."

He jogged off down the path behind the buildings, waving for Lily to follow.

A pair of Army lorries rattled past, packed with crates. Lily could still hear the drilling on the green. A few officers clustered by the steps to one of the cottages.

"Smoke, Lieutenant?" one offered.

"Not those gaspers you favor, Phillips," George called back in return as they passed.

The men gave her no notice.

They paused at the Vauxhall, where George popped the boot and tugged out a rucksack. He swung it over his shoulder and led her to the wall that bordered the barracks.

A barrel stood by the stones. George hopped easily up onto it, reaching to run his fingers along the top of the wall beneath the vicious curls of razor wire. He grasped something in his hand and tugged. The sharp coils shifted apart, revealing a gap in the barrier. He secured the thin wire in his hand around a brick that protruded a bit from the wall. Lily could see where some of the mortar had been chipped away.

"Some of the lads have girls in town," George explained.

He let her climb over first, then followed. They found themselves in a little copse of woodland. A few birds trilled in the bare branches of the trees, the half-frozen underbrush crunching under their feet.

They walked in silence for perhaps half a mile, then George stopped, tossing Lily the rucksack.

"Go ahead and swap up," he ordered. "I'll look the other way."

He resolutely turned his back.

Lily ducked behind a tree and shivered out of her borrowed uniform, pulling back on her own blouse, skirt, and coat. She was particularly grateful for the coat. She tucked the uniform back in the bag.

"Thank you," she said, extending it toward George.

He accepted it, smiling.

"No thanks required. That was a brilliant lark. Oh!" he exclaimed, reaching into his coat pocket. "Nearly forgot."

He handed Lily the sheet of paper they had stolen from the records room.

Captain Hugh MacMahon's date of commission was listed as January 1905 at Armagh in Ireland. As Felix Brockmeyer, the man hadn't revealed so much as a hint of an Ulster accent. It was one Lily knew well, as Gardner shared it. His physical description was also listed, the height, weight, and eye color matching those of the man she had met at Taddiford. If she had doubted that Brockmeyer was MacMahon despite Strangford's reading of his tags, the statistics made a strong argument.

The back of the page listed a few medical incidents—two hospitalizations for influenza and a sprained knee.

There was nothing that so much as hinted at why this man had given up his identity to plant himself in the office of the First Lord of the Admiralty.

Lily turned back to the front of the paper, frowning at a particularly illegible scrawl at the bottom. George peered at it shamelessly over her shoulder.

"Here, let me try," he said, snatching the page from her hand. "I'm well practiced with translating officer scrawl. Says . . . he was transferred to the Royal London in March 1913."

The frustration wrenched at her. The records for the Royal London would be kept at that regiment's headquarters, one she likely lacked the connections to break into.

"That's not what you were hoping to hear," George surmised.

"No," Lily admitted.

"What's all this about, anyway?" he asked, handing her back the paper.

George had taken quite a risk smuggling her into the barracks. He would have been well within his rights to demand an answer, but his question was very clearly more casually intended. Perhaps that was what made Lily feel like she could answer it.

"Captain MacMahon showed up somewhere he shouldn't have been," Lily replied.

It was something short of admitting that George himself had actually met the man, had drinks with him, and ended the evening by staring down at his corpse, but still more than she had planned on sharing.

"Oh," George remarked. "Sounds like they ghosted him."

"Ghosted?" Lily blurted, surprised by the oddly accurate turn of phrase.

"That's my own word for it," George admitted. "Sometimes a transfer to the Royal London isn't actually a transfer to the Royal London if you catch my meaning."

"I don't," Lily bluntly returned.

"The Royal London has roughly an extra battalion's worth of men attached to it," George said. "We had a fellow under my commanding officer who was transferred there a few weeks ago. The captain still writes him letters, but they aren't addressed anywhere the Royal London is stationed. I got curious and had a look at the regimental lists. He wasn't attached to any division. He's just a name hanging out there in the ether. So, I asked around, and rumor has it that the Royal London is a catch-all for fellows transferred to special duty with one of the intelligence bureaus."

"Like the Secret Service Bureau?" Lily pressed.

"That's it," George happily replied. "Who knows where those intelligence blokes go off to? If your fellow turned up someplace out of the way, perhaps he got there by way of a little espionage."

Lily took a step away from him, pacing on the frost-dusted leaves that covered the ground.

If MacMahon had been working for the Secret Service Bureau, it would certainly explain why Kazi had turned up at the scene of his murder so quickly. The death of one of their own would obviously raise an alarm. It still didn't explain why an Army intelligence officer would pose as a Navy lieutenant.

Unless . . .

Her father had said there were suspicions of a high-level spy in the Navy. Brockmeyer was a clearly German name, and MacMahon—whom she now knew was actually Irish—had lied about having close family connections in Germany.

To all appearances, he would have been an officer with a German name and German connections working in the office of Winston Churchill, one of the highest-ranking men in the Admiralty—a position that would grant him access to any number of sensitive documents.

It was a picture that must seem very appealing to anyone looking to recruit agents to the German cause . . . like, perhaps, a spy already working in the Navy.

The pieces clicked into place, shocking in their audacity.

"He was bait," she blurted, surprise spilling the words out of her.

Suddenly Strangford's strange impressions of the objects in Brockmeyer's Scarborough house made sense. The place really had been a rummage sale. Brockmeyer had never actually lived there. The house was a fiction staged by the SSB in case anyone thought to look into Brockmeyer's background.

None of it was real.

Felix Brockmeyer had been an invention of the SSB. He had been created to draw out the Navy spy . . . and he must have succeeded.

Only his cover was blown before he could alert his handlers, and the spy took action to silence him for good.

Brockmeyer had gone into the hall to place a telephone call after dinner. Had he been calling headquarters to share his suspicions about someone in the house? She remembered the words she had overheard thinly from the telephone receiver.

... believe it's who, then?

If Brockmeyer had been able to reveal the name, Kazi would have arrived at Taddiford knowing full well who was responsible for the murder. He had been interrupted ... by the falling of that damned vase.

Lily was abruptly certain that if she had not moved it, the vase would not have crashed. Brockmeyer would have been able to complete his call. It might not have prevented his death, but it would have ensured that the suspicions were on the real spy and not Strangford.

This was all her fault.

The fact of it swept over her like a wave, threatening to drown her in guilt. She had blindly trusted a power she wasn't even close to understanding, and it had inflicted unthinkable disaster on the man she loved.

"Are you feeling well?" George asked with concern.

She could not tell him. He could not possibly understand, and she had put him in enough danger already.

"Thank you," she said, forcing her voice to steady. "You've been enormously helpful."

"No trouble," George replied. "That's what friends do for each other, isn't it?"

He looked so hopeful, so eager. Lily managed to force out a smile. She couldn't bring herself to let him down just yet.

"You ought to be getting back," she said.

"Nonsense," George replied. "My captain's on leave until noon today. I can get away with running about a bit longer. I'll walk you into town."

THIRTEEN

HE WOODLAND GAVE way to fields. George crossed them with confidence, knowing where to find the stiles that allowed them to easily mount over the rambling stone walls that lined the pastures. This was clearly a well-trodden track from the base to the town, soldiers finding their way along it for women or drink or contraband cigarettes.

Lily's half-brother kept up a running monologue as they walked, chatting happily about the woes of a vegetarian private and the corporal who came out every morning to do stretches in his drawers. Apparently, a pair of his fellow lieutenants had accidentally set fire to the latrines. George was a gifted storyteller, the men he described coming to life as they walked. Lily tried not to think about how they would all soon be shipping off to the trenches from which many of them would never return.

Last summer, when she went dizzy in the middle of Lord Bexley's drawing room, the young men around her shifting into corpses, George's face had still been clear. Was that because his words snapped her out of that terrible foresight, or because he would be safe?

She could try to find out, of course. It was the sort of question she might put to her power, and perhaps it might deign to grant her a response. Lily found she didn't want to.

They stopped at the train station in Chichester. It was bustling with midday traffic.

"I suppose this is where I see you off," George said, dropping his stream of anecdotes.

He put his hands in his pockets, looking just a little bit awkward.

"I'll have a few days leave before I ship out. There's a splendid curry house in Holborn if you don't mind a bit of pepper. Would you like to meet me there for lunch sometime?"

The invitation sounded lovely. Lily couldn't possibly accept it, not without prolonging George's hopes. It would only make her that much more of a rotter when she inevitably had to disappoint him. It would be better to do it now before things went any further.

She was searching for the words as an automobile engine rumbled to a stop behind her. A familiar voice called out as the door to the vehicle opened and then closed with a slam.

"There you are, you useless prig. I've been over half of Sussex looking for you. Quit flirting and—"

The words stopped as Lily turned around.

The face of her half-brother Simon, Lord Deveral, paled with surprise, then narrowed into something sharper.

Lily hadn't seen Deveral since the night she interviewed him about the murder of his lover, Annalise Boyden. That had been nearly a year ago. He had done everything he could in that conversation to make her feel small and miserable, throwing his words at her like weapons.

Her father's heir hated Lily with a bone-deep passion.

By identifying and facing down Joseph Hartwell, the man actually responsible for Annalise's death, Lily had exonerated Deveral of suspicion for the crime. She had no illusions that he felt he owed her anything for that. Deveral was not a man given to charity or goodwill.

"*You,*" he hissed.

He was tall, like George and their father, with the same patrician nose and the signature gray eyes. But where George was hale and bright, Deveral was thin and dissipated, perhaps the result of the cocaine he used for reasons that had nothing to do with medicine.

At the moment, he looked as though he wanted to spit in her face. He restrained himself, instead turning to unleash a stream of verbal bile at his younger brother.

"This is where you've been while I was out looking for you? Cavorting about town with the likes of her?"

Her—Deveral's tone twisted that simple pronoun into the basest insult.

"She's our sister, Simon," George pushed back.

"She's the bastard spawn of an Irish whore," Deveral snapped in reply.

"I say, that's not—" George protested, uncomfortable and shocked. Deveral left him no room to continue.

"She tossed up her skirts as a Covent Garden chorus girl and took on who knows what other sources of income. Her very existence is an insult to our family's honor, and you stand here nattering with her like she's some debutante in the park?"

Deveral's voice was now loud enough to turn a few heads in the street. Lily could smell the wine on his breath, remnants of the night before, or an early start to the day's debauchery.

Eyes flickered over her, measuring, judging. It was everything she feared—people staring and whispering on a respectable cobblestone street.

This was why she had known she must push George away, even though in her heart she desperately wanted to believe that at least one of these men who shared her blood might be something more to her than a name in the society columns.

Now she faced the reality of that nightmare, but what she felt was something rather different than shame.

"Enough," Lily said.

The word carried a cold authority. Deveral paused, surprised by her tone—by the fact that she was speaking at all.

"George is a grown man," she continued. "He wears the uniform of his country. He is more than capable of making his own decisions, and if he wishes to pursue a connection with me despite all that you have so helpfully pointed out about my history and upbringing, I will welcome it regardless of your own childish opposition. This choice is his to make, not yours."

Deveral loomed over her, a ghastly and outraged specter. Lily's hands itched for her walking stick. It was probably best she had left it at home. If she'd had it, she might very well have whacked him across the knees with it.

"How about that curry, then?" George said.

There was an edge to his usual cheerfulness, and he had taken a protective step closer to her.

"I should be delighted," Lily replied without looking away from Deveral.

"As for you," George continued. "Should you insult our sister again, I shall happily burst your nose."

Deveral's eyes narrowed.

"You're a fool," he retorted, pointing sharp finger at them. "Mark my words. This woman is poison. Blood will out, one way or another."

"Cheerio, brother. On your way, then," George said.

Deveral glared for an extra breath, clearly searching for some further way to strike and failing to find it. He turned on his heel and stalked back to the automobile.

The door slammed, engine grinding. The road spit dust and gravel as he tore out of the street and away.

Lily watched him go. The onlookers who had stopped to gape picked themselves up and hurried along their way.

"You alright?" George asked quietly.

"Entirely," Lily replied.

She found, surprisingly, that it was true. Deveral's presence was deeply unpleasant, but he had no power to hurt her. His verbal darts were just noise and air.

She looked up at her half-brother.

"This won't be uncomplicated," she warned.

"He already does his best to make me miserable every chance he gets," George easily returned. "I can't see it'll change all that much."

Lily pressed on. She needed to be sure he understood.

"It could also be hard for your mother."

George absorbed this a bit more seriously. He toed at a pebble on the road.

"It was never you who caused her any harm," he concluded. "And we can't spend the rest of our days protecting her like some china teacup."

The reply sparked a little glow inside of her.

"Come on," he said. "Let's get you on the train. If you get trapped here and have to come back to the barracks for lunch, your taste buds will die a wretched and ignominious death."

~

The sun was beginning to set when Lily returned to March Place, the winter gloom settling in. A few more of the shops had strung up garlands in their windows, wreaths warming the doors. Christmas was only a week away. She could not begin to guess what the holiday would look like for her this year. The thought of that left her feeling hollow and a little frightened as she walked past the townhouses glowing with candles in the windows, lamps lit against the encroaching darkness.

She was a little bedraggled from her walk through the woods. She had decided to go back to her flat to wash and change before going to tell Strangford what she had learned today.

Was part of her postponing going to Bayswater? Her conversation with Strangford yesterday had been so troubling. Of course, he must feel powerless, trapped in the house by Kazi's men, but instinct told Lily there was something more behind his unsettled mood.

She climbed the steps to her building and nearly bumped into someone coming out the front door. Estelle had swapped her turban for a soft purple felt cloche hat, wrapping herself in an overcoat and boots.

"Well?" the medium demanded without ceremony. "Did you find anything?"

"A bit," Lily replied. "Though I'm not sure how much it will help."

"I was just headed to the patisserie," Estelle said. "Gwendolyn is sleeping again, and I wanted to pick up something nice for when she wakes up."

"How is Miss Bard?" Lily asked.

"Her head aches, and she's very tired, but the doctor was here earlier. He says she is healing up well."

"Thank God."

"Thank you, rather," Estelle returned. "It would have been far worse had you not warned us it was coming."

Lily felt a burn of shame.

"If I had warned us a little sooner, she wouldn't have been hurt at all," she bit out.

Estelle's hand firmly clasped her arm.

"Don't," the older woman ordered, her hazel eyes clear and intent. "We can't fix everything. We are not gods."

She looked tired. The lines around her eyes were more pronounced than usual, her cheeks a bit thinner. Estelle had been extending herself for weeks now, squeezing in more spiritual readings in response to the upswell in demand from those grieving men lost in the war.

It lent extra weight to her words. Lily was certain Estelle had needed to turn people away to grant herself time to eat and sleep, to replenish the energy she used when contacting the dead.

Lily knew Estelle was right, but it didn't make her feel any better. She pushed the conversation onto what felt like safer ground.

"I saw Lord Deveral today," she reported.

"You have my sympathies," Estelle dryly replied. "I hope you told him to stuff it."

"I rather did, more or less," Lily admitted.

"Good," Estelle concluded.

Her expression shifted, becoming more careful.

"I had a letter from James this morning."

Lily didn't have to ask which James. She knew Estelle was referring to Cairncross.

"Oh?"

"He has found a tenant for the house on Bedford Square," Estelle said.

The house on Bedford Square ... The Refuge.

It felt like a boulder tumbling onto her.

Lily knew she should have anticipated this. The last time she had seen him, Cairncross had admitted he was considering letting out the two buildings that constituted The Refuge. Much of Ash's fortune had been tied up in entailments, leaving very little to maintain the property he had built into a place of learning and solace for those he called charismatics. Cairncross, the sole trustee, was left in the unenviable position of determining the fate of the building that had served as a kind of home to each of them.

"A school," Estelle continued. "Looking to expand to a satellite location in Bloomsbury. It seems quite appropriate."

"Yes," Lily blurted in reply, at a loss for anything else to say. "I'm sure that will be very nice."

It was not nice. It felt like the brink of an avalanche, the snowflake that tipped the whole mess into threatening to consume her—the threats to Strangford. Deveral's awfulness. The injured woman upstairs. The ever-present terror of the war—all the little ways Lily had failed to make things better.

Estelle was watching her carefully.

"Would you like to come in for a vermouth?" she asked. "I could run my errand a little later."

"No," Lily replied, snapping out of it. "Don't worry about me."

"You will tell us if there is anything more we can do to help Strangford," Estelle ordered.

"Of course," Lily replied.

The medium gave her hand a squeeze, and then descended the stairs, her posture straight and elegant as always. She paused as she reached the pavement, turning back to where Lily stood with her hand on the knob of the door.

"It's alright to be angry with them, you know," she said.

"With whom?" Lily replied.

"The dead, darling."

Then she turned and strode down the road, slipping into the shadows of the winter dusk.

~

The house smelled a little of boiled nettles, as it often did. There was a clatter of pans in the kitchen as Mrs. Bramble prepared supper. Lily had never been particularly fond of either the smell or her landlady's cooking, but both momentarily provoked a beat of nostalgia. She would only walk through this door a few more times. Everything was changing.

Her rooms at the top of the stairs were freezing, the little parlor stove unlit. The enormous orange tabby the household knew as Cat had burrowed into Lily's pillow. The animal cracked open a single yellow eye as Lily entered.

She was quite certain Cat had not been in her flat when she shut the door that morning. Not that it mattered—Cat had always been impervious to doors.

Sam shared that trait. Lily recalled what he had told her the last time she found him inside her flat—that Cat considered himself hers. Certainly, no one else in the house had ever claimed him. Did that mean she needed to pack the animal up along with the rest of her belongings and move it to Lancaster Gate? The thought was alarming. Lily realized she had never asked Strangford his feelings about felines. She seemed to recall him once mentioning that they made him sneeze.

Not that it mattered. Lily felt rather certain that packing the beast was irrelevant. If Sam was right, Cat would simply show up in her room some morning, sleeping on whatever shawl or hat she most wanted to stay free of orange fur.

The thought of Sam reminded Lily of all the things she hadn't yet had the courage to say to him. Her eyes fell to the letter-writing paper on her desk.

There was so much she still needed to do tonight, but she found herself sitting down in the chair, picking up her pen. She set it to the page, scribbling out the words before she could think better of them and shoving them into an envelope.

She reached into her wardrobe to change. As her hand brushed the fabric of one of her afternoon dresses, her onmyōdō sparked.

It was a distinct repulsion that pushed against her fingers, urging them away.

Lily hung suspended in a moment of indecision. Should she ignore the impulse or see where it led her?

She felt as though she were facing a wild animal in some wide, deserted space and could not know whether it meant to befriend her or turn and attack. Taking a deep, shaking breath, she tentatively extended her fingers back into the wardrobe.

Electricity buzzed. She felt that tense pressure pushing against her bare skin as she brushed across the assorted gowns and blouses. Then it twisted, inverting into a hot pull. Lily blinked to find herself gripping the worn canvas of her motorcycle trousers.

Her heart thudded against her ribs, the familiar geometry of the room around her narrowing.

"Fair enough," she whispered tentatively aloud.

~

The envelope with Sam's letter burned quietly in her pocket as she stepped into the back garden. She rolled the Triumph out of the shed where she stored it, wheeling it quietly into the gloom of the alley. Swinging her leg over the motorbike, she quickly spun the pedals and flicked the igniter.

The engine roared and caught. It lurched her forward as she flipped on the headlamp. It shone into the surprised face of a constable watching at the mouth of the alley.

Lily blew past him.

She paused by a postbox on Tottenham Court Road, slipping her letter into the waiting red mouth. The Triumph wove back into the snarl of traffic, heading for the West End.

Lily swung the motorbike into a narrow alley that ran between two of the fine Georgian townhouses that lined Lancaster Gate. It was largely used to store rubbish. She hid the Triumph behind a pair of bins and headed back to the road.

She nearly spilled into someone walking quickly and intently the other way, a small figure with hunched shoulders and a thick coat bundled against the cold.

"Oh! I'm terribly sorry," a feminine voice gasped.

"That's alright," Lily replied.

The girl's head shot up, and Lily found herself looking to a pair of familiar hazel eyes.

"Miss Albright?"

"Bonnie?" Lily replied, surprised. "Whatever are you doing here?"

Virginia Eversleigh's housemaid responded by grabbing Lily's arm and tugging her back into the alley. Her grip was surprisingly strong. Words tumbled out of her.

"I came to see his lordship, but when I reached the house, the place was crawling with Peelers going in and out, and I just couldn't..."

She was clearly upset, holding back tears. Lily found herself trying to comfort the girl.

"You needn't mind them. They've been here for days. It's all quite ordinary after a murder."

The maid's grip on Lily's arm tightened.

"You must tell him for me," she declared.

"Tell who what?" Lily returned.

Bonnie looked about nervously. Something about her reminded Lily of an animal about to bolt.

"I saw Mr. Anstruther-Fields coming out of the conservatory the night the lieutenant was killed."

The alley narrowed, focusing to a single point. Lily could hear the slow beat of her heart in her ears.

"What do you mean?" she quietly demanded.

Bonnie released her arm to wring her hands together.

"It was just before midnight. My room is at the top of the house near the nursery in the southeast corner. It looks down over the terrace. It was dark, but there was enough light from the rooms along the wing that I could see him. He walked from the conservatory up the terrace to the door to the billiards room and just . . . stood there. Like he was waiting for something."

"That's very odd," Lily admitted. "But perhaps it was when Dicky—Mr. Anstruther-Fields—went out to relieve himself. The inspector said he'd done that a little before Lieutenant Brockmeyer retired for the evening."

"No, miss," Bonnie pushed back, her eyes bright and nervous. "The inspector said the lieutenant left to go upstairs at eleven-thirty. This was eleven-forty on the nose. I've a clock in my room with a radium dial. It was a present from my gram. I could read the time perfectly."

Lily's pulse leapt. If it was true, it changed everything. Eleven-forty was right within the window of time for Brockmeyer's murder. He had left the room at half-past eleven, and Lily and Strangford had found him around eleven-fifty.

Except that Dicky had been asleep in the chair when Lily passed the room herself at around quarter to midnight. Would he have come in from murdering a man and promptly pretended to fall asleep? But even that was impossible. George and Walford had both claimed Dicky had not left the room after Brockmeyer retired for the evening.

Somebody had to be mistaken—Bonnie or George and Walford. Either that or Dicky had been in two places at once at precisely eleven-forty that night.

"Did you tell this to the inspector?" Lily demanded.

"I tried to, but the sergeant who was with him said I must've been dreaming or that my clock wasn't wound. Only I was awake—I know I was. And I wind up the clock every night before I lay down. How else can I be sure to wake up on time in the morning? I know Mr. Eversleigh and Mr. Carne said that Mr. Anstruther-Fields was in the room with them the whole time, and who are the police going to believe? The toffs or a housemaid? But my clock wasn't wrong."

Bonnie's voice was small and fierce.

"Lord Strangford is a good man," she pushed on. "He doesn't deserve to be suspected like this. If the police wouldn't believe me, I thought I could tell him myself. It's the least I could do after..."

Her voice trailed off, but Lily could put the rest of it together. Strangford had intervened when Dicky had gone after the girl with an indecent proposal. It had clearly earned him Bonnie's loyalty.

Lily felt certain that Bonnie was telling her the truth, but she would've said the same about George and Walford. There were two truths, and they didn't add up. It made her head ache to think about it.

None of this made sense, but it wasn't her job to figure it out on her own. She needed to bring it to Strangford.

"Thank you, Bonnie," Lily said, squeezing the girl's hands. "I'm grateful you told me."

"Take care of him, won't you?" Bonnie blurted, then hurried away into the darkness.

Lily turned to the glowing windows of Strangford's home.

She knocked at the front door. Approaching the house in her motorcycle gear would have been scandalous in the broad light of day, but at this hour, she was more or less concealed in the gloom. A curious neighbor would likely take her for a courier.

Light shone from between the curtains of the drawing room, and she realized something was wrong.

There were no constables stationed at the steps. Kazi's men had been there religiously since Taddiford. And Strangford never used his drawing room.

Alarm sang through her as the door swung open. It was not Roderick holding it but a constable. The hallway behind him was crammed with men.

A gentleman in plainclothes stood at the center of the knot of activity. He turned at the draft from the door, and Lily found herself locking eyes with Inspector Kazi. An animal instinct sang for her to bolt, but if she did, she wouldn't be able to learn what was going on.

Lily stepped inside.

"Inspector," she said.

"Miss Albright," he returned thinly.

"I would like to speak to Lord Strangford," she announced, putting as much authority as she could muster into the words.

"As would I," Kazi replied.

Her stomach lurched.

"He's not here," she blurted.

"No," Kazi said. "And I rather hope you might tell me where he has gone."

The police weren't just milling about. They were searching the house. Two men to her right were dusting for fingerprints, others pulling the paintings from the wall and peering at the paper lining at the back of the frames.

"What happened?" she demanded.

"The House of Lords indicted Lord Strangford today—a late addition to the agenda of a closed session. I have a warrant to take him into custody."

He flashed Lily a piece of official-looking paper.

It felt as though the floor had disappeared from beneath her boots. An indictment meant a trial in the Lords. It meant Kazi had stopped looking for other suspects, that the evidence he had presented was enough to convince the other peers of Lord Strangford's guilt. Lily knew her politics well enough to recognize the Lords wouldn't indict one of their own, risking all that noise and scandal, unless they felt the case was unavoidably clear.

Something ripped away from her. Lily vaguely recognized it as the hope that she might enjoy a life that in some way resembled normal—one of warm windows and holiday garlands. A family. Love.

"Do you have any idea where I can find him?" Kazi asked.

The question felt more like a challenge than a genuine inquiry, as though he did not expect her to answer it.

"I do not," she replied.

It was true. She had no idea where Strangford had gone, and it terrified her. She was hardly about to admit that fear to Kazi. Let him think she was hiding it from him.

He seemed surprisingly unbothered by her resistance.

"It has come to my attention that a woman matching your description was seen fleeing the scene of a train derailment in Ludgate last August," Kazi remarked casually.

The hallway began to spin.

"What?" Lily said numbly.

"A man resembling Lord Strangford was witnessed at the scene as well. I have learned his lordship was admitted to St. Bartholomew's Hospital later that day with severe injuries to his face and arm," Kazi continued relentlessly.

The memory swept over her like a wave.

The weight of the mortar in her pocket. The close dungeon of the train's engine room, stinking of burning coal. The screams of the Army officer guarding the deadly shipment trailing behind them.

Strangford's hands on her chest, shoving her out into the warm rushing air.

The blood dripping onto the gravel of the rail bed.

Lily's father had seen them all released, quelling any suspicions about their involvement by pulling his quiet and powerful threads of influence. Lily didn't know what story he had told to make that happen. The plot they had risked everything to stop had never been made public. Somewhere high and secret, someone had decided that exposing a conspiracy on the evening of a declaration of war against Germany risked tearing the country apart.

How much had Kazi learned? It seemed just enough to deepen his suspicions of Lily and Strangford, reinforcing his theory that they were collaborating with her father in a scheme to benefit England's enemies.

Fear washed through her. It left something unexpected in its wake—a quick, cold fury.

Strangford had risked everything to stop that train. He had saved countless lives. He didn't deserve this suspicion—for this man who knew nothing to brand him a traitor.

"If you know about the train, you should know what it was carrying," Lily replied, her words edged in ice. "Read the bloody timetable. Use your powers of deduction to figure out what would have happened had it not been stopped before it reached the bridge."

"The train was carrying rations and gear for forces mobilizing to head to the continent," Kazi said.

"The devil it was," Lily returned flatly.

His golden eyes flashed with surprise. Something in him was irresistibly calculating, sorting the various pieces of the puzzle. He clamped it down, forcing his focus back to the hallway.

"Take her into custody," he ordered.

Hands grasped her arms.

"I am arresting you for suspicion of complicity in the murder of Lieutenant Felix Brockmeyer and the sabotage of Army property in August of this year," Kazi formally announced.

She wanted to scream, to rail at him that they both knew perfectly well there was no Lieutenant Felix Brockmeyer. The dead man was a fiction. She bit back the words. Revealing she knew that would only make him suspect her even more.

The two constables who held her yanked her into motion, dragging her to the front door.

She stumbled down the steps, her mind whirling. Going with them cooperatively might help demonstrate her innocence—but if she was imprisoned, who would give Strangford the information she now possessed—information he needed if he had any chance of clearing his name?

Lily could not let them take her.

The policemen were powerful hulks on either side of her. Her boots barely touched the ground as they propelled her forward. She had no staff she could use to try to break their holds . . . but she did have one weapon at her disposal.

If there was a way to reshape this future, Lily could find it.

She burned the demand down into the house of her power. *Show me the way out.* It hung there, suspended and crystalline, as they approached the black prisoner's wagon on the curb.

Where was the answer? The need for it pushed panic up into her throat, threatening to choke her.

Then she realized it was an answer—quiet and confident, a single thought clear as a word spoken aloud into the still December air.

Wait.

Time slowed to a crawl. The constables carried her forward—one step, then another. The dark mouth of the wagon loomed closer, promising the end of her chance to change things.

She became conscious of a lorry rumbling toward them up the road.

The sound of the engine glowed, resonating with significance. Lily suddenly understood.

Now.

The lorry loudly backfired, the crack of the engine like a gunshot snapping against the facades of the elegant townhouses. The two constables jumped at the unexpected sound, one of them startled into releasing his grip on her arm.

Lily was ready for it. She pivoted, twisting her body, using her arm like she would her walking stick in a move she had practiced for years. It broke the remaining officer's grip.

She bolted, diving in front of a rattling omnibus.

The driver pounded on his horn, shouting through the window.

Lily didn't slow. She raced forward, skimming within inches of the fender of a passing Daimler. She twisted around it, sprinting for the narrow alley near the end of Strangford's road.

The constables were right behind her. She could hear their shouts, the slam of the door as others from inside the house ran out to join the chase. Her veins flooded with a sweet exhilaration as she pivoted around the corner into the alley and snatched the handles of the Triumph.

She vaulted into the saddle, feet swinging onto the pedals, and with the flick of a switch, the motorbike sparked to life.

It tore up that narrow space, dodging a pile of cinderblocks and a discarded wheelbarrow. She blasted out the far end of it, facing the park.

The sharp call of a whistle echoed behind her, but it didn't matter. On the broad expanse of the road, Lily opened up the throttle, weaving through the carriages and automobiles until Lancaster Gate had faded behind her.

FOURTEEN

$\mathcal{L}$ILY DIDN'T KNOW where she was going. She let the Triumph decide for her, the motorbike choosing which corners to swing around. She found herself following the pale, narrow path of Regent's Canal west into the quieter, respectable suburbs to the northeast.

The tidy row houses broke against a tall stone wall, iron gates offering glimpses of ghostly stones crowded together on a shadowy lawn, and Lily realized where she had unconsciously steered herself.

She stopped her motorbike at Kensal Green Cemetery.

She stared through the gate, the engine ticking quietly as it cooled. The graveyard was cloaked in dusk, the monuments softly reflecting the glow of the streetlamps outside the walls. The low rumble of the gasworks could be heard from across the canal. The circular iron scaffolding of the gasometer rose in the distance like the frost-ringed crown of some giant gazing out over this city of the dead.

Lily gripped the iron bars of the grate, then scrambled over, moving nimbly in her trousers and motorcycle boots. She dropped onto the soft grass between the graves. Carriage wheels clattered slowly past as she waited in the shadows, her eyes adjusting to the gloom.

She picked her way through the leaning, lichen-encrusted tombstones, stopping at a simple marble slab and reading the words carved into its surface.

Robert Ash
March 5, 1851 to August 2, 1914
没身不殆
Cairncross had once translated the row of characters for her. *Do*

not fear the decay of the body. It was a line from the *Tao Te Ching*, the book Ash had so often referenced when trying to teach Lily and the others about the great order he believed moved the universe, infusing harmony into the patterns of life and death, pain and joy.

The waters of the canal glittered darkly at the edge of the cemetery. A low horn sounded from the gasworks, signaling a shift change. Outside the walls, a group of revelers staggered down the street, singing carols loudly and badly.

Lily stared down at the grave.

"You were supposed to be here."

The words fell into the quiet of the cemetery. Nothing answered her.

Her chest tightened, eyes burning. A tangle of emotion welled up inside of her like a coiled beast. It stunk of the explosion at Blackfriars, sulfurous and metallic. It sang at her of everything Ash's Tao—his Parliament of Stars—had denied her.

The mother who sang careless tunes at her mirror. The family she had never been permitted to know. The teacher who deserted her, leaving her with a mess of conflicted feelings about a power she did not even begin to understand.

Everything Strangford offered her had always been tainted with fear—because of this. Because the Tao was cruel, a deluge that wanted only to drown her.

She should have been able to change it. She possessed a power out of myth, the fodder of legends made flesh and blood. It hadn't helped her save her mother or Ash. It was clumsy and awkward in her hands, like trying to shape wet sand into something that could stand. Now it was failing her again with Strangford.

Her eyes fell closed. She could feel the endless rows of graves that surrounded her, and for a moment, the world seemed to shift.

Warm sunlight dances across her eyelids. The breeze smells of wildflowers. Rustling leaves sing in some ancient language to the dead that lie under her feet. Her hands touch the rough surface of a wooden cross.

There is a soft flutter of wings.

Lily opened her eyes. In the gloom of Kensal Green, an ordinary brown sparrow perched on top of the cold slab of stone in front of her. The bird looked at her curiously, tilting its head from one side to the other.

She thought of the others like it she had seen flitting through the parlor of The Refuge, Sam's constant companions. Remembered the crooked joy of his smile and thought of all the things they had both been too guarded to ever say aloud to each other.

She tasted Estelle's vermouth on her tongue, heard the bold crack of her laughter. Felt Dr. Gardner's big, warm hand squeeze her shoulder. Smelled the dust and wisdom of Cairncross's books as he rattled on in some language the rest of the world had forgotten.

Saw the quiet, careful respect in Zhao Min's fierce eyes.

The quick, loving chaos of the Eversleighs. The brilliant glow of George's grin.

Her father's arms around her back, holding her in spite of his regret, his sadness.

Strangford's hands dancing electric over her skin. The knowing in his gaze—an unmitigated acceptance of all that she was, all that she could never be.

It swept over her like a tide, and everything was changed. The fear and pain were still there, but something else had shifted—growing roots and anchoring her to the ground.

Her own words came back to her, the ones she had said to Sam when he bared a part of his soul to her on a Limehouse street corner.

It doesn't have to be like that.

No? And why not?

Because you aren't alone.

Lily found that she knew exactly where Strangford had gone.

She cast a final look down at the grave of the man who had promised her all the answers, heard his voice inside her mind.

The door has always been open. You may walk through it anytime you choose.

She did not know where this would lead her—what the future was going to bring. But she knew where she had to go next.

~

The streets were quieter as she rode the Triumph back into the city, slivers of light through curtained windows hinting at the lives that went on within. The rich were sitting down fashionably late to dinner, the ordinary already clearing their plates, preparing to douse the lamps to save on gas. Lily wove past the garlanded houses, cold air frosting her lungs until she finally turned into Bedford Square.

She stopped, gazing up at the front of The Refuge. The windows were dark. Dry leaves covered the front step. She thought of what Estelle had said the first time she brought Lily here and put her hand to the door.

It's never locked.

Lily throttled up the motorbike, swinging around the square and then ducking into the mews that ran behind the buildings. She stopped at Ash's carriage house. The rooms upstairs where Sam once had his apartment were tightly shuttered.

He had showed her the trick to opening the carriage house bay doors. Lily felt the lock give under her fingers and wheeled the Triumph into the gloom.

Ash's car, the enormous Rolls Royce Silver Ghost, rested in the quiet darkness, shrouded in a canvas tarpaulin and a layer of undisturbed dust. She let the motorbike rest against the wall and passed into the garden.

It had grown wilder in the months since she had seen it. The hedges were untrimmed, dry stalks of flowers spilling out of their beds. The laurels were still green, but the rest of the space was all angles and textures in monochrome hues of gray and brown, edged with frost.

It was even quieter here than Kensal Green had been, the sound of passing automobiles muffled into a dull hum in the background.

Lily gazed up at the back of The Refuge.

Black glass glittered down at her, capturing the tiniest slivers of light filtering in from the street. The elegant conservatory was an empty shell. Mr. Wu had taken all the plants out of it, knowing that if they were left, they would slowly die and rot.

Lily had avoided coming here for months, ever since the funeral, going well out of her way not to drive past it. The house felt like another sort of tomb, a four-story monument to a life that no longer existed, one rife with memories of both belonging and frustration.

She walked up the path, her boots scratching softly against the stones.

There was an empty pane in the kitchen window where the glass had been broken. The latch was turned. Lily pushed the sash up. She climbed through, noting that the floor was clear of any broken fragments.

The kitchen had been Mrs. Liu's domain. It was stripped of all the signs of her occupancy, from the smiling porcelain god and his altar to the bamboo steamers and the paper calendar. Everything was covered in a fine film of dust. The desiccated corpse of a beetle rested on the kitchen table, limbs turned inward.

A faint band of light glowed from under the door that led into the cellar.

Lily had never been in the cellar. The warren of rooms beneath the house were used for storage, housing Mrs. Liu's cleaning supplies and the surplus items from Ash's collection of books, antiquities, and esoterica—anything that didn't fit in the enormous two-story library that had been Lily's first introduction to this place.

The library shelves would be empty now. Cairncross had said he was packing it up, taking whatever he could to his flat in Rotherham, where he was now teaching at a girl's school. The rest had been put into a rented storage bay somewhere near Deptford. She did not know if he had finished sorting through the archives squirreled away below. She supposed he would have to soon enough now that the building had been let out.

Recalling that threatened to break something inside of her open again. She pushed on, quietly opening the cellar door.

The stairs were dim, only a little light from some distant source spilling onto the rungs. They did not creak as Lily descended. Sam's father kept things too well-tuned for that. He had cared for the bones of the house with the same careful attention to detail he had exercised in the garden.

At the bottom, she faced not an open space, but a long hallway lit by a single electric bulb. Thick wires strung along the low ceiling led into each of the rooms that branched off to either side. It was clear that Cairncross still had work to do. A stack of crates nearly blocked her way forward, topped by the bust of a Roman orator.

The chill began to seep through her coat, the air still and smelling of earth.

She glanced into the nearest room. Like the hall, it was lit by a single bare electric bulb, buzzing softly. The walls were covered in shelves dotted with artifacts. Some rested in crates labeled with Cairncross's spidery hand. Others stood free, like a pair of Grecian helmets, their brass green with age. One was split down the back as though from the blow of some ancient blade.

An enormous gold-framed mirror leaned against the wall beside a pair of rolled-up carpets. A half-dozen paintings rested beside it, the backs of their canvases facing out. Lily wondered if they were works by Ash's wife. Evangeline Ash's art was far from comfortable to look at, woven through as it was with obscure threads of fate.

Curiosity warred with dread and won. Lily pulled back the first of the canvases.

It was not Evangeline Ash's work. The painting was a portrait of a wise-eyed man in puffed sleeves and a ruffled collar, a thick gold chain around his neck. He sat at a table covered in glass beakers, burners, and scales.

The next work was in a completely different style, obviously by the hand of another artist. It depicted a veiled woman in colorful silk. Gems sparkled from the tassels of her headdress. She held out her hand, and above it burned a disembodied flame.

Looking closer, Lily realized that small labels had been carefully affixed to the back of each work, written in Cairncross's distinct hand. She read the last one, pasted to the back of a framed piece of silk depicting a warrior in shingled armor, his thick black hair tied into a topknot, face distorted into something monstrous over the pile of severed heads at his feet.

白起, *the Human Butcher. Qin general. Possible berserker?*

Lily gently let the portraits fall back into place.

The shelves beside them held a rusted, primitive sword and a jeweled reliquary containing a mummified foot, but it was the book that captured her attention. It was dull-looking, bound in tanned hide and chained into place on the shelf with links of iron.

There was no label on it, nothing to indicate what it contained or why Cairncross had decided to bind it into place like an unruly prisoner. The chain was clearly new, clasped by a modern padlock.

The leather of the binding looked soft and supple, worn by centuries. Lily found herself wanting to know what it felt like. She longed to run her fingers over the skin. Then she would pick the lock and expose the pages. Everything she had ever wanted to know was inside, everything that mattered to her. The chains would fall away, and the book would reveal the most secret yearnings of her heart...

A gloved hand closed over her arm, holding her back.

"Best leave that be."

Strangford's voice was warm and familiar at her ear. Lily should turn to him. He was the reason she had come here, and yet she was still staring at the volume on the shelf.

"What is it?" she asked.

"*The Book of Days.*"

She recognized the name. She had heard Cairncross mention it before. She wanted to touch it, but Strangford hadn't let her go.

"Is it very valuable?" she asked absently.

"No," he replied. "I believe it is rather dangerous."

His words cut through the fog clouding her thoughts. Lily blinked down at the ordinary object ruthlessly bound to the shelf.

"How on earth could it be dangerous?"

"Cairncross says it tells you the day you're going to die. You and everyone else you care about."

That broke any lingering remainder of the spell of fascination the thing had cast over her. Lily knew all too well what that sort of knowledge meant. How much it could hurt.

The skin binding it was stained and weathered with age. The yellowed pages were thick, clearly cut by hand.

"That's impossible," she noted.

"So are we," Strangford returned. He cast a wary glance at the book. "I'm not inclined to test it."

Cairncross was constantly rattling on about how the saints and heroes of the past were something more than just legends. History was also full of stories about magical objects. Lily supposed it shouldn't surprise her to learn that some of those might be true as well.

She studied the object on the shelf, but it was merely a rather dull-looking old book. Beyond the chain, there was nothing all that compelling or interesting about it.

If Cairncross's story was true—if there really was a book that allowed you to know when the people you loved would die—it might tell her whether Sam would make it home from France. Or whether Strangford would ever succumb to the vision she'd foreseen of him.

She asked herself whether she was tempted.

The answer rose up like bile in her throat.

No.

"I need to fetch some coal," Strangford said.

"I'll come with you," she quietly replied.

He finally released her arm.

Once out of the room where *The Book of Days* was chained, Lily could take in more of the details of Strangford's appearance. He had forgone his usual black suit and was instead dressed in the trousers, boots and jumper she had last seen on him at Taddiford.

Lily glanced into the rooms they passed. Some were empty of everything but cobwebs and the odd mousetrap. Others still held assorted curiosities or boxes labeled *Books: Incunabula* or *Scrolls: Hebrew, Byzantine, Med. Irish.*

Strangford pushed up the sleeves of his jumper before grabbing the shovel for the coal bin. He filled the bucket he had brought down and then led her to the stairs.

He stopped to pick up a battered tin lantern. It was the type used by thieves with a panel that could be slid open or closed to reveal just a narrow beam of light. Strangford pulled a box of matches from his pocket, struck one, and lit the lamp. He closed the shutter to a sliver.

At the top of the stairs, he punched the button to kill the electric lights, plunging them into darkness. Lily found herself acutely and uncomfortably aware of the secrets lurking in the shadows behind her.

The walls were bare on the main floor of the house. The familiar artifacts Lily remembered from her many visits here were gone.

At the door to the library, Lily paused, glancing inside. The clouds shifted, allowing a beam of moonlight to spill through the windows. It fell across the rows of empty shelves, the comfortable chairs covered in dust clothes like so many ghosts gathered around the cold hearth. An empty square of carpet marked the place where Cairncross's desk had once been.

It was gutted, the corpse of the room Lily had once known—the space where they had gathered, learned, joked … *belonged.*

She stepped away from Strangford, moving inside and forcing herself to take in the whole of it, all the emptiness, gloom and dust.

This was supposed to be the place where she would figure all of it out—what her power meant. What her role was in the world. Fate had robbed her of that, the fate the woman who was once mistress of this place had known like her own breath. Lily was not sure she would ever be able to forgive it.

The moonlight washed over her skin. There was no warmth in it, but somehow Lily felt comforted all the same. She closed her eyes, soaking it up, letting it whisper to her of all the things that had been lost, then opened her sight to what was still here.

Strangford stood in the doorway, the bucket of coal at his feet, the scars of the past marking his face. The world seemed determined to run him to the ground like a stag in the woods, but his shoulders remained straight under the wool of his jumper.

"Why did you come here?" Lily asked.

He looked around at the empty shelves.

"I had to go somewhere. This was the only place that made sense."

"But how did you know that Kazi was coming for you?"

"Ah," Strangford replied softly. "I suppose that should not be surprising."

"You didn't know?"

"How did you find it out?" he returned.

"I found him at Lancaster Gate along with a dozen constables."

"Did he give you any trouble?" Strangford pressed.

"Nothing I couldn't handle, though I won't be going back home for a while," Lily replied.

The line of his mouth tightened at that bit of news. Lily could feel the frustration rising off of him.

"If you didn't know Kazi was coming, why did you run?" she demanded.

"Your father sent a messenger with news of the indictment."

"Did he tell you to try to escape?" Lily asked, startled by the notion. Surely running would make Strangford look even more guilty. She found it hard to imagine her father recommending it as a course of action.

"Rather the opposite," Strangford replied.

"Then why on earth did you do it?"

He turned to the window, his eye patch a deeper blaze of darkness against the shadows of the night.

"I couldn't just sit there waiting. Doing nothing."

He bit out the word like a curse, the sharpness of it alarming her. There was something in his gaze—something she had seen before. She had been seeing it for months now, always too afraid to ask what it meant. She had told herself she was respecting his privacy, but here in the stark, empty shell of a place she had once loved, she finally admitted that wasn't entirely the truth.

"This isn't about Brockmeyer."

It was a statement, not a question, and it surprised him into looking at her.

"Of course, it is," he countered.

"But not entirely," she softly pushed back.

Something gave in him, a taut cord finally releasing.

"No," he agreed.

Lily crossed to him. She took his gloved hand in her own.

"Tell me."

His eye closed. He dropped her hand and moved past her into the library, gazing out the moonlit window into the barren sprawl of the winter garden.

"What happened last November with Jack Cannon," he started.

Lily's pulse kicked up. She hadn't known what she expected him to say, but it was not this.

"I know you've wondered why I haven't brought it up," he continued. "You've been afraid of it."

It was true, of course. She was afraid of it even now. Recalling that encounter in Limehouse always stirred up a terrible mix of fears—the fear of how easily it could all have gone wrong. The fear that the decision she made had irrevocably cost her Sam's friendship. The fear of what that fierce capacity for violence revealed about who she was. And, of course, she had feared Strangford's anger and hurt.

"You're bringing it up now," she pointed out.

The words were careful, every part of her scared of all the ways this conversation could go wrong.

"I was angry, Lily," Strangford said, still not looking at her. "It was recklessly dangerous. A complete disregard for your own safety—your own life. I wanted to shake you. Lock you up in a tower where you could never so much as contemplate something so risky again."

"Why didn't you say anything?" she asked softly.

His head lowered. Dark hair fell over the scars on his cheek. His hands were clenched at his sides.

"How could I?" he returned. "What right would I have to call you to account for it when I want the same thing for myself?"

The room was still. Cobwebs shrouded the high corners of a bookcase. Outside the windows, Lily heard the muffled clacking of carriage wheels, a cabbie calling cheerfully to an acquaintance.

"What are you saying?" she asked, forcing herself to speak the words aloud.

"It's the war."

His words dropped into the quiet of the room like stones, too heavy for any echo.

The pieces clicked together, the puzzle reshaping itself into a coherent picture—the look on his face when he stared out over the channel. His horror when the woman in Scarborough mistook him for a soldier. Flashes of uncomfortable reaction to newspaper headlines, thoughtless talk in drawing rooms. The long black procession of a funeral passing through the soft green grass of the park. The answer to all of it became clear to her and was more terrible than she had dared to guess.

"You want to go," she filled in, trying not to let her voice tremble.

"I don't know. I'm not . . . driven by some idiot impulse to throw myself into where the bullets are flying. I just need to do something. To be of some *use* instead of sitting here while the world tears itself apart."

He raised his head, his dark gaze fierce.

"I am not an invalid."

"No," Lily agreed, knowing it was true.

He had lost a great deal at Blackfriars, but not his strength, his intelligence. Loyalty. Courage.

He flexed his hands.

"This . . . power. This gift," he said, the word edged like a knife. "There must be some point to it. Something I can *do.*"

She felt the resonance of that somewhere deep under her skin, an echoing need. It cut through the raw terror that had clenched at her since he said that terrible word—*war*. Lily had yearned for the same thing all her life. It was what had driven her to try, time and again, to change the futures she foresaw—to throw herself against the jagged rocks of failure over and over again until it finally became too much.

Hopelessness hadn't made that need go away.

She knew now that her power was far more complicated than she had suspected when she was a girl. The future wasn't a straight line anymore but a network of roads. Lily could find the turnings, but she was terribly far from understanding them. She still did not know what she had unleashed when she moved that vase in the hall. How much would it cost her? Cost Strangford? She had followed the impulse of her onmyōdō on trust because that was all it offered her—a leap of faith. She was still tortured by the idea that she might have been horribly wrong.

Strangford turned back to her, confronting her as though they were in a fight.

"But if I were to seek a commission, I'd be walking into the future you foresaw for me. I know what it is, Lily. I have felt it in your skin."

He did not have to tell her what he meant. Lily remembered. The horror of it was burned into her mind—his mud-streaked face, the deafening roar of the noise, the earth tearing itself apart. It was more terrifying than even Kazi and his suspicions, than the threat of a murder indictment—a beast waiting to devour him like some dragon out of myth.

"That's why I couldn't blame you for what you did with Cannon," he said, his voice raw. "Because despite every shred of common sense, I also feel the need to go running into my own destruction."

"You don't know that's where it would lead," Lily weakly pushed back.

He came closer, taking hold of her arms. His grip was rough.

"How can I do that to you?"

It was not a rhetorical question. It was real, as solid as the weathered boards under their feet. He wanted an answer, and at the same time, she could hear that he did not expect to find one.

Of all the people in the world, Strangford knew better than anyone what abandonment meant to Lily, ever since the day they had laid her mother in the ground—the day her father had walked away from her. Even talking about it here, now, threatened to spin her into a panic.

She fought against that, anchoring herself in the spill of moonlight across the bare boards of the floor, the rows of empty shelves. They were not in France. They were here, now, in the ruin of what had once been her sanctuary.

In the low, sprawling attic that crowned this space, Evangeline Ash's last work covered the walls. Lily remembered the portrait that loomed there—the dark figure with the gauntlets of a warrior on his hands, the halo of a noble cause crowning his brow, the detritus of rough beauty scattered at his feet.

The truth dawned through her, as frightening as it was undeniable.

"This is who you are," she said, the words spilling from her. "And I love you. I don't want you to become something else."

Her words only seemed to deepen the conflict in him.

"Lily—" he began.

She stopped him.

"Enough. Please."

She wanted to touch him, and yet she was afraid of what that touch might reveal. She wanted to choose what he would learn of her reaction to the revelation he had just shared with her, and yet she knew it was futile. He would know it all eventually. He always did.

"Cairncross kept his room intact upstairs. Let me fix it up for you," Strangford said.

"Thank you," Lily replied evenly and followed him to the stairs.

FIFTEEN

They moved past rooms like empty shells—the studio where Strangford had learned the dance of his tàijí, the quiet corner where Lily had stared into mirrors and candle flames, then kicked over a chair with frustration when Ash's quiet disappointment finally broke her.

They reached the stairs to the attic, still whispering with a lingering scent of smoke, and Lily stopped, gazing up at the dark door that concealed the final work of Evangeline Ash.

She didn't know what Cairncross would do with the secrets that lay on the other side. Certainly, he could not leave them open to the predations of a batch of schoolboys. It would take something more than a mere locked door to keep them out, which meant that this might very well be the last opportunity Lily would have to view Evangeline Ash's opus before it was hidden away from the world for good.

She went up.

The smell of smoke grew stronger as she neared the top, tinged with an acrid chemical aftertaste that made her heart beat faster with the memory of flames.

The curtains that had always covered the panels of the mural were gone. She wondered if Cairncross had pulled them down before the mice could start tearing them into nesting material. The Dendera ceiling with its whirling stars and Egyptian gods had a great black scorch mark in the center of it, unchanged since she had last been here with Robert Ash.

He was still here now, painted onto the wall in the panel that faced the door, right at the heart of the whole terrible array of Evangeline's work. It was too hard to look at Ash's face, so exquisitely rendered by the brush of a woman who had loved him. Lily found herself staring at the object he held in his hands.

The structure was woven together from shining silver threads that wound back to all the other figures crowding the attic walls. In Ash's hands, those delicate filaments connected to form something geometric, powerful and resilient.

It was a bridge.

Evangeline Ash did not see the future. She had not painted her husband holding a bridge in his hands because she had foreseen that he would lose his life on one, blown away by the hubris of powerful men and a poorly made battery. She had painted it because she had known that the bridge had meaning for him—layers of complex meaning that threaded not only through his death but through his life.

All the symbols of the attic were like that. They reflected significance, the people, objects, or places that would act like the pull of a magnet on someone's existence, reshaping and aligning it in accordance with a force that science would never be able to measure. As she finally brought herself to look around the attic, she recognized how many of the objects in the mural now also represented events that had come to pass. It was evidence of how successfully fate had shaped the lives of those Evangeline had woven into her tapestry, pounding at their days like the waves of an inexorable tide.

Ash had been the bridge that had connected Lily and her fellow charismatics, and a bridge had stolen him away from them. The keys on Lily's gown were the doors of her onmyōdō, the ones she was only just uncertainly learning to open with a power thrust upon her when she went into the waters of Regents Canal.

The gauntlets on Strangford's hands, painted when he was barely born, were the gloves he donned as armor against a world that assaulted him with every touch.

At Gardner's feet, a pile of bloody rags spoke of his choice to serve in the war. Lily could now see that the skeletons that danced with Estelle wore military medals and bars on their bony chests, symbols of the dead soldiers she now exhausted herself trying to serve.

Evangeline herself floated, suspended, in a sea streaked with the red-gold of sunset—or of flames. That water had eventually claimed her, consuming her during the wreck of the *Princess Alice*.

The attic whispered, soft and relentless, of inevitability—of the hands of great and impersonal gods meddling in each of their lives. Lily found herself thinking of the hundreds of premonitions she had failed to change—how all of her attempts to fix things felt like a struggle against some terrible inertia indifferent to the horror it inflicted on those trapped in its currents.

That inertia felt like an enemy, a nemesis against which she was bound to struggle for the rest of her existence.

For decades, it had seemed a battle she was bound to lose. The onmyōdō had changed that, giving her the power to do what had once seemed impossible—shift the path of things to come. But how would that new and largely untested ability stand if pitted directly against the weight of destiny?

She didn't know the answer, and that terrified her. It was a fear woven through with the scream of falling shells and the smell of blood and dirt.

Strangford waited in the doorway.

"Do you dislike this place as much as I do?" Lily asked.

"Dislike it?" Strangford asked, confused. "No."

The answer made her feel just a little more alone.

"Then what do you think about it?" she quietly pressed.

She wasn't looking at him. Somehow it was easier not to. His answer was a voice behind her, coming a step closer.

"It's ... true. All of her work was. This more than anything. There's a very great deal of truth in it. I suppose that's what makes it so ... "

"Hard," Lily filled in for him.

Her hands clenched at her sides. She glared at the figures on the wall in their rich raiments of significance—at the scattered jewels Evangeline Ash had painted at the feet of the flame-haired woman in her gown of keys, glittering crimson with old pain.

"I hate it," she asserted, the admission bursting out of her. "I hate what it's done to us. What it's still promising to do."

The details leapt out at her as she said the words, the symbols Lily knew would matter but couldn't yet understand. There were the great black mechanical wings that hung from Sam's shoulders. The words and phrases that made up the threads of Zhao Min's web, rogue bits of French and German and other languages Lily did not know. The rusted, bloody sword at Cairncross's side.

Something in the shape of the torn-up earth at Strangford's feet sent a deep bolt of fear through her.

A black-gloved hand slipped over her fist. His fingers softly wove themselves with her own, loosening the tension that clamped at her. It should have been a comfort, but all Lily could think of were the two figures on the wall beside her—the woman with the bloody jewels at her feet and the man with the gauntlets on his hands. Even this was tangled up in Evangeline's terrible truth.

"I won't let it take this from me," Lily blurted.

The words had the weight of a vow.

The voice of a dead woman came back to her, torn from a memory that continued to fade and twist until Lily felt as though she were only holding on to the faintest tatters of it—the scent of brine and mud, the croak of a raven.

There is more than one right path.

"Let's go back," Strangford quietly offered, and Lily allowed him to pull her gently away.

~

Back in the upstairs hall, they rounded a corner, turning into the other building that made up The Refuge. Strangford led her to a door at the very end. Lily had never been through it though she knew where it led. This was Cairncross's space. The idea of entering it now felt a little like a violation, but Cairncross wasn't here. Nothing was here anymore but the echoes of old dreams.

It was a narrow room with a window that would have overlooked the garden if it weren't covered in thick curtains. A single bed was made up with blankets folded neatly at the corners. A small table beside it was ornately carved with Persian motifs, but Lily sensed it had been chosen more for utility than beauty. It held an unlit lamp and a half-finished book. A drying rack stood by the opposite wall.

There was no dust here. It smelled of lemon polish. The walls were papered in a warm red but stripped of any other decor. The whole arrangement had a Spartan feel to it, reminding her that Cairncross had served in the military in Afghanistan, a part of his life Lily knew almost nothing about. It had always struck her as strange that Cairncross the scholar had once been a soldier.

Strangford carried the coal to the fireplace. He opened the shutter on the dark lantern, allowing a bit more light into the room.

The paper was already laid under the grate. Strangford shook out some of the coal and struck another of his matches. The fire caught, brightening the room with its glow. It was cold, like the rest of the house, but would warm up quickly enough.

He stood, looking down at the little blaze.

"I think Cairncross kept it like this for the days he works late at packing," he said. "You'll be most comfortable here. I can make up a pallet in the studio."

The decision stole over her, warm and gradual as the flames licking up at the dry tinder Strangford had laid. Lily wondered at it only for a moment. Once it was there, she found she had little motive to doubt it.

"No," she said.

He turned sharply, surprised, but as his dark eye took in the expression on her face, everything shifted, an exquisite tension seeping into the room.

"I want you to stay," Lily added with quiet determination. "Here, with me."

There was no mistaking her meaning. That Strangford understood was clear from the emotions that marched across his features, the sharp flare of desire warring with a careful self-control.

"Lily, I know how you feel about this," he breathed, grasping for the latter.

And he did. He had known since the first day he touched her. He knew about the looks respectable women had cast at her mother as they walked down the street, knew the click of the door all the times her father left to go back to the family he belonged to. He'd heard the words in her ear, the label she'd carried all her life: *bastard*.

Felt her father's hand on her shoulder in the cemetery as he made a promise he could not possibly have kept.

All will be well.

He had meant every word, spoken them from the depths of his heart, but duty had made them a lie. That was what it meant to be split between two lives. One would always have to win.

Lily had spent her life being illegitimate. Doing this right had been important to her... but not as important as this.

She held out her hand, her bare skin dancing with the light of the fire.

"See for yourself," she said.

He stripped off his gloves—first one, then the other, exposing his elegant hands to the soft light of the room. He took a step closer to her, hesitating for a breath before entangling his fingers with her own.

The brush of his touch was electric. The energy of it skittered across her palm, raising the fine hairs of her arm.

She didn't have to do anything. What she felt was there, pulsing through her blood. Lily simply waited, opening herself to the power that flashed through her core, racing over her most secret thoughts.

His grip tightened. He tugged her closer, raising their clasped hands between the breath of space that separated them. His gaze burned with the fire of a dark need, then flickered with uncertainty.

"It's been ... I haven't ..." The words failed him, his throat dry. "Done this ... in a very long time."

There was so much in those words, a history Lily knew only in fragments. For Strangford, a kiss could never be casual. It must be wrapped up in guilt over what he could do, how inevitably he must invade the souls of those he touched, exposing every idle thought— each flash of ennui or disappointment. Wishing it was someone else or growing attached to a man who didn't really exist.

When Lily met him less than a year before, he had been wrapped in armor that shielded him from the world. He had been wrapped in it for years.

She raised her free hand, running it through the thick, dark waves of his too-long hair, feeling the familiar warmth of it.

"Don't worry," she replied, an irresistible impulse pulling her mouth into a curve. "I can show you how it works."

He let out a burst of helpless laughter, and Lily's heart grew a little warmer.

His arm slipped around her waist, pulling her firmly closer, and then his lips brushed against her own.

Tenderness quickly shifted to need. Lily knotted her hands in his jumper, pulling him closer. His own fingers were more careful, weaving into the short auburn waves of her hair. His touch raced tingling fires of sensation through her body, flaring into a blaze at every point where his strong frame pressed against her.

His mouth moved to her throat, the delicate skin beneath her ear, and Lily gasped.

Strangford paused, taking in a deep and uneven breath, his forehead pressed against her own. His hands—exposed and vulnerable—hovered at her sides.

"Your tailor," he said, voice a little shaky.

"Mr. Ducasse?"

"He is … distracting."

"Ah," Lily said, a wicked understanding dawning. "You require some assistance."

She stepped back.

She felt a moment of self-consciousness. She was not wearing a fine evening gown. The boots, trousers, and coat of her motorcycling gear belonged more to a working man than a lady, but then this was how he had first known her. It was more honest, perhaps, than jewels and lace would have been.

Lily shrugged out of her coat, letting it fall to the floor. Setting her fingers to the buttons of her blouse, she flicked the first one free.

His gaze darkened, zeroing in on the place where the cool air brushed against her collarbone.

Lily didn't need to be psychometric to know what he was thinking—what he wanted. It was written into every line of his body.

She reached the end of the buttons and slipped off the blouse, the chill of the room shivering over the exposed skin above the silk of her chemise. Unlacing her boots, she set them aside and tugged free her stockings.

The canvas trousers were a bit loose on her to begin with. They slid easily over her hips after she unfastened the waistband.

Lily stepped out of them, her bare feet soft on the worn carpet covering the floor.

The fire had caught, but the room was still far from warm. She felt exposed in her underthings, vulnerable in a way she had never let herself be in the past. It was like standing at the edge of a precipice.

With a breath, Lily launched herself over it.

She tugged off what was left, tossing it aside, and then faced him, standing tall—revealing everything.

She knew her waist wasn't as narrow as was fashionable. Her arms were unusually muscled for a woman, the result of her rigorous training in kali. Her hair was too short. Freckles dusted her skin.

She offered him all of it, apologizing for nothing.

The room was still, the quiet of the night deep around them, the bones of the house long settled. Threads of heat touched her skin, the first gifts of the fire.

Strangford looked at her. Words fell helplessly from his lips.

"You are perfect."

Lily flushed with pride. The vulnerability shifted into something else, something powerful. She stepped over the pile of discarded fabric to where he stood and slipped her hands under his jumper. She could feel the hard planes of his body through the linen of his undershirt.

"I don't share your handicap," she noted.

"No," he agreed, his voice rough in his throat.

She tugged at the wool. He gave way to her, helping her pull it over his head. He was left in his white shirtsleeves and black trousers, just as she had caught him back at Taddiford. It was not enough.

"Your shirt," she ordered.

He obeyed, peeling it off. Firelight danced over the curve of his shoulder, the line of his biceps. Dark hair lightly dusted his skin.

Memory flashed back to her of her vision in the scrying glass months before when she had been searching for clues to the threat that faced Estelle. She had seen him like this, his bare hands gliding over her skin—possessing, worshiping.

She had been so frightened of it then—of how thoroughly this man could upend her world.

She'd had no idea.

He reached for her, pulling her in. Her fingers slid into the dark silk of his hair, the heat of his skin blazing against her own.

His hands devoured her. They glided down the length of her spine, pressed against the curve of her hip. His touch was hungry, drinking her in like a man in a desert might meet a pool of cool, clear water. His kiss sent bolts of awareness shooting into her toes, every nerve raw, sparking up new fires of her own need.

He paused for breath, tracing a finger carefully down the line of her cheek.

"Thank you," he said. His throat rasped with the weight of the words—with how much they meant—and her heart cracked open a little further.

She offered him a smile, otherwise afraid she might start to cry. She touched the black cord that held his eye patch in place.

He tensed, his grip on her waist tightening reflexively. Lily paused for a moment, giving him the chance to stop her.

She pulled the circle of cloth away, taking the time to set it down carefully on the table, then rose to face him again.

The patch didn't hide his scars. Those extended too far above and below, but there was a greater damage here, the price he had paid for trusting her—for choosing to risk his life to protect her own.

He had put himself between her and the fire. Lily knew he would do it again without hesitation. He was a warrior, and he was pledged to her cause.

His look shifted, flashing discomfort.

"I wish I was—" he began.

"Don't you dare," she cut in gently.

She traced the rough skin, following the elegant angles of his jaw. His breath drew in with a shudder, then released. A tension in him uncoiled. It opened the way for something hotter, like oxygen feeding the blaze inside of him.

Strong, powerful hands took hold of her, pulling her closer, molding her to his body. She could feel every inch of his need.

"I want you," he growled, his skin like fire where it brushed her own.

"I'm yours," she replied helplessly.

He lifted her, carrying her to the bed. They fell into it together, entangling further, limbs and flesh and the wild electric energy of his touch. She reached greedily for the clasp of his trousers. He helped her free it, and then there was nothing but Strangford.

He held himself poised over her, the lines of his face outlined by the orange glow of the coals. The hesitation clearly cost him. His forehead fell to hers for a moment. He pulled back, looking down at her.

"Are you sure?" he demanded.

He didn't have to ask. Lily knew he must feel her answer in every cell of this delicious avalanche of connection between them. It moved her that he did so anyway—a mark of honor and respect.

"I have never been more certain of anything in my life," she replied.

~

Lily lay boneless, every muscle softened like bending grass. A draft from the window cut through the warmth of the room. She welcomed it, the cool air a relief against her passion-heated skin.

She was sprawled across Strangford's chest with her head against his shoulder, her fingers smoothing over the strong lines of his torso. The world nipped at her thoughts, trying to push in and remind her of the threats that waited with the dawn—of all that she stood to lose, so much more now even than there had been before. She pushed it back. It took less effort than it ought to, a mere lazy impulse, but there was a greater power in this stillness, in the even pattern of his breath under her breast.

That other subliminal hum was missing—the prickling energy of his psychometry.

"Can you read me right now?" she asked, lifting her head to look down at him, curious.

Strangford lay beneath her, his dark hair mussed, skin glowing. He raised a brow, then opened his eye, surprised.

"No," he replied, wondering. "Not at all."

Lily curled her mouth into a smile.

"Well. Perhaps we should practice this instead of your tàijí," she suggested.

His laughter was tangled through with threads of joy. Lily soaked up every note of it. A truth dawned over her, clear and unquestionable as she let herself fall once more against the man sprawled beneath her in this borrowed bed. She embraced it fearlessly, her own power thrumming warmly through her veins.

She would fight the world for this.

SIXTEEN

Saturday, December 19th
Ten in the morning
The Refuge, Bedford Square

LILY PLUCKED THE steaming kettle from the cooker in the bare kitchen of The Refuge. The window behind her was patched with a bit of cardboard where Strangford had broken one of the panes. The sun had risen a couple of hours before but still felt low in the sky with the solstice just around the corner.

She had lain in far later than usual that morning. She'd had a good excuse for it.

Spooning tea leaves into the pot, she let her thoughts dwell on that excuse. Her body still ached from the night before . . . and the gloom of pre-dawn, and again after the sun had just peered over the horizon.

She had left Strangford asleep a few minutes before. The curtain was still drawn upstairs, the dying light of the embers painting the perfect lines of his body as he sprawled on the narrow bed. His hand lay relaxed and open against the pillow. There would be elements of Cairncross he would inevitably pick up on from lying in his bed, echoes of careful routines and restless sleep, but she suspected the force of what they had shared on those sheets would render them fairly pale.

She looked down at the dark swirl of the Oolong leaves, a slow and elegant storm in the steaming water of the teapot. If she were a witch, she would spell the house out of the world, pluck it from time and lie here with Strangford until the end of all days.

Lily knew that was impossible. The world lurked outside the garden walls with all its threats and responsibilities. Kazi would be playing bloodhound on their trail. He would find The Refuge eventually. He was too clever not to. The murder charge awaited, as did the murderer, a man who it seemed was likely passing England's secrets to her enemies.

The violence of Scarborough couldn't be forgotten. It would happen again if the spy wasn't stopped.

She recalled Strangford's words to her in the library the night before.

There must be some point to it. Something I can do.

Lily understood. The same need echoed through her own heart in response as she stood in the pale winter light of the empty kitchen. The vision of Strangford in the trenches filled her with a bone-deep fear, and yet she knew she could not run from it forever. The man she fell in love with had always believed in fighting for what was right.

Lily had no illusions that her own government was free of sin. She'd faced too many of its demons already, but that did not mean this conflict lacked clear lines of right and wrong. Someone had to hold those who would use, violate, and destroy the innocent accountable.

It was what Zhao Min had demanded of her in the street near St. Pancras Station the last time Lily saw her.

We call it bàoyìng—that good or evil deeds are repaid in kind. But who does the repaying?

She lifted the pot, pouring the tea. Usually, she preferred a little milk and sugar, but there was none to be had in the house. She drank it black. The liquid was tannic, bracing but not unpleasant. She let the bitterness of it slide over her tongue as she stood at the narrow kitchen window, looking out into the winter-dry wilderness of the garden.

A raven settled onto the bare branches of a cherry tree. It was a lean, ragged city bird, grasping the wood with thick black claws. It made her uneasy. Ravens always did, ever since the night she fought Joseph Hartwell and won. She had paid a dark price for that victory.

Sam had told her that Strangford had earned a boon from the birds for his sacrifice at Blackfriars. Lily knew the ravens could find anything or anyone you wanted. They might even be able to find Brockmeyer's murderer—though Kazi would hardly take the word of an animal on the subject.

It felt like there was something more to that word—*boon*. It brought to mind djinn trapped in lamps, the sort of wishes that easily twisted into curses.

Even if what the ravens offered truly was a gift, was now the time to use it?

Lily was still contemplating the question when the door to the carriage house opened, and a tall, lean figure in a thick wool coat stepped into the yard. The raven startled from the branch, cawing its way back up into the pale morning sky.

It was James Cairncross. Lily found she was not particularly surprised to see him. Setting down her tea, she picked up her own coat and went out to meet him in the garden.

The air was crisp, the dry brown stalks of the flowers dusted with frost. The old Scotsman raised his cool blue eyes as Lily emerged from the kitchen.

"I thought it must be you," he noted.

His northern brogue was a bit more apparent than usual, but then he would have had to rise early to get here at this hour from Rotherham.

It had been over a month since she'd last seen him. Lily's relationship with The Refuge's librarian had always run hot and cold. His loyal role in some of Ash's tests and manipulations had occasionally made her want to throttle him. Today, she found herself oddly glad he was here.

"How did you know?" Lily asked.

Cairncross's hands were stuffed into his pockets, his shoulders a little hunched against the cold.

"The sparrows," he replied. "Blasted things started pecking at my window at two o'clock in the morning. Sam set them to watch after the place and must have told them I was the one to harass if they found something amiss."

"That sounds like something Sam would do," Lily admitted.

"I take it something is indeed amiss," Cairncross noted, his sharp eyes moving to the cardboard patched onto the kitchen window.

"Strangford is wanted for murder," Lily replied.

"Did he do it?" Cairncross asked bluntly.

Lily raised an irritated eyebrow.

"I'm not saying it wouldn't have been for good reason," Cairncross returned. "Μούνοι θεοφιλέες, ὅσοις εχθρόν το αδικέειν."

"English, please?" Lily said.

"*The gods love the enemies of injustice,*" Cairncross returned. "From Democritus."

He looked down at a stone that had come loose from the border of one of the flower beds, bending to neatly set it back into place.

It was Cairncross who had been left with the responsibility of caring for this place. The words spilled out of her before she could think better of them.

"You're giving it up."

Cairncross didn't look at her. He appeared to be studying the flower bed.

"A boys' primary school out of Kent. They wish to open an auxiliary location closer to the city. There will be twenty-five pupils and three staff."

It was a sensible solution, however terrible it sounded. Buildings did not maintain themselves, and a place like The Refuge must be especially costly to keep up. And what would be the point? There was no one here anymore.

She thought of small feet pounding up and down the grand staircase, the familiar rooms echoing with young voices. Chalkboards hung on the walls of the library and the parlor, the upstairs bedrooms lined with bunks. It was an entirely appropriate use for the space.

The light over the garden was brightening, sparkling against the little crystals of ice covering the dried geometry of the dead blossoms and neglected herbs. It was quiet, as it always was in this place, a strange island of peace in the middle of the city.

However painful these changes were for Lily, they must be even worse for Cairncross. The Refuge hadn't just been an emotional sanctuary for him. It had been his literal home. However stuffy and irritable he had seemed, Lily knew he had found a great deal of peace in his books and his artifacts—in the wisdom he was able to lift from them and pass on to those who might be able to use it.

And Ash had been here. Lily didn't know much about the history between the two men, but Cairncross's loyalty to Ash ran ferociously deep. That didn't come out of nowhere. It had to be earned.

"Why did you come here?" she demanded.

"I told you. The sparrows—"

"I mean in the first place," she cut in.

Cairncross's expression grew more guarded.

"Ash brought me."

"But why? How did the two of you come together? You've never told me."

Cairncross didn't answer. His hands remained resolutely tucked into his pockets, his collar turned up against the chill. He turned to the southwest, the movement an instinct, looking to someplace Lily could sense was very far away.

"He found me at Lahore," he replied. "In the Punjab."

"After you fought in Afghanistan?"

"Yes."

Cairncross had never spoken of his military history with Lily. She only knew of it because of a slip of the tongue by his old colleague, Eddie Adler, the boatman who had piloted them through the Essex marshes last summer. Even without Adler, it should have been obvious. She could see it now in every line of him—the close cut of his silver hair, his neatly trimmed mustache, the rigid straightness of his bearing. She wondered how she had ever failed to notice it before.

Lily waited for more of the story, but Cairncross didn't offer it.

"Were you already studying charismatics then?" she prodded.

"No," he replied shortly.

"So, it was Ash who sparked your interest?"

"No!"

Cairncross's tone had sharpened. Lily startled, but of course it must a sensitive subject. Ash had been very important to him. She couldn't guess what his grief might be like, but it likely ran much deeper than her own.

If it wasn't meeting Ash that drew Cairncross to the study of charismatics, what had it been? She wanted to ask, and yet it was clear to her that her questions would be far from welcome.

"This murder," Cairncross said, firmly changing the subject. "I take it the matter is serious?"

Lily nodded, feeling the weight of it settle back onto her shoulders.

"What can I do to help?" he asked.

The offer was genuine, but Lily wasn't sure how to answer. It was all such a horrible puzzle. A dead man in a room no one could have been inside of—other than the lover she had left sleeping upstairs. A spy disguised to draw out another spy. The threat it all might pose to the outcome of the war loomed over her. Even the information Bonnie had shared with her outside Strangford's house about seeing Dicky on the terrace only muddied the waters even further.

"Can you tell me how a man could be in two places at once?" she muttered.

Cairncross frowned.

"You mean bilocation?" he offered.

The garden seemed to grow even quieter, its details suddenly etched with a deeper precision—dry leaves, brown stalks, the delicate veil of frost.

"What did you say?" Lily demanded.

"In September of 1774, St. Alphonsus de Liguori was meditating before Mass in Campania when he announced that Pope Clement XIV had just died. Later, there were multiple reports that the saint had been seen in Rome ministering to the dying Pope—that he was, in fact, present in two geographically distant places at the same moment in time. He is one of several saints said to have possessed the ability."

Echoes of old memories rose in her mind—the hard pew of St. Patrick's in Soho under her dress as she sat there beside her mother, the priest droning on about men she knew only as tonsured figures in stained glass windows.

"But that's a miracle," she replied automatically. "How can that have anything to do with us?"

Cairncross raised an eloquent white eyebrow.

"We have discussed this," he noted.

It was true. The history of charismatics was one of Cairncross's favorite subjects. Lily had heard his theories on the subject a dozen times over.

"But we were talking about seeing the future or speaking to the dead. If people were capable of popping up in two places at the same time, surely the world would know about it."

"The world did know about it. There are several excellent cases among the more advanced Hindu mystics. Pythagoras himself was said to have appeared in both Thurii and Metapontum on the same afternoon."

"You know what I mean," Lily countered.

Cairncross sighed. He looked tired.

"You would be surprised what people can ignore when they put their minds to it," he noted. "But by my estimation, it was historically a very uncommon form of khárisma. There aren't many reliable accounts of it, and even those peter out around the mid-eighteenth century. It is almost certainly extinct."

He said the word casually, but it caught at Lily's mind.

"What does that mean, extinct?" she demanded.

He didn't answer right away. In the distance, Lily could hear the low rumble of a passing train.

"There are forms of khárisma described in ancient literature which are not observed in modern contexts," he said. "Bilocation is one of them. There are others. Raising the dead, for example. Levitation or flight. Achieving immortality. The animation of inanimate objects or substances, as in the creation of a golem."

He swallowed thickly.

"The transformative battle-rage of a berserker," he finished flatly. "These phenomena are described over millennia across widely disparate cultures but are not so much as whispered of in modern times. It could be that these powers were mere fantasy on the part of the authors of those stories, but I have theorized that the truth is more Darwinian in nature. Such powers are sensational and obvious in their effects, inevitably drawing a great deal of attention to those who exercise them. Charismatics who draw a lot of attention to themselves frequently end up dead."

The conclusion was harsh, but Lily didn't need to be convinced that it was valid. Less than a year ago, she had fought a man who systematically murdered those who spoke to the dead, searching for a way to claim their power for himself.

"Those who are dead can't make more charismatics," Cairncross said.

The conclusion surprised her. It reminded her uncomfortably of some of the things she had heard Joseph Hartwell say. The man had been a eugenicist, after all, convinced that controlling human bloodlines was the secret to launching the species into the next phase of its evolution.

"You think khárisma is inheritable?"

"Perhaps," he replied, then corrected himself. "I haven't the foggiest idea. There are indications it sometimes runs in families, particularly some of the lesser powers, but there are also countless cases of charismatics who are the first among their relations."

"Gifts of grace," Lily said, quietly echoing Ash's translation for the word he had used to describe what she and Strangford and the others were.

"Robert's theory, yes," Cairncross noted. "The divine impulse of the Parliament of Stars."

"You don't agree," she countered.

He looked away to somewhere far beyond the walls of the garden. He seemed to have aged since they began their conversation.

"A berserker in full battle rage could tear a man in half with his bare hands. I find it hard to see the will of God in that."

Cairncross's careful, wary tone spoke of old secrets. It reminded her that there was still so much she did not know about khárisma— about people like her and where they had come from. There were other things to worry about now.

"How does bilocation work?" she demanded.

"The details of the accounts vary, but as best I can determine, it's a form of spiritual or psychic projection. The physical body remains in place, but an energetic form that can be made to appear whole is sent abroad. Certain Taoist adepts were said to be able to do it if they had acquired sufficient qi and shen to sustain two distinct life forces. I honestly couldn't tell you whether the projection actually appears in space or whether it is a working of influence on the minds of those present, convincing people they saw something rather than actually presenting it to them."

"Could it speak? This projection?" Lily pressed.

"There are stories of bilocating priests preaching sermons," Cairncross answered.

"What about physically impacting things? Could a projection lift something? Strike someone?"

The question came out with more urgency than she intended, but Lily found that her pulse was drumming.

"The projection of a bilocator has no physical form," Cairncross replied. "It's only spirit. It would require an immense mustering of energy to make any kind of physical impact in that state."

Brockmeyer's murder had been committed by someone inside the house. Only Strangford and herself lacked alibis for the time of the lieutenant's death, but if it was possible that someone else at Taddiford could be in two places at once . . .

It was hard for her to even consider it. They were speaking of the impossible, the stuff of legends and fairy-tales—but Lily lived in that world. Faced with the reality of her own abilities, how hard was it to believe that there might be someone else out there who possessed an even stranger power? That a khárisma that had existed in the past might still linger, however rarely, in the present?

Her head spun with notions of what else might be real—dragon-haunted mountains or men with the bloodthirsty strength of monsters. She had to focus.

Dicky Anstruther-Fields had been seen passed out in his chair by both Walford and George during the time of Brockmeyer's death . . . and yet he had also been witnessed out on the terrace by Bonnie at the same time. Of course, one of them could be mistaken, but there was still the unalterable fact that someone had driven Brockmeyer's skull in with a shovel, and it had not been Strangford. If there were no other possible suspects, then Lily must consider the impossible ones.

Lily tugged at the memories, trying to shuffle them into some kind of sense. Kazi had said that Dicky got up to relieve himself shortly after eleven, neglecting to close the door after he stumbled back in. George had needed to rise and do it for him. He had lain there, seemingly insensate, until after Brockmeyer's corpse was discovered.

But even if Dicky was capable of bilocation—a mad notion Lily allowed herself to consider—his projection still would have been incapable of delivering the fatal blow to the lieutenant's skull.

She paced down the garden path, boots cracking against the gravel. It felt as though she were trying to put together a puzzle with the pieces turned around the wrong way.

"Could someone bilocate invisibly?" Lily demanded.

"I haven't the foggiest idea," Cairncross replied.

"But could they project themselves anywhere they liked?" she pressed.

"Again—I cannot know precisely how it works, having never met such a charismatic myself—but I strongly suspect it would require some sort of connection to the space they wished to enter. One would have to be able to visualize it, connect with it on a psychic level. That must be very hard to do with a location one had never been before."

But if the spy were someone who already knew the Admiralty—someone who worked there … any room might be open to him. Perhaps he couldn't yank loose file drawers, but a page might be left carelessly out on a desk in a place thought to be secure. Conversations might be overheard.

Dicky also had connections to the continent. Celia had spoken of how they had stayed at the Duke of Saxe-Coburg and Gotha's estate on their honeymoon—the duke who was Dicky's old school friend as well as a general in the Kaiser's army.

If Dicky was somehow able to project himself into the duke's residence—relay some of the secrets he had uncovered in the Admiralty…

And of course, it need not have been Dicky's projection that Bonnie had seen leaving the conservatory. He had been outside earlier in the evening. His physical body might have gone into the glasshouse to wait for Brockmeyer while his projection went back into the room with Walford and George.

That, of course, was why he had not been able to close the door behind himself when he came in.

Her head spun with it, every shred of modern sensibility rebelling against the idea, and yet the logic fit. He had been *seen in two places at once.*

Dicky Anstruther-Fields was the spy threatening England's future in the war. He had murdered Brockmeyer for it, but that was not what rooted her to the spot, dizzying her with its implications as she stood in the shadow of what remained of The Refuge.

"He's one of us," Lily gasped, raising her eyes to Cairncross's weathered face. "Dicky is one of us."

Discovering others like herself had been the most important moment of Lily's life. It had given her a family, the strength to accept herself for what she was.

"Are you talking about the murderer?" Cairncross pressed.

Lily put her hands to her temples, her head pounding.

"Ash would have reached out to him. Wouldn't he? Is that what I should do?" she demanded.

The question twisted inside of her, threatening to tear her in half. Dicky was a charismatic. He belonged at The Refuge . . . and he was a murderer and a spy. He'd cornered Bonnie in the upstairs hallway, either thoughtlessly or deliberately leveraging his superior social position to coerce her into sex.

Lily's skin still revolted against her own memories of uninvited hands on her arms, her breasts.

"I . . . don't know how to answer that," Cairncross replied, paling.

"Ash said we were gifted with it. That we were chosen."

Her voice was shaking.

"Robert Ash had a great deal of faith," Cairncross carefully returned.

Yes—Ash had faith. It was faith that had led him to transform his home into a sanctuary for those afflicted with powers that tormented them with knowledge they never asked for. It was faith that made him drive Lily to further extremes with tests that bordered on torment until the day he had nearly burned the two of them alive.

She did not know what it was that made him take a pair of wires in his hand so that Lily and Sam could escape the disaster that devoured half of the Blackfriars rail bridge. Perhaps faith had done that too.

She found herself thinking of the charred black glove on Taddiford's conservatory floor. Strangford would have been perfectly visible alone in the library to someone standing outside those glowing windows on the terrace. Dicky had *meant* for him to take the blame for Brockmeyer's death, knowing the world would be incapable of imagining the flaw in his own alibi.

It was too much—anger and fear muddling together with guilt and responsibility. It shouldn't be left to Lily to sort it all out. That was Ash's job, but Ash was gone.

Strangford pushed through the kitchen door, striding quickly through the garden.

"Kazi has found us," he announced, taking Lily's arm, burning with purpose. "We have to run."

SEVENTEEN

EAR SNAPPED THROUGH her. If she was right about Dicky, the story was far too fantastic for there to be any hope of convincing Kazi to take it seriously. They needed more evidence, and they couldn't acquire it if they were in jail.

"He'll have men in the mews," Lily pointed out as Strangford propelled her toward the carriage house, Cairncross following.

"I know," he replied. "That's why we're taking the Ghost."

Lily dug in her heels as he pushed through the door to where Ash's silver Rolls Royce lay shrouded.

"But you don't know how to drive," she protested.

"I'm not going to drive it," Strangford replied. "You are."

"I've only ever driven a motorbike!"

"And a hijacked Army lorry," Cairncross helpfully pointed out.

"You told me Sam was starting to teach you," Strangford pressed.

"Barely. He just pointed out the controls while we were driving one afternoon."

"It's that, or you escape alone on the Triumph," he cut back.

"And leave you to him? Absolutely not."

Strangford smiled knowingly.

"Shall we, then?"

Cairncross pulled free the canvas covering the vehicle with a snap of his wrists, a new layer of dust swirling into the dim air. The Ghost gleamed in the semi-darkness. Even with its canvas top folded neatly back against the boot, it looked enormous.

"I've read the manual. I can tell you the starting sequence,"

Cairncross offered, oblivious to Lily's rising panic. "Start with the fuel valve. It's outside on the driver's side, just above the fender."

She hated everything about this plan. The Ghost was neither a motorbike nor an Army lorry. She had no idea what she was doing.

Strangford watched her quietly as Cairncross moved to unlatch the carriage bay doors.

"You'll need to activate the battery under the driver's seat," the librarian continued. "Then pump up the fuel pressure to exactly one half-pound."

Lily bit out a curse that would have turned Sam's East End ears blue and stalked to the automobile.

Strangford smiled at her and went to join Cairncross, holding the other side of the two wooden panels that would slide back to open the carriage house to the alley.

"Now what?" she called once she'd picked out the fuel pump from the dizzying array of levers and gauges on the Ghost's dash.

"Turn on the magneto and adjust the carburetor—no, it's there, on the steering wheel! Then feed it some fuel and hit the starter."

Lily looked to Cairncross and Strangford, who stood ready to yank open the doors.

"You'll both have to jump in as I pull through," she warned. "We'll only have the element of surprise for a moment."

"Both?" Cairncross startled. "But I'm not going."

"He'll arrest you if you stay," Lily returned.

"That's perfectly fine with me," the librarian asserted.

"You can't help us if you've been arrested," she shot back. "We need you."

Cairncross closed his eyes, fighting some quick inner war. His gaze moved inexplicably to Strangford.

"Do you know?" he demanded.

His voice was thick with a tense significance Lily did not begin to understand.

"Know what?" she demanded.

"We're out of time," Strangford carefully replied, meeting the older man's gaze.

It was not an answer. It was also true.

Lily pumped the accelerator, extended her finger to the ignition, and took a breath.

She wanted to see the future, to push her awareness forward into what waited for them in the alley. Whether the car would start when she pushed the button or choke on a surplus of fuel or a dearth of pressure. The Rolls Royce was a beast, an enormous monstrosity of chrome and steel. How could she possibly do this?

The door behind them smashed open. Kazi stood framed in it, four constables at his back.

She jammed her finger into the starter button.

The engine blazed to life. Cairncross and Strangford yanked open the doors as Lily threw the car into gear and slammed her foot into the pedal.

Kazi bolted toward them.

The Ghost responded with alacrity, leaping forward like a lion waiting to pounce. It flew out into the mews, Strangford leaping into the seat beside her as Cairncross half-tumbled into the rear.

Kazi's hand grasped the back of the automobile.

In the mirror, Lily glimpsed how Cairncross twisted, nimble as a cat, his left arm flashing out. It caught the inspector on the shoulder, tossing him into the wall of the carriage house like a child's thrown toy.

Strangford pivoted in his seat, catching hold of Cairncross with a black-gloved hand. The librarian whirled, something a little wild and strained in the movement.

"James," Strangford said, his voice low and forceful.

Lily tore her attention from the two men, forced to contend with the task of piloting this massive silver missile. She wrenched the wheel, the tires screaming against the macadam as the automobile pivoted. A pair of startled policemen stared at her from the end of the narrow way.

Lily stomped the pedal to the floor and felt the Ghost lurch in response, flattening her back against the seat as it roared forward.

The policemen scattered, falling to either side as she blew past them, skidding around the corner. Bedford Square flashed by, and then the Rolls Royce was flying towards Shaftsbury Avenue.

Strangford settled more comfortably into the seat beside her as Cairncross slumped down in the back, covering his face with his hands.

"So, where are we going?" Strangford asked.

Lily gave the wheel a quick tug to avoid a post office lorry blocking part of the road. The Ghost responded neatly, dancing into an opening in the traffic.

"Dicky Anstruther-Fields' house," she replied. "If you happen to know where it is."

She could see that the direction surprised him.

"Putney," he replied, studying her thoughtfully. "Near Wandsworth Park."

"Probably best if we avoid Whitehall," Cairncross noted from the rear, his voice just a bit ragged.

He was right, of course. There did tend to be rather a surplus of police around the heart of Britain's government.

Lily glanced back at the librarian through the mirror, aware that something strange had taken place during their escape from the house. Now was certainly not the time to ask about it.

"Right, then," she replied and swung them neatly around the glowing marquees of Piccadilly.

~

Lily ground the clutch once or twice as they wove through the posh streets of Belgravia and Chelsea, neighborhoods where the Ghost blended in comfortably. Driving the auto was an altogether different experience from piloting her Triumph. She missed the way the motorbike responded nimbly to subtle shifts in her weight. Turning the Rolls Royce required muscle, but the vehicle thrummed with strength and power, cocooning her as they glided along the streets.

Strangford had taken off his glove, asking her the needed question with a look. Lily nodded, and he slipped his hand to the back of her neck, the only exposed skin he could touch without interfering with her driving. It was easier than trying to shout explanations over the noise of the road and the rush of the chill winter wind.

From the corner of her eye, she could see his expression shift from surprise to a flash of simmering anger.

Nearing the river, the far less posh environs of Battersea loomed into view, the gasworks, factories, rail yards, and slums rising across the water. They finally bridged the Thames at Wandsworth, the river reduced to a tamer gray band here in the westernmost reaches of London's sprawl. Painted houseboats and pleasure barges were tied up at the short little wharves rather than the great oily freighters of the docks.

In Putney, the houses were tidy, window boxes stuffed with holly and evergreens. Everything had more air. The buildings were granted ample room to breathe, generously interspersed with graceful trees. People walked dogs or strolled to the shops down quiet little streets. It was the sort of place that had been built recently but very artfully made to look as though it had been there forever.

They passed the lovely green of a park, the glittering water of the Thames visible on the far side of it, flashing in and out of view between the trunks of old oaks.

"Just ahead on the right," Strangford said.

Lily slowed where he directed, bringing the car to a brief halt alongside the house. It was large by Lily's standards, perhaps five bedrooms encased in sedate gray stone. The narrower side of the building fronted the street, the longer frame of it looking out over an acre of walled private garden set right on the banks of the river. There was money here, the kind that showed itself off with quiet good taste.

She pushed the Ghost a little past it, pulling into a tidy side street. Strangford lowered his hand.

"Do you understand?" Lily asked.

"Perfectly," Strangford replied thinly, tugging on his glove.

"We'll need much more than this to convince Kazi," she pointed out.

"Then let us go acquire it," Strangford returned grimly, pushing out of the automobile.

Lily joined him on the pavement, staring across the road at the house. Access to the inside would give Strangford a chance to read objects that were more personal to Dicky and perhaps uncover evidence that would tie him more concretely to either the murder or the espionage—evidence someone like Kazi would actually believe.

She winced at the thought of the inspector. He wasn't a monster. Lily believed he truly wished to understand the truth about Brockmeyer's death. Had their escape from The Refuge only cemented his suspicions, turning him definitively into an enemy?

Lily looked to Cairncross, who was still hunched quietly in the rear seat.

"Could you ring the door? Distract the staff long enough for us to find a way in?" she asked.

He didn't answer.

"Cairncross?" she prompted.

"Yes," he abruptly blurted. "I'll manage it."

He climbed out, stalking toward the house without any further comment.

"Are you up for this?" Strangford asked.

She understood what he left unsaid. This was the home of a wealthy gentleman in the middle of the day. It would be packed with servants, perhaps even the family. Getting through it undetected would take more than stealth and luck.

"Yes," she replied.

Lily quickly assessed their options. She settled on the narrow alley at the back of the house, where the property was separated from the estate next door by a high brick wall. It was a service corridor, something only utilized by servants and tradesmen.

She jogged across the road, Strangford following beside her.

The alley was long and narrow, shadowed by the high walls to either side. A little sliver of the water was visible at the far end of it, even that view an unimaginable luxury to a woman who had once shared a room over Covent Garden with a bevy of noisy chorus girls. It still felt like a gauntlet Lily was about to run.

She pushed the fear aside, along with her confusion about what they would find once they got inside the house, and drew on her power. It rose up in response, quick and oddly joyful, as though it had been waiting for her. Lily let it pour into every nerve, infusing her with its energy.

The feeling was familiar, like stepping into a well-worn shoe, but something had changed. She felt it as a darker current twisting through her core, tasting of copper on her tongue. It whispered to her of violence, speaking in the tongue she had heard at the Poplar Hippodrome the night Jack Cannon fell.

Recognition snapped her out of it, the power shivering apart, leaving her mundane and exposed at the mouth of the alley. She gasped at the impact of it.

It hadn't been like this when she last deliberately used her power at Taddiford. Why was it happening now?

The answer presented itself to Lily with perfect clarity—*because I am approaching my enemy.*

She forced herself to reconnect to that quiet readiness that would tell her how to navigate them to their goal. It still tasted of blood. She ignored it, directing her will at what mattered.

"This way," she ordered, leading Strangford forward.

Two doors opened from the house into the alley. One lay midway along the building, the other at the far end, near the river. Lily's instincts led her to the first.

Strangford waited beside her.

Not yet, her power whispered, even as it warned her of a disturbance, something about to crack the quiet of the service corridor. Panic bolted through her at the thought of it, but Lily forced herself to steady, putting her hand on Strangford's arm to keep him still.

The farther door slammed open. A kitchen maid stalked out, holding a bucket of refuse. She dumped it into the tip, then pivoted neatly and strode back into the house without so much as a glance up the alley to where Lily and Strangford were standing.

The door at the far end snapped firmly shut. Lily let out a breath, returning her attention to the entrance in front of her, the one that called with subtle pressure.

"Now," she said at last.

Strangford turned the knob, and they slipped inside.

The hallway was narrow and sparsely furnished, signaling to Lily that they had entered the area of the house reserved for the servants. The clatter at the far end revealed the presence of the kitchens.

Lily crept the opposite way, a murmur of voices there becoming clearer. She could make out Cairncross rattling on about overdue library books.

They had made it inside, but what now? Strangford knew something of the layout of the place, but which room was most likely to hold what they were looking for? Some kind of study, perhaps? Or a breakfast room?

The power that granted her knowledge of what was coming next wouldn't answer that question. She had to ask something else—and trust whatever answer it gave her.

Lily reached for her onmyōdō.

The smell of salt and decay rose, the brine and rot of the marshes. Shimmering threads of possibility moved through her. Lily let herself glide along them, tossed in their currents as she pressed her question against them.

Where should we go?

Her awareness shot forward, racing along the threads.

Strangford grapples with a swarm of policemen, arms pinned, boots striking out.

The nervous rustle of the House of Lords, full of gilt and crimson pomp. Strangford's black shoulders holding steady against the crack of a gavel. The clang of bars, chains scraping against stone.

It was the broadest thread, the one paved almost like a road. Lily would not accept it. She must find another.

Show me, she ordered, remembering the lessons a dead woman had once whispered in her ear. *Show me how to change it.*

Another thread glimmered delicately, whispering with strange music as Lily reached for it.

Night-dark waves crash against the shore. Ice stings her cheek. Tariq Kazi, dark hair plastered to his forehead, raises a pistol in his hand.

She falls further, deeper.

A cave of ice glitters with a pale and unworldly blue. Flower petals fall softly through drifting clouds of smoke.

Strangford's face streaked with mud, framed in an alley of wood and wire. The shriek of death cutting through the gray air.

Lily lurched back from it, terror freezing her blood.

Not that—anything but that.

She held herself suspended between the two possibilities in a salt-scented abyss. Uncertainty twisted inside of her, threatening to tear her apart.

"I can't do this," she breathed, surfacing enough to recognize that strong arms were wrapped around her body, holding her upright. The solid strength of Strangford's chest was a wall against her back.

Somewhere nearby, Cairncross's voice continued to drone.

He pressed his lips to her temple. She felt his arms tighten around her as he absorbed some fragment of her conflict. His power would focus on the most powerful emotion. This time she knew it would be fear.

"This is about more than us, Lily," he said, his breath warm against her cheek.

He was right. There was so much more at stake. Others had already died for this. More would join them if Lily and Strangford didn't find a way to stop it.

She took a deep, shuddering breath, letting herself lean into his strength. She pushed herself back into that other place—the one that whispered of unseen grasses, echoing with the harsh call of a carrion eater—and felt for the threads once more.

Lily grasped the weaker line, the less certain one, plummeting into it once again.

Cold rain stings against her cheek. A light flashes over dark water.

Blood seeps across the ground toward a pair of pale green slippers.

A staff balances in her hand, both familiar and strange.

The rustling of black feathers. The screams of monsters in the smoke.

She opened herself to all of it, letting it spill through her, all those whispering possibilities.

Yes, she told it. *This.*

The answer rose, glowing softly with certainty.

Shaving oil and the scent of cedar. A narrow window framed in rustling wool and tweed.

"We need to go to his dressing room," Lily whispered.

It was not the answer she had expected. Nothing about it made sense.

"The master suite is upstairs, facing the river," Strangford murmured in reply. "There's a service stair by the kitchen."

He started to move back that way. Lily's hand flashed out to stop him.

"No," she said, instinct flaring.

With a leap of something that felt oddly like faith, she stepped from the servant's hall.

She stood in the wide, high-ceilinged entry to the house. The walls were papered in pale blue silk, hung with tasteful landscapes. A fine Turkish carpet covered the floor.

In the doorway, Cairncross loomed over a handsome footman. The young man's broad back was to her. He looked ready to slam the door in Cairncross's face.

The Scotsman's blue gaze flickered to where Lily stood. She jerked her head to the staircase that rose beside them. He shifted his attention neatly back to the footman.

"Does Mr. Anstruther-Fields have a library? If I can browse the shelves, I'm sure I can find it. Lord Thornberry requires the book most insistently. I'm quite sure Mr. Anstruther-Fields would prefer the matter be settled promptly. This way, is it?"

Cairncross didn't wait for an answer, stalking past the footman and pivoting into the depths of the house. The footman hurried after him, sputtering.

Lily dashed forward, hurrying to the stairs as quickly as she could without her feet pounding on the floorboards, knowing Strangford would follow. Her hand glided along the smoothly polished surface of the banister as she twisted around the corner.

"End of the hall," Strangford said from behind her as she reached the top.

She followed the direction, nearly running, then threw herself abruptly to a stop just shy of an open doorway.

The knowing held her for six beats of her heart, then urged her forward. She crossed the opening just as the maid turned to make up the bed.

At the end of the hall, she put her hand to the door and hesitated, a brief flicker of panic pulling her up short.

It was Saturday. Dicky Anstruther-Fields was a man of licentious habits. Though it was nearly half-past ten in the morning, it was entirely possible he was still in bed.

Her power continued to urge her forward, oblivious to this logic.

Lily pushed her way inside. The bed was empty, already neatly made. Broad windows behind it looked out over the Thames, spilling the soft light of an overcast morning into the room.

She could hear someone humming.

Two doors led off the bedroom, one to either side of the bed. The sound emanated from the one on the left. Lily slowly turned to look through the door and saw Celia seated at a vanity table in front of an enormous mirror. She was looking down at her jewelry box, her fingers picking through an assortment of glittering earrings.

Lily and Strangford were framed perfectly in the reflection of the looking-glass.

Lily reacted on instinct, pushing Strangford back against the wall beside the door. They were out of Celia's view for now, but she would see them the moment she left the dressing room.

Where could they hide? How would they explain why they were here?

The fear burnt through her connection to her power, frying her sense of what was coming next. She turned to Strangford, the panic written large on her face.

He took her arm, his lips at her ear.

"Close. Low," he ordered with a breath, pulling her down.

He crouched at the side of Celia's dressing room door, glancing in and then darting—quick and silent—across the open doorway, tugging Lily along behind him.

She glanced inside as she passed by, glimpsing Celia gazing at herself in the glass as she set a dangling ruby into her earlobe.

Strangford caught her, pulling her to her feet and pressing her behind the looming shadow of a tall dresser. It was a poor hiding place. Celia would see them immediately if she came back into the room and turned toward the river.

"Be ready," Strangford breathed at her ear.

Celia stepped out of the dressing room, pushing a button to kill the electric light. She crossed to the foot of the bed.

Strangford pulled Lily around the dresser, spinning her into the gloom of the dressing room.

It was almost as large as Lily's bedroom on March Place, though much of that space was consumed by racks of dresses and gowns. Shelves held elaborate hats and an assortment of shoes. The only light was a soft, cool glow from a narrow window.

It seemed like a safe enough place to wait until Celia had left—until Lily's power flared with a sharp warning.

She grabbed Strangford and pushed him into a thick forest of silk gowns. The dresses rustled back into place with a soft clicking of beads.

Lily pressed against Strangford in the shadows, waiting.

Celia strode back in. She plucked a shawl from the chair by the vanity and pulled it around her shoulders.

Then she was gone. Lily heard the click of a door.

Strangford stepped out, offering her a gloved hand.

"Shall we get on with it, then?" he asked.

"Yes," Lily agreed, climbing out of the nest of evening wear.

EIGHTEEN

THEY STEPPED OUT of Celia's dressing room. The river gleamed softly outside the windows, framed in bare branches. Lily could hear voices in the hall. She tested the future for another threat. The sense that echoed back to her whispered of urgency but not an immediate danger. There was certainly no time to waste.

Lily crossed to the opposite door, the one that must lead to their destination, and pushed the button for the light.

Dicky's dressing room was identical to his wife's, with the same small window looking out over the water. Instead of dresses, the racks on the walls held trousers, shirts, jackets, and waistcoats. A preponderance of gray and navy was brightened by flashes of color—a red scarf, the glimmer of gold thread in an embroidered waistcoat. There was a vanity table here as well, smaller and less crowded than the one in Celia's room. An open jewelry box glinted with cuff links and tie pins.

Lily tried to feel for some further sense of direction, but nothing presented itself.

"I'm not... entirely sure why we're here," she admitted.

Strangford stepped past her.

"Because these will be the things that know him most intimately," he replied.

It made perfect sense once Strangford voiced it. A chair in the parlor might grant them layered impressions of Dicky sipping his morning tea. If there was a study in the house, Lily found it unlikely a man like Dicky would spend much time in it.

The objects crowding this dressing room would spend hours close to his skin. They would go with him wherever he went.

Strangford took off his gloves, tucking them into his pockets. He extended his hand to the sleeve of a jacket, then hesitated.

She had some idea of what demons he must be confronting. Dicky was a friend of the family, and Strangford was about to tear into all of his secrets. It was something he had scrupulously avoided for most of his life because it so often led to complications and disappointment or left him feeling wretched about peering into the private universes people kept carefully hidden from the rest of the world. If they were wrong about Dicky's involvement in the murder, Strangford was about to learn the darkest truths about someone who was married to his sister's best friend.

She could remind him of all that was at stake, but Strangford already knew. Lily kept quiet, and a moment later his fingers brushed the pinstriped wool of Dicky's suit.

He moved down the row of jackets with his eyes closed, as though feeling his way through darkness, pausing here or there to linger on a waistcoat or a necktie, his mouth twisting with a frown. Something about his movements reminded Lily of her onmyōdō, the way using it required her to glide through the space around her—through possibility—until something lit up in her awareness.

She watched him for a few moments, then turned away, feeling she ought to grant him a bit of privacy as he worked.

A cricket bat leaned against the corner of the table. There was a comb, some hair cream, a delicate pair of silver scissors. Nothing about any of it was extraordinary.

She searched the vanity. There wasn't much to it. Lily was careful not to touch anything, not wanting to mar any impressions Dicky might have left on the assortment of objects. She skimmed over the contents of the jewelry box, the bottle of cologne, stopping at a little leather book. It lay open on the table, the pages neatly marked with the odds for what Lily recognized as a football match set to take place at two that afternoon in Southampton. The newspaper lay beside it, open to the sporting section. There had been some controversy lately about the football leagues—that able-bodied men were playing sport while scores of others died in the mud of Flanders.

Dicky had placed a wager.

She turned, sensing movement from the doorway behind her, but Strangford had gone further into the closet. The door to the bedroom was empty, a square of paler gray light. It must have been the shadow of a passing cloud.

By the window of the dressing room, Strangford let out a huff of frustration.

"What is it?" Lily demanded.

"It's all just…clubs and brandy and horses. Mulling over what he wants for lunch. Women," he added thinly, his hand clenched on the blue silk of a necktie. "Not his wife."

Lily thought of Celia's tear-streaked suspicions. Their confirmation wasn't much of a surprise, given what she already knew about Dicky's proposition to Bonnie.

The sordid mundanity of it left a sour taste in her mouth. She wondered how many such impressions Strangford would have to sift through before they found something useful—or determined that there was nothing more to find.

She moved to the small window, feeling extraneous. She couldn't even search the dressing room for incriminating relics. Her touch would only confuse any memories Strangford might otherwise be able to draw from the objects here.

The Thames was pale and gray outside the glass, framed by the bare branches of the stately trees that punctuated the grounds. A breeze was stirring up little waves on its surface. The water captured the dull winter light, turning opaque with it. It was impossible to see what might lay beneath.

"You haven't said anything about the rest of it."

Strangford raised his head behind her.

"What I nearly did to Jack Cannon last month in Limehouse," Lily continued softly. "What I became for a moment."

"There's a lot going on in your mind that night," Strangford replied. "It isn't all clear to me."

It was his way of offering her an escape, an opening through which she could deny the more terrible aspects of what had passed that evening. A day ago, she would happily have taken it. Too much had now changed.

"It wasn't just Cannon," she said.

She refused to look at him as she spoke, keeping her eyes on the slow, eternal movement of the river.

"It happened again in Scarborough. I was so angry about the attack. I wanted to tear those German ships apart, but I couldn't reach them, and it just . . . looked for something closer. Kazi," she added, almost choking on the name. "I could've killed him, right there on that pavement. I wanted to."

Her hands were clenched. Lily knew she was shaking, but she didn't know how to stop. She still couldn't face him.

"Lily—" Strangford began.

"I'm sorry—I can't. Not here. I shouldn't have brought it up. We need answers, and we don't have very much time."

Her words were quick and hard, leaving no room for argument. If she was the one with the hands that could plumb into someone's most authentic and private thoughts, perhaps she would have touched him then and found a way to know for certain how he felt about what she was. She couldn't, and she wasn't at all certain she really wanted to know.

"What else do you see?" she demanded, firmly changing the subject.

She had finally turned and could see that Strangford wasn't satisfied. If he wanted to protest, he held it back, whether out of respect for Lily's decision or because he recognized the validity of her point about the timing.

"That hat was a gift from his father-in-law."

"The admiral?" Lily asked, recalling what Virginia had told her of Dicky's background. Celia's father was top brass at the Royal Navy, heavily involved in war operations.

"Dicky doesn't like him. Thinks he's a stuffy fool." He pointed to a pen forgotten on the windowsill. "That's from the Admiralty. He's bored when he holds it. It's wrapped up in a sense of doing as little as necessary. It's all like that." He swept his hand over the dressing room. "Ennui and self-indulgence. Nothing . . . matters in here. Nothing is of consequence."

It would be uncomfortable for him to be here, even without Lily muddying the waters further with ill-timed confessions. Strangford was a man for whom appearances meant nothing and substance everything. There was little substance in Dicky Anstruther-Fields' dressing room. Lily could practically sense that herself in the excessive rows of starched collars and polished shoes.

They needed more than this. She scanned the racks of clothing, trying to identify what Dicky had been wearing on the night of the murder. It had been evening dress, she recalled, the standard uniform of an upper-class male.

There were four identical sets hung in a row.

"Try these," Lily ordered.

Frustration sharpened her tone, but it took Strangford only a breath to follow her line of thinking. He set his hands to the flawless ebony fabric, the elegant white waistcoats.

Lily watched his face, following the parade of emotions that played out across his features. His lip curled with irritation as he felt his way through night after night of parties and dinners. Another infidelity was revealed in a quick intake of breath, a flinch.

Then his focus shifted, sharpening. He went utterly still, and Lily could hear that his consciousness was divided when he spoke—both here with her and somewhere else.

"He's being blackmailed," he said, his fingers twisted into the black silk of a bow tie.

"What?"

"Someone is blackmailing him," Strangford carefully repeated.

"Can you see why?" she demanded.

He pushed himself back into the tie, trying to draw out more information.

"It's . . . unjust. Someone he trusted. His own fault . . . knew better than to let it slip, but how was he to know what would happen?"

A note of petulance had crept into his tone, one that sounded far more of Dicky than Strangford.

"The blackmailer," Lily pressed. "What does he want?"

"Has to go someplace he isn't meant to," Strangford replied. "Blue walls. Tastes like champagne. Ships in a bottle . . . tawdry things. The old man's study. Plenty of stiffs about in blue uniforms. Makes it easier, the crowd."

He frowned, his brow creasing.

"I can't... grasp anything. The feeling's gone blurry."

"Too much champagne?" Lily suggested.

Strangford looked as though he were starting to sweat, his fingers clenched around the bow tie.

"Not drunk. Something different. It's like . . . someone's smudged the lines."

Ships and blue uniforms, and old man's study . . . it had to be the admiral, Dicky's father-in-law. But what blackmailer would want something from the admiral's sanctum? Could it be one who was forcing Dicky to spy for him?

Voices softly echoed up to her from downstairs, a quick murmur of conversation. She wondered if Cairncross was still there or whether he had gone back to the Ghost already. They could not have very much more time.

"Try the others," she ordered. "Feel for Taddiford."

Strangford set his hands to the rest of the evening jackets, his fingers dancing over the fabric. He stopped at a perfectly pressed lapel, twisting it in his hand.

"This one," he declared.

"How can you be sure?"

"He despises me in it," he replied. "Pretty girl. Upstairs hall. Thinks I'm a meddling prig."

His voice revealed an uncanny mingling of feeling, his own disgust with Dicky mingling with Dicky's disgust of that week-ago Strangford, impressed into the fabric of the jacket.

"What about Brockmeyer?" she demanded, trying to shift his focus.

He leaned in, his grip on the jacket tightening.

"On the earthworks. Something the lieutenant said."

Her thoughts flashed back to the excursion to the Roman encampment outside Taddiford where Dicky and Brockmeyer had scrambled up the steep grade of the palisade.

"But he wasn't wearing this then," she protested.

"He's . . . picking at it, over and over. The words . . . one word."

"Can you hear it?" she asked, knowing it was rare for Strangford's power to elicit something so specific.

"*Vaterland*," he replied.

Lily didn't speak German like Strangford did, but even she could feel out the meaning of the word—*fatherland*. Except, of course, that Brockmeyer didn't actually have family connections in Germany. He was Captain Hugh MacMahon of County Armagh in Ireland, playing a part.

"He took a chance. Feels like . . . flashing his cards. He was worrying while he wore this. Had he played it right? There's something he wants—needs. Papers. Some kind of papers. Brockmeyer can get them, but it's all . . . danger. Suspicion. Anything could happen. Putting it all on an unknown horse. After dinner, Brockmeyer stepping out . . . he had to take the chance. Can't risk . . ."

He stopped, brow furrowed, looking almost ill.

"What is it?" Lily demanded.

"That feeling again. Like everything is turning itself inside out."

Her pulse skipped, awareness sharpening. She could smell wool and starch, pick out the little reflected glimmers of light from the river dancing on the ceiling.

Brockmeyer had left after dinner to make a telephone call—a call that was interrupted when that vase crashed to the floor.

She knew the call must have been to his handlers at the Secret Service Bureau. It was the only explanation for how Kazi had shown up so quickly at the scene of the murder. Brockmeyer had been a creation invented to draw out a spy, and he had succeeded, but he had not been able to give them a name.

It all came back to that vase—that blasted rotten vase. Why had it chosen that precise moment to tumble to the floor? Was it just some whim of fate?

She remembered what Cairncross had said, his careful theory that someone bilocating might be able to impact the physical world around them if they could muster enough energy. How much qi would it take to knock over a bit of porcelain?

Not so much, perhaps, if it happened to be sitting at the very edge of the table.

Lily had put it there. Lily had made it possible.

The implication spun through her, shattering her world like glass.

She had done this. Brockmeyer's death, the suspicions against Strangford . . . it was all her fault. She had chosen it when she gave in to a whim of her onmyōdō.

The horror of that was still choking her when she was startled by the sound of a voice from the doorway.

"Well, this is unexpected."

Dicky Anstruther-Fields stood framed in the light spilling in from the bedroom.

Her heart pounded. Why hadn't they heard him come in? Why hadn't her power warned her? She had let herself become distracted by her own guilt, losing her focus—dropping her connection to her khárisma.

He was dressed for travel in a twill driving coat and a flat cap. Brown leather gloves covered his hands. He held a black walking stick, clearly an accessory rather than a practical implement, though Lily knew all too well the alternative use it could be put to. A walking stick was a weapon in the right hands, and many men of Dicky's class trained in how to use it. Was Dicky one of them?

"I forgot my wager book. Can't place a proper bet if I don't know the odds for who's going to score, and here I find my friends rifling the closet."

His eyes shifted to Strangford.

"Fine trick, that," he noted, nodding towards Strangford's hands.

A chill seized her. How long had he been there? How much had he heard?

The answer was written there in his features, in that mix of curiosity and the gloating pleasure of someone who knew he had the upper hand.

He had heard enough.

The thought was terrifying, evoking bonfires and blood. Lily fought against the panic it provoked in her, searching for a way to strike back.

"You killed Felix Brockmeyer," she blurted.

"Now, Miss Albright," Dicky replied easily. "You know perfectly well that would be quite impossible. I was sleeping off an excess of whiskey in front of two reliable witnesses at the time of the poor lieutenant's demise."

"I think we both know that doesn't make it impossible," Lily returned evenly.

They stared at each other a moment across the quiet, dim space of the dressing room. Dicky looked mildly amused, eyes sparking as though he were facing a clever little game.

"Someone is blackmailing you," Lily pressed, searching for a way to turn the conversation to her advantage—to lure him into revealing something that she could actually use with the inspector. "I'm sure that must be terrible."

Dicky rolled his eyes.

"You have no idea," he complained easily. "And here I thought Charles Edward was a proper mate. One drunken night at school, I decided to show off a bit, and he turns it into a liability."

The name clicked into place.

"Charles Edward—the Duke of Saxe-Coburg and Gotha?" she asked.

"No, the other German general I ran around with," Dicky returned sarcastically. "Yes, the duke. It was all a dozen or so years ago, but two years back, he turns up and tells me I'm to start delivering him information from the Admiralty or he'll spill my little secret to all and sundry—Celia, her old man, my superiors at the office. It wouldn't do, of course. And we weren't at war at the time. Rather friendly with the krauts, really. After all, half their ruling families are married to our own. So what's the harm in sharing a little information?"

"We're at war now," Strangford noted thinly.

"Thank you for pointing out the wretchedly obvious," Dicky returned. "Yes, we're at war. And that would make things even more awkward were Charles Edward to reveal that I've been feeding him his little tidbits for the last two years. These suits have all been precisely tailored to fit the length of my neck—I've no desire to have it lengthened by a hangman's rope."

"What about Scarborough?" Strangford demanded, taking a step forward, eyes glittering darkly.

"I don't know anything about that," Dicky replied unconvincingly.

As long as he was talking, there was a chance he'd reveal something they could use. Lily tried another tack.

"And Brockmeyer?" she pressed.

"Not what he seemed to be, was he?" Dicky returned. "Though he nearly had me until he went out to make his telephone call. It's a good thing I thought to pop along for a listen, or I might've been rather caught out."

"But you were in the billiards room with me when Brockmeyer left," Strangford said.

"Was I?" Dicky mused. "Silly me."

Lily's mind churned, quickly filling in the missing pieces of the uncertain picture that had been tormenting her since Taddiford. Dicky must've let something slip that triggered Brockmeyer's suspicions—perhaps an attempt to recruit him to provide Dicky with more information about the Navy's plans. When Brockmeyer stepped out after dinner, Dicky projected himself into the hall to eavesdrop.

And when he heard Brockmeyer prepare to name the person he suspected of being the spy, Dicky had mustered the energy to interrupt . . . by shattering the vase Lily had so conveniently positioned for him.

Blood pounded in her ears, the dressing room starting to spin.

Dicky was still talking.

"I couldn't let Brockmeyer run back to London after that. I knew I needed to take care of the situation. The stairs to his bedroom were right next to the door to the conservatory, so I hid in there and made sure to make a bit of a racket when he came down the hall. He came in to have a look, and that was that," he finished easily.

The horror of it sickened her. She could feel the wet slick of Brockmeyer's still-warm blood on her hands, the thick smell of orchids in the air.

"Why are you telling us this?" she demanded, feeling dizzy.

"You asked," Dicky replied. "And it's not as though you can do anything with it, can you? It's all the wildest stuff and nonsense. What difference is it to me whether they put you in prison or the asylum?"

Something was itching at the back of her brain, a tiny sliver of fact that didn't fit into the picture before her. Lily felt stuck on it, unable to move forward.

"You're after something," Strangford said, stepping forward. "Papers—the plans Brockmeyer brought to Eversleigh."

"The ones for the new steam engine," Lily filled in.

Dicky startled, revealing a flash of surprise and perhaps just a little hint of fear. The walking stick tapped against his shoe, swinging in neat, ready arcs. Lily was conscious of the threat of it even as her mind continued to whirl.

"Two o'clock," she murmured, catching on the number.

As she grasped it, the rest of the picture spun into clarity. Her head snapped up, meeting Dicky's gaze once more.

"Two o'clock in Southampton. Your football match. You couldn't make it there from London in three hours. It doesn't make sense to come back for the wager book—not if returning would make you miss the game."

Dicky's mouth shifted into a grin. It was an expression of genuine delight.

"Aren't you clever?" he remarked.

Somewhere downstairs, a door slammed. Loud and authoritative voices echoed up from below. What they signified popped abruptly into her head with a snap of foresight, and suddenly the reason for Dicky's easy loquaciousness over the last ten minutes became clear.

"Police," Strangford said, giving voice to the word that was blaring like an alarm in her mind.

Dicky regarded her with a twist of a smile.

"Did I neglect to mention I had the butler call for them on my way up? I gather they've been looking for you."

Panic rooted her to the spot. Her thoughts raced from the narrow window to where Dicky stood, blocking the only way out of the dressing room.

Beside her, Strangford snatched one of the hats from the shelf and sent it spinning through the door.

It passed through Dicky like a flicker of light, slipping into his body and out the other side again, gliding to a stop against the bedpost.

Dicky's gaze moved to Strangford, carefully appraising.

"Touché," he mused and then blinked out of existence.

The shock of it froze her for a moment. It was the stuff of miracles. It could not possibly exist in the same space as mundane, self-absorbed Dicky Anstruther-Fields.

Dicky, who had just been projecting himself into this room from somewhere else.

Strangford grabbed her arm, snapping her to attention.

"Can you get us out of here?" he demanded.

Lily forced herself to focus, pulling on her power. It surged up in response.

"Yes," she replied.

She took a step toward the door, then halted, something tugging her back. She turned to the vanity, eyes falling on the object there that sung with the clarion tone of her onmyōdō.

"The newspaper," she blurted.

Strangford reached back, snatching it from the table. He stuffed it into his coat and took her hand.

They dashed out into the bedroom. Lily could already hear feet pounding up the stairs.

"Which way?" he demanded.

She pushed the question down through wood and plaster and stone into the earth, through roots and bones and water.

Which way?

The answer glowed at her—the hall and the door, the twist to the left. The great white elephant outside the window.

She didn't pause to question it. There was no time.

"Get ready to break glass," she said, pulling him into a run.

NINETEEN

$\mathcal{L}$ILY CHARGED OUT into the hall, Strangford at her heels. The police had reached the top of the stairs. A shout rose up at their appearance, black boots pounding toward them.

She pivoted, swinging into the room on her left. It was a spare bedroom, nicely made up with windows looking out over the narrow alley behind the house.

Strangford grabbed a small table as they ran in, swinging it up into his hands. As they ran toward the window, he threw it.

It shattered through the glass, glittering shards spilling across the hardwood floor.

She did not hesitate, could not slow. The police at her heels, Lily put everything she had into the power thrumming through her, into the single word it presented to her.

Jump.

She dove through the window, landing hard on top of the white delivery lorry parked below.

Lily hit the roof of the cargo hold, the impact bloodying her lip. She grabbed on, fighting for traction. The engine of the vehicle was already rumbling, the great beast of it slipping into gear.

Strangford landed beside her, rolling. Lily flashed out an arm to catch him, halting his momentum. The lorry jerked forward as the driver slammed the pedal, shocked by the racket from above.

They burst from the alley into the road. The driver pressed the brakes, jerking the wheel. The momentum threw Lily sideways, sliding her across the roof.

She let it happen, readying herself. She slipped over the side, hitting the ground boots-first, the impact jarring through her knees.

Strangford landed beside her, grabbed her arm, and yanked her into a sprint.

They raced across the road, shouts rising up behind them as Lily burst into the alley where they had left the Rolls Royce.

"Cairncross!" she shouted.

The Scotsman was sitting in the driver's seat. He pulled a quick lever, hitting a button, then half-tumbled into the passenger side.

"It's running!" he called back.

His eyes widened at the sight of the men racing after Lily and Strangford.

Lily leapt behind the wheel as Strangford dove into the rear seat. She could feel the warm vibration of the engine, the banked power of it as she eyed the cluster of constables pouring across the street. A dark sort of pleasure tugged at her, and Lily threw the Ghost into reverse.

The tires screamed, burning against the macadam. The automobile flew backward down the street, leaving a trail of burned rubber behind it.

She yanked the wheel, spinning them into a half-turn, then switched the gears and pounded the accelerator again.

The car responded, tearing away.

~

Lily drove them east, instinct pushing her back toward the familiar heart of her city. Putney gave way to the far less posh environs of Wandsworth and Clapham. Beside her, Cairncross had his sleeve pressed across his eyes. He looked ill.

"Do we have a destination?" he asked as they passed by another row of terraced houses.

She jerked the Ghost to a stop. They were at the edge of Clapham Common. A cluster of boys was playing football on the shriveled winter lawn.

The impact of it all roiled through her—the shouts of the police, the lingering smell of burnt tires. The hat sailing through Dicky as though he weren't there ... because he hadn't been.

She sat in a silver luxury vehicle at the edge of a working-class football pitch, the street lined with narrow brick houses, windows covered in faded curtains. The gray sky smelled of burning coal. Her stomach rumbled, reminding her it was likely lunchtime.

For a brief moment, she ached for something different—something normal. A life like those that went on behind the bland facades of the row houses.

Even that was an illusion. Behind those doors, women watched the death notices. Families worried about funds if the draft took their breadwinners away. Nothing was normal anymore.

"Richard Anstruther-Fields can bilocate," she reported.

Cairncross absorbed this.

"You suspected as much," he noted.

"But I never…"

She trailed off, at a loss for the words. She could not have imagined what it would feel like—talking to a man that wasn't there. Finding another charismatic to discover he was nothing like the rest of them, nothing like Sam and Estelle and Dr. Gardner. It felt wrong. It felt like she had failed somehow.

She had been broken when she stumbled into Ash's sanctuary, fractured by grief and isolation. Ash had changed that—they all had, everyone at The Refuge. Discovering them had healed her, put something together inside of her that she'd thought was shattered for good.

If it had been Ash who discovered Dicky, could this all have turned out differently?

She forced herself to set that guilty confusion aside. Dicky was a spy. He had murdered Brockmeyer—or rather the man who was pretending to be Brockmeyer. Scarborough was his doing, with all its death and destruction. He was a threat to her, to Strangford—to England. He had to be stopped.

"He wasn't in the bedroom," Lily noted. "So, where was he?"

Strangford pulled the newspaper from his coat. He was wearing his gloves again, having pulled them on while they drove. He glanced up at Lily, meeting her eyes in the mirror.

"You told me to take this," he noted.

"I don't know why," Lily admitted.

Cairncross studied it.

"It's today's edition," he pointed out. "If he read it, he did so just this morning."

Strangford pulled off his glove, laying his hand on the page. The paper bent as his grip tightened.

"Taddiford," he said, the word thin with urgency. "He was going to Taddiford after the match."

"He won't bother with the match now. He's after the papers," Lily exclaimed. "The ones in Eversleigh's safe."

Urgency pressed at her. She grabbed the fuel pump. Strangford reached over the seat, taking hold of her arm to stop her.

"We can ring," he said, nodding to the small post office a few doors away, the sign for a public telephone hung in its window.

Strangford hopped out, Cairncross joining him. Lily moved to follow. The librarian stopped her, clearing his throat.

"It might be best if you stay with the car. In case the police should arrive."

Lily nodded, hating being left behind but knowing he was right.

She nudged the engine into idling, feeding it a little fuel as the two men disappeared into the post office.

The waiting was more terrible than it should have been. Something felt dreadfully wrong, pulling at her in a way she had to consciously resist in order to stop herself from throwing the Ghost into gear and tearing down the street. With the two men gone, Lily finally recognized it for what it was—a dark nudge from her power.

She pushed at it, demanding more. It coughed out a response, quick and bright as a flashbulb.

Her hands turned red.

She lifted them from the wheel, looking at them with surprise. The hue had texture. It was wet, glistening in the cool gray light of the overcast day. A drop pulled loose, tracking its way down her forearm. Another followed.

Lily began to shake, the dread welling up in her like oil from a well. It choked her, yanking her into somewhere else, the rest of the vision spilling across her mind.

A shirt soaked in dark crimson, rising and falling with a shallow breath.

Light flashing from a pair of gold-rimmed moons.

Cold air spilling across her skin, scented with the sea.

She thrust her hands against the fabric of her shirt, desperate to get them clean. Her shirt remained dry, her hands bare, pale skin unblemished.

They were still shaking.

Horror washed over her, cutting off her air. She knew this. She had done this before as a ten-year-old child crouched on the floor, tortured by the foresight of her mother in a red dress, sprawled on the pavement. Jewels glittering darkly like stars around her.

The visions twisted things, swapped symbols in for facts. A crimson gown for a white one soaked with blood.

"God, no," she gasped, falling forward to the steering wheel.

She clutched the gear shift of the Ghost like an anchor, willing the solid shapes and textures of the automobile to ground her in the present, to what was happening now and not the horrors of both the future and the past.

"The line to Taddiford is down again," Strangford said, yanking open the passenger side door as Cairncross followed behind him. As he saw her, his tone immediately shifted to concern.

"What's wrong?" he demanded.

Lily clung to the Ghost, knuckles white as though the tension in her grip could stop the shaking that threatened to overwhelm her.

"We need a doctor," she gasped out.

"Are you hurt?" Strangford returned urgently.

"Not me. Someone else. Soon."

The knowledge washed over her as though her brain were finally catching up with what her power was telling her. Fear had made her slow.

She looked to Cairncross, still standing on the pavement beside the Ghost.

"Ring Gardner. He has to get to Taddiford. Please."

Her voice broke on the word, desperation shaking it.

Cairncross's eyes widened, face paling.

"I-I'll telephone the hospital now," he stammered.

Strangford tugged off his glove, putting his hand to her cheek. Lily held it there, needing the comfort of his touch as much as she needed him to know.

His mouth firmed with his own desperate intention.

"Contact Scotland Yard as well," he ordered. "Tell Inspector Tariq Kazi where we have gone."

His words cut through the fog of fear enveloping her.

"Strangford—" she protested.

He cut her short.

"We need help, and he's an honorable man. There's too much at stake."

An honorable man who thought Strangford was a killer—and yet Lily accepted it, knowing he was right.

"Go on. I'll manage it," Cairncross replied. "Go!"

Lily didn't wait. The urgency of the vision still pulsed through her veins, tightening her with panic. She threw the car into gear and tore away from the curb, aiming south.

~

Lily pushed the Rolls Royce, tearing around the curves of the narrow roads as fast as she could without smashing them into a wall or carriage. They passed acres of vivid green fields and tangled hedgerows, flying through picturesque little villages. The clusters of houses were nothing but obstacles to her, places where she was forced to slow as she raced toward Taddiford.

The clouds had thickened overhead, turning from uniform gray to something more ominous, the chill air growing damp with the promise of winter rain. The first drops began to sting down as they passed the road to Aldershot.

"Stop," Strangford quietly ordered from beside her.

"We don't have any—"

"For a moment, Lily," he cut in.

She gritted her teeth, forcing her foot to obey, shifting it from the accelerator to the brake. She tugged the Ghost into the packed dirt before a pasture gate, just off the narrow pavement of the road.

Strangford got out and unclasped the canvas top, wrestling it up. Lily finally rose to help him snap it into place. He rolled up the windows.

The sky was darkening with more than foul weather, the early December twilight settling in. Drops plopped dully against the canvas overhead. Lily gripped the steering wheel, unable to bring herself to move.

"This is my fault," she said, forcing out the words in the close, dim confines of the Ghost, which smelled of leather and oil. "I chose this. The onmyōdō made it feel like it was the right thing to do. I trusted it. No—I gave in to it," she corrected herself, words laced with bitterness. "I did what it was asking because I didn't like how it felt *not* to, and it brought down all of this on us. On you."

Silence lingered after her words. Strangford sat beside her, leaning back against the seat. His dark hair curled around his temples, his eye closed.

"It would be easier, wouldn't it—if you could always know the right thing to do?" he said quietly.

Lily gasped out a laugh that was half a sob, still clutching the steering wheel of the unmoving vehicle.

"Ash would tell you it all happens for a reason," he continued. "Even if it doesn't seem like it. That it's part of something bigger."

"You say that like you don't really believe it," Lily pressed.

His smile had an edge.

"It's complicated."

Something in the words made her think of that dark space beneath the roof of The Refuge where stars and gods marched across the ceiling, looking impersonally down at the mortals crowded below.

Ash's wife had understood. She had seen that bigger something, felt its currents chasing through her bones, and it had drowned her.

"What if I don't want to be part of something bigger?" she quietly replied. "What if all I want is to be happy with you for as long as I can?"

His gloved hand slipped around her neck, pulling her gently to his shoulder. She let herself fall into him, soaking up his warmth, his smell—like cedar and cool water. How could she risk this? How could she ever let it go?

"We'll muddle through it," he said, and she could almost hear the ache in his throat. "That's all we can do."

The rain pattered lightly against the canvas.

"Are you ready?" he asked.

Lily pulled herself upright, wiping the damp skin under her eyes.

"No," she replied grimly, then hit the starter.

~

Taddiford came into view through an opening in a stretch of wood-lands, and Lily tapped the brakes. The manor was a darker, jagged line painted against the gloom of the horizon, punctuated by the warm golden glow of illuminated windows. She could smell the sea through the open sides of the Ghost, the sharp, briny scent of it mingling with the rain that still tapped against the windshield. A pinprick of light flashed on the headland, the lighthouse making another turn.

Lily's mind churned through all the uncomfortable questions. Was Dicky already there? Would they walk in to find some illusion of him sitting down to tea?

No—a ghost could not break into a safe. Dicky had to come himself, in the flesh. That much Lily could be certain of. There was also the issue of how he was going to get the papers to Germany. There must be a plan for that, or Dicky would not risk coming here—not now that Lily and Strangford knew his secret.

She closed her eyes. What were they going to tell Walford and Virginia? How could they possibly explain this?

"Can you drive without the headlamps?" Strangford asked from the darkness beside her.

"If we go slowly enough," Lily replied.

"Do it. Turn down the service road."

"Right," she said dully.

She flipped the switch for the headlamps, plunging them into a deeper gloom, and pressed carefully forward.

Gravel crunched under the tires as they pulled up to the back of the carriage house. Strangford hopped out to yank open one of the bays as a few more icy drops of rain splattered against the windshield.

The inside of the long building smelled of horses. Lily could hear the animals snort in protest from their stalls at the far end, beyond the empty space where the Eversleigh's motorcar was normally parked.

She met Strangford at the door, looking out across the damp grass to the great stone sprawl of the house.

The beam of the lighthouse glanced over the landscape, its light weaker here than it would be on the beach. Taddiford looked quiet, the lamps glowing steadily behind its windows, regular beacons set in gloomy walls of ancient rock.

"This way," Strangford said.

He led them across the shadow-swathed open ground toward the back of the manor. The rain pinged against her skin, beading on the canvas of her motorcycle jacket. They stopped at the kitchen, Strangford yanking open the plain wooden door.

He slipped inside silently, something in him going coiled and ready in a way Lily recognized as the stance of his tàijí.

The kitchen was warm and golden. Mrs. Metzger stood at the stove, peering into a pot. The cook started with surprise as Strangford came in, her eyes wide.

"M'lord," she said in greeting, quickly collecting herself.

"Where is Mrs. Eversleigh?" Strangford demanded.

Mrs. Metzger could hear the urgency in his tone. She set down her spoon, wiping her hands on her apron.

"In the library. Is there something—"

Strangford didn't wait for the rest of her words, stalking past her toward the hall.

Lily lingered behind for a moment.

"Stay here," she ordered. "Lock the door."

She joined Strangford in the hallway. It was quiet, unchanged from when she had seen it a few days before. Tastefully chosen paintings hung on the walls, the clock ticking with irritating regularity. They made their way across the thick carpet to the library.

Virginia was tucked into a chair, dressed for comfort in a wool skirt and blouse. Horatio snored on a hassock at her feet. She held a magazine in her hand and looked up with a frown at the interruption.

When she saw them, she set the magazine down and stood. The pug raised his head from the cushion tiredly, blinking at them with disinterest.

"What's wrong?" she demanded.

"Is Anstruther-Fields here?" Strangford pressed.

"Dicky?" she echoed, surprised. "He arrived about an hour ago."

"What about Gardner?" Lily asked, hope and fear warring inside her chest.

"The doctor?" Virginia said, clearly bewildered by the question.

Strangford crossed the room to her, taking her arm.

"Collect the children. Get them out of here—somewhere safe."

"They've already gone," Virginia stammered. "Nanny and Mr. Lewis took them into town in the motor for a bit of shopping, everyone but Portia. Anthony, what the devil is going on?"

"He murdered Brockmeyer. He's after Walford's papers."

"He must be having you on," Virginia protested. "I know Dicky has a rotten sense of humor, but this is beyond the pale—"

"He didn't tell me, Ginnie," Strangford ground out, still holding his sister's sleeve. Something desperate in him began to crack. "I felt it. I saw it with my hands."

Time held its breath, his words echoing dully off the books that lined the walls as the rain pattered against the windowpanes.

Virginia's eyes widened—first with surprise, then something like a quick-dawning recognition.

"Anthony—"

Lily cut her off.

"Time for that later. Where is Dicky now?"

Virginia was clearly reeling, her skin paling in contrast to her rich dark hair, so much like her brother's, but her voice was steady when she spoke.

"He went into the study."

In the study with the safe—with the papers. Lily's heart pounded. Were they already too late?

Then a crack like thunder split through the quiet of the house.

TWENTY

$\mathcal{L}$ILY HAD BEEN waiting for it.

The knowledge came to her as soon as the sound whipped through them, splintering the world. The import of it was perfectly clear to her—and utterly terrible.

"Oh God," she burst out, reeling, her knees abruptly weak.

Strangford caught her, reading the truth in her face. Then he turned and bolted into the hall.

Lily forced her body to obey. She raced after him, Virginia lifting her skirts to follow. They sprinted past the elegantly appointed rooms of the wing and pivoted around the corner into the main body of the house.

Strangford kicked through the study door.

It was the room Lily remembered, files stacked on the shelves, the Roman spear mounted on the wall. The French doors to the yard were open, admitting the cold, salt-scented wind. Threads of chill rain flew in, peppering the desk. The seascape oil painting rested on the floor, revealing a hole in the wall that stood open—the mouth of Walford's safe, where he kept both the plans and the gun he never used.

Something groaned on the floor, and abruptly everything else went out of focus, Lily's attention homing in on the only thing that mattered.

Walford Eversleigh lay on the ground, his hand clutched to his chest. Red liquid spread from around his fingers, soaking the white cotton of his shirt.

The world narrowed to a pinpoint. The sound of the rain faded, the rustle of the wind blowing at the loose papers on Walford's desk. All Lily could hear was the resonant ping of false gems bouncing against the pavement as crimson flowers bloomed on a white silk dress.

I'll see you in the morning, a stóirín.

Virginia's scream cut through the memory, shattering it like glass.

Lily snapped clear of it. She dove to her knees, pushing Walford's limp hand aside and putting her own pressure on the wound.

Strangford stood over her. His gaze moved from his brother-in-law to the open door.

Dicky had gone outside. He could not have left more than a moment ago.

She could feel Strangford weigh the decision, torn by the terrible pressure of it, and then he pulled off his coat, pushing it at Lily.

She wadded it up, pressing it against the wound in Walford's chest, hoping it might slow the bleeding, but she knew by the position of the injury that it must be critical. She did not know what else to do. She was not a nurse. She was a woman who could see the future, and in even that, she had failed.

"I'm sorry," she blurted out, the guilt pressing down on her. "I'm so sorry."

Strangford knelt at her side. His hand came to her shoulder.

"Lily—" he began.

"He apologized as well," Walford said, his voice thin. He half choked out a laugh. "The bastard. Right after he shot me."

He groaned, and a fresh pulse of blood welled up under Lily's hands.

Virginia cried out again, cradling her husband's head in her lap, and a familiar voice boomed to them from the hall.

"Just bloody show me where they are!"

"Gardner!" Strangford shouted, the word tearing out of his throat.

The doctor strode into the room, his uniform on, bag in his hand, and Lily's arms went weak.

He had come. She had called him, and he had come.

He took in the scene with a glance, and then he was crouched on the floor on the other side of Walford. He took a razor from his bag and ripped it up through the fallen man's shirt. Pushing Lily's hands aside, he carefully removed Strangford's bloodstained coat, exposing the wound.

James, the footman, followed him to the doorway. He stopped there, eyes wide, face paling with shock.

Portia Eversleigh pushed neatly past him. She wore a pale green dressing gown and slippers, her spectacles perched on her nose.

The light from the chandelier glinted off those two round circles of glass, blanking them momentarily into pale moons.

Fresh red blood welled up urgently now the pressure of her hands was gone. Any relief Lily felt at Gardner's appearance was tempered when she saw the grim line of his mouth as he assessed the damage.

"Hold it down again," he ordered, and Lily leaned back in. Walford's breath felt shallow under her hands.

"I don't understand," Virginia said weakly, still stroking Walford's hair. "How are you here?"

Gardner glanced instinctively to Lily.

"Please," she said. "Please do whatever you can for him."

The doctor put his large hands to Walford's chest, lowered his head, and closed his eyes.

Virginia's attention slipped back to her husband, but Portia, standing at her father's head, stared at the doctor. She had gone pale and rigid, but her eyes were carefully focused behind her spectacles.

Lily wondered how much she could see—if she could possibly guess what Gardner was doing as his mind traveled through the muscles and veins and tendons of the man who lay before them.

"The bullet has passed through," he said, his voice low. "Small caliber, thank God. It missed his heart, but one of his lungs is collapsing."

Her heart skipped. It was as much as a confession, drawn from him by the urgency of the moment. He had weighed Walford's life against his secret and made his choice.

"What do you need?"

The words were Portia's. She stared down at them, drawn but resolute, her voice steady.

Gardner met the girl's eyes over the bleeding body of her father as Bonnie stumbled to the door. The maid gasped with horror at the scene, James grabbing her arm instinctively.

The doctor seemed to come to a decision, directing his instructions at Portia.

"Boiled water," he ordered. "Lots of it. Clean towels. Rubbing alcohol if you have any, or whatever in the house has the highest proof." He glanced to Virginia. "Do you have any laudanum?"

"She doesn't use it," Portia replied. "But Mrs. Metzger has some in her cabinet. She takes it occasionally for her arthritis."

"Bring it," Gardner said.

Portia pivoted, snapping out instructions.

"James, see to the towels. Bonnie—the water. I'll get the laudanum and the alcohol."

"Yes, Miss Eversleigh," Bonnie replied, swallowing her fear. She raced back into the hall. James followed a moment later, staggering back a bit but managing to pull himself together as Portia stalked after them.

Virginia grazed her fingers over Walford's cheek as his eyes flickered open, his mouth twisting in a grimace of pain.

"You terrible fool," she said gently. "How dare you let yourself get shot?"

"Dreadfully irresponsible of me," Walford gasped in reply.

Gardner tossed aside the coat of his uniform, rolling up his sleeves. He opened his bag and unrolled a canvas wrap of tools—scalpel and forceps, needle, and a tin of catgut.

Portia was the first one back, James following at her heels.

"The laudanum?" Gardner demanded as Bonnie hurried in, carrying a steaming kettle. Mrs. Metzger stepped into the doorway and froze, shoving her hand to her mouth in horror.

Portia set a small brown bottle into the doctor's extended hand. He scanned the label.

"Give him two teaspoons," he ordered, pushing it back at the girl.

Portia knelt at her father's side, lifting his head.

"No complaints," she snapped. "I have swallowed my medicine for you a hundred times."

Walford's hand came up to clasp his daughter's wrist. His eyes drifted, the drug taking hold.

"Strangford, Lily—hold him down," Gardner said.

He pointed to James.

"You. Keep pressure on the wound."

James looked green. He took a hesitant step forward.

"I'll do it," Portia cut in. She shifted around her father's body, grabbing a clean towel. Lily pulled her hands back, allowing the girl to push Strangford's blood-soaked jacket out of the way and replace it with the towel.

Lily set her hands to Walford's arm and shoulder, Strangford mirroring her on the other side as Gardner carefully rinsed his hands in the alcohol, the sharp scent of it cutting through the aroma of the blood.

He rubbed clean the scalpel, tossing aside another towel. The blade winked in the glow of the chandelier.

"Do you need more light?" Portia asked, her voice breaking only slightly.

"No," Gardner replied.

He set a hand back to the bare, crimson-stained skin of Walford's chest, his focus veering inward.

No, he did not need more light. He was feeling his way through the pressure collapsing Walford's lung, using his khárisma to navigate to exactly the place he would cut.

He lowered the blade. Virginia closed her eyes, turning her face away.

The cut was small but deep. Walford cursed, jerking, forcing Lily to put her back into holding him in place. Gardner slipped the scalpel into the opening, slicing deeper.

Then he dropped the blade onto a clean towel, big hands pressing firmly down around the incision. Blood foamed up in delicate pink bubbles. Gardner grabbed another towel to catch the flow.

Lily was not a doctor. She had nothing of Gardner's power, but it seemed to her that she could feel the difference. Walford's next breath was deeper, longer, and some of the tension went out of the doctor's shoulders.

He looked to Strangford and then Virginia.

"He'll live," he announced.

Portia closed her eyes for a moment, body shuddering with a silent relief. Virginia let out a sob, half-falling against her daughter.

Gardner moved to the catgut and needle.

It had been an eternity, but the hands on the clock had moved only a handful of minutes.

"Strangford," Lily urged.

The safe stood ajar on the wall, the winter rain still pattering softly off the gravel outside the open French doors.

Strangford stood, tearing off his gloves. He put his hands to the safe, running them over the dial, the handle—the emptiness of the interior.

"He's gone to the beach," he announced.

Portia looked up, the light glinting off her spectacles.

"Get him," Virginia said.

She still sat at her husband's side, his blood splattered across her blouse. Her voice was low, trembling with intensity.

"Run him down, Anthony."

A gust of wind blew into the room. It was cold and damp. Something about it smelled faintly of horse and campfire. A whisper of it crawled across her skin.

Lily looked to the spear on the wall as Gardner set his needle to Walford's flesh. The decision took only a moment.

She vaulted up with one foot on Walford's chair and plucked the weapon from the hooks on which it hung. She swung it in her grip. It was longer than her walking stick, but the balance was good, the wood strong. Ash, she thought distantly. It felt like ash.

She met Strangford's eye by the door, saw his grim approval.

"Let's go," she said, and they dashed together out into the night.

~

Darkness had fallen, the stars drowned out by the thick clouds overhead. Gloom shrouded the landscape, cloaking the brown stubble of the field and the abyss that was the sea beyond the cliffs. The only relief was the brief spill of illumination as the beam of the lighthouse swept over them, then swung away again. Pinpricks of light were just visible across The Solent, signs of distant life on the Isle of Wight.

A chill drizzle coated her skin, dripping down the back of her neck as she ran, the spear gripped in her hand. Her boots slipped against the mud, and Strangford caught her arm, tugging her back into balance.

They stopped at the edge of the cliff, looking down. Strangford waved her into a crouch as the lighthouse beam swung by once more.

The light raced across the dark sand of the beach, then hit the ragged chop of the water.

Something lurked there.

The beam revealed it in a glimpse lasting only a little longer than the blink of an eye—the silhouette of a low tower like an old fortress rising up from the sea, a cluster of dark figures huddled at its ramparts. It was as though some relic of a ruined kingdom had pressed itself up out of the water, a thing that made no sense to her until Strangford gave it a name.

"U-boat," he muttered from beside her.

Memories of Scarborough forced themselves back, shivering a kind of animal fear through her, but she knew it was irrational. Submarines could only fire their missiles under water, not at targets on the land. They were weapons made to sink ships, only there were no other vessels here.

This was not an invasion. It was an extraction. The Germans had come for their papers—providing an escape route for their spy.

Strangford bolted along the cliff, racing for the top of the path. Lily hurried after him, her feet feeling less sure. A stumble slowed her, forcing her to be more cautious as she turned the corner and started down the packed ridge of red clay that descended to the shore.

Another flash from the lighthouse revealed the dark shape of a man on the beach, tugging Walford's dinghy toward the water. He turned as the light passed over him, wincing against the brightness.

It was Dicky.

They could not let him get that boat into the water. If he managed to escape the beach, it was over. He would reach the U-boat with Eversleigh's papers, and it would sink under the waves, hiding beneath the surface until its cargo was safely delivered to Germany.

Strangford leapt down the rest of the path. He sprinted across the wet sand, throwing himself at Dicky. The spy turned as Strangford approached, sensing him over the rush of the surf. He plucked a metal document case from the little boat and swung it up to block Strangford's blow.

Strangford flinched back, shaking his arm with a curse, but the impact had sent Dicky sprawling back against the sand.

And then he doubled.

The lighthouse beam glided over them, painting its pale ribbon across the strand. Dicky rose from the sand on either side of Strangford—two men clad in identical rain slickers, each pulling a pistol from his coat. Then the light was gone.

The fear split her like a knife. Walford's blood was still on her hands. How much more deadly would such a wound be out here in the rain and the darkness?

The twin threats stalked Strangford, moving at either apex of a slow circle, shoulders hunched under rain-darkened hair. Strangford held himself carefully in the center, poised in the ready stance of his tàijí, watching.

He could not know which way to strike.

Lily's boots hit the sand at the bottom of the cliff path, the damp wind pulling at the short waves of her hair. She breathed in the sharp brine of it as she anchored herself, finding her balance, muscles coiled and ready.

The lighthouse beam moved toward them, rippling over the dry grass of the cliffs. Then it arrived, blazing across the beach.

She raised the shaft of the spear, twisted, and let it fly.

It arrowed across the sudden light and slipped through the nothingness of the man who appeared to be standing to Strangford's right.

On his left, Dicky dropped his jaw with surprise.

Strangford pivoted, boot digging into the rich softness of the sand. His leg snapped out, foot connecting with Dicky's wrist. The gun flew from his grip, disappearing into the gloom.

Strangford attacked.

He landed a punch, struck out with another, sending Dicky falling back to the ground. Lily felt a quick pulse of victory as she ran toward them—then Dicky turned, throwing a handful of sand up into Strangford's face.

Strangford flinched back, instinct forcing him to close his eye, and Dicky doubled again.

Lily ran for her spear, conscious of the direction she had loosed it in through the darkness. The lighthouse beam approached once more, the glow of it gliding over the rough face of the cliffs.

She glimpsed the weapon just a few steps ahead of her when her power flashed a warning.

Lily threw herself behind a stone jutting from the sand as the light crossed her path and the world exploded with the unmistakable rattle of a machine gun.

The blast tore through the surf, throwing up saltwater and bits of shells. Fragments of stone blew away from the rock she crouched behind.

The beam passed, sliding across the water and revealing how the U-boat had moved closer. She could see the sharp edges of the artillery mounted on its tower.

She had perhaps a minute before the light returned again.

Lily crept from behind the stone, reaching out in the gloom to grasp the shaft of the spear. Clutching it, she scrambled to her feet, running across the beach, keeping herself low. More rocks rose jaggedly between her and the dinghy.

Pinpricks of light flickered from the top of the cliff, dancing like the glow of fireflies. Voices sounded distantly, sharp and masculine, the echo of a barked order. There was something familiar about it even through the obscurity of the roaring surf.

She prayed it meant help, but she could not afford to wait for it.

The lights winked out.

From behind another stone, she watched two versions of Dicky Anstruther-Fields frame the place where Strangford stood. The nearer of the two knelt in the sand, his hands pressed into the fine, damp grains of it. The other stood on the far side, rain dripping from his slicker as he called out.

"I'm terribly sorry about Walford," he said. "The stupid bastard simply wandered in at the wrong moment. He was supposed to be out in the garden."

Strangford was rigid as a bowstring, jumper plastered to the hard line of his shoulders.

"If I hear one more excuse from you, I swear I will tear you apart," he replied, his voice breaking on the words.

"It's your hands, isn't it?" Dicky pushed back with all his characteristic insolence. "That's how you knew I had my eye on the maid. How you knew about the plans. It's damned intriguing, I'll admit. I'm sure we'd have a great deal to chat about if we had the time."

Strangford had turned toward the speaker. Behind him, the other

Dicky, the one with his hands in the sand, climbed awkwardly to his feet.

"You aren't alone," Lily called out, the words spilling from her.

The speaking Dicky glanced to her, head cocked with interest.

"There are more of us," she pressed on, needing to say it. "Others like you. We could help."

Her voice cracked on the last word.

It was Ash's offer, Ash's revelation—the one that had changed her life, transformed her into something else. In that moment, she desperately wanted Dicky to take it, even as another part of her felt ill at the thought.

"How dreadfully kind of you," he drawled in response.

His silent double whirled, gun in his hand, and aimed the barrel at Lily's skull.

"Anyone moves, and I shoot."

He was at her in three long steps, the cold steel pressing against the back of her head. It was no illusion.

"The document case," the Dicky with the gun shouted, nodding in the direction of the metal box lying in the sand in front of her. "Bring it to me."

The beam of light passed over them once more, illuminating the scene with unmistakable clarity. Rage and fear mingled on Strangford's face, his dark hair dripping with damp. His gloved hands clenched at his sides, and then the beam passed, spilling over the rough little waves to the con tower of the U-boat. The machine gun was silent. Dicky must be close enough that they would not risk a shot.

She wondered what was happening on the cliff path. Had the light she glimpsed been help approaching? She dared not turn her head to look, afraid to draw Dicky's attention to it.

They could not let Dicky get the document case. The dinghy was right behind her. If he got into the boat, delivering those plans to Germany, England's hopes of winning the war could very well be lost. Who knew how many lives that would cost?

She still gripped the spear in her hand, wet fingers clenching the damp wood. She adjusted that grip carefully as the barrel of the gun pushed into her hair, staring at Strangford's shadowy form across the sand, frozen with the weight of an impossible decision.

This is about more than us.

The light approached once more, spilling down the face of the cliff. Lily dared not turn, conscious only of a flicker of movement at the corner of her eye, a ghost slipping behind an outcropping.

Strangford took a step toward the document case, and Lily struck.

She dropped, twisting as she fell to whip back with the spear. It hit Dicky's arm, and his shot went rogue, thudding dully into the wet sand.

The gun was still in his hand.

Dicky's expression was grim with frustration and fear as he swung the weapon back toward her, the lighthouse beam reaching them, gleaming off the polished steel of the pistol.

There was an unexpected crack. The pistol spun away, Dicky clutching his hand with a curse.

Lily whirled toward the cliff. A dark figure stood framed against the softer blackness of the night, wool greatcoat falling to his boots. His arm was extended, hat blown clear.

Her eyes recovered from the glare of the beam, making out the familiar elegance of his face.

It was Kazi.

"You will halt!" he ordered, voice strong enough to carry clearly over the crash of the surf.

The instruction was indiscriminate, taking in all of them. Lily wondered desperately how much he had seen—how much he knew.

The gun in the inspector's hand swung to Strangford, lingering there for a breath—then returned to where Dicky stood.

Lily watched from where she had spilled onto the ground, the spear still clutched in her hand. Dicky's gaze moved from the armed policeman to the metal case five steps away—from the dinghy to the U-boat lurking in the darkness of the water, the cluster of men just discernible in the tower.

Strangford bolted toward her.

The lighthouse beam paled the distant grass of the headland, racing toward them once again. It picked out the men hurrying down the cliff path, following in Kazi's footsteps. Two of them had reached the sand, sprinting forward, weapons in their hands. They wore Army uniforms.

Dicky looked at Strangford, and abruptly the future became perfectly, dangerously clear to her.

The lighthouse beam spilled across the sand, revealing another Dicky Anstruther-Fields standing by the document case, directly between Strangford and the approaching soldiers.

The double raised a pistol, light glinting off the steel.

Kazi's gaze snapped between the two identical figures, his jaw dropping open.

Lily screamed.

"*No!*"

Strangford dove as the Army men opened fire, bullets strafing through Dicky's projection. The sand behind him exploded into wet bursts, clumps of it falling dully back into the encroaching surf.

The cry tore from her lungs.

"Strangford!"

"I'm alright," he called back.

He was unharmed, and yet the rage fired through her, hot and clear as she crouched on the sand. It buzzed along her limbs with a dark energy, one Lily had felt before.

As the waves rushed against the shore, the men on the cliffs shouting in confusion and alarm, Lily welcomed it, letting herself fall into its familiar embrace.

She rose, the spear coming with her, fluid as an extension of her body. It swept out, taking Dicky in the jaw, his head snapping sideways with enough force to half-spin him around. He pulled an arm back to swing at her, but she already knew his reaction. She was waiting for it. She brought the spear up, deflecting his blow to the side, then swung it back, taking out his ankles.

Dicky collapsed to the wet ground, breath coming out of him in a whoosh.

What came next flooded across her mind, simmering with dark beauty.

How she would rise with the weapon in her hand. How she would drive its point down into his throat. The blood welling up, rich and thick, ebony as the night.

It was terrible, and it was perfect. Lily chose it, letting that future settle into her bones.

Then something knocked into her from the side.

She staggered, thrown off balance, but warm arms grasped her, holding her by her waist and shoulders.

"No, Lily," Strangford whispered at her ear. "Not like this."

The wool of his jumper was damp, crusted with sand. His face was rough with a day's growth of beard. The ferocious urge inside of her rose against him, then broke, falling apart like a wave meeting the land.

She let herself crumble against him, the spear falling from her hands. Behind them, Dicky scrambled to his feet, a disarray of rain slicker and wet sand. The soldiers shouted, feet pounding closer as they pursued him.

The light spun through again, blinding in its clarity. It sparked off the forgotten document case which lay by one of Dicky's boots, spilled over the place where his twin stood in the surf, pushing the dinghy into the sea.

The world went still, the crash of the waves silencing to a whisper, the men on the beach stilled to statues, frozen like Olympians on an ancient frieze.

In the quiet, Lily heard the distinct click of a mechanism switching to readiness.

The warning of it blazed at her, turning the world to red. She gave it voice, the words tearing from her throat.

"*Get down!*"

Strangford's weight shifted in response. He threw them both to the sand. Behind them, Kazi dove for the cover of the rock she had concealed herself behind earlier.

He added his voice to the call, urgency stripping it raw.

"*Down! Down! Down!*"

The swarm of bullets from the U-boat machine gun exploded through the night, falling indiscriminately across the strand. Chips of rock burst into the air, wet sand blowing up around her. Strangford pushed her head to the ground, holding her down, covering her with his body.

She forced her face back, needing to see.

From his place by the dinghy, Dicky jerked abruptly—first a shoulder snapping back, then a twist of his torso. He took two more shots to the chest, falling backward into the edge of the surf.

By the document case, another Dicky Anstruther-Fields turned with a look of surprise. Then he flickered, a skipped frame in a moving picture, and blinked out of existence.

Kazi swung from the cover of the rock, aiming his pistol at the black silhouette of the submarine, snapping off the rest of his clip. More gunfire joined him from the cliff, swallowed by the sea.

The U-boat turned, making a slow arc back out into the deeper waters of The Solent. The dark figures on the tower disappeared, then the black shape of it sunk down into the waves and was gone.

A few more shots were fired at the indifferent black water, then torches flared to life, their pale beams urgently crossing the beach. A trio of uniformed policemen joined one of the soldiers as he pulled his wounded colleague across the sand.

Lily rose, running her hands quickly over Strangford, searching for damage. His jumper was split at the shoulder, blood staining the white sleeve of the shirt he wore beneath.

"Just skimmed me," he assured her. "Nothing deep."

She let herself fall against his chest, the relief of that washing over her—that he was here, that he was whole. His arm came around her, his hand slipping into the damp mess of her hair.

Kazi crossed the beach to where Dicky lay face-down in the shallow water, his body shifting softly with the movement of the sea. He took hold of the fallen man's slicker, dragging him up onto the shore and rolling him over, then pressed his fingers to Dicky's throat.

After a moment, he brushed his hand over Dicky's eyes, pushing them closed.

Lily stepped closer.

"He's dead," she said.

"He is," Kazi confirmed as he rose.

There was a relief in it, and also a sense of failure. He had been one of them, a kindred in his power, and now he was gone.

Behind them, the sergeant Lily recognized from Kazi's interrogations at Taddiford a few days before started shouting orders, plucking up the document case from the edge of the surf. The rain continued to fall in light, cool drops.

The inspector squinted out at the water, the line of it unbroken now, the U-boat vanished.

"They must have had orders. What to do if things went wrong," he said.

Strangford faced him, blood dripping slowly from his shoulder, his wet hair thick with sand.

"Am I under arrest?" he demanded.

Shouts echoed down from the cliff path, a pair of men working their way along it with a stretcher carried between them. A little distance down the shore, the injured soldier wrapped a bundle of gauze around his bleeding leg, laughing through a strongly voiced curse.

"It is clear enough to me which side you fight on," Kazi replied.

The waves rushed in, then pulled back again, tugging at Dicky's boots. Exhaustion seeped through Lily, fueled by the cold and the aftermath of fear.

"Let's go home," she said.

TWENTY-ONE

Taddiford, Barton-on-Sea
Sunday, December 20th
Eight in the morning

$\mathcal{L}$ILY SAT IN THE library, a blanket around her shoulders and a hot cup of tea in her hand.

The rain had stopped, giving way to a gray, cool December morning. Bonnie had set a fire, the coals glowing warmly against the chill.

She wore a set of Walford's spare clothes. The soft wool trousers and white shirt were large on her but clean and dry. Her hair was still damp, clinging a bit with sand. She desperately needed a proper bath but lacked the energy for it. There had been too much to do with one soldier shot through the leg, and a policeman grazed by a bullet on his temple—so many questions to answer and to ask.

And of course, there was Dicky, who had to be carried off the beach on a stretcher. There would be no treatment for him.

The door to the library opened, and Gardner stepped in. The trousers of his uniform were speckled with blood.

He dropped into the chair beside her own, leaning back, eyes falling closed for a moment. His large, capable hands spread across the blue upholstery.

"I don't suppose you've any holes need repairing," he asked.

In answer, Lily reached across the narrow space that separated their chairs. She took his hand.

349

He was quiet for a moment, then let out a satisfied sigh.

"Good," he concluded. "I'm not sure I have the energy to pull out another bullet."

"How is Strangford?"

"His lordship is cleaning himself up. He has four very fine stitches in his arm and a few bruises, but you will find him otherwise intact," Gardner reported.

Lily kept her hold on his hand. She gave it a squeeze.

"Thank you," she said.

There was more in the words than appreciation for the update. She felt all of it—the gratitude for how he had answered her call, arriving in time to save Walford Eversleigh's life, risking who-knew-what trouble with his regiment on nothing but her vaguest word.

"It's what you do for family," he replied.

Family. Lily felt the truth of it. It was how she felt about Gardner, Cairncross, Estelle and Miss Bard—all the people who had risked so much to help her over the last few days. It fit Sam as well, even though he wasn't here. They were all family, those that Ash had brought together at The Refuge. It didn't matter that the building was gone. The bonds—the things that mattered—were still real.

"And Walford?" she asked, thinking of her other family—the one she still couldn't quite believe she would be joining in another two days.

"I had some of the lads move him upstairs," Gardner replied. "So long as he stays put, the only risk to him now is infection. I feel better about his chances with that here at home than I would at the hospital. The last thing he needs is to catch a cough."

"But he'll be alright?" she pressed.

"He'll be fine. He's one of those damnably hearty types. I wouldn't be surprised if he's up and about in a fortnight."

Lily soaked up the relief of that as a companionable silence settled over the room, wrapped in the warmth of the cold fire and the thick gray clouds moving slowly outside the window.

Finally, Gardner sighed, pushing himself up.

"I should be getting back. I've a bit of explaining to do about running off in the middle of a shift, though your inspector kindly offered to smooth that over a bit."

Lily rose. She put her arms around the big Ulsterman, letting her face fall against the olive wool of his uniform. He hugged her back.

"I'll see you on Tuesday," he said.

Tuesday. That in two more nights she would wake to her wedding day felt like a hallucination, and yet the thought of it warmed her, steadying something that had been pounding frantically inside of her.

As though in answer, the door opened once more. Strangford came in.

His dark, too-long hair was mussed, his eye patch in place. A bruise was starting to darken his jaw. He still hadn't shaved, and his feet were bare. His boots, like hers, were waterlogged and full of sand. It made him look even more like a pirate. Lily wondered if Dorcas had seen him yet. The nine-year-old would be delighted.

"Doctor," Strangford said, extending his hand. Gardner took it, clasping him back.

"My lord," he replied. "Mind that shoulder. I don't want to have to reset a stitch before you marry this woman."

"I'll do my best," Strangford returned warmly.

Gardner took his leave, and Strangford crossed the room to her. She leaned into him, letting her head fall against his shoulder, soaking up the pure relief of having him here in her arms.

"Where is Kazi?" she asked, her voice a little muffled by his borrowed coat.

"At the telephone. I overheard him badgering the switchboard operator about a secure line."

Lily still wasn't entirely certain where they stood with the Secret Service Bureau. Both she and Strangford had provided a statement about what drove them back to Taddiford, but it was necessarily full of holes. There was so much they couldn't explain, including how Dicky could have murdered Brockmeyer while still apparently in the room with George Carne and Walford. The story didn't hold together, and Lily knew enough of Kazi by now to feel certain he would not fail to notice those disconnects.

"Anthony."

The voice came from the door. Lily lifted her head from Strangford's shoulder to see Virginia watching them. She was clearly tired but had taken the time to dress in a mutedly elegant day gown. Somehow Lily wasn't surprised. Strangford's sister wasn't the type to fall apart.

"May I have a word?" Virginia said.

It was less a question than a demand.

"By all means," Strangford replied carefully.

Lily flashed Strangford a look, wondering if she should make a polite excuse and depart. Virginia answered first.

"You might as well stay, Lily. I doubt any of this will be a surprise to you."

She stepped into the room, quietly pulling the door shut behind her, then whirled on her brother. Her petite figure radiated emotion, some of it clearly outrage.

"Tell me how you knew where Dicky had gone," she demanded.

Alarm flashed through Lily. She thought of the moment in the study when Strangford stripped off his gloves and read the open safe, declaring Dicky's intention to go to the beach. There had been no time for anything else, not if they'd stood any chance of stopping him.

Strangford had gone tense beside her. Lily waited, pulse pounding, for what he would say.

"I can read the past in the things I touch."

It was a simple statement, but she could hear the tumult under the surface of the words.

Virginia didn't scoff or flinch. She glared at him, her small figure rigid.

"The gloves," she demanded.

"They block it," he admitted. "Prevent me from seeing things I don't want to see."

He was wearing them now. Lily's gaze inadvertently drifted down to where they were clenched at his sides.

Virginia's eyes were on her brother's face.

"It isn't just objects," she stated.

It struck a blow. Lily could feel it from where she stood. Slowly, she reached out, taking Strangford's gloved hand.

"No," he confirmed.

Virginia closed her eyes, fighting her way through some morass of feeling. Lily wondered what would be there when Strangford's sister opened them again. Rage? Denial?

Then the moment came, and Lily's heart broke a little at what she saw.

"Did you think I wouldn't believe you?"

"No, Ginnie," Strangford protested. "It wasn't that."

"Then why?" his sister demanded.

Silence stretched for a breath, the time it took Strangford to muster the words.

"It makes everything so complicated," he said softly.

There was another shift in Virginia's expression, a kind of falling. Her eyes moistened.

"Oh, Anthony . . ." she said.

She crossed the room to him, lifting one of her slender hands to his face, to the tear that was falling down his stubbled cheek.

"You wretched dolt," she concluded warmly.

He gasped out a laugh.

"But honestly—it's so typical that you would insist on keeping it all to yourself when there are perfectly capable people around who would be happy to help you," Virginia protested.

"I lied to you," Strangford countered, pushing as though he couldn't quite believe this wasn't going worse.

"Well, you've never been particularly good at it," Virginia snapped in response. "It's not as though I didn't know *something* was going on. I thought perhaps you tended the Oscar Wilde way—until Lily came along, of course. I was hardly alone," she protested, seeing the surprise on his face. "How else was the world to explain why you threw over Annalise? Though, of course, I always assumed you'd merely come to your senses. I never did like the woman. I suppose now you must have found your own reasons not to trust her."

Strangford didn't answer. The story of his first love was a complicated one.

He raised his head, looking down at his big sister.

"Can you forgive me?"

"I'm sure that I can, once I've sufficiently humbled you," she replied. "How could you keep something so terribly interesting from me for so long? It's dreadful of you. You may expect to be at my mercy for at least a month over it."

His ragged face brightened with a smile, and something warmed in Lily's chest.

He took a breath, shifting again, sadness deepening in the lines around his eye.

"There's something else you should know. About Mother."

Lily's heart skipped. In all the madness of chasing Brockmeyer's killer, she had pushed aside the terrible truth Gardner had revealed about Lady Strangford. That had not made it disappear.

"You mean that she's ill," Virginia stated.

"She told you?" Lily blurted, shocked.

"She didn't have to," Virginia replied. "I don't need magic powers to know that something is wrong. I can't tell you what it is," she continued, raising a hand to forestall Strangford's next question. "If Mother wanted us to know, she would have said something about it. I have chosen to respect that—and you know how much of a meddler I am. Honestly, the unnecessary secrets in this family … If you are ever irritated at Mother for what she keeps from us, you must know that you are just as bad as she is. No—worse," she corrected firmly. "I don't know how I put up with it."

Strangford took a step toward her, looking down at her with a great deal of love.

"No more secrets," he said.

"Don't make promises you can't keep," Virginia countered, a little edge coming into her voice.

She looked up at him, frowning.

"If I hug you, will you know what I'm thinking?"

"Very possibly," Strangford admitted.

"Good," his sister replied and put her arms around him.

She fit neatly under his chin. He let his nose fall into the dark waves of her hair. Lily could see the relief in him.

A firm knock sounded at the door, and Virginia pulled back.

"Come in," she ordered.

It opened to reveal Inspector Kazi. He looked no worse for having been out half the night, his boots somehow miraculously free of sand, his elegant mustache and dark brows unruffled.

"Mrs. Eversleigh, your husband is asking for you. And I require a moment to speak with Lord Strangford and Miss Albright."

Virginia fixed him with a glare.

"I hope you are quite done with your suspicions against my brother," she said, her voice dripping with both authority and disdain.

"I am," Kazi replied simply.

Virginia brightened.

"Then you have my permission to otherwise make things as difficult as you like for him. Brother," she concluded, giving Strangford a regal nod before sailing out of the room.

"Perhaps we might speak more privately outside," Kazi suggested once she had gone.

~

He led them to the cliffs. The grass was still damp, water beading on the leather of Lily's borrowed boots. Below them, the sea was a paler gray, moving with heavy calm against the shore. The tide had swept in, covering most of the evidence of last night's events. Only a few indiscriminate footprints at the base of the cliff remained.

The breeze was cool but gentle, tugging at her hair. Across the waves, the Isle of Wight rose as a distant shadow on the horizon. As Lily watched, a Navy cruiser moved past, heavily armored.

"They've been patrolling," Kazi reported, answering the question she hadn't asked. "There has been no sign of the German submarine."

It did not surprise her, but Lily still felt a flash of relief.

"We found highly sensitive government property in the document case Mr. Anstruther-Fields brought to the beach," Kazi continued. "Mr. Eversleigh has confirmed that he came across the man removing the papers from his safe. That he was shot during the encounter lends additional credence to his account. The presence of the U-boat indicates that Mr. Anstruther-Fields had a line of communication to German High Command and was able to arrange a rendezvous. There is no other explanation for why the vessel would have been this close to shore in an area which is otherwise of no military interest."

The inspector turned to them, his dark eyes missing nothing.

"I don't suppose either of you knows anything about what that line of communication might have been."

"I can tell you it likely leads through the Duke of Saxe-Coburg and Gotha," Strangford replied.

Kazi absorbed this. He did not look particularly happy about it.

That might have had something to do with the fact that Dicky's old school friend, the duke, was also a first cousin of King George's.

"What are my chances of finding physical evidence to confirm that connection should I go looking for it?"

"Non-existent," Strangford replied.

It was clearly not what the inspector had been hoping to hear.

"Could anyone else transfer sensitive information using the same means?" he demanded.

"No," Strangford returned flatly. "Not anymore."

It was the truth, and yet so much remained unsaid. Kazi must have a thousand more questions—questions she was not certain they could answer. Would they be forced to lie or admit things that must sound impossible?

She remembered the answer she had given him when he pressed to know what had woken her the night Brockmeyer died.

I heard a ghost.

He had not scoffed at it, instead subjecting her assertion to the same ruthless questioning as any other piece of evidence.

That was how Kazi would measure all of it—by weighing, assessing. She recalled the look on his face as he whirled from one Dicky Anstruther-Fields to another on the beach the night before.

The question was not whether he would believe. It was what he would do with that knowledge once he had it.

The thought set her pulse racing.

The wind rustled the blades of pale, bending grass. The sea hushed against the sand below, the tide dancing around the rocks.

"I checked the timetable," the inspector said.

It seemed a non-sequitur. Lily struggled to catch up.

"August 2nd. A special Army transport en route to Dover. It would have crossed the Blackfriars rail bridge at quarter past six in the morning. There was an unfortunate industrial accident, it seems, at precisely that time. Half the bridge was blown away in the process. The cargo of the train was classified, of course, but I believe all of us here know what it contained. Don't we, Miss Albright?"

"Yes," Lily confirmed, rasping out the word.

The nightmarish memory of the day rushed at her—the terrible struggle to reach the engine, to stop an apocalyptic prophecy from coming to pass. The horror of Strangford crumpled on the rail bed under a pillar of black smoke.

Ash's blue eyes gazing at her steadily over the top of a bomb.

Lily forced herself back to the present, to Strangford's rigid tension beside her and the lean, striking figure of the inspector at the edge of the cliff, the wind tossing the hem of his greatcoat.

"I will not presume to say I understand the whole of it. Not yet," he added carefully, pinning her with his golden-brown eyes. "But I believe we may owe you both a very great debt."

Something inside of her cracked apart, a fault line that spilled out an emotion she did not know how to name. It felt like joy, relief, and a terrible and beautiful sort of sadness.

"We do what we must, Inspector," Strangford replied.

"To the best of our abilities," Kazi finished, sharp intelligence in his eyes. "And you are a man of rather extraordinary ability."

The world held its breath for a moment, that habitual fear stealing over her. Instinctively, Lily reached out to slip her hand into Strangford's, anchoring herself in the familiar feeling of the leather of his glove.

Kazi stepped back, then paused.

"Another party has taken an interest in your involvement in this affair. He would like to call on you later this week. Would ten o'clock Tuesday morning be acceptable?"

"I'm being married that afternoon," Strangford replied, clearly thrown.

"Then you should be available in the morning," Kazi concluded. "Good day, my lord. Miss Albright."

He tipped his hat, then stalked off across the grass.

TWENTY-TWO

Lancaster Gate, Bayswater
Tuesday, December 22nd
Nine forty-five in the morning

S TRANGFORD STILL HAD not repaired his garden gate.

It had been nearly a year since Lily kicked her way through it, forcing her way into his home and his life. A year since he had first touched her, blackmailed into it when Lily refused to allow his mind to be devoured by an encounter with the dead.

The damage wasn't obvious, mostly hidden under a fall of ivy, but Strangford didn't neglect things. There might not be much money to keep up the house at Lancaster Gate, but everything was carefully maintained. That the lock had not been replaced felt like something else—something deliberate. An invitation.

Lily pushed inside.

She might have gone to the front door, but Virginia had strong feelings about the groom seeing the bride before the wedding. On the chance that Strangford's sister was still there with her mother, Lily decided to use a less obvious entrance. She would not miss this meeting.

The small back garden was still and quiet, framed by overgrown rhododendrons. The perennial beds were neatly trimmed around a small wrought-iron table and a pair of chairs.

She blinked, and for a moment, it was springtime. Flowers

359

bloomed, the grass a startling new green. There was a tea set on the table beside an old book, binding worn from use. Sparrows danced through the branches, sunlight dappling across the ground.

A hand slipped over her own, the warmth of bare skin. A low voice from across the table.

Your tea is getting cold.

Lily shook her head, and it was winter once more, crisp and cool.

She mounted the short flight of steps and slipped through the back door of the house. Someone had left it unlocked.

The hallway was empty. Dishes clattered downstairs in the kitchen. Theresa, the maid, hummed as she worked in one of the rooms at the front of the house, a tune Lily remembered from the music halls.

Strangford was in the study, as Lily had known he would be. The room was his sanctuary. It was simply furnished with a plain desk and chairs. The walls were covered in art. The paintings were strange and expressive rather than literal. Strangford had told her once that he chose them because he saw the truth in them, something that felt more like the world he perceived through his hands—the one that lay under the surface of things.

He was gazing at the gallery wall. Like Lily, he hadn't yet dressed for the ceremony. He wore one of his ordinary black suits, a little worn at the cuffs, and had foregone a necktie. His hair was too long. She was sure Virginia would be railing at him for neglecting to cut it before the wedding. It curled beautifully around his collar.

His gloves were on. Lily slipped her hand into his and joined him in contemplating the art on the wall—the splendid explosion of a sunrise, the delicate knowing in the geometric eyes of a woman stroking a black cat. A watcher in a bright red cloak held vigil over the swirling tempest of the sea.

He didn't jump at her arrival. Strangford might not see the future, but he knew the woman he was about to marry.

"You look beautiful," he noted.

"I'm not dressed for the wedding yet," Lily countered.

His mouth quirked into a smile.

"I know."

A knock sounded from the front door. Lily started at the sharp rapport of it, but Strangford was more ready. He turned, preparing to face whatever was coming next.

There was an exchange of voices from the hall, one high and nervous, the other bellowing. A moment later, Strangford's wide-eyed footman opened the study door.

"T-there's a caller for you, my lord," Roderick stammered.

His gaze flickered to Lily. To his credit, he did not look terribly surprised to see her there. Perhaps Roderick was also getting to know her.

"It's Lord Admiral Winston Churchill," he announced with a hint of terror.

"Show him in, Roddie," Strangford replied.

Her mind spun. Kazi had warned Strangford there would be another interested party calling on them that morning, but Lily had never imagined it would be Churchill. He was one of the most powerful men in the realm, more so even than her father. She had met him once before in the halls of Parliament, an accidental and brief encounter. She could not possibly imagine why he would have insisted on meeting with a minor baron on a Tuesday morning.

Of course, she recalled that Brockmeyer had worked as an aide in Churchill's office. Was that why he had come? But what could he possibly want to know? And what could they dare to tell him? The latter question had her gripping Strangford's hand a bit more tightly as the man himself stepped into the study.

He was tall, broad-shouldered, and solid, projecting an immediate and overwhelming presence that made the room seem like it had just grown smaller.

"Lord Strangford," he boomed, extending a hand.

Strangford met it and was treated to a firm and energetic handshake.

"And you must be Miss Lilith Albright," the admiral noted.

Something in his tone told her that Churchill knew exactly who she was—the illegitimate daughter of one of the realm's most influential peers. She instinctively checked for the disdain or disapproval that often followed being recognized as Lord Torrington's bastard but heard none of it.

"Lord Admiral," Lily said, offering him a curtsy. "Would you care for tea?"

"I would prefer a whiskey and soda," Churchill comfortably replied.

The world spun a little.

She remembered Parliament, the suffocating heat of summer—the smell of cigars and expensive cologne. He had been standing in the hall with Chancellor Lloyd George, quizzing Strangford about his work as a translator when time had bent, and those words spun through her mind.

Would prefer a whiskey and soda . . .

The sense of significance overpowered her—the feeling that something important was about to happen.

Caution flared. In Lily's experience, important things were often rather dangerous.

She crossed to Strangford's small liquor cabinet. Strangford hardly ever drank, but Virginia made certain it was stocked with whatever he might need for callers—however rare those might be.

Lily realized that would likely be her responsibility after today. She hadn't the foggiest idea how to do it. The thought made her hands shake a bit as she poured out the whiskey and squeezed the lever of the soda siphon.

Churchill had turned his attention to the gallery wall. He looked over the pieces as Lily fixed his drink.

"They are too disparate to be the work of one artist, so I must suppose you are a collector rather than a creator," Churchill noted.

"You are correct," Strangford confirmed.

The big man studied the pieces with careful attention.

"They are not to my taste," he concluded bluntly. "But they are thoughtfully chosen."

"Thank you," Strangford replied as though that were a compliment. Lily supposed in a way it had been.

She handed the whiskey to Churchill, who treated her to a charming smile.

"Thank you, my dear."

"Will you sit?" Strangford offered, extending a black-gloved hand to one of the chairs.

Churchill took it. There was something leonine about him, the banked power of a pack leader who did not need to constantly assert his position. It made the green-upholstered armchair feel like a throne. Lily supposed any chair this man sat on must take on something of that energy.

"Lily," Strangford said, nodding for her to take the other chair. She did so, Strangford hovering behind her.

"I have received a complete briefing on the death of the man we both knew as Lieutenant Felix Brockmeyer and its relation to an unfortunate breach of security at the Admiralty," Churchill said. "I must say I find the whole matter quite infuriating—that a few upstarts in our intelligence services thought to place an agent in my personal staff without informing me of the matter. Captain MacMahon's work would have been greatly aided and his life very well preserved had he been working with my support rather than against my ignorance."

The admiral's irritation was genuine, but Lily wasn't sure she agreed with it. There was something so large about the man, something that demanded attention. He was so clearly convinced of his own capability, and instinct told her that he felt as though he had missed out on a grand adventure. That seemed a potent and dangerous combination.

She was equally certain Churchill's briefing had not been as complete as he believed. No one knew the full story of what Dicky Anstruther-Fields had been and how he had been stopped—no one but her and Strangford.

Though there was perhaps one other who might possess some inkling of the truth.

"However much I might disagree with the execution of the scheme, I cannot deny that it exposed a very dangerous threat to the security of our nation and led to its elimination. Had Mr. Anstruther-Fields been allowed to remove those plans from England, our narrow edge in the war at sea would be lost, and in a year's time, we might very well have seen German boots trampling British soil."

Lily's pulse quickened.

Had Mr. Anstruther-Fields been allowed to remove those plans...

What had stopped Dicky from succeeding in his mission? How easily might all of this have turned out differently? If Strangford hadn't immediately become Kazi's prime suspect in the murder, if Dicky had been subjected to greater scrutiny from the start—what might have changed?

He would never have been pinned for Brockmeyer's death. No one could have possibly imagined how Dicky overcame his ironclad alibi. Only Lily and Strangford were equipped to even guess the truth of that.

No—had Kazi's suspicions ranged more widely, it would only have pushed Dicky to greater caution until things cooled down. It was only the extremity of the moment that forced him to show his hand. And without Strangford's freedom—and possibly life—on the line, would the pair of them ever have dug deeply enough into the murder to uncover the truth about Dicky?

It all came back to that phone call—the one Brockmeyer placed to his Secret Service Bureau handlers from the hall at Taddiford. If he had been able to give them Dicky's name, they would all now be facing an entirely different future.

But he hadn't... because of the vase.

The implications pulsed through her with each beat of blood in her veins, the flashes of vision the onmyōdō had granted her finally making sense.

In that moment, her power had been asking her to risk Strangford's safety for the sake of something greater.

She supposed it should be reassuring. It wasn't. What she mostly felt was rage overlaying something deeper and colder... a terrible fear.

"It is my understanding that we have you to thank for identifying and stopping Mr. Anstruther-Fields," Churchill said, forcing Lily to focus her attention back on this room, this moment—one she could not help but feel was equally critical.

"My role was largely peripheral," Strangford countered, his hand tensing on the back of Lily's chair.

Lily felt certain Churchill would not simply accept that. He was a man who came into a conversation certain of the point he would make, but instead of confronting them, he changed tack.

"You're a translator," he said. "French and German."

"And a bit of Latin," Strangford returned.

"Useful skills in our current situation," Churchill noted. "As are intelligence and valor, which I have been given to understand you possess in spades."

The statement surprised her.

"Kazi said that?"

Churchill turned his watery blue eyes on her. The lines of his face were soft, his hairline receding. It gave him the look of a gentleman of leisure, but there was nothing leisurely about the way he was looking at her.

"Do you disagree?" he asked.

It was an unsettlingly direct question. It was possible this was a trap, but she would not lie—not about this.

"No," she replied.

Strangford's hand shifted, moving from the chair to her shoulder. Lily felt the strength in it and lifted her own fingers to touch him.

Churchill gave the whiskey and soda in his cut crystal glass a little swirl before taking another sip.

"The Admiralty has its own intelligence service," he said.

"So I understand," Strangford replied.

Churchill raised his eyes, pinning Strangford with them.

"We could use a man of your talents."

His words hung in the still air of the room as it suddenly became clear why he was here.

Lily's mind whirled, trying to catch up. Fear flashed into the space left by uncertainty. It tasted of mud and gunpowder. In her vision of Strangford—the one where he fell—what uniform had he been wearing?

She fought to call up the detail and failed. The memory, worked over and over in her mind, had lost its edges, growing indistinct. She could not trust it any longer.

That sparked a new kind of panic. Lily fought against it, thinking instead of what Strangford had admitted to her in the shadows of the empty library at The Refuge.

I need to make a difference.

Strangford's fingers had tensed on her shoulder. Lily could not read what he was feeling. She could not ask—not here, with Churchill watching them.

"I am disqualified from service," Strangford carefully replied.

Churchill regarded him keenly, his posture in the chair deceptively casual.

"There are men on my staff who've lost far more than an eye," he said. "A medical exemption is easily obtained for someone of particular value. The commission would be temporary for the duration of the war. I can offer you only the rank of lieutenant—you lack the experience as a sailor for anything greater. The posting is at the Admiralty here in London, but I cannot guarantee you would not eventually be needed at sea. Or elsewhere."

The last word made the room go a little colder.

Churchill rose, moving with surprising grace for someone of his size. Lily rose with him. The instinct to do so was automatic.

"I won't press you for an answer now. You'll need to think over the matter. You may send your response to me at the Admiralty."

He extended his hand. Strangford took it after only a moment's hesitation.

Churchill released him and plucked his hat from the table, setting it on his balding head.

"My felicitations to you both," he announced, and then he was gone.

She turned to Strangford, knowing how this must have rattled him—how he must be torn. She searched for the right words to move them forward, but before she could find them, another voice sounded from the hall. It was bright and strong, quick with purpose.

"I can see myself in, Roderick."

A moment later, Virginia stepped into the room. Her eyes widened at the sight of Lily, then narrowed.

"I would very much like to know what Lord Admiral Churchill was just doing here," Virginia demanded. "But first, it seems I must spirit your bride away before she ruins the entire day for us."

She fixed Lily with a glare.

Lily accepted it, releasing Strangford's hand. What came next would have to wait. There was other business to attend to.

"I suppose I had better get dressed," she said.

TWENTY-THREE

Lancaster Gate
Seven o'clock in the evening

ILY HAD NEVER imagined the house could look so busy. An hour before, the rooms had burst with garlands, holly, and people. A tree dominated the rarely used drawing room, illuminated with glass-shielded candles. Tables were jammed with punch, pastries, and the remains of a roast. Fire glowed in every hearth, the place warming to the point where someone had started cracking open the windows. It had been strange but not unpleasant.

This was better. Most of the other guests had gone home, though the wedding had been small to begin with. Those left were gathered in Strangford's study. They had carried in chairs and a small settee, the room bursting with uninvited furniture. She was reminded oddly of the library of The Refuge, though the ceilings were lower, with far fewer books and more art.

The room was packed, every corner echoing with the clink of glassware and the rumble of conversation. Miss Bard reclined on the settee, leaning against Estelle. Dr. Gardner bent over her, reaching for the bandage on the folklorist's head as she shooed him away. Her eyes were bright, and Gardner looked very dashing in the elegant red jacket of his mess uniform.

Virginia had tugged Strangford out a moment earlier. Mrs. Liu hovered over Walford Eversleigh, who sat in a wheeled bath chair.

He had insisted on coming despite his injury. The chair had been the compromise between tying him to the bed in Taddiford and Walford making his own far riskier escape. He had also submitted to being carried onto the train on a stretcher. Sam's nǎinai pinched the skin on the back of Walford's hand, then turned for a quick exchange in Mandarin with her tall, quiet son, who stood beside them. Lily felt fairly certain Walford was going to end up with a packet of healing herbs tucked into his luggage tomorrow.

George Carne also looked very fine in his regimental red coat, flanked by the Eversleigh children. In her frilly white dress, Dorcas was peppering George with questions about what one might do with a bayonet while Lysander quietly untied his boot laces and Rosalind browsed a copy of Debrett's Peerage for eligible dukes.

Cat sat at his feet, staring with ill-intent at George's currently fur-free lap. Lily was not entirely certain who had brought the animal to the house. It was entirely possible it had simply materialized here the moment she exchanged her vows with Strangford in St. Patrick's church.

Somewhere in the hall, she was fairly certain she heard Strangford sneeze.

Portia was curled up in a chair in the corner, quietly studying Strangford's art gallery. Her bespectacled eyes occasionally shifted over to her father, carefully assessing how Walford was faring.

At any moment, Lily thought she might blink and find the room empty—but that was an illusion. The warmth around her was real in a way that had nothing to do with the fire glowing in the hearth.

Her father stood by the curtained windows with Cairncross. They were too far for Lily to eavesdrop. She wondered what the two men had found in common to talk about and doubted any guess she made would be close.

The wedding had been a whirlwind. Since Churchill left the house, Lily had been spun through dressing and pins and a tasteful brush of Virginia's rouge. They had rushed her to the church, stuffed flowers into her hand, and then she had been standing at the door to the nave, her father's hand on her arm.

Are you ready?

The moment had stretched, time drawing itself out as she looked up to see Strangford waiting for her. His hair was still too long. He had taken off his gloves. It struck her that they had actually made it— they had somehow pulled through it all to reach this—and then time kicked back into gear. Even the Mass had seemed to fly past, followed by a dizzying parade of rings and rice, clasped hands and hugs.

Spilled wine, a lost shoe—Lysander's, of course. George nearly setting himself on fire by the Christmas tree … and now she was here.

Everything in the room felt right, even the pang of grief over who was missing—those who were far away and those who would never be back.

"Lady Strangford," someone said from beside her, breaking her reverie.

It took Lily a moment to realize the comment was directed to her. She turned to find Strangford's mother nearby, managing to look stern even in the festive gown Virginia had picked out for her to wear to the wedding.

"May we have a word?" she asked.

The woman was no longer Lady Strangford, Lily realized. That title was hers now. Strangford's mother had officially passed into the status of a dowager.

The dowager's question sounded more like a demand, sparking up Lily's nerves. They had exchanged only a few quick words since she had returned to London from Northumberland the day before.

Lily knew the foal had been safely birthed and that the train had been running ten minutes late. She did not know what the dowager Lady Strangford thought about Lily joining her family.

"Of course," Lily replied politely.

She followed her mother-in-law into the hall, then froze for a moment with indecision. She could hear Mrs. Jutson and Theresa at work clearing the tables in the drawing room. Lily didn't want to interrupt them.

"Do you mind the cold?"

"No," the dowager replied.

The older woman put her hand to the back door, tugged it open, and stepped into the dark chill of the garden.

Someone—likely Virginia—had thought to set a few lanterns around the path. They cast a soft light over the glossy leaves of the rhododendrons, spilling gently over the gravel path. An ashtray sat on the wrought iron table, holding the remains of someone's cigar. An empty wineglass stood beside it.

The noise from the house was muffled here, dulled by the walls and the drawn curtains to a low murmur. The air was still as the space between breaths, clear and chill. Lily thought briefly of a scarf, then dismissed it. The sleeves of her wedding gown were long. She would manage.

"What did you wish to say?" Lily asked.

The dowager Lady Strangford was a tall woman, solidly built, but now that she knew to look for them, Lily could see the signs—the way her dress hung just a little too loose, the pale tone of her skin.

"I have never been very good at this," her mother-in-law replied flatly.

"At what?" Lily returned.

The dowager looked back at her, her dark eyes disconcertingly similar to Strangford's.

"Affection," she replied.

Surprise lowered her guard.

"I don't understand," Lily admitted.

Strangford's mother folded her hands in front of her. She stood straight, unsmiling.

"I am not a demonstrative person. It is not in my nature to give the little signals of esteem that come naturally to others. I do not understand them very well. They are therefore tools I do not like to use."

As she said it, Lily realized it was true. She thought of the dowager's stilted handling of the embraces of her children and grandchildren. It was never something she initiated. She didn't show the younger ones the same easy affection Virginia and Walford did, her comments to them always more practical—pointing out that a shoe didn't match or that a toy had been left behind. Yet the Eversleighs seemed to move effortlessly around that, including her in the warm chaos of their lives like water finding its way around a stone.

Lily had been more sensitive to the lack of those signs of acceptance when it came to her own relationship with the woman, but she had never doubted that Lady Strangford cared deeply for her family.

It seemed to shine through her in other ways, in her protectiveness and her honesty, even if they were sometimes awkward.

She was different. Her emotions didn't spill out for all to see. They ran down less familiar channels, finding subtler ways into the world.

Lily knew something about being different.

"I see," she said.

"No," the dowager countered flatly. "You do not. You could not because I failed to inform you."

"Inform me of what?"

"That I believe you well-matched with my son," she replied.

It was not what Lily had expected to hear. She could only blurt out the first question that came into her head.

"But why?"

The dowager frowned as though finding the question rather strange, but she answered it.

"You know what he is and chose him because of it rather than in spite of it."

Lily's heart skipped at her words. Did the dowager mean what Lily thought she might? Could it be possible that Strangford's mother was perfectly aware of the unique talents he had worked so hard to keep hidden from his family?

She could not ask, not without risk of giving something away if she was wrong. As she stood in the cold and quiet of the garden, Lily realized it didn't matter.

"Yes," she confirmed. "I have chosen him. And I would choose him a thousand times over again."

"It will be difficult," the dowager continued matter-of-factly. "But I think you are very strong."

"You have no idea," Lily quietly replied.

"Am I wrong?"

"No. You are entirely correct."

The dowager absorbed this.

"I believe you bring him joy," she concluded.

She turned for the house, seemingly satisfied, but there was more that Lily needed to say. She thought of Gardner's terrible message, of the extra fabric in the woman's gown. Suddenly answers were less important than making certain that another truth was heard.

Lily called to her.

"You know that we are here for you as well. All of us. No matter what."

The woman paused for a breath, her skirt in her hand. That was all the sign Lily had that her message had been heard.

"Thank you," she finally replied.

The door to the house opened, Strangford framed in the soft light that fell from the hall.

"Hello, Mother," he said. "Ginnie could use your help. Lysander got into the inkpot."

"That is not surprising," the dowager concluded and strode past him.

Strangford shut the door behind her and descended to where Lily stood on the gravel path.

She hadn't found a moment alone with him since Churchill descended on them that morning, swept through the day on currents of ceremony and celebration. She allowed herself a breath to relish in him now—in the familiar angles of his face, the curve of his lip, the fall of his hair over the dark circle of his eye patch. He had, of course, lost his tie somewhere in the course of the evening.

She could vividly recall what it had felt like to take his hand at the altar of St. Patrick's a few hours before. How it had felt to take him inside of her two nights earlier in the warmth of the temporary oasis they built among the ruins of The Refuge.

What it meant to fight beside him, to risk everything in the name of what they knew to be right.

She brought him joy. The thought warmed her, sparking a glow that easily out-burned the chill of the evening.

Lily raised her hand to his cheek, letting her fingers graze over his skin, already a little rough with the regrowth of his beard. She soaked up every dancing note of the sensation it provoked, peppered as they were with that subtle electricity she always felt when they were in contact with each other.

"Has it been a good day?" he asked.

"It has," she replied.

She smiled at him, letting some of her own joy show through.

Something in the crisp night air shifted, and a few flakes of snow began to drift down around them. They moved slowly, hovering in the air as though this moment hung suspended in time.

In truth, nothing was holding still for them. The world waited outside the quiet of the lamp-lit garden.

Lily knew what she needed to say.

"Churchill's offer. Have you decided whether to accept it?"

Trouble clouded his brow, his gaze shifting. He took a breath, preparing to answer, and suddenly everything shifted, clicking into place. The truth became as clear to Lily as the chill of the snow. It was not easy, and it still terrified her, but that did not make it any less real.

"Lily, I—"

She took a breath, cutting him off.

"I think you should take it. It is who you are, Strangford. It is who we both are," she added.

He did not miss the look of challenge she gave him.

"But what you saw . . ." he started.

"We have fought the future before. We can do it again."

Her voice trembled on the words, but his face showed her everything—the guilt, the need.

"Are you sure?" he asked.

Her mouth curled into a smile.

"You tell me," she ordered.

The electricity of his touch surged, blazing through her. He took hold of her waist, pulling her close, and then his mouth was on hers, hungry and powerful.

He broke from the kiss but not the embrace. Their breath mingled in the gentle fall of the snow. The sounds of the party rose through the windows behind them, warm with an outburst of laughter, and Lily was conscious of how close she was to so many people that she loved.

It could not last—this perfect peace. The war waited, and it would not be content to leave them as they were. It would find them, eventually, even if they did not march into it. In the meantime, Lily would drink deep of every moment like this she could find.

They were interrupted by a musical ping, the sound both lovely and strangely out of place. Another followed it, and Lily turned to see a sparrow perched on the wrought-iron table. As she watched, it pecked its beak against the forgotten wine glass once more, making it sing.

Something white was tied around the bird's leg with a piece of red thread.

Intuition drove her closer. She moved cautiously to avoid startling the creature. It watched her warily but hopped only one step away, then waited.

Lily reached out and carefully untied the delicate little bow, removing a thin scrap of paper that had been wrapped around the sparrow's leg.

A word was written there in careful print. The letters were small, but Lily recognized them nonetheless. She had seen that hand scrawled onto orders for carriage parts and reports for Cairncross or on notes that found their way to her old flat at March Place.

It was Sam's handwriting.

She thought of her own letter, the one she had finally mustered the courage to write and post a few days before. It had been received. She was looking at the response, one that somehow said far more than the fifteen letters carefully inked onto the paper.

Congratulations.

As Lily read it, the bird flew from the table, and suddenly there were more of them—a swarm of brown sparrows filling the air of the garden, whirling around the place where she and Strangford stood. They were like so many snowflakes dancing in a wind of their own making—an answer that shone with a warmth that Lily could feel across continents. Strangford held Lily in the center of it, laughing aloud with joy, and her own happiness rose up to meet him.

NOTES FROM THE AUTHOR

Lily and Strangford's adventures conclude in *What the Ravens Sing*, Book Four of The London Charismatics, available now at Jacquelyn-Benson.com/What-the-Ravens-Sing.

~

Please take a moment to rate or review *Bridge of Ash*. It's a simple thing that has a real and powerful impact for independent authors like myself.

What the Ravens Sing

A world torn by war. A castle full of secrets. And the darkness of the space between the stars.

In a Europe devastated by four years of conflict, a platoon of elite Italian soldiers is horrifically and mysteriously slaughtered. Strangford's arcane ability can uncover the truth behind the massacre, but a violent fate stalks him from the trenches. It's up to Lily to change its course.

To succeed, she'll need the help of unlikely allies, from the brilliant police inspector who once accused Strangford of murder to an elusive spy full of dangerous secrets—and a friend that Lily once terribly betrayed. Together, they'll follow a trail of whispers from ice-dimmed caverns to forests haunted by more than wolves where a terrible threat rises, born from the blood-soaked work of Lily's greatest enemy.

Strangford's life. The outcome of the war. The future itself. All of it hangs in the balance, carried in the implacable call of a black-winged oracle over a devastated landscape of wire and mud—where Lily must open herself to the darkest potential of a power that could tear her apart.

And hope there is someone left at the end to pull her back together.

.

Read What the Ravens Sing now and fall into the shattering conclusion of The London Charismatics series.

ACKNOWLEDGMENTS

As always, the writing of a book is not something one does alone. My beta readers—Matthew Dow, Kaitlyn Huwe, Chris Mornick, Anna Leone-Brown, and Cathie Plate—are so much more than just cheerleaders. They provide the thoughtful and incisive comments that pull the manuscript into something greater.

Suzannah Rowntree is owed much for correcting my Latin (and her own Miss Sharp's Monsters gaslamp fantasy series is highly recommended).

Casey Fenich and Mike Dunbar polished up my grammar, and Cathie Plante created the layout for the original edition of this book.

Sahrish Nadim provided valuable insights into Inspector Kazi's experience while Zhui Ning Chan once again put her eagle eye to the text.

The men and women of the Lamplighter's Guild have my deep gratitude for their continuing advice and support. *A Wrath of Sparrows* never would have existed if not for Nicholas Atwater, who apologizes for nothing. Please go check out his witty and adventurous *Tales of the Iron Rose* series.

My hero, Dan, is owed much for waiting on me hand and foot for weeks as I finished this book on bed rest for one of those surprise medical anomalies that sometimes flatten us out.

And as always, I thank you, my lovely readers, for your continuing support of Lily and her motley crew of friends and allies.

ABOUT THE AUTHOR

Jacquelyn Benson writes smart historical thrillers where strong women wrangle with bold men and confront the stranger things that occupy the borders of our world. She once lived in a museum, wrote a master's thesis on the cultural anthropology of paranormal investigation, and received a gold medal for being clever. She owes a great deal to her elementary school librarian for sagely choosing to acquire the entire Time-Life *Mysteries of the Unknown* series.

When not writing, she enjoys the company of a tall, dark and handsome English teacher and practices unintentional magic.

If you'd like to be friends:

- **Join the email list on her website:** JacquelynBenson.com. You'll also get a free download of an exclusive novella, *The Stolen Apocalypse.*

- **Follow on Bookbub:** BookBub.com/Authors/Jacquelyn-Benson and stay informed about deals and discounts

- **Follow on Goodreads:** Goodreads.com/JacquelynBenson

- **Find her on social media:**
  Instagram: @jbensonink
  BlueSky: @jbensonink.bsky.social
  Facebook: Facebook.com/JBensonInk
  Pinterest: Pinterest.com/JBensonInk